Praise f[...]
Ghostland and *Spid[...]*

"Strong's terrific tale should win her many new fans. Really good stuff!"
—*Romantic Times*

"The world is gorgeous, the characters are fantastic, and the plots will draw you in!"
—*Errant Dreams Reviews*

"*Ghostland* is well-defined, intriguing from the start, and deliciously erotic."
—*Darque Reviews*

"Jory Strong will leave you hooked and hoping for more of this dark world."
—*Romance Junkies*

"Urban fantasy readers will relish *Ghostland* and look forward to more escapades in Jory Strong's new California (and beyond)."
—*Genre Go Round Reviews*

"Jory Strong writes an enthralling story which will quickly immerse readers in a futuristic fantasy."
—*Romance Reviews Today*

"The world-building is nothing short of stunning. Rich and deeply detailed, the grim post-war Earth is both unique and intriguing."
—*Genre Fiction Reviews*

HEALER'S CHOICE

Jory Strong

BERKLEY SENSATION, NEW YORK

THE BERKLEY PUBLISHING GROUP
Published by the Penguin Group
Penguin Group (USA) Inc.
375 Hudson Street, New York, New York 10014, USA
Penguin Group (Canada), 90 Eglinton Avenue East, Suite 700, Toronto, Ontario M4P 2Y3, Canada
(a division of Pearson Penguin Canada Inc.)
Penguin Books Ltd., 80 Strand, London WC2R 0RL, England
Penguin Group Ireland, 25 St. Stephen's Green, Dublin 2, Ireland (a division of Penguin Books Ltd.)
Penguin Group (Australia), 250 Camberwell Road, Camberwell, Victoria 3124, Australia
(a division of Pearson Australia Group Pty. Ltd.)
Penguin Books India Pvt. Ltd., 11 Community Centre, Panchsheel Park, New Delhi—110 017, India
Penguin Group (NZ), 67 Apollo Drive, Rosedale, North Shore 0632, New Zealand
(a division of Pearson New Zealand Ltd.)
Penguin Books (South Africa) (Pty.) Ltd., 24 Sturdee Avenue, Rosebank, Johannesburg 2196,
South Africa

Penguin Books Ltd., Registered Offices: 80 Strand, London WC2R 0RL, England

This book is an original publication of The Berkley Publishing Group.

PRINTING HISTORY
Berkley Sensation trade paperback edition / September 2010

Library of Congress Cataloging-in-Publication Data

Strong, Jory.
   Healer's choice / Jory Strong.—Berkley Sensation trade pbk. ed.
      p.   cm.
   ISBN 978-0-425-23653-6
1. Women healers—Fiction. 2. Werewolves—Fiction. I. Title.
   PS3619.T777H43—2010
   813'.6—dc22   2010018550

PRINTED IN THE UNITED STATES OF AMERICA

10 9 8 7 6 5 4 3 2 1

Thanks once again to my editor, Cindy Hwang,
and my agent, Ethan Ellenberg. Your support of
and faith in my work is greatly appreciated.

Thanks also to Leis Pederson for her behind-the-scenes
efforts and assistance, and to copyeditors Luann Reed-Siegel (Healer's Choice)
and Rick Willet (Ghostland, Spider-Touched), *the unsung heroine and hero*
who've kept me from erring too egregiously.

One

THE demon caught Rebekka in the forest, turning day into night and nature into a seething weapon. He arrived in a tornado swirl of fury, encircling her in a wind of dirt and shattered trees and rocks from which there was no escape. Trapping her there until her heart threatened to burst and only terror filled her. And then he relented—allowing what was left of the trail she'd been running on to fall back to earth in a twisted, horrifying demonstration of his power—and that was worse.

In the unnatural calm following the violence, he took form. A creature of nightmare. A dark-skinned thing heralding damnation.

Leathery, batlike wings spread out to block the sight of anything but him. Fingers ended in wicked talons and yellow eyes danced with sinister glee. His forked tongue flicked out to taste her fear while a barbed tail coiled around his thigh like a living thing.

His smile held a wealth of cruelty. His gaze held her immobile, trembling in the face of her own death.

Lightning-fast his hand wrapped around her throat, a razor-sharp claw digging into her flesh, slicing through it with ease. But instead of delivering torment and death, he released her, drawing his hand back to lap at blood-covered fingers.

"So there are other players in this game than the one I so recently encountered," he said. "Your father's involvement is a surprise. He had no love for humans when I was last among my kind."

He laughed, a sharp-edged sound sending shards of ice sliding into Rebekka's spine. And then as quickly as he appeared, the demon dissolved into nothing, leaving her shaking as she surrendered to terror and sank to her knees at the center of the destruction he'd wrought.

Rebekka pressed trembling fingers to the wound at her throat, stopped the flow of blood despite the wild pounding of her pulse beneath her fingertips. Nausea swelled in the aftermath of surviving the encounter.

The sweat from her run became a cold clamminess on her skin. Shudder after shudder racked her frame as the demon's words played over and over in her mind.

Her features were those of her mother, as were the deep brown of her hair and the blue of her eyes. There was nothing in her looks to identify who her father had been, and she'd never asked. What child of a prostitute wanted to hear her mother admit she had no idea which man had left more than his money behind?

Rebekka's thoughts went to the place above her pubic mound where an ugly black circle with a scarlet red *P* in its center had been forcibly tattooed onto her skin. A terrifying memory from that day skirted at the edge of her consciousness. She reached for it but it eluded her as it always did, and she let it go, ashamed at the gratitude she felt for not having to confront whatever truth lay repressed by her mind.

A different horror had her standing, frantically looking around for the Weres who'd been somewhere on the trail ahead of her when the demon arrived. Relief came with the absence of twisted, broken bodies. It swept through her and brought with it sweet denial and a refuge in purpose. Her ability to heal using her hands and will alone was proof there was no stain on her soul, no taint of it in her blood despite the demon's words.

Rebekka began running, scrambling and jumping over the demon-created debris. She caught up to the Weres a short time later. Of those waiting, only Levi appeared fully human, his lion form lost forever unless her gift deepened, strengthened.

The six Weres she and Levi and Tir had freed from the maze less than an hour ago were grotesque mixtures of human and animal, made that way by a man using witch-charmed silver and torture to twist them into an abomination of form.

Levi's eyes flicked to the wound on her neck and his nostrils flared, his senses Were despite no longer having a lion form. "I smell the demon Abijah. What happened?"

"He caught up to me then left. I'm okay."

She didn't want to reveal what the demon said. In truth, she didn't want to think about it at all or lose the shield of denial she'd managed to erect.

Lion-gold eyes met hers for a long moment, as if Levi sensed an evasion. He let it go, and she turned her attention to the waiting Weres.

There were five of them. Two Wolves, a Leopard, a Tiger, and Cyrin, Levi's brother.

Pity and anger and sadness churned together inside her. Horror for what they'd endured and for what they'd lost.

"I've told them what their choices are and what to expect," Levi said. "They all want you to heal them."

She looked at the gathered Weres and asked, "Who's first?"

The sole female stepped forward. Her body was wolf but her head was human. She was almost the complete opposite of the male. He had a wolf's head on a body that was human except for the genitals.

Rebekka knelt on the ground, telling the female, "It will be easier if you lie down."

The Wolf complied, stretching out though her body vibrated with agitation.

Rebekka trusted Levi to have spoken the truth about what the Weres desired, but she couldn't bring herself to use her gift without making sure the Wolf understood fully what her choice meant. "I can push the parts of you that are human back or I can push the animal away, so you're one or the other. But if I change you, there's no going back. You will remain in animal form or in a human one. Do you understand?"

"Yes." The answer was growled with lips pulled back and eyes darkening with rage. "I am Wolf. My mate is Wolf."

Rebekka looked up to find the male had moved close enough to attack. He was tensed, but she'd lived in the Were brothels since she was sixteen, and with Levi at her back she felt no fear.

She turned her attention to the female, reaching for calm and projecting it outward. She wasn't telepathic but her gift allowed her to touch emotion, to use it when dealing with animals and Weres.

"This won't hurt, but it'll feel strange, almost like you're a piece of clay in the hands of a sculptor." She placed her hands on the female's furred shoulder. "Try not to offer any resistance. It'll go faster and be easier for both of us if you don't."

"I'll try."

Rebekka closed her eyes, gathering her will to her as though it were something with form and substance. Her fingers tingled where they touched the Wolf, but the feeling passed quickly. In its place came the stomach-dropping sensation of fingertips passing through furred skin, like the sliding of a blunt knife into soft clay.

She became both sculptor and tool with the use of her gift. It was a melding that took her completely, sucked her in and blocked everything external out.

It was instinctive, complex. In her mind she saw what needed to be re-formed, reshaped. She felt her will driving the human parts back and tugging the wolf forward, forcing change where it wouldn't willingly come.

By the time it was done and her hands dropped to her lap, she was light-headed.

The Wolf sprang to its feet and backed away, telegraphing distrust despite Rebekka's help. The male took his mate's place, positioning himself on hands and knees rather than lying down.

Weariness washed through Rebekka. Sensing it, Levi said, "Take as long as you need. The Tiger, Canino, is accompanying Cyrin and me to Lion lands. The three of us will make sure you get back to the brothel safely before we leave."

Rebekka reached for strength and found it. "I can keep going."

She placed her hands on the Wolf's back. Though his mate had spoken for him, she still asked if it was his choice to become fully wolf. He yipped in answer, howled, and once again Rebekka let herself become her gift.

The healing took longer. Rebekka knew it by the change in light, by the hunger pains reminding her it had been a long time since morning and breakfast.

As soon as she lifted her hands from the male's fur he sprang to his feet. But unlike the female, he didn't back away in distrust. He stared, intelligent eyes meeting hers, holding a promise that if it ever came to pass that she needed his aid, he would help her.

"Thank you," she said.

He turned away then and, with his mate, melted into the darkening forest.

"You need food," Levi said. "The others can hunt while I build a fire."

Rebekka glanced at the three remaining Weres. They were all big cats.

Cyrin, Levi's brother, had the flattened, maned face of a lion. His arms were furred, ending in paws with deadly, nonretractable claws.

The Leopard had animal arms, legs, head, and back but human chest and genitals. A short distance away was the Tiger, a beast from his armpits down.

Rage filled Rebekka looking at the men. It poured strength into her.

What had been done to these Weres was criminal. It should never have been allowed by the vice lords who ruled the red zone.

There were Weres in the brothels who were an abomination of shape, too. She knew some of their stories but none of them had been trapped and created through torture so they could be used for entertainment purposes.

"I can do another before eating," Rebekka said. Her gaze fell on the Leopard. With only his chest and genitals human, he would be the easiest—or so she thought until he indicated his choice, to take a man's form.

She was shaking with exhaustion by the time it was done, so tired it sounded as though the ocean thundered in her head. So weary she couldn't find the strength to stand despite the smell of meat cooking in a fire pit.

"Thank you," the Leopard said.

Curious, Rebekka asked, "Why?"

"Because I have people to kill and this form will serve me best."

Levi returned to help Rebekka to her feet. The Leopard lingered only long enough to eat some of the cooked deer; then after accepting a knife from Levi, he, too, entered the forest, startling a bright red cardinal into flight as he passed under the branch it sat on.

Food restored Rebekka's strength enough for her to heal the Tiger, Canino, and then Levi's brother, Cyrin. Both chose to take their animal forms.

"Stay here for the night? Or go back to the brothel?" Levi asked.

Rebekka looked at the rapidly darkening sky. "I've been away too long. By now I'll be needed in the brothels. If we hurry we can make it back to Oakland."

Two

BLOOD and bowel and death. The shallow grave was an afterthought. The burial meant to delay the discovery of the bodies, hiding scent until predators had destroyed answers to how and when and who, and nature had eradicated the trail leading back to where.

The attempt failed. In jaguar form Aryck could easily find the answers to all those questions. Even *why* didn't evade him, not when he felt the same seething emotions over the presence of human intruders in territory held by the Weres.

Giving up the Jaguar's black form, fur yielded to smooth, deeply tanned skin. Bones and organs reorganized, the pain sharp, excruciating, lasting only long enough to mark the transition between beast and man, to serve as a reminder of the covenant between his kind and the Earth that had given birth to them.

Aryck remained crouched at the graveside, looking down at the man and woman he'd unearthed. His pack mate Daivat's scent rose, intermingled with that of the dead.

Arrogant fool, Aryck thought, lips tightening into a grim line as he surveyed the carnage.

He reached in and grabbed the man's blood-drenched shirt. Pulled the corpse from the shallow blanket of earth with easy strength.

The head dropped as though it would follow the shower of dirt back into the grave. It remained held to the body by sinew alone, a testament to the powerful swipe of Daivat's claws in what would have been a fatal strike, though whether it had come first or last was unanswerable.

The human had been mauled. He'd been attacked in a rage Aryck knew stemmed from an urge not only to drive out an intruder but to prove himself, to issue a challenge to both the interlopers and, subconsciously, to the pack's alpha.

Aryck released the corpse. It landed on the rich loam of the shallow hole with a soft thud.

He took more care with the female, rising to his feet as he lifted her. Her skirt fell open as he stepped backward, stirring the air and adding the smell of sex to that of death.

Aryck placed her on the ground before returning to his crouch. The front of her blouse was torn and, like the skirt, opened to leave her bare and exposed.

Bruises marred her skin. Black and yellow. Purple. Old and new alike. A long history of them on her arms and legs.

His gaze flicked to the dead man in consideration, then back to the woman. Between her pubic mound and left hip she bore a tattoo, a solid circle of black with a bloodred symbol set in its center.

Dried semen on her inner thighs told a complex tale. Not a single man, but many. All of them human. Except one. Daivat.

Was it rape? Aryck growled low and deep in his throat. The thought of it was abhorrent, regardless of the species involved in the act.

He studied the woman, looking for evidence to either condemn or vindicate Daivat of at least one of his crimes, then growled again in frustration at not finding any. Neither his jaguar senses nor his human ones could tell whether she'd given herself to Daivat willingly or not.

The blood on her clothes and skin belonged to the dead man. Her death had been as quick as her companion's, but not as messy, a snapped neck instead of a throat ripped open.

Both killings happened more than a mile away in a tangled stretch of wild grapevines. And like the burial place, the attack was on Coyote land. It was forbidden territory to any Jaguar except those sent for the purpose of gathering information about the humans who'd arrived in a caravan of heavy trucks.

Their encampment was guarded by uniformed men anxious to send bullets into live targets. The rattle of machine guns cut across the valley daily, scattering predator and prey alike with random bursts of violence and the senseless brutality that was the hallmark of the only-human race.

Aryck rose from his examination of the female. He wondered what Daivat's explanation of events would be.

Entering the forbidden area alone was enough to warrant punishment. Killing the humans without sanction, then hiding the deed rather than coming forward and explaining the necessity of it, made what he'd done worse.

Weres were three-souled. Man soul and beast soul living harmoniously and perfectly entwined in the physical world while the eternal soul resided in the shadowlands with the ancestors.

In another Were, killing and hiding the deed might signify the beginning of a rogue state, an imbalance or separation of the man and animal souls. Aryck didn't think that was the case with Daivat.

This challenge had been a long time in coming. It was inevitable, but only a fool blinded by arrogance would issue it now, and under these circumstances.

Pure jaguars were solitary creatures by nature, with males fighting to establish and defend their territories against other males. In Weres the animal need of their beast soul was tempered by their human one. It drew them together into communities, for fellowship and safety and to keep from losing themselves in beast form and beast mind. Even so, an alpha couldn't afford to show weakness or he would find himself challenged by another male.

Aryck's fingers flexed in jaguar reaction, instinctively preparing for a fight as he reached mentally for the pack's alpha, his father, Koren.

The ability to communicate telepathically was rare among Weres, but it ran strong in his father's bloodline. *You found something?* Koren asked without preamble.

Yes. Aryck transferred images and perceptions to his father, starting from where he'd come across Daivat's scent and traveling to the kill site, before ending with what he'd discovered in the shallow grave.

Prostitute, his father said at the sight of the woman's tattoo. *There are settlements in the San Joaquin still following many of the laws enacted during The Last War.*

Though he didn't elaborate further, Aryck knew his father hadn't lain with one of the prostitutes, but had seen the tattoo in the days when he himself was an enforcer hunting Weres who fled a death sentence. The mating bond between his parents had been so strong that even though his mother died giving birth to him, his father had never sought another female, much less a human who sold herself.

Do you want the bodies brought back to serve as evidence?

No. Dispose of them as you see fit. Daivat remains away from camp. I will summon the pack to the challenge circle and confront him with his crimes once you've both returned.

Aryck's fingers flexed and phantom claws emerged. Inherent in his father's words was a warning he should be ready to serve as the pack's enforcer.

The mental connection fell away, leaving Aryck to contemplate the corpses he'd unearthed. Jaguars carried their dead high into the trees in a place deemed sacred by a shaman. They left them for the carrion birds and insects to pick clean, then for the sun to purify. Later, those bones that could be gathered by the elders were placed in the ancestral cave dug deep in a steep hillside.

He was no shaman to know the disposition of these only-human souls. Nor did they matter to him. Pack came first, and these dead represented nothing but danger to his kind.

He and Daivat had both covered their tracks to this burial site. Still, until more was known about the human encampment, Aryck was hesitant to leave the bodies so close to it. If there were gifted humans among those who'd invaded Coyote lands, it was possible they could find these corpses.

Even in the cities, where rule of law was said to prevail, Weres were protected only while in human form. Evidence of a jaguar attack might well offer an excuse for those in the encampment to come hunting with their guns, killing his kind regardless of whether they wore fur or not.

Aryck once again lifted the dead man from the shallow grave, slinging the carcass over his shoulder as he would have done to a slain deer. He did the same to the woman, balancing the weight before settling into a smooth, mile-eating run.

He traveled well-worn game paths until he drew near a pack of spotted hyenas. It was Jaguar land, but like most of the other Were alphas, his father allowed pure animals to move about freely as long as their presence didn't threaten the pack.

Aryck grimaced in reaction to scrub marked with oily excrement from hyena anal glands. He stopped on a sheltered rise above the den area and lowered the corpses to the ground.

The wind favored him, carrying the smell of death toward the direction he'd come from. He carefully stripped the bodies, dropping the torn and bloody clothing into a pile before creeping forward to peer down at the gathered pack.

Humans thought of hyenas as scavengers, but they were predators to be respected. Aryck had no desire to become their prey. There were almost thirty animals present, including two he didn't recognize. From their subservient behavior and small size he guessed they were males.

Several cubs played near a watchful female. They wrestled and tumbled, making Aryck smile in remembrance of a simpler time in his life, and reminding him, too, of the four mischievous and adventurous Jaguar cubs he often found himself hunting and chastising for the danger their curiosity led them to.

He took a moment to study the slope leading down to the lounging pack. It was steep enough to serve his purpose.

Given the lack of threat coupled with the promise of food, he doubted the hyenas would give chase. Still, he hurled the corpses as far from his position as possible.

A rattling growl sounded immediately. It was echoed tenfold then followed by loud whooping, a rallying call announcing a meal as the first animal reached the bodies.

Aryck paused only long enough to gather the discarded clothing then began running, confident that by the time he reached camp nothing would remain of the murdered humans, not even a bone.

FIREFLIES lit the dusk and swarms of tiny, winged fey raced for their nighttime hives as Rebekka and the others reached the forest edge closest to the street lined with Were brothels. Her breath caught when she spared a glance in the direction of the maze. It was leveled, reduced to rubble and chunks of brick that made the demon's destruction in the woods seem like nothing.

He'd been a prisoner there as much as the Weres had been, used by the former priest, Anton, not just to guard the maze but to provide entertainment by hunting humans and beasts in it for the benefit of the gaming clubs. For Abijah to escape it, to wreak such damage . . .

Fear settled in Rebekka's chest for Araña, who'd entered the maze in payment of a debt owed to vampires, sent there in order to destroy the urn once housing the demon. And for Tir, who'd left to find Araña after helping to free the Weres.

Levi whistled softly and, guessing that she worried, said, "If Abijah didn't kill you, he probably left them alive as well. Let's hope Araña and Tir were also successful in killing Abijah's master."

Rebekka couldn't suppress a shudder. If Anton lived, he would never stop searching for those responsible for his loss.

"Let's go," Levi said, a hand on her arm drawing her away from the sight of the destroyed maze. "We don't have time to savor our victory. The brothel doors will lock soon."

They stepped from the woods. Movement drew Rebekka's eye. A ragged street boy scurried along the front of buildings, probably having delayed to eat whatever food he'd managed to scrounge so he wouldn't have to share it with those he took shelter with.

Cyrin and Canino left the trees. Rebekka started to tell them to remain hidden but Levi said, "This close to nightfall the feral dogs will already be out. They're getting bolder. It'll be safer staying together than separating."

"I can make it the rest of the way on my own," Rebekka said, forcing confidence into her voice because the thought of losing Cyrin and Canino to a bullet now was intolerable. The red zone was no safer for Weres in pure animal form than the areas of Oakland where laws were enforced by police and guardsmen.

"We'll see you to safety." The growl in Levi's voice was echoed by the deep rumble of the other big cats.

"Then we'd better hurry."

Like the street boy, they kept to the shadows. Moved along the sides of buildings boarded up for the night, shutters and doors closed tightly by shopkeepers who didn't rely only on bars to keep predators out.

The red zone was as varied as Oakland itself. Pockets of wealth, clubs and homes owned by the vice lords and their associates, were surrounded by places where the poor lived.

They entered the area holding the businesses and homes of outcast Weres. As they passed a bar with a skinned human nailed to the front of it, raucous noise drifted through the open windows along with the smell of beer and meat. Unlike the Were brothels, which were locked against the night to keep prostitutes and patrons safe, places like the bar remained open, daring predator and prey alike to enter.

They were close enough to their destination to be recognized by those who frequented this area of the red zone. Rebekka moved into the middle of the street so they could be seen and use the fear of the vice lord Allende to keep them safe the remaining distance. Most knew she was under Allende's protection when she worked in the Were brothels, and viewed Levi as her bodyguard.

Cyrin and Canino stayed lost in deep shadow but Rebekka could sense where they were. Intensified by proximity to the maze, their desire to kill licked at her like hot flames and erupted into action when she and Levi rounded the corner and were rushed by five strangers, three of them armed with heavy iron pipes.

Cyrin and Canino reacted instantly, without offering warning. In a bounding run Cyrin knocked the first of the pipe-wielding men down.

A sickening crunch marked the crushing of a skull and the first death.

It was followed by a second, and a third.

By a shriek of terror as Canino dragged the man who'd grabbed Rebekka's arm to the ground and mauled him as the fifth fled.

It was over in seconds. The attack and counterattack so fast Rebekka barely had time to understand what was happening.

Out of sight, an engine roared to life and a vehicle sped off, leaving the dead behind. By daybreak the corpses would be gone, taken care of by the creatures who ruled the night.

Levi rifled through the dead men's pockets and found nothing. He joined Rebekka, taking her arm and allowing her only a quick glimpse of the bodies before urging her forward, forcing her into a run that kept her from trembling in reaction to the sudden shock of violence.

"Did you recognize them?" he asked.

"No. But if I saw the one who got away again, I would. He had a birthmark on the left side of his face, a port-wine stain."

Canino edged closer, flanking her. Cyrin did the same for his brother.

"Who do you think sent them?" she asked.

"The Church maybe, if they're still trying to recapture Tir. Or the vice lords who own the gaming clubs. There are cameras in the maze. Before it was destroyed we might have been seen freeing the animals and leaving with Cyrin and the others."

They reached the first of the Were brothels connected to others by secure passageways. Rebekka gave Levi a hug, her stomach cramping at the thought of him out in the night, trapped in human form. "Go."

"You first. Make sure Feliss knows I'll be back as soon as I see Cyrin home." He hugged Rebekka against him before she could step away. "Don't leave the brothel. You're safe there, even from the other vice lords."

"I won't."

Caphriel's Pawn

THE cool evening air brought the sound of wolves howling in the distance and the nerve-racking yipping of coyotes. Goose bumps pimpled Radek's skin at hearing them so close to the encampment with the arrival of night.

"Filthy beasts," he muttered, casting an involuntary glance at the concertina wire stretched along the tops of the walls. It, and the threat posed by machine gun-carrying humans, was the primary defense against being overrun by Weres.

By law, this area was his now to salvage in—as long as he could hold it. But he was well aware of being deep in hostile lands.

Anger flashed through Radek. He shouldn't have to scurry around like a man afraid of his shadow. By rights the entire encampment should be bright with light. He shouldn't have to pay the Ivanov militiamen premium wages to patrol by lantern light in groups, gossiping and joking at his expense.

Radek purposely slowed his pace, not wanting to show any fear to the conscripted criminals and poor human trash who made up his workforce, or to the militiamen who answered to his father, or to the handful of guardsmen who probably spied for the other Founding Families of Oakland.

The scent of fresh-cut timber drew him to a shored-up opening leading downward, into space no human had been in for hundreds of years until he was responsible for it being unearthed. Pride filled him. Satisfaction coursed through his veins.

He'd done what he'd set out to do. After years of collecting and studying texts created in the days before The Last War, he'd identified the site of a laboratory dedicated to energy-related technology.

The bitter taste of having to grovel for money to fund this expedition into Were lands filled Radek's mouth for an instant, only to be replaced by the sweetness of success as he relived the moment when the overseer's shout called him to where tons of broken concrete had been cleared to reveal a hollowed-out spot and a safe still set in what had once been a wall.

It took a full day and almost every laborer in the encampment to get the safe out. Another to get it open and locked in the privacy of the building he'd claimed as his own. He was still going over the contents on the computer storage drives, the files upon files of schematics and designs for harnessing energy.

Much of it was useless, the technology no longer in existence to produce the parts or even the plants necessary to create them, but some of it, enough of it, was clearly viable—not in his hands; he had no desire to manage a commercial empire, but in a buyer's . . .

A surreptitious glance and Radek found Captain Nagy, his brother's loyal dog, leaning against a building, cigarette tip glowing red in the growing darkness. No doubt he'd already managed to get word of the safe to Viktor.

Radek laughed softly, imagining Viktor's face turning furiously red as he desperately tried to outbid those gathered at an auction—only to lose.

Or perhaps not.

It would be immensely satisfying to sell whatever information and physical items were salvaged here to the family, taking back a share of the profits they later generated by it and making it a condition that each month, Viktor, his father's smug, condescending heir, had to personally deliver Radek's due.

With a smile on his face Radek turned away from the opening.

There was plenty of time to consider the best way to handle the gold mine of information contained in the safe. This was only the very beginning of the discoveries. So far his workers had excavated just a small part of what he knew lay beneath the rubble of the valley floor.

As he neared the building housing the prostitutes whose contracts he'd purchased from a vice lord in the red zone, the guard captain, Orst, emerged. Radek braced himself. It was too much to hope he was there to make use of the women.

When Orst hailed him, Radek stopped rather than be followed back to his quarters and have his work interrupted. He didn't trust anyone in camp when it came to the contents of the safe, wouldn't have allowed the guard's presence at all if it hadn't been a requirement attached to using the convicts. That it *had* been a requirement only served to make him more suspicious.

If his brother-in-law Felipe were still running the guard—

But then Felipe and Ilka had played one time too many in the Oakland red zone. They'd become part of the entertainment when they were tossed out of Sinners, the club they favored.

A fitting end, Radek thought. They were savaged by werewolves and feral dogs as the gathered crowd sipped brightly colored drinks and watched from the safety of the old Victorian house.

Another strain of coyote song pierced the evening air. Radek shivered before he could stop himself. "What is it?" he snapped, irritated at having shown any reaction.

Captain Orst's expression remained flawlessly neutral. *A feat in itself*, Radek thought sourly, *considering the pole that must be rammed up the man's ass*.

"The prostitutes tell me one of them has been missing for over a day. Apparently she was called from their quarters to service a convict yesterday morning and didn't return. The man in question is also absent. His foreman says he reported it to you. Under the terms of the conscription contract you were supposed to inform the guard immediately."

"It slipped my mind. Consider yourself notified. The workers and prostitutes were warned not to leave the encampment. The fate of those who do is not my concern. One might even consider it a validation of Darwin's principles. Now if that's all, I have work waiting for me."

"I will return to Oakland within the next day or so and file the necessary paperwork."

Orst turned away, heading in the direction of the building housing the guardsmen. At the sight of the man's straight back in its neatly pressed uniform, Radek allowed himself the small fantasy of the captain encountering a pack of coyotes in the woods and being ripped to shreds as a reward for conscientious duty. *Sanctimonious prick.*

Irritation flashed to anger in Radek. If his father had been willing to give him more money instead of calling this venture a pipe dream and turning over what little was officially Radek's inheritance, then he wouldn't have needed to supplement his workforce with criminals. He wouldn't need to tolerate the guard's presence and, worse, pay for it as insurance that the conscripted men were treated fairly and not thrown to the Weres as the situation warranted it.

Radek snorted at the ludicrousness of it all. Civil rights for criminals. Concern for whores and the worthless poor. Ridiculous. If there'd been enough of his brother-in-law left to bury then Felipe would have spun in his grave at the direction the guard was taking as the various factions, including the Iberás, fought for control of it.

Radek paused long enough to turn on his personal generator before entering his quarters. He double-checked the locks on the windows then took a seat at his desk, turning on the computer so he could resume his study of the files.

It was a tedious, mind-numbing process.

Open the file.

Read through pages filled with complex words and ideas.

Decide whether any of it needed further study or not.

His alertness faded quickly, though it returned for an instant when he stumbled upon mention of a top secret government-sponsored project being worked on elsewhere in the laboratory complex currently being excavated.

Radek's eyes grew gritty, the lids heavy. The drone of the generator outside and the increasing stuffiness inside made it difficult for him to stay awake.

He succumbed to sleep, to a favored dream.

In it he smiled as he surveyed the reclaimed valley that was his domain. Where there was now rubble and ruin, much of it covered in tangled vines and rot-created dirt, a city stood.

Its entrance and the roads leading to it were controlled by him. And like the city itself, they were patrolled not by guardsmen or the private militia answering to his father and Viktor, but by men who owed their allegiance to him and wore a crest of his own design rather than the one created by an Ivanov ancestor.

His wealth surpassed that of all the Founding Families of Oakland combined. It rivaled that of the Tassonc vampire family who ruled San Francisco.

In his sleep Radek smiled as he stood at the entrance of a grand estate and watched the motorcade containing his father arrive.

A chauffeur emerged from a sleek black limousine to open the back door. His father exited, pride wreathing his face as his gaze encompassed the city and the mansion behind Radek. "You've done well, son. Better than your brother, Viktor."

There was a short, pain-filled hesitation. "And God rest her soul, your sister, who was taken from us too soon."

Radek aped his father's sadness over Ilka's death even as he pressed his lips together tightly to keep from pointing out she'd brought her fate on herself. Death made saints of grasping bitches and sinners alike, and his sister was both.

He escorted his father along a hallway filled with priceless artwork and into his study. Poured two glasses of expensive, imported brandy as his father claimed a plush chair covered in jaguar hide so black there was only a hint of the rosette pattern present in the fur.

The sleeping Radek frowned, recognizing a deviation in the recurrent fantasy. But the thread of concern dropped away when his father said, "I've arranged a parade through Oakland celebrating your achievement."

His father lifted his glass in salute, pulling Radek more firmly into the altered dream. "To your vision. And to your courage for pursuing it when few would have dared."

Radek touched his glass to his father's and the scene changed, veering into new territory but making his chest swell with pleasure. He was riding in an open-topped jeep through the wealthiest section of Oakland.

Flags bearing his standard fluttered on the vehicles in front of him, as well as the one he was in. Men and women and children, all of them members of the elite, waved from their balconies while their servants lined the street. Even his sour-faced brother tipped his head as the motorcade passed, while at his side, Viktor's tight-lipped wife regretted turning Radek down when he had expressed an interest in her first.

Oh how sweet it is, Radek thought, accepting his due as he reflected on the long nights he'd spent locked in the tiny quarters of the original encampment, the generator droning as he painstakingly went over the items salvaged by a crew made up of society's dregs.

The computer screen he'd been staring at before falling asleep slipped into the dream, a sinuous thread working its way into his consciousness.

Numbers and letters rearranged themselves like a divine gift for the worthy, giving up the details of the government-sponsored project being conducted in a separate lab.

A thrill swept through Radek, followed by a chill. The scientists had known about the existence of Weres. They'd anticipated their emergence and thought they would one day attempt to rule over humans. They'd made plans for that day, to wipe them out using viruses tailored to individual species and tied to nanites.

Fear nearly woke Radek. He'd grown up viewing the stark images of plague and anarchy, the nightmare masterpieces hanging on the walls of every Founding Family to glorify their part in restoring order to Oakland and reclaiming it for mankind.

Before icy horror could force him from the dream, the dark, hungry place in his soul pulled at him, and he was once again in the jeep. Next to him, his father murmured, "Nothing can bring your sister back, but by freeing us forever from the threat the Weres present, you're a hero to the human race."

It was a golden dream of power and wealth and glory, a temptation so sublime there was no turning away from it. "I did what needed to be done," Radek said, drinking in the sound of the crowds calling his name.

Three

REBEKKA climbed the brothel staircase. There was nothing she could do but wait, and hope Levi remained safe. Even with her gift she wouldn't be welcomed in Were territory. No humans were.

Levi would be accepted only long enough to tell his pride family what happened to his brother and to him in Oakland; then he would be forced to leave. Or he would die there. Trapped in a man's form, he was viewed as outcast.

Early on in their friendship, she'd been certain if they managed to free Cyrin from the maze, Levi would choose death among his kind over life in the red zone. Worry he would change his mind about coming back gripped her. He was her closest friend and the thought of never seeing him again was intolerable.

At the top of the stairs she punched in a code allowing her access to the second floor. Along the length of the hallway the doors were all closed. As she passed by them she could hear music coming from some of the rooms, but most were empty.

Those prostitutes who worked during the day and had somewhere else to go would be off the premises so they couldn't be called upon to service clients. Those who worked during the night would be downstairs or in one of the other houses.

The vice lord Allende owned them all—buildings and outcast Weres alike. He'd taken control, killing the previous vice lord, a Wolf, the year before she approached Dorrit about working as a healer in the brothels.

Rebekka couldn't suppress a shiver at the thought of being bound by contract to Allende. Some said his animal form was Hyena. Others Jackal. Levi said Allende smelled like Leopard. She'd met the vice lord only once, but she'd heard tales of what he did to those who tried to flee without fulfilling the terms of their agreements—even when those terms were dictated by someone else, a debt-holder or a family member or a court of human law.

For room and board and safety she healed those who worked in the brothels owned by him. She was free to come and go as she pleased, yet she couldn't escape this world of prostitutes or the red zone where they plied their trade. She felt bound by her gift, by her upbringing, by the tattoo marking her as a prostitute though she'd never given herself to a man.

Rebekka reached the end of the walkway and once again entered codes allowing her to pass. Unlike the building she'd just left, serving only Weres, this one held rooms for hosting parties of sexual excess.

The walkway continued, a bridge built on top of the hallway separating the three front rooms from the three back rooms. Weres patrolled it, walking back and forth, a leap away from preventing trouble or delivering punishment, a menacing presence there to ensure patrons got what they paid for, no more and no less.

All of those supervising the activities were pure, able to shift between human and animal forms. Their presence in the red zone made Rebekka assume they were outcasts forced from Were lands by their deeds.

She barely glanced at scenes playing out in the six rooms. The only difference between these and the ones that had taken place in the brothels she'd grown up in was that here men—and sometimes women—played out their fantasies with prostitutes they considered little more than animals.

Oakland was a port town and the red zone thrived as a result of it. The Were brothels provided something humans who lived elsewhere couldn't easily experience.

She passed into the next building, going down to the first floor. Plush carpet and walls painted in erotic murals created a feeling of luxury and entitlement. A higher class of client was served here but not an exclusive one like the three brothels on the other side of the street.

It was too early in the night for her services to be needed in this building, but they would be. Just as they would be needed in the one she entered next, a place dedicated to those who thrived on giving and receiving pain.

The sounds of screams and growls, of whips and paddles, dominated. There were few private rooms, as those who found sexual satisfaction in the dungeonlike setting enjoyed an audience.

Rebekka hurried through, the flash of wedding bands glinting as hands rose and fell, delivering blows. Once again she climbed stairs and entered a walkway. Relief came at reaching the last building, and then the small room that was hers.

She sat on the bed, legs suddenly wobbly, and wished she could stay. She couldn't.

She'd already been away too long. There'd be those who needed her, and she had a message to pass on for Levi. This was the worst of the brothels Allende owned. It served the dregs, the humans who were that in name only.

Rebekka forced herself to stand. She allowed herself the luxury of a hot shower and a change of clothes before going downstairs.

In the alcove just beyond the parlor where Dorrit negotiated with clients, Feliss waited. She was delicate and beautiful, doe-eyed with a timidness attracting both the best and the worst of the men who visited the brothel.

Like the other prostitutes, she wore little in the way of clothing. From the front she could pass for human, hiding the black, horn-tough finger- and toenails underneath polish. But when she turned around, her shoulders, back, and buttocks revealed her Deer heritage.

Because they were friends, Rebekka knew Feliss's story. Her mother was a Deer trapped by a hunter who rarely left the woods. Rather than accept death, she shifted into human form, erroneously thinking it would be easy to escape.

The trapper never dropped his guard. He kept her chained or caged, used her as whore and wife and ultimately the mother of his child.

When the opportunity arose, and Feliss managed to free her mother, her mother *changed* and returned to the forest. If Feliss had been able to shift between forms, instead of being born in a mixed one, then her mother wouldn't have abandoned her.

But because Feliss wasn't pure, she was left behind. And when she hit puberty, she was forced to take her mother's place as whore and wife until the hunter who'd fathered her came to Oakland to sell the pelts he'd taken years to gather, and sold Feliss as well to the vice lord before Allende.

Rebekka's stomach turned thinking about it. She raged at the horror, the injustice.

It shouldn't be possible to hold a woman against her will, human or Were. It shouldn't be possible to sell someone into prostitution.

But if the history books were to be believed, even in the United States, before The Last War, sexual slavery existed, with the masses turning a blind eye, not wanting to know about the plight of girls lured to this country and forced to sell themselves, or about the millions who had no choice in other places around the world.

Rebekka crossed her arms over her chest, rubbed her palms against the material of her blouse. This was the first time she'd been to the brothel since escaping from the Iberá estate after being held there in the hopes she would lead the patriarch to Tir.

For the Iberá patriarch, the hunt was now over. She had no fear of being made a prisoner at the estate again, though a tightness swelled in her chest at a remembered conversation. He wanted the red zone eliminated. But as horrible as the brothels were, if he succeeded, the prostitutes would find their contracts sold.

Some would be sent to other cities. Some would be placed on ships like the *Pleasure Venture*, or sold to brothel caravans like the one she lived in until her mother's contract was bought by a vice lord in Oakland. And some would simply disappear, sold to places like the maze, or to hunters like Feliss's father.

If only she could heal them completely, free them from being trapped between forms and make them whole, able to *shift*. If only—

"Are you okay?" Feliss asked, drawing Rebekka from the turmoil of her thoughts.

"I'm fine. Levi found his brother. He wanted me to tell you he'll be back after he sees Cyrin home."

Feliss looked down but not before Rebekka saw the doubt, the hopelessness, in her friend's eyes. She took Feliss's hands in hers and gave them a gentle squeeze.

"He'll be back." If they'd been alone, Rebekka would have added, *He won't forget his promise to buy out your contract so you never have to let another man touch you if it's not your choice*. But they weren't. And she couldn't. Like the human brothels of her childhood, there was jealousy and plays for power here, too.

Feliss pulled free when the sharp clap of hands summoned her into the parlor. Rebekka retreated to the small room that served as her workplace unless someone came to get her. Most of the time she healed using her touch and her will, but she also kept supplies on hand, salves and bandages, formulas meant to reduce pain or cleanse.

Word of her return spread. Within minutes a male Lynx arrived, shuffling in painfully, his human testicles swollen and bruised and his buttocks smeared with blood. He was followed by another prostitute, and another, a steady stream testifying to the brutality of those who visited the brothels.

She'd lost count of how many she'd healed by the time one of the pure Weres who served the dungeon madam arrived. "You're needed in the next building."

"Give me a moment more."

He nodded and left. She finished healing a Cat whose teat hung by a thread of flesh, nearly bitten off by a drunk patron in the bar.

Rebekka rose to her feet, swaying with crushing fatigue. The Cat looked at her without expression, turned away, and left without comment, emotions deadened except for an underlying hatred of all humans.

Rebekka drew in a deep breath, trying to suck strength in with the air. Her gift wasn't inexhaustible. There were limits and she had far exceeded them already with the healing of the Weres in the woods.

She forced herself forward. Passed by the leather-and-fur parlor where Dorrit dickered with a client as female prostitutes stood in a line, Feliss no longer among them.

The bouncer who'd brought the message peeled away from a spot near the doorway to accompany Rebekka down a hallway with glass-fronted windows. Inside the rooms, prostitutes performed the acts required of them while humans paid to walk back and forth, watching from the hall.

Rebekka kept her attention focused forward but it didn't save her from getting a glimpse of Feliss on her knees before a burly, unwashed man. From seeing his fingers wrapped in Feliss's hair as his cock thrust in and out of her mouth with no care for the pain he caused or the damage he might do.

It was a relief to turn onto a hall with the doors closed, to have several moments away from the brothel atmosphere as she and the bouncer entered the stairway, climbing upward before stepping onto the connecting walkway and going to the next building.

They descended once again, and, even muted by the walls separating the passageway from the dungeons, Rebekka could hear screams and cries and the sounds of paid-for violence.

Instead of remaining in the parts of the brothel off-limits to clients, the bouncer punched in a code and opened a door leading to the area set aside for play. The scent of sweat and blood and sex hit Rebekka.

"This way," he said, placing a hand on her back and guiding her, his presence a deadly deterrent.

They walked past men and women gathered around prostitutes bound onto pieces of equipment, gagged and made helpless.

Servers moved among the clients, selling liquor that would erode all boundaries and control by morning, the waitresses and waiters themselves available for a price.

Jewels glittered in the low lighting. It took money to play here, not as much as in the buildings across the street with their private entrances and suites so the rich and powerful could do exactly as they wished with no audience and no threat of discovery, but enough to make this a favorite of the younger sons of wealthy families, many of them guardsmen.

Ahead a crowd gathered in front of an open-faced dungeon. As Rebekka neared she heard girlish laughter, then several female voices shouting in unison, "Twenty-eight!"

It was followed by the sound of a whip cracking, by delighted giggles, and another count. "Twenty-nine!"

At "Thirty!" the crowd began wandering off, the show complete.

Rebekka's breath caught in her throat at the sight of the Lioness, Kala, chained to the gray wall. Her back was raw hamburger with tawny fur mixed in, her tail striped with blood and bent at odd angles, cut and broken by the whip. Clear, curved nails extended from human hands, claws unsheathed in reaction to the pain.

A human woman stood admiring her work, hands bloody as they caressed the whip she held. Her friends protested when the bouncer went to Kala, unlocking first one manacle and then the other. He ignored them, and when Kala slipped into unconsciousness as he scooped her up in his arms, they, too, wandered off, reliving their fun in animated conversation.

Hate raged in Rebekka, listening to them. For a shimmering instant she allowed herself to imagine healing Kala, making her purely Were so the Lioness could hunt down these women and slaughter them.

The force of the desire to see it shocked her. A chill swept down her spine, stripping away some of the shield she'd managed to erect against the demon's mention of her father. A single act of violence was all that was required to turn her gift into a thing causing pain and suffering.

Kala's low moan allowed Rebekka to block out thoughts of the demon and once again escape into purpose. She followed the bouncer to a camouflaged door and keyed in the code, opening it so he could enter. After placing Kala facedown on a blanket left ready on the floor, he asked, "You want her tethered?"

Rebekka glanced at the restraints set in the floor, then at Kala's still-unretracted claws. Healing unconscious Weres and animals was always dangerous.

Awake she could touch emotion, instill calmness and trust long enough to repair damage and end pain, though she rarely needed to do so with the prostitutes since they knew her. But without the connection, she risked being attacked with the sudden return of her patient's consciousness, especially when rage and remembered suffering would be at the forefront of their minds.

Kala moaned again. "Can you stay a few minutes and hold her arms to the floor?" Rebekka asked as she knelt next to the Lioness.

The bouncer answered by crouching down and pinning Kala's wrists. Though he appeared fully human, he was stronger than one. A big cat of some kind, she guessed, but like the reasons for his being in the red zone, he wouldn't reveal his animal form unless forced to.

Rebekka placed her hands on Kala's back and closed her eyes. She called her gift to life by willing flesh and muscle to mend, urging skin to be covered in sleek fur.

When it came to those trapped between forms, she could heal their injuries but couldn't alter how they wore the mixture of animal and man. She could offer those like Kala a choice between appearing fully human or fully animal, but it came with the risk of being punished by the vice lord. And beyond that, few wanted to live out the rest of their lives in animal form, or take a human's when they saw little advantage to it.

The Lioness returned to consciousness with a snarl, with a furious struggling that ended when her head whipped around at the sound of Rebekka's voice saying her name, projecting calm and urging her to relax and allow healing to take place.

Kala subsided, claws retracting but body remaining tensed in pain. "You can let me go now."

The bouncer looked to Rebekka for conformation.

"We'll be okay alone," she said.

He released Kala and stood. "How long?"

Rebekka fought the anger that came with knowing he meant *how long until Kala can be sold again*. She hated that in using her gift, those who worked in the brothels would endure more in a night than they could otherwise. That seeing Kala return to the dungeon, restored to health, perpetuated the belief among humans that Weres could take more abuse and would heal rapidly from it.

The pure Were did heal by shifting between forms. Rebekka's bouncers were rarely injured severely enough to need her.

It was different for the prostitutes who couldn't change. Rebekka's function in the brothel was a guarded secret known to few outside those connected to them.

A hard, cold fist wrapped around Rebekka's heart, squeezing mercilessly, whispering in a demon's voice, telling her that using her gift extended pain, allowed for the oily spread of human evil.

No! she told herself, slamming the door against the insidious doubt caused by Abijah's words. What happened in Were brothels was no different than what she'd witnessed when she lived with her mother among human prostitutes.

"How long?" the bouncer asked again.

"I don't know."

He scowled and gave Kala a hard look. "I'll be back in an hour if you're not out on the floor."

Kala shrugged, though the hiss of pain following it revealed that it cost her. The bouncer turned and left the room.

Rebekka placed her hands on Kala's back again. Closed her eyes and resumed concentrating on the weave of flesh and muscle, the return of fur.

Time ebbed and flowed, meaningless except her strength drained away with it.

Exhaustion returned like pounding surf as she used the last of her reserves to mend the bone in Kala's tail and close the gashes left by the whip.

She would have stretched out on the floor if the Lioness hadn't guided her to the cot kept in the room for use after a grueling healing.

"Thanks," Rebekka murmured.

"I'm the one who should be thanking you. Do you want a blanket?"

"I'm fine." She wouldn't be allowed to sleep long, but if she was lucky, it might be a while before another emergency arose.

Kala knelt next to the cot. Rebekka forced her eyes open. Like Feliss, Kala looked fully human from the front. She was beautiful and sleek.

And very interested in Levi, who worked as bouncer, guard, or bartender, depending on the need.

"Is he working tonight?" Kala asked.

Rebekka didn't need to ask who. "No."

Feliss was the only other person beside Rebekka who knew Levi's brother had been held in the maze, and even she didn't know Levi had also once hunted there, or that he'd played a part in today's destruction of it. Like Cyrin, when Levi was a prisoner, he'd had the head of a lion. In human form, he was unrecognizable even to the brothel clients who also visited the gaming clubs and had once watched him on big-screened television sets.

"He's working another job?" Kala asked.

"No," Rebekka said, deciding she needed to tell Kala something or the questions would never end. "He's in the woods but I don't know where."

"And Feliss? Is she with him?" It was said in a light tone, but the look in the Lioness's eyes didn't match it.

Only years spent among Weres kept Rebekka from reacting to the hidden menace with fear. "She's in Dorrit's lineup tonight."

Kala's nose wrinkled. Her lips pulled back in a show of distaste and disdain that was shared by all of the prostitutes who no longer had to work in the brothel catering to the lowest class of humans and Weres.

The Lioness leaned forward, the intensity of her gaze warning Rebekka she'd have to be careful not to let her body tell the truth while her words said something else.

"I heard a rumor today," Kala said, whispering despite it only being the two of them. "I heard Levi intends to buy out Feliss's contract and set her up somewhere as his little snack."

Kala made a show of licking her lips.

"I don't think the rumor is true," Rebekka said, and thought she must have done a credible job of lying when Kala leaned back and cocked her head, then shrugged and stood.

"I'm glad. She's prey and always will be. Bad enough he takes what she offers him, but for Levi to elevate her above the other females he mounts and treat her like a mate . . ." Kala's lips pulled back once again in disgust. "It's perverse."

Rebekka closed her eyes as Kala left the room. Sleep descended, claiming her until she was roused by a bouncer from Dorrit's house.

"You're needed," he said, accompanying her through the dungeon and then the passageway connecting the two buildings.

Rebekka heard drunken sobbing and pleading well before she reached the parlor. When she got there, two bouncers held a man between them. He was on his knees, begging for his life.

Dorrit stood in front of him, boar tusks and small black eyes in a round human face giving the impression of cold savagery. She lifted her hand, halting Rebekka and the bouncer in the doorway.

Gathered into the small space was a collection of other humans. Most were bleary-eyed from drink, rounded up from the bar and brought in to serve as witnesses.

Few of them were looking at the man. Instead they feasted on the lined-up prostitutes, stared with tongues darting out to moisten their lips as they fantasized about being able to afford sex that was more expensive than what was offered in the bar.

"The vice lord Allende is tolerant," Dorrit told the kneeling man, receiving murmurs of agreement when she glanced around. "But this is your second offense."

With a signal from her the prostitutes moved, parting in the middle to reveal a woman lying on the floor behind them, her body curled in a fetal position, her face a bloodied, broken mess.

One of the gathered humans vomited, spewing beer onto brown tile at the sight. Rebekka gave a cry, recognizing Feliss, but was stopped from rushing forward by the bouncer's grip on her arm.

Dorrit turned everyone's attention back to the kneeling man by saying, "The vice lord Allende is tolerant but a second offense can't go unpunished. Put him out."

The man began struggling then. Fighting in earnest.

Those brought in from the bar or pulled from the rooms moved deeper into the parlor, as far from the front doors as they could get.

Dorrit pressed her thumb to a pad. She was one of only a few who could open the doors once the locks were engaged at nightfall.

Unlike the humans who played in the Victorian clubs with names like Sinners, Envy, and Greed, the Were bouncers didn't arm themselves with guns or wear padded protection to step out into the night. They threw the brothel patron to the mercy of the predators, lingered for a moment before stepping inside, doors closing and locks engaging behind them.

The humans who'd pushed to the back of the parlor rushed forward to enjoy the free entertainment. The Weres were less obvious, yet their eyes darkened and flickered with satisfaction, and more than one of them wore a hungry expression as outside feral dogs and wolves attacked, tearing and shredding and growling as they made sport of their meal.

Rebekka went to Feliss. Anger swelled inside her with the knowledge that the human whose screams ended abruptly died not because of what he'd done, but because he lacked the money to pay for the damage to Allende's property.

A hand settled on her shoulder. Dorrit said, "You're broadcasting your emotions, Rebekka. Wherever you've been these last few days, it hasn't been good for you. It's made you forget there are always eyes watching and mouths ready to spread gossip."

Fingers dug in, adding to the warning. Rebekka looked up and saw a hint of compassion in the brothel madam's face. Admitted, "I'm exhausted."

"I'll have Feliss taken to your room. You can take care of her there and stay to get some sleep unless the need for your services is urgent."

Dorrit glanced at the unconscious prostitute. "Feliss can remain out of the lineup for the remainder of the night if she chooses." A shrug said it didn't matter. In the end, the debt owed Allende would be paid.

Four

THE pack members gathered in the clearing, called there by the deep, coughlike roar of their alpha. Men and women and children slid silently from the woods, some in their jaguar form, most in a human one.

At his father's left, his hair and skin still wet from a morning swim, Aryck frowned, noting the absence of the four adventurous Jaguar cubs who so often found trouble—and a fifth, Caius, a Tiger born to a Jaguar female. When this was done, someone would have to find and chastise them for straying so far from camp they didn't hear Koren's summons.

The bloody clothes of Daivat's victims lay piled on the ground in front of the alpha. Aryck had brought them back not to serve as evidence, but so they could be thrown into the fire at the center of the challenge circle to ensure nothing remained of the dead man and woman.

Murmurs arose from those gathered as the scent of human death and Daivat's involvement reached them. Tension built—in anticipation, in dread—stirred to life by what the clothing represented. Threat.

Sound flowed into silence when Daivat arrived, shifting easily from his jaguar form to his human one. Several of the lower-ranked females edged closer, jostling for the attention of a male in his prime, some of them seeking only transitory pleasure while others were ripe and fertile and intent on gaining a permanent mate.

Daivat ignored them, sending a challenging look to Aryck instead.

Aryck met the gaze with a cold one, uncaring about the females who openly courted another male after having presented him with swollen vulvas earlier in the day when he was in jaguar form.

Daivat's fingers flexed in subtle challenge. Rage flared to life in his eyes as a female Jaguar emerged from the woods and rubbed the length of her furred body against Aryck's before changing to human form, her bare breast pressed to Aryck's arm.

Aryck resisted the urge to step away from her but couldn't remain quiet. "This isn't the time or the place for your overtures, Melina."

She purred and pressed a pebbled nipple to his upper arm. "Later then, when this matter is settled."

The deepening of her scent indicated she was aroused by the prospect of violence, by the thought of two dominant males fighting in her presence as though they fought over the right to mount her.

Several male human-formed Jaguars standing nearby hardened in reaction to her heat-scent and sultry voice. Aryck's cock stirred, making him glad he'd pulled on loose shorts rather than coming to the clearing naked in preparation for changing form. He wanted to give Melina no encouragement.

Across from them Daivat's expression darkened with hatred and jealousy when Melina's hand settled on Aryck's belly. Aryck captured her wrist and squeezed in warning. "Not now," he growled. "Not later."

He turned his head to give Melina a deadly stare, Jaguar to Jaguar, one that ordered her away from him. One she couldn't refuse.

Her eyes flashed, resenting him even as he knew his ability to resist her only increased her hunger for the feel of his cock thrusting inside her.

He regretted taking her in the past. He'd only coupled with her for a season, and not exclusively, but that didn't matter to her.

She'd now reached the age when the Jaguar soul wanted to breed.

But unlike the other unmated males in the pack, he had no desire to answer her yowling calls or to end up with her as a permanent mate.

True jaguars took no life-mates; they bred and separated, with the duty of raising the cubs to adulthood falling entirely on the mother. Among Jaguar Weres it was different, nature's way of keeping them from indiscriminate breeding.

When a child was conceived, a bond formed between the parents. It was nearly impossible to break.

If he was foolish enough to cover her and sire her young, then he'd never be free of her.

He understood the compulsions driving Melina. And because he did, he tried to avoid her in jaguar form despite his father's attempts to throw them together.

Deep inside him the beast soul longed to pair, to find a female and claim her thoroughly, completely, in every way a male could take the mate who belonged to him. The man's soul wasn't far behind in wanting a woman to call his own. But even though beast and man, instinct and rational mind, agreed *the one* they wanted for a lifetime wasn't among the pack, when he wore fur, scent became a prime motivator, as did the powerful, natural urge to procreate.

He wasn't so vain as to think Melina's interest in him was only because of his prowess when it came to lovemaking. One day this pack would be his with his father's blessing, or he would leave it to claim a different territory, taking many of its members with him when he did so.

It was their way. It spread their rule over the lands few humans dared venture into and prevented battles of dominance between fathers and sons, as most often, bloodlines ran true and those who ruled were born to it.

That Daivat, too, might one day lead a pack of his own made him a worthy mate in the eyes of many of the females. His father was Nahuatl, the pack's shaman. And a bloodline filled with telepathic alphas was strong on his mother's side.

Like Aryck's mother, Daivat's had gone to the ancestors. And though her bones were never recovered and placed with those in the ancestral cave, Nahuatl knew of her passing through their mate-bond and because he was shaman.

Koren straightened to his full height, signaling the beginning of the proceedings. With his foot he nudged the clothing on the ground, releasing more of its scent. "I call Daivat before me to answer charges of law breaking."

Daivat crossed the circle boldly, skirting the fire blazing hot in its center as if he had no fear of what its being lit meant. He stopped beyond the shredded clothing, nostrils flaring and eyes holding defiance as he spat on the bloodied trousers in challenge and insult.

The muscles along Aryck's back and arms rippled as the Jaguar rose inside him, instinctively preparing to defend the alpha or enforce his will.

"You were in territory forbidden to all but those sent by my order," Koren said. "You killed two humans and thought to conceal it. What defense do you offer?"

"I am only just now returning to camp. I heard the summons and came immediately. As soon as I saw the clothing I knew it was too late to approach you about what I'd done and why I'd done it. My reason for entering Coyote territory was simple. I intended to capture one of the humans and learn what they hope to find and how long they intend to stay.

"I encountered the human female first and accepted what she offered. She was seemingly alone, a whore well used by the men in the encampment. Her companion came upon us afterward and took exception to her fucking an animal when his witch-amulet flared in my presence. He killed her and I returned the favor."

Daivat glanced at Aryck, his lips pulling back in a snarl. "Or did your enforcer tell a different story?"

"The enforcer told no story at all, nor did he find the amulet you mention. He merely gathered the facts. By your own words, you have admitted to defying the law I set down when the humans arrived, and to taking lives without sanction."

Daivat met Koren's eyes in unmistakable challenge. "And I would repeat my actions on behalf of the pack. We cower, hoping the humans will leave on their own and not enter Jaguar territory, when we should be hunting and killing the interlopers one by one if that's what it takes to get rid of them."

Discord rippled through the pack, uneasiness. Many of those gathered felt as Daivat did about the humans.

Aryck agreed with the sentiment. A subtle attack might work where open warfare would bring the military and could all too easily lead to the suspension of laws specifically forbidding hunting Weres in their furred form. But he also saw the wisdom in his father's caution, in gathering information over hasty action.

Daivat's gaze shifted to meet Aryck's. It burned with a desire to fight a battle for dominance, one heightened by Melina's presence at Aryck's side, by her shameless pursuit of another when she was also letting him mount her.

"The enforcer has failed our pack," Daivat said. "It's time another took his place, someone who has already shown courage and gotten closer to the humans than he has. I issue challenge."

"A man who stands accused of law breaking has no right to do so," Koren said, his voice little more than a rumbling growl. "You claim your motive for entering Coyote land was pure, done for the benefit of the pack. Yet the taking of the human female and the death you left in your wake are both signs of one on the rogue path. There is also the curious lack of the amulet. By your actions you could be cast out, but I will let the ancestors judge your heart."

If Daivat feared the ancestors' judgment, there was no sign of it in his scent or expression as he was forced backward when those gathered moved forward, not stopping until they were standing shoulder to shoulder just steps away from a circle marked in the dirt.

Aryck stripped off the shorts, entering the challenge circle naked. Heat from the fire at its center stroked his skin in a deadly caress, reminding him that he, too, would soon be in the presence of the ancestors and subject to their judgment.

The shaman, Nahuatl, joined them. Black eyes stared out through a snarling Jaguar headdress. The hide it was attached to formed a patterned cape and matched the silver-clawed gloves he held, both pairs of them altered to fit human hands.

Nahuatl sang an invocation over the gloves, offering Daivat first choice of them then giving Aryck the remaining pair. When they'd put them on, the shaman stepped from the circle and began a different song, one meant to draw the ancestors' attention.

Pack elders standing at points marked north, south, east, and west struck the drums they carried, a heartbeat rhythm tying pack to ancestors, symbolizing the fragile, ethereal barrier between life and death and between the two worlds.

Daivat lunged quickly, attacking immediately, as if he wanted to have the battle over with before the ancestors arrived.

Aryck danced away, retreating, sweat already coating his skin from the fire's heat.

"Coward," Daivat baited. "Is this why you've brought nothing back? Why we still know nothing important about the humans?"

"And you know more after covering the female and filling *her* with your seed instead of Melina?"

Daivat closed the distance instantly, swinging savagely. Mercilessly. Making Aryck regret answering taunt with taunt as silver-tipped claws tore through the flesh of his upper arm.

In the center of the challenge circle the fire flared at first blood and the heat grew more intense. Around the circle the elders responded by increasing the tempo of their strikes against the hide-covered drums, driving the combatants' heartbeats into a faster pace.

Aryck's blood mixed with sweat, no longer a sheen coating his skin but drops pouring off him like sacrificial rain.

Nahuatl began chanting welcome to the ancestors, and Daivat struck again.

This time Aryck was ready. He deflected the attack, ducking and swiping across Daivat's unprotected belly before moving out of range.

Fear flashed in Daivat's eyes at the opening of his skin. He came at Aryck fast and hard.

Aryck scored another hit, raking claws along Daivat's forearm but sustaining an injury as well.

The silver burned as it cut through the skin over Aryck's collarbone. He hissed in reaction, bared his teeth against the pain.

His heart thundered in time to the nonstop beat of the drums. His blood poured down his chest in a tide of red.

Heat from the fire siphoned strength and will. Aryck fought the effects of it and attacked.

Daivat snarled and leapt at the same time as Aryck did.

Talons grazed Aryck's cheek, leaving a clawed trail. He twisted, savaging Daivat's side.

The fire flared higher, drinking the spray of blood and demanding more of it.

Nahuatl's voice rose, moving from welcome to a prayer for judgment.

Aryck and Daivat circled each other, and as they did Daivat's form changed. Fur replaced the skin on his arms and face and chest, turning him into something neither man nor beast.

Chant and drumbeat ended, the abrupt silence signaling the fight was over.

There was no sound other than the crackle of flame and the panting of the combatants.

Around the circle the pack members' expressions were grim, condemning. Nahuatl stepped forward, hands out to accept the gloves. When he held them he said, "Change," and Aryck did so, accepting the sharp pain with welcome as his bones and organs reorganized and he became Jaguar.

In front of him Daivat remained standing, trapped between forms. Judged so all who looked at him would know the ancestors had sundered Daivat's eternal soul, casting it out of the shadowlands as unworthy to live among them.

Koren spoke. "I name you outcast. Leave Jaguar lands before sunset or be hunted and killed."

A cry followed the pronouncement. Not one of protest but the terrifying wail of a cub in grave peril.

The circle dissolved immediately. And as Caius came into view, horror filled those gathered, pulsing and vibrating in the air like a living thing. The Tiger cub was in human form, the skin on his arms and torso and face an open, hungry wound.

The smell of vomit and raw, exposed muscles reached Aryck even as Caius crumpled to the ground before the first of them could reach him. In a thready, pain-filled voice the cub whispered, "I tried to help them."

He succumbed to shock and unconsciousness before he could say more. But Aryck knew by *them* Caius meant the four Jaguar cubs he so often trailed.

At a caution from Phaedra, the healer, Caius was left where he lay until a blanket could be brought to serve as a stretcher, and leather gloves put on in case his skin was contaminated.

Around Aryck others changed form to lend their noses in retracing the cub's route. *Lead*, Koren said. *Others can follow with blankets and gloves. I will remain here with Phaedra so you can report what you find and she can advise you on how to proceed.*

Aryck loped out of camp in answer, his fight with Daivat forgotten.

Addai

CLOAKED in light, Addai witnessed events unfold among the Jaguars. In thousands of years of existence he had yet to tire of the beauty and the savagery of those this lush planet gave birth to.

In the challenge circle the fire burned and the shaman chanted softly in supplication and sorrow as he reached out and placed his hand over his son's heart, ceasing its beat with a spoken word. Preferring to halt the stain he feared would only deepen and spread outside of Were lands.

He knelt next to the son he'd slain, a father who'd administered harsh punishment, hoping to gain salvation for his child's soul in the wake of what the ancestors' judgment meant, what Addai knew to be truth.

Daivat lied when he said the woman was willing. He lied in saying she died first and at the hands of the human male.

The wind brought the scent of brewing infection and the raw smell of a living creature turned into meat. Addai watched the still form of the injured child being carefully placed on a blanket and the makeshift stretcher lifted so it could be carried to the healer's home.

As the boy and those attending him disappeared from sight, leaving only the shaman and the corpse in the clearing, speculation edged out

Addai's pity. He contemplated the possibility the Djinn were responsible for the child's condition. They were capable of great cruelty in the ruthless pursuit of their goals.

A smile of amusement curved his lips. Then again, his kind was capable of an equal ruthlessness.

Addai looked toward the path the Jaguar, Aryck, had taken. He paused long enough to wonder if the other children survived and if the enforcer would prove himself worthy in the days ahead. Then he descended, taking flesh, the essence of light becoming the form of a man.

Nahuatl gave no sign of being aware of his presence at the edge of the circle. The shaman's song to his ancestors continued, rising and falling, pitching higher with each new refrain until it reached a crescendo and ceased with the plunging of a ceremonial knife into his dead son's chest.

Bone and muscle gave way with the force of the thrust and the sharpness of the blade. A new song began as Nahuatl pulled the heart from its mortal cavity and threw it into the flames.

The taste of blood and fire coated Addai's tongue.

He laughed silently, appreciative of the drama, the rite.

The passion of faith.

When the heart had been consumed in a hungry blaze, the shaman turned, Jaguar cape swirling, the snarling headdress hiding everything but the dark eyes of a man who spirit-walked among the dead.

"You asked for a sign that the things revealed to you in the shadowlands, and the part you will play in their unfolding, are true," Addai said, letting all Earthly pretense fall away in a spread of white wings and a haloed show of angelic glory. "I am that sign."

Five

REBEKKA slept, and blissfully it was free of dreams and fears. Free of demons and doubts, and worries.

Hunger finally woke her, making her stir from the warm cocoon of blankets. She opened her eyes, breathed in the scent of herbs and familiarity.

This was home. More so than the house she'd homesteaded in the area set aside for the gifted. More so than the brothel she grew up in, and yet less than what her heart craved.

She rose and dressed, closing her mind to wishes and hopes that seemed impossible. She had time only to eat before one of the prostitutes summoned her to the front door.

A street child stood there, a girl who was ten at the most, her eyes already far too old for her face. Small feet in worn-out shoes stayed in motion, barely touching the ground before lifting again as if in readiness to sprint away at the tiniest hint of danger.

She used her thumb to point to the right, sending Rebekka's attention to a parked car. It was a silver sedan with dark windows. A flag bearing the Iberá crest fluttered from the antennae.

"Your services are needed," the girl said, not able to hide the hint of revulsion in her voice. "When you're done, they'll bring you back."

Indecision held Rebekka in the brothel doorway. She'd promised Levi she wouldn't leave, and yet despite the street child's assumption, there was only one service she performed and if she was needed . . .

Rebekka couldn't ignore the request. She left the brothel doorway, thinking how odd it was that now she hurried to a car flying the Iberá flag, when for days she'd wanted to escape their estate after being held there in the hopes she could be used to find Tir, and Tir, in turn, could be used to heal the dying Iberá patriarch.

The driver emerged to open the door for her. Instead of finding the backseat empty, Annalise Wainwright waited inside the car.

With her presence came the crawl of magic over Rebekka's skin, like a hundred tiny spiders. She'd felt the same thing the first time she'd met the witch.

Annalise said, "The child was sent with the truth. Your services are needed but not at the Iberá estate. We thought it best to let anyone watching believe that's where you're going. The person who sought our aid is known to the Iberá patriarch. The terms are set and you will be paid by my family. Your silence is required. Do you agree?"

Rebekka trusted the witch enough to say, "Yes."

A strip of cloth lay across Annalise's lap, her hands on the ends of it. "I need to blindfold you."

Rebekka acquiesced, leaning forward so the soft material could be tied around her head.

They drove for an indeterminate amount of time. Longer, Rebekka guessed, than was truly necessary.

A radio tuned to a news channel was the only sound in the car. The chauffeur's presence prevented them from speaking freely.

Eventually they slowed to a stop. The chauffeur got out rather than roll down a window. In the brief instant the door was open, Rebekka heard nothing, though the scent of flowers flooded the interior of the car.

Annalise made no movement, nor did the back door open. Rebekka imagined armed guards and a gate with a distinctive crest on it. She'd already guessed whoever had sought out the witches was wealthy and powerful and didn't want it known they had dealings with the gifted. It was easy to picture the chauffeur waiting outside to gain entrance to the estate, so there'd be no risk of her hearing a name.

Long minutes passed before he returned to the driver's seat, bringing with him another burst of flower-scented air. The car began moving, traveling in a straight line before making several turns as if going to the back of the house, to a servant's entrance maybe, or one where absolute privacy was guaranteed.

They stopped again and this time Annalise placed her hand on Rebekka's forearm. "I'll guide you."

The door on Annalise's side opened. The air was cool and smelled of diesel and hot car. *A private entrance*, Rebekka thought, *a garage probably*.

"This way," a female voice said, the sound of her voice telling Rebekka the woman was old.

They traveled in silence, leaving the firmness of concrete to walk first on wood, then plush carpet. The flower scent was present, blending in with the smell of wealth and power.

Until her involuntary stay at the Iberá estate, she'd never considered that either had one, but now Rebekka knew differently. Wealth and power smelled of rich fabrics and subtle perfume, of wood polish and an immaculately kept home, of time and luxury and freedom from the everyday struggle for survival.

The texture underneath her feet changed again. Annalise halted her.

Doors closed, a whisper of sound broke the silence. They rose with a low hum, the motion revealing they were in an elevator. When it stopped Annalise urged Rebekka forward and they were once again on plush carpeting.

Even with the ever-present smell drifting in from what Rebekka imagined must be extensive gardens, she knew the moment they'd arrived at their destination. Sickness tainted the air, the scent of medicine and age, and something else—the unexpected smell of reptile.

She'd healed only a couple of them before, women with exotic scales on sections of their bodies instead of skin. Snake outcasts were rare. Rebekka guessed they were probably as rare as those who could shift purely between two forms—at least here in the United States with its lack of rain forests.

It explained the secrecy. She would never have imagined a Were among Oakland's elite. Then again, despite the association with the Iberás and the drive, they could just as easily be in a vice lord's home or that of a magic practitioner who didn't dare live outside the red zone.

Behind them a door closed firmly and a lock clicked into place. "Can you heal without having the blindfold removed?" Annalise asked.

"I don't know. I need touch at least. I need to know the nature of the injury."

"May I?" Annalise asked, her question directed to the left, telling Rebekka they were positioned at the unknown person's torso or lower body.

The answer was given silently, revealed in the rustle of bed clothing.

Annalise guided Rebekka's hand to rough, ridged, and creviced skin. "You're touching a woman's leg. The other is the same, covered in what looks like alligator skin. Until days ago she had a severe infection, something like gangrene. Are you familiar with it?"

"Yes."

"She was under a doctor's care, a man who would never think to seek help from the gifted. Some combination of the drugs he used in his efforts to combat the infection compromised her immune system. When that happened, genetics lying dormant in her were triggered. It is not so rare an occurrence as you might think. The Last War and what followed created millions of orphans and erased knowledge of their heritage.

"Amulets used to detect shapeshifters would not have reacted in her presence before this happened. Now they will. The amulets can be countered, but only you can restore her to a completely human form."

Rebekka's mind spun with the implications. She wondered how many of the brothel prostitutes had started out life fully human, only to have something happen to change them, trapping them in a nightmare of shape and a life no one would freely choose.

Beneath her hand the leg moved, drawing her back to the task she'd come to perform. She gathered her will, but even knowing the details, her gift remained dormant. "I need to see."

In response there was the sound of a sheet being pulled up. It was followed by the feel of Annalise untying the blindfold and removing it.

Rebekka blinked against the brightness. Sunlight glinted off fragile crystal flowers, a vast collection that sparkled in rainbow hues of light and artistry.

Nothing of the woman who owned them was visible, save for where human skin turned into dark alligator hide at the thigh, and human feet became reptilian claws.

One glance was all it took. Rebekka closed her eyes, her will and gift combining, tugging at the exposed skin, pulling it downward and forcing the retreat of anything nonhuman in its path.

When it was done Annalise replaced the blindfold and they retraced their steps, taking a circuitous route until they were once again parked near the brothel entrance and the strip of cloth covering her eyes was removed.

"You have a choice of payment," Annalise said. "Between gold coins and the favors we can call in, enough to buy the freedom of several prostitutes, or this."

She lifted a leather-bound book from her lap and offered it to Rebekka. "Take a moment to examine it before deciding. It was written toward the end of The Last War, after chemical and biological weapons had been widely used. It belonged to a healer who was also Were. He didn't have your gift, nor was he a medical doctor. He treated any who came to him regardless of whether they were human or his own kind."

Rebekka carefully opened the book and scanned the neatly printed index. The script was small and concise, written by a man who lived in the days before the supernaturals made their existence known.

There were entries for salves and potions that aided in healing, as well as those used to reduce pain—and worse, to counter the effects of weapons she prayed no longer existed.

Her hands tightened on leather, instinctively resisting the urge to touch the hated tattoo. The Last War had been started by religious zealots, by people determined to cleanse mankind of sin. When terror and mayhem didn't achieve their goals, they let loose a virulent strain of a sexually transmitted disease.

Millions had died as result, and with countries fighting for their survival and governments descending into chaos, there was no money for research or cure. Only time and the mutation of the virus had ended it. But even so, for years afterward, any human who was labeled a whore or a prostitute was marked, not just as a warning to those they lay with, but so they could be gathered up and exterminated like vermin should the engineered disease return. All this, when the weapons let loose in the name of ending war had nearly destroyed the world.

Rebekka forced her thoughts away from a past that had played out well before her birth. She paged through the book, reading the healer's accounts of his work. If they were to be believed—and she did—then many of the salves and potions he'd discovered and recorded were better than what she left in the brothel for those times when she wasn't there.

"Have you reached a decision?" Annalise asked.

A fist tightened around Rebekka's heart at the choice between helping only a few, Feliss among them, versus easing the suffering of many, of gaining knowledge that could be shared and passed on and didn't depend on her presence or her gift.

For long, agonizing moments she tormented herself with remembered images of the horrifying damage done to those prostitutes she called friends, the repeated healings. But in the end, despite the raw, jagged ache in her chest, she said, "I'll accept the book in payment."

THE mewling sounds of acute distress reached Aryck as he cleared the weed-covered metal fence and collapsed walls of what had once been an exclusive residential development. He shifted form, urgency making the change so fast and smooth that between one leaping bound and another he went from four-footed to two.

All of the cubs were in jaguar form. One lay still while the crying of the other three grew more piteous when they realized help had arrived.

Great patches of fur had been consumed, just as Caius's skin had been. The scent of raw muscle and blood was heavy in the air, and, underneath it, infection.

A glance told Aryck what had happened. Debris had shifted, fallen, creating a pit and tumbling the cubs into it.

They'd struck a canister left over from the days of war, crushed through rust, and let loose a portion of the contents. Small, bare footprints and drag marks revealed Caius's presence, probably emerging from a hiding place to help the others since Aryck doubted the older cubs had invited him to explore with them.

"Don't touch them with your bare skin," Aryck reminded the Jaguars shifting into human form around him. "Wait for the blankets and gloves to arrive."

He crouched next to the still form of the oldest cub, hands clenching into fists to obey his own orders and keep from using them to determine the extent of the damage. Along the mental link with his father he sent images and a request for instructions.

Take them to the stream. Whatever weapon this is, Phaedra has determined it's safe to touch the skin after it's been washed off.

It would mean taking the boys farther from camp, extending their suffering before it could be relieved. *Are painkillers being sent?*

Yes, with instructions on their use.

How is Caius?

Phaedra has done what she can for him.

His father's mental voice held no inflection, but it still conveyed a truth Aryck already knew. There was no guarantee any of the cubs would survive.

The Jaguars who'd followed with blankets and gloves arrived. Aryck felt his horror mount when the unconscious cub was lifted. The entire side he'd been lying on, including the fur on his face, had been eaten away.

He must have been first to fall into the crater, and if not the one whose body landed on the rusted canister and opened it, the one who'd been closest to it, with the others following him into the pit, perhaps landing on top of him so when it came time to drag him out, Caius's strength had been drained.

There were teeth marks on the cub, indicating at least one of those wearing fur had helped. But given the damage Caius had sustained, and the fact he was in human form, with hands to grab and lift, he'd done much of the work.

Shock could account for the unconsciousness, as could concussion. Or there might be more serious injuries.

Aryck wrapped the blanket around the cub before scooping him up and standing.

Thanks to whatever painkiller they'd been given, the other cubs were now silent bundles in the arms of pack members.

"They need to be bathed as quickly as possible. We'll go to the place were the stream pools in the cedar grove."

"And the Tiger cub?" one of the Jaguars asked.

"He remains alive." *For now.*

Caphriel's Visitation

PROPPED up by pillows on her bed, Rebekka became engrossed in the journal. It was more than a healer's collection of cures. It was a window into his soul, a view of a world where bombs might just as likely hold contaminants capable of slowly eating a person alive as be constructed to kill anything living while leaving buildings untouched.

She shivered, glad she hadn't been alive in the final days of The Last War. And when reading about them became too much to bear, she closed her eyes, preferring a fantasy where she healed the Weres fully, allowing them to *shift* and escape the brothels and the red zone.

Sleep came, leaving her defenseless. It held her under with an unnatural awareness, a disjointed sense of being awake even while dreaming.

In that state she looked up from the journal and saw the urchin standing next to the bed. He was thin and scabbed and pale. His clothing nothing more than grubby rags.

Her heart raced in terror at the sight of him, its frantic beating beyond the fear of seeing a stranger in her room. He smiled then, making his face beautiful as he reached out and touched her before she could scramble away.

"Tag, you're it," he said, laughing, his voice following her as she tumbled into a nightmare she'd suppressed since she was eight years old, his touch ripping away the shield hiding the memory of her first encounter with him.

It was before Oakland, when her mother was a caravan prostitute. They were in the San Joaquin, sweltering in the heat, as nearby the drivers and guards worked on the broken bus.

She was hot and sweaty, but curious, so curious about a world she never got to explore. When they camped her mother made her stay in the old bus that served as a bedroom for the prostitutes.

At eight she already knew to stay out of sight of the men who snuck away to visit the brothel trailer. She'd already learned she'd be beaten, or her mother would be, if she let herself be found when the policemen came around to collect sin taxes.

With the bus broken down, the prostitutes sat under shade trees, some of them beading jewelry to sell, others sewing clothing or, like her mother, sleeping, while a couple of the teenage girls splashed happily in the deeper portion of a wide stream.

No one complained about the delay. They were all content to miss a day's work underneath sweaty farmers and self-righteous businessmen.

Rebekka hoped the bus stayed broken. So far she'd seen a rabbit with a little white tail, two black squirrels, a deer with a spotted fawn, and five lizards.

She stepped into the stream and crouched down, turning rocks over and squealing in delight when a tiny crawfish darted away. A yellow salamander followed, then a frog, which she gently scooped up in her hands.

The joy of each new discovery made her unaware she'd wandered out of sight until she felt someone watching her. She looked up then and saw the urchin.

He stood on the bank, gaunt and ragged, a rat perched on his shoulder. With amusement dancing in his eyes he reached up and stroked his pet. His smile and her own curiosity held her in place despite the trembling of her limbs.

"Looks like I found your hiding place," he said, his voice beautiful and terrible at the same time. "Welcome to the game."

The rat jumped, sailing across the distance to land on her bare arm. Its claws and fur were ice-cold and the feel of it touching her skin filled her with nameless dread.

In her sleep, Rebekka's heart sped up as visceral terror swept through the younger version of herself, so strong it freed her from the spot she'd been rooted to and sent her running back to where the prostitutes were rising, returning to the bus so they could be under way.

That night she dreamed of plague, of thousands dying of infectious disease, of whole cities filled with the dead. She woke screaming so many times the others insisted she be drugged. And the next day—

A shudder nearly woke the adult Rebekka. In her sleep she whimpered, remembering herself as a child climbing out of the hiding place that was also where she slept. She'd been groggy from the drugs. Otherwise she would have made sure it was safe to leave the bus.

The police from a nearby settlement were there, four of them collecting the sin tax. They saw her before she could retreat. Caught her before she could escape.

It was an area where the ultraconservative and the religious ruled. They followed the old laws, requiring prostitutes to bear a tattoo, not so much because they feared disease, but because it was a mark of shame meant to deter patrons and protect the unwary from marrying a whore.

She fought them as they tugged her clothing aside to look for the tattoo. And when they didn't find one, their leader ordered her marked.

Her mother struggled, the caravan guards holding her back. She pleaded with the policemen, begged them with tears streaking down her face. Told them her daughter was no prostitute.

Their leader quoted the scripture of Exodus. "*He* doesn't leave the guilty unpunished. Unto the third and fourth generation, *He* punishes the children and their children for the sin of the parents."

Rebekka screamed as they held her down. The needles pierced

her flesh repeatedly, until the pain and horror were too much for her young mind.

She escaped into her memories, leaving her body behind to wander through the woods where she'd seen the deer and rabbit and squirrels. And when it was over the police collected the sin tax for the "new whore."

Her mother gathered her up, held her tightly as they both cried. But where the child Rebekka had thought her mother's trembling and tears were like her own, the dreaming adult saw terror on her mother's face.

She looked around and saw the black dog, remembering it now. It came from the woods, sickness radiating from it, and something inside her unfurled. The desire to ease its suffering, the first stirrings of her gift.

The settlement police saw the dog, too. They fired on it with their guns, killing it, but not before it had bitten one of them.

"You brought the rabid dog here, little healer," the urchin said, suddenly there, standing next to her mother though no one else seemed to see him.

He smiled and stroked the rat on his shoulder. Leaned forward and laughed when she struggled wildly, her mother's arms preventing her from escaping.

"I've given you a piece of myself," he said, his ice-cold lips touching hers, breath tasting of disease slipping into her mouth as his words slid into her mind. *Forget now, until it's time for you to join the game.*

Rebekka woke retching. Shivering. Coated in cold sweat.

The healer's journal tumbled to the floor as she rolled off her bed, disoriented, shaken by the dream.

She bent down and picked up the book. Smoothed a bent page with a hand that trembled before closing the journal and putting it into the pocket of her pants.

"It was only a dream," she whispered into the silence of the room, telling herself the horrors she'd been reading about before falling asleep had triggered the nightmare memories of being held down and tattooed, telling herself the encounter with the demon and his talk of games had woven the image of the urchin into her dream.

She told herself that, and yet the scent of disease filled her nostrils. The taste of it coated her tongue, driving her to the bathroom to brush her teeth and rinse her mouth.

In the mirror above the sink her face appeared haunted, frightened. A hard pulse beat against her throat, visible evidence of a heart that wouldn't stop thundering in her chest.

Knowledge pounded in her skull even as she clung to denial. There were diseases with no cure. There were others where survival was possible only for those with enough money to pay for the cost of doctors and hospital care.

She shuddered, remembering the nightmare within the nightmare, the images of thousands dying from plague, of whole cities full of the dead. It was like some of the scenes from the healer's journal, she argued with herself. But she couldn't shake the need to escape her room and clear the images from her mind with fresh air.

Thinking of the men who'd attacked the night before, and her promise to Levi to stay in the brothel where it was safe, she paused long enough to stop by Feliss's room and borrow a distinctively patterned cloak, hooded so its wearer could shield hair and face.

It was a ploy used by the Weres to routinely wear something identifiable when they left the brothel, so other times they could slip away unnoticed by wearing a concealing garment associated with another should overinterested clients or those with grudges be watching for them.

Rebekka used the private exit, first checking to make sure no one loitered in the alleyway between brothels before stepping through the door.

The smell of warm dirt and brick filled her lungs. Relief poured into her but it was short-lived.

Cold blossomed in her chest, while at the same time her fingers warmed, tingled in the same way they did before she used her gift. A small cry of denial escaped when a rat entered the alleyway. Bile rose in Rebekka's throat along with horror at the sight of the open sores on its body.

It came toward her as no normal animal would have, so intent on reaching her it didn't notice the scrawny feral cat that rounded the corner seconds later to pounce and kill and carry away its prize while Rebekka was still wrapped in the horror of a nightmare made real.

Without conscious thought she turned and fled. Terrified of remaining in the brothel and bringing death to the Weres trapped by both their forms and their debts to Allende.

Six

THE blood red of the cardinal's feathers drew Rebekka's attention like an omen waiting for interpretation. It perched where a raven had on her last visit to the witches' house, a glossy black bird of death that had shifted into a supernatural being so powerful at masking his nature not even Levi could see beyond the human facade.

The conversation she'd had with Annalise Wainwright on that day swept into Rebekka's thoughts like an icy wind.

There's a war brewing between supernatural beings, not unlike one occurring at the dawn of human creation. It will be fought and, depending on its outcome, the world as we now know it may change again. As alliances are forged, healers will emerge who can make those Weres trapped in an abomination of form whole. You are one of them.

If I'm willing to pay the price.

There is always a price to pay.

Rebekka's hand closed on the engraved pentacle in her pocket. It was the Wainwrights' token, given to her first in summons, and then as a sign of alliance.

She'd come here instinctively, without conscious decision. Being able to call the diseased to her would be a death sentence. If the humans didn't kill her, then the Weres trapped in the brothels would. But now Rebekka trembled as she forced her gaze away from the cardinal and to the house in front of her.

Dark stones absorbed the sunlight. A myriad of small windows, each with elaborate glyphs carved into their frames, made her think of soulless eyes looking out on the world.

Did she dare tell the witches what Abijah had said about her father? Or about the being who appeared as an urchin and claimed to give her a piece of himself? Did she dare reveal the cold blossoming in her chest, the tingling warmth in her fingers that had preceded the appearance of the rat?

Rebekka's stomach tightened into a knot. The Wainwrights offered an elusive promise that she might become a healer who could make those Weres trapped in an abomination of form whole, but she couldn't bring herself to trust them.

She might be gifted, but she'd lived among Were outcasts since she was sixteen and had absorbed their suspicion of witches. She might be human, but a childhood among prostitutes had set her apart from all society but that of the brothels.

The back of her fingers brushed against folded paper, the pages she'd torn from an old journal on the Iberá patriarch's desk just before her escape from the estate. The pages held an account of urns said to hold trapped demons in them, and except for her soul, her life, and her gift, they were the only thing of value she could use in a bargain with witches.

Desperation kept her from turning away. And when she felt cold blossom in her chest like a hand unclenching while at the same time warmth spread through her fingers, fear for those in the brothel made her take a step forward.

She opened the sigil-inscribed gate and entered the witches' domain. The sense of cold and warmth vanished, as if the wards set in place prevented her from drawing the sick to her.

On the porch she grasped the ring held in the mouth of a brass gargoyle. Used it to announce her presence.

Out of the corner of her eye she caught the red flash of the cardinal taking flight. She turned her head slightly, in time to see a thin boy of eight or nine running down the street.

He had the look of a street child instead of one who belonged in the area set aside for the gifted. For an instant he reminded her of the child she'd seen the previous night, shortly before she and Levi were attacked near the brothels.

The door opened and there was the familiar crawl of magic over Rebekka's skin. Rather than usher her into the house, Annalise's attention remained on the boy until he disappeared around a corner.

"The Church has watchers posted now," she said. "Father Ursu still hunts for you in the hopes you'll lead him to the others."

Not the Weres she and Levi had helped free from the maze, but Araña and, through her, Tir, a being Rebekka now knew was more than human, just as she knew the Church sought him because they believed his blood healed and with it they could perform miracles to strengthen their hold on Oakland.

Fear tightened its grip on Rebekka at the thought of ending up in the Church's hands. But better theirs—where death would come after torture proved her worthless to them, or they discovered she could bring plague to the city—than to learn the vice lords who ran the gaming clubs and had profited from the maze were after her.

Annalise stepped back out of the doorway. "The matriarch will wish to see you. There are allies we can call upon on your behalf, beings who can turn the Church's attention away from you."

The knots in Rebekka's stomach grew worse. She made no response as she followed Annalise down a hallway lined with prewar artwork.

Paintings of glorious color and celebration hung on the walls. Depictions of naked men and women dancing, coupling in ancient rites of fertility and worship.

The sound of a baby crying loosened the bindings of fear and worry. It filled Rebekka with soft, impossible longing.

Unable to resist, she stopped at an open doorway and looked inside. A girl, no more than seventeen, picked up a tiny infant and quieted it with the offer of a nipple.

"My grandson," Annalise said. "Born yesterday."

There was love in her voice. Its presence and the sight of the baby held against its mother's breast sent an ache through Rebekka's heart.

She wanted a child of her own, a family that included a husband at her side, a helpmate and partner to share her life with and serve as a safety net so no son or daughter of hers ended up living in the street or selling themselves to survive.

It was a dream she rarely allowed herself. The human men she encountered regularly were those who visited the brothels. She'd never accept one of them.

Among the gifted humans, she doubted her talent would help overcome the stigma of being the daughter of a prostitute, of growing up in a brothel and then continuing to work in them, caring for Were outcasts.

And the Weres who called the red zone home . . . Marrying one of them was to be trapped between worlds, just as they were. It meant hardship not just for her as a human, but for any children who might come.

There was a time, at the very beginning of their friendship, when she might have considered such a thing with Levi, but . . .

She thought about the wedding bands that so often glinted in the subdued lighting of the brothels. Even Levi, who routinely slept in Feliss's room and intended to buy out her contract, took what was offered free by the prostitutes.

Hopelessness settled like a heavy weight in Rebekka's chest. She knew there was a difference between intimacy and sex, believed the act itself was meaningless for those who visited the brothels. But she wasn't sure a man was capable of being faithful to only one woman over the course of a lifetime together. And she didn't think she could handle that kind of betrayal by someone she'd given her heart to and created children with.

"Would you like to hold him?" the girl on the couch asked.

Rebekka moved forward in answer, looked in wonder at tiny fingers. Prostitutes rarely carried their children to term. And those who did—

She knew she'd been lucky in so many ways. To be born at all had been the first stroke of it. And it had been followed by so many more, including being gifted.

Her mother hadn't abandoned her on the street or in the forest, leaving it up to fate whether she survived or not. She hadn't ended up in an orphanage or been sold.

Even in the red zone, those who trafficked in children didn't operate openly. But it was common knowledge, especially in the brothels, that unwanted pregnancies could be turned into profit in any number of ways.

There were men whose sexual fetishes involved pregnant women. And after the baby was born, there were brokers willing to sell to those with sexual perversions, or to dark mages looking for sacrificial victims, or to supernatural beings with an appetite for human children.

"He's beautiful," Rebekka said, taking the boy into her arms and inhaling the baby scent of him, knowing this child would never fear the fates waiting for so many others in Oakland, not just those born in the red zone, but for the poor who scraped and struggled to survive.

"He's gifted," the girl said, pride in her voice. "The matriarch said one day he'll have the strength and skill to call upon the ley lines. She's never wrong when she does her scrying using fire."

Mention of the matriarch reminded Rebekka of what had driven her here, forced her to turn away from a dream that always brought with it the ache of hopelessness. She handed the infant back to his mother, noticing the loss of his warmth before closing her mind to it.

Rebekka turned away from mother and son, followed Annalise to the parlor where the Wainwright matriarch sat draped in black, hunched and bony, her eyes made sightless by cataracts.

A tremor of fear went through Rebekka, deep and instinctual.

Annalise took a seat on the couch next to the old woman. Rebekka sat across from them, separated by a coffee table, though the distance wasn't enough to keep her skin from crawling.

If Annalise's magic felt like a hundred spiders pouring over her, the matriarch's felt like a thousand of them, blanketing her as if they sought to measure what she was made of.

Darkness formed at the edges of Rebekka's consciousness. She swayed, on the verge of passing out, combatted it with the same determination and focus required in healing.

As quickly as the shroud of power had covered her, it disappeared, leaving her breathing fast, sweating, but less afraid than when she'd stood in front of the witches' house. She'd be dead now if the matriarch had wanted it. She knew it with absolute certainty.

"It's done then," the matriarch said. "The maze is destroyed and Araña has set Abijah free."

Rebekka's pulse sped up at confirmation of what she'd guessed was the witches' true goal. It was only while being held prisoner at the Iberá estate that she'd learned demons could be bound to urns. She'd thought at first the Wainwrights meant to gain possession of the urn the maze owner had stolen from the Church, so they could command Abijah. Only later had she thought otherwise.

A suspicion slithered into Rebekka's thoughts. She wondered if the witches had originally sought her out, ensuring her path crossed Araña's because somehow they knew a demon's blood ran in her veins.

Despite the pounding of her heart, she asked, "Why did you involve me in this?"

The matriarch answered, "Because your father is like the one Araña freed."

Rebekka felt the cold drenching of fear. The same she'd felt when Abijah found her, tasting her blood and claiming to know her father.

Denial screamed through Rebekka once again. She argued internally against believing without further proof, without speaking to her mother. She reminded herself witches couldn't be trusted. The Wainwrights had their own agenda and had already used her once in achieving their goal, arranging for her to meet and help Araña, who in turn became a tool to free the demon Abijah.

But already Rebekka felt cut by shards of truth that left the life she knew bleeding away and a terrible acceptance seeping in. As soon as she'd gone to live and work in the Were brothels, her mother left the red zone for a life among the Fellowship of the Sign, a religious group that had carved out a community in the forests beyond the Barrens.

In desperation Rebekka latched onto the purpose that had driven her to cross the Wainwright wards and enter their home. Through the fabric of her pants the folded pages in her pocket seemed to burn, like a hint of the fiery hell promised to those the Church condemned. Her throat went dry even as her palms grew slick.

She had no confidence she could bargain with the witches and come out ahead, but she had no choice but to try. Her hand shook as she pulled the pages from her pocket and set them on the table. Her voice trembled as she said, "There were other urns, like the one Araña destroyed. They may no longer exist but they once did. These pages came from an old journal in the Iberá patriarch's possession. He showed them to Father Ursu."

Ice slid down her spine at the memory of how hard the priest had pressed the Iberá patriarch, urging him with each visit to the estate to turn her over for questioning—a questioning that would surely have ended in her death. With its public face, and solely for political purposes, the Church might accept those humans having supernatural gifts, but it hadn't truly turned away from a doctrine it'd carried with it from its inception and through all the different names it had called itself. Those humans with unnatural powers should be killed, just as the Weres were deemed abominations with no right to life.

Annalise picked up the pages and carefully unfolded them, her eyes scanning the text and studying the drawings. To the matriarch she said, "The names on the urns are those you heard whispered by the flame."

"The hunt for them begins soon, then, with the aid of a Finder." The matriarch's milky, sightless gaze returned to Rebekka. "You've come here seeking the deepening of your healing talent."

"Yes."

"It is not a gift I can bestow on you."

Bone-white hands appeared from beneath her shawl. The subtle jangle of amulets hanging from bracelets sounded as the matriarch's skeletal fingers opened a cloth-wrapped package on her lap to reveal a necklace.

Strung on leather with knotted black beads along its length was an amulet that reminded Rebekka of dream catchers she'd seen in history books. It was made of supple wood and woven string. At its center were two red beads on either side of a small black feather that seemed to shimmer and cast off a thousand different colors.

"The pages you brought have value. It's fair you be given something in return. This amulet offers a measure of protection for one with your gift. Blood is required to bind it to you."

Rebekka rubbed damp palms against her pants. She couldn't trust the witches with the remembered encounter with the urchin, or how the rat had come to her in the alleyway, and yet she also couldn't afford to turn down the amulet and what protection it could offer. "I accept."

Annalise drew a silver athame from a sheath on her belt. Rebekka's stomach cramped at the sight of the sigils running the length of its blade. She held out her hand anyway.

Annalise leaned forward, making a shallow cut across the lifeline on Rebekka's palm. Blood welled up quickly, unnaturally.

"Take the amulet now," the matriarch said.

Rebekka did. She gasped as fire streaked through her, going from her hand to the center of her chest. And when she opened her palm, she found the cut completely healed, the red beads woven into the weblike design of the amulet darker, dry, as if they'd absorbed her blood.

Hands shaking slightly, she lifted the necklace and tied it around her neck. At some hidden signal, Annalise rose and helped the matriarch to her feet.

"Come," the matriarch said, "Annalise and I will escort you to the back door. It's hidden from the Church's watchers. Do you wish for us to intercede on your behalf?"

Rebekka licked suddenly dry lips. "At what cost?"

"A favor owed."

Rebekka only barely suppressed a shiver at the thought of being in their debt. She'd brave a return to the Iberá estate and ask for the patriarch's intercession with the Church before she promised a favor to witches.

"No," she said, and on the heels of her answer came a stirring of hope that they'd lied about her father being demon. It would serve their purpose to make her believe it, to pull her deeper into their elaborate web.

"As you wish."

Levanna Wainwright allowed her granddaughter to support her as they slowly left the room. Rebekka's refusal of help brought a stirring of worry, a tiny measure of pity. So many children of the Djinn died during their testing.

It was only afterward, when the fullness of the pattern was revealed, that the choices, the places where failure originated or might have been averted, could be identified.

Not that it mattered to those administering the tests.

A waste, the matriarch thought, her hand tightening slightly on her granddaughter's arm. *A terrible waste.*

In this she was glad she was born human and gifted, and when it came to those of her family, her will—Anna's will—ruled. Occasionally magic took one of them, or they died at the hands of their enemies, but their testing was meant to make them stronger, to determine position in coven hierarchy, not to separate out the weak, often at the expense of their lives.

Theirs was a harsh world, one where everything came at a cost. She'd learned the lesson well enough when she was in her teens, on the fateful night of her initiation ceremony.

She'd thought to show herself powerful enough to one day become not just matriarch of the Wainwright coven in Oakland, but of all those covens bound to the Wainwrights. And so she had. But at a price that altered not only the course of her life, but the destiny of the covens.

How foolish the girl born Anna Wainwright had been. Proud and headstrong and overly confident.

She'd thought to free a demon contained in an urn and command it. Instead she'd died at the hands of a female Djinn.

If it hadn't been for the quick action of those gathered, she'd be in the ghostlands, her spirit bound to that of the Djinn who killed her, her body nothing but a collection of ashes in the Wainwright burial vaults.

She and the Djinn were still bound and, ultimately, when the thread tethering the both of them to the mortal plane—as Levanna—was finally and irrevocably broken, she and the other—Levaneal en Raum of the House of the Spider—would enter the spiritlands as one, their souls forever tangled unless the battle they prepared for was won and the Djinn once again claimed Earth as home, ruling it with those allied to them.

As they stepped out of the house and Rebekka passed them, the matriarch felt only a coldness of purpose in the other, Levaneal. A ruthlessness tied to ancient memories of friends slaughtered or made prisoner by the alien god's army of angels.

Rebekka's death would mean nothing to the Spider Djinn. The healer was only important if she proved herself worthy of her Djinn parentage, if the thread of her life strengthened the fabric of a future that had been in the weaving for thousands of years.

"Take the path through the thornbushes," Annalise told Rebekka, drawing the matriarch from her thoughts. "It leads to the other side of our garden and onto the next street. If you change your mind and wish us to arrange for the Church to stop pursuing you, come back."

With a thank-you, the healer hurried off. Shades of brown and a swirl of gray in the matriarch's mind, offset by a flash of red just beyond the fence marking the warded boundary.

The emotionless resolve defining Levaneal's spirit presence gave way to a burning, hungry desire to be among the Djinn again. A face rose from ancient memory, spilling the image of a sharp-featured man into the matriarch's mind. Torquel en Sahon of the House of the Cardinal.

Surprise at his continued presence flickered though the matriarch, the emotion echoed by the other. In the eyes of the Djinn, Levaneal was tainted, feared.

This was the first time Torquel had approached directly, risking what few of his kind dared. It made the matriarch wonder if perhaps he had grown tired of losing the daughters he created with human women.

Few of his kind managed more than one or two children, either in this world or in the Djinn kingdom deep in the ghostlands. But since shortly after the initiation ceremony that left Anna's soul bound to Levaneal's, five of Torquel's daughters had come to this house before Rebekka. All of them had failed their testing and died.

With a tightening of her fingers on Annalise's arm, the matriarch said, "Take me to where he waits."

The Watcher

ONLY a will honed over thousands of years of existence and tempered by being a healer prevented Torquel en Sahon from retreating as the old witch whose foolishness in youth had cost the Djinn one of their own approached. With each step she took he fought against retaking the form of the cardinal and escaping the presence of the *ifrit*—one of the soul-tainted, a being whose name was crossed through in the Book of the Djinn and whose spirit couldn't be guided back and reborn into a new life.

He stood his ground by reminding himself the loss of the Djinn whose name was no longer spoken had ultimately served The Prince's vision. Only by forming alliances with those they would have seen destroyed in the past would the Djinn return to Earth.

The Wainwright witches served as intermediaries. Even so, as the *ifrit* drew near, he couldn't stop himself from turning his face away to look in the direction his daughter had gone.

He'd taken no pleasure in her creation. In truth, he preferred not to remember any of the human women he'd lain with.

Rebekka was the last of his children. Out of all of them, her gift as a healer held the most promise.

He'd spent more time observing this particular daughter. Found himself caring about her fate more than was wise. But whatever the outcome of her testing, his time among humans was drawing to an end. When this was done he would return to his House and to the Kingdom set deep in the spiritlands that was both refuge and prison for the Djinn.

"Did she give you the pages she took from the Iberá estate?" he asked, directing his attention and question at the younger witch, because for all his courage in remaining in the presence of an *ifrit*, he wouldn't risk inviting a similar fate by speaking to it directly. Nor did he want to hear or see the Djinn soul tangled with the human's.

"Yes, and she accepted the amulet."

A wisp of guilt drifted through him. A private acknowledgment he'd failed to hide Rebekka well enough and Caphriel had found her.

Torquel brushed the emotions aside. Caphriel's games were the price for his silence about the alliances the Djinn sought and formed in this world.

Caphriel's gift could be countered. And in the end, both game and gift would be made to serve the Djinn.

The necessity of the amulet added to the complexity of Rebekka's trial, deepening her talent for healing and strengthening the blood tie between them, and with it her connection to the Djinn and the Earth that gave birth to them. He would have preferred otherwise, but when all was said and done, this daughter would succeed or fail, live or die, as the five before her had.

"And the rest of it?" he asked.

"Her mother never spoke to her about you but she might have encountered Abijah in the maze before he destroyed it. She didn't deny the possibility she'd been fathered by a being she believes is demon, nor did she seem shocked by the disclosure."

"You guess correctly. Abijah sought her out, but I didn't witness what occurred between them." He felt pride in his daughter, for not easily trusting the witches, though had she, there were things they could have revealed that would have helped her.

The decision to have Rebekka think she was a demon's child was his, made after Caphriel found her and when it seemed likely her path might one day cross Abijah's. Until she proved herself worthy, she couldn't know of the existence of the Djinn.

The witch said, "We offered to turn the Church's attention away from her in exchange for a favor owed. She refused."

"Will she continue to?"

"I believe so."

Torquel looked again in the direction Rebekka had gone. It was his right to mark an end to the part of her trial that had begun when she'd agreed to wait outside the maze the night Araña ran in it, not knowing she'd been made a participant in a Spider Djinn's testing.

This daughter had courage and intelligence as well as honor and loyalty, all of which had prevailed in the face of fear. She'd withstood both the temptation of The Iberá's protection and the terror of being turned over to the Church.

The desire to intercede was strong, to separate this part of her testing from what remained. It was matched by his desire to have Rebekka prove herself worthy of being known by the Djinn, her name entered in the books kept by his House.

The fierceness of his pride in her, the depth of his will for her to succeed, gave Torquel pause. He hesitated over the words that would make Rebekka safe from one threat, finally saying, "The Church's part in this is done after the sun rises tomorrow. See that one of our allies visits the priest Ursu."

"It will be as you wish."

Caphriel's Pawn

RADEK'S palms were slick. The green thermos nearly slipped as he pulled it from the knapsack.

At the sound of rustling paper he startled guiltily, heart racing. It was only the map spread out on the ground next to him, lifting and dropping with a small breeze.

Sweat slid down the back of his neck. He felt eyes on him.

A glance over his shoulder told him he wasn't imagining it. Captain Nagy leaned against the rear of the Hummer, a cigarette between his lips, watching.

Two other militiamen wearing the Ivanov crest were a short distance away. Alert, but at ease, playing dice on the hood of the vehicle as he'd given them all permission to do when he told them he needed a few minutes to study the map and take a water sample from the small pond.

Radek licked his lips. His heart stuttered in his chest.

His gaze went to hoof tracks captured in the mud. Elk. He was pretty sure of it. They matched the picture he'd slipped from his pocket and studied surreptitiously.

The thermos in his hand trembled. Inside it was the subtle movement of liquid.

He set it down on the ground before him. Losing his nerve for opening it and emptying the smart-virus into the pond.

What if the scientists were wrong? What if the virus mutated into something that affected humans?

Radek took several deep breaths. He pulled the map over in front of him, pretended to be concentrating on it, but instead of seeing elevation markings and penciled-in notations of where man had once built, he looked into his memory.

The laboratory was exactly where the file he'd recovered from the safe and decoded said it would be. It'd taken less than a day for the convict workers to get to it, and none of them had seen him remove something from the site.

So far he'd uncovered three canisters, unmarked except for a symbol indicating the virus's ultimate target. Each coming with a sealed data file containing information on how the scientists planned to use the weapon they'd created in the event the Weres emerged from hiding.

Radek picked up the thermos. His stomach churned.

Activating the virus had been relatively simple. The scientists had factored in lack of technology and the possible collapse of civilization when they designed their postwar weapon.

Having the courage to use it was more difficult than Radek had envisioned in the safety of his private quarters. He closed his eyes and sank into a dream that had changed from one involving discovery and riches to one of glory.

The tightness in his chest eased as he imagined the crowds chanting his name. Heard again his father calling him a hero to the human race.

Courage returned. Nervousness became anticipation.

Radek opened his eyes and got to his feet. He knelt next to the pond. By his calculations, the smart-virus targeting werewolves by using elk as a vector should reproduce and be present in every mouthful of water by nightfall.

He uncapped the thermos. Submerged it in the pond so the watching militiamen would see what they expected to.

Fear returned with the irreversibility of his actions, the possibility he might be unleashing another plague on mankind.

Vomit rose in his throat.

He swallowed it down.

Drew strength from the golden dream of power and wealth and glory.

"I'm doing what needs to be done," he whispered.

Seven

THE smell of slow, horrifying death drifted through the dense foliage of trees hiding Phaedra's house. It blanketed the Jaguar camp in a noxious, unseen cloud of puss and raw flesh, exposed muscle and the scent of voided bodies.

Anywhere other than a Jaguar's lair the smell would have drawn every scavenger in the forest. Already, some of the pack members couldn't be trusted not to lash out, driven by an instinct at the core of their being that said none but the strongest deserved to survive.

Only those wearing a human form could enter the house and be in the presence of the cubs. And had the five boys been allowed to emerge from their drugged, pain-free cocoons, their mewling cries would have been unbearable, adding to the helpless torment, the edge of violence seething in the Jaguars.

Aryck knelt next to the pallet where one of the cubs lay. The slow spread of whatever was eating through skin and into muscle, devouring them while they still lived, put them at risk of greater infection if they were moved to their own homes.

They were like burn victims, only nothing Phaedra had tried, no potion or salve handed down in the oral tradition of their kind, worked. Nothing known by the Lion healer had helped either.

Locked in their furred forms, the four cubs were denied the chance to talk to their parents, to find comfort in words where touch was increasingly denied as their injuries worsened.

Rage ate at Aryck but he had no way to strike out at the long-dead humans who had created such a horrible weapon. His fury was fueled by a helplessness to change the course of events, by the heartrending knowledge that ultimately, when all hope of survival ended and they could no longer be shielded from the pain, the cubs would be killed to end their suffering.

He moved to the pallet were the Tiger cub lay still as death. For his bravery, for changing into a human form so he could help the others, Caius's condition worsened more quickly than that of the others, probably because whatever was eating him alive had been keyed to and designed for mankind, with animals just collateral damage.

Grief welled up inside Aryck, obliterating his rage and bringing guilt with it. He should have recognized Caius's quiet courage and the strength of spirit allowing him to rebound despite repeatedly being left out of Jaguar play. He should have made more of an effort to befriend this lone Tiger cub and in doing so help him fit more quickly into the pack.

It was rare for Weres to mate outside their species, but because they shared a human form, it was possible. Caius's mother had done so, disappearing when Aryck was a teen only to come back recently with a white Tiger cub at her side and no mate.

Aryck reached out, pushing the boy's hair off his forehead. He should have done more for this cub who'd lost his father to death and his mother to her grief.

Given time, the Jaguar cubs would have accepted Caius, but now . . .

A hand touched Aryck's shoulder. He looked up into Phaedra's age-lined face and saw compassion there.

"Leave," she said. "Don't come here anymore or torment yourself. There is nothing any of us could have done to prevent this. I played in those ruins as a child; so did you, so did your father, and his, and the ones before, all the way back to the claiming of this land for the Jaguars. It is in the hands of the ancestors now."

Aryck rose from his crouch. As he did so, his father's voice sounded in his mind. *The council of elders gathers in the circle. Tell Phaedra we meet, then join us.*

Seven old men and five old women sat on seats made from the branches of the trees in the sacred place where the Jaguar dead were placed. They were the oldest members of the pack, seemingly ancient and feeble in body but with minds that were an immense library of Were history.

They had no authority. But an alpha would be foolish not to ask for their opinion on important matters, and heed it unless there was a compelling reason to do otherwise.

Aryck took up his position next to his father. Phaedra sat on the ground beside one of the elders.

Nahuatl stood with his back to a small fire. It crackled in the center of the circle, signaling a meeting of importance. He was dressed in the light loincloth he favored but he carried a staff made of Jaguar bone and skull, signifying his position and that he would speak as a representative of the ancestors.

Beyond him, members of the pack gathered, called there by curiosity instead of the alpha. Melina appeared, shifting easily from jaguar to human form and placing herself so Aryck couldn't avoid seeing her naked breasts and the tuft of pubic hair arrowing down to draw attention to her vulva.

Several males jostled into position next to her, touching their bare skin to hers. Aryck turned his head to look at his father, wondering at the purpose for being called here.

Koren addressed the elders, saying, "Nahuatl came to me with a vision sent by the ancestors. They have shown him a face and given him the name of a woman capable of healing our cubs."

Outside the circle, murmurs met his announcement. Like a fever, hope sped through those gathered. Inside the circle, the elders remained stoic, waiting as Aryck did, knowing there was more to the vision.

"She is human," Koren said. "Gifted."

Hope became edged with fear and distrust. Whispers held anger and hate but were silenced with a glance from Koren.

"And the cost to us if we bring this human into our midst?" one of the elders asked, his voice querulous.

Nahuatl tapped his staff on the ground, drawing every eye to him. "The ancestors have bid me to say this: The decision must be made quickly, and it is the enforcer who must be sent for her. They also issue a warning. If she does not agree to providing aid, then Aryck will die before returning to Jaguar lands."

Those gathered in the circle weighed what was said, to what lengths they should go to save the cubs, but for Aryck the decision was easy. "I will go for the healer."

Murmurs met his declaration, but none of the elders objected. Koren placed his hand on Aryck's shoulder. "It will be done then, and the cubs healed because of it. Melina will accompany you."

REBEKKA emerged from the thorn-lined path and onto a broken, cracked sidewalk a block away from the Wainwright house and on a different street. Hidden beneath her shirt, the dream catcher-like amulet was warm against her skin.

She reached up and touched it, grateful for its presence. The cold blossoming in her chest hadn't reappeared when she passed beyond the wards protecting the witches.

Fear gnawed at her stomach at the thought of returning to the brothel. Denial continued to scream through her with the witch's claim she was fathered by a demon.

She wouldn't believe it. Couldn't without seeking answers from her mother.

A glance at the sky confirmed it was too late to cross the Barrens. Even if she had the courage to enter the wasteland of burned and collapsed buildings by herself, she'd never reach the Fellowship settlement where her mother lived before nightfall.

She couldn't return to the brothel, not until she knew she wouldn't draw disease there. And she didn't dare go to her homesteaded house in the area set aside for the gifted while she was being hunted.

Rebekka glanced at the sky again. If she hurried she could make it to Levi's lair in the woods.

It could be secured at night. And at least she wouldn't put anyone else at risk there.

She began running, part of her recognizing the danger of it, how moving quickly would draw more attention to herself. But the intense desire to escape the nightmare that had begun with the demon Abijah's appearance, and grown worse with dreams and memories of the urchin, rode her.

Where it was possible she remained in shadow, using vegetation and the piled debris that had once been houses to shield her from the street and the places reclaimed by humans.

Sticker bushes tore at her clothing, scratching at bare skin. Still, she hurried. Driven, hoping to outrun her thoughts and fears.

Over the pounding of her heart she heard the rumble of an engine drawing closer. It could be anyone, she told herself. In Oakland the rich and powerful often sought out the gifted.

They bought the services and products of those they required to live apart, just as easily and openly as they entered the red zone, arriving in chauffer-driven cars to indulge in their chosen vices.

She forced herself to slow long enough to look around, and cursed herself for a fool when she saw the darting movement of a street child taking cover, this one older than the one she'd seen watching the Wainwright house.

Renewed fear spiked through her, bringing with it a surge of adrenaline. For enough coin to pay for a meal or buy shelter for the night, the boy would point her out to anyone hunting her then turn away, uncaring what his actions meant for her.

Rebekka pressed a hand to her side. Ran again, lungs and muscles burning with the effort.

She reached the place where the gifted section bordered that of the non-gifted instead of the red zone. Despite what the witches said, she couldn't discount the possibility it was the vice lords who had benefited from the maze who now hunted her.

Piles of stone and rusted metal hidden by curling, tangled vines made it treacherous to stray too far from livestock paths used by those who took their animals to graze during the day. She did it anyway. Taking cover when the sound of an engine drew closer like a hungry mechanical bloodhound on her trail.

The street boy came into view, panting. She became aware of her own harsh breathing and pulled her shirt away from her body, pressed the material to her mouth in an effort to mute any sound that might give her away.

Moments later a sleek silver car drew alongside the boy. The back-seat window rolled down, and Rebekka stifled a gasp when she saw the man's profile. The port-wine stain on the left side of his face made him unforgettable. He was one of the men who'd attacked near the brothel, the only one to escape.

He turned his head, following the direction the boy pointed. She huddled deeper into her hiding place as two additional boys joined the first. One of them was the boy outside the Wainwright house. It made her sure he was the one she'd seen the night before.

The boys held out their hands for payment. The man glanced at the sky and cursed as he dropped coins into their hands before rolling up the window.

They fanned out as the car drove away. Rebekka remained hidden, not daring to make any movement at all, not daring even to close her eyes.

The car disappeared from sight but the sound of it lingered. Each moment slowed to feel like a hundred of them. When the car reappeared it kept going, heading in the direction she'd come from. The boys gathered a short time later and did the same.

She couldn't be sure they were calling off their search so they could get to shelter before night fell, or if they were lying in wait, knowing she was defenseless against them, that even to save her life, she couldn't inflict harm, not without it turning her gift into something evil.

Rebekka shivered, sweat cold against her skin, the amulet warm, as if reminding her that with the appearance of the urchin, her gift was already changed, perhaps tainted.

The distinctive rumble of a bus's engine cut across the waiting silence, bringing the hope of escape—if she dared risk it.

In her mind she traveled the distance to the nearest stop. Imagined herself climbing into the bus and going to a place few in the red zone went to willingly—the building housing the police and guard.

Her pulse accelerated and her breathing grew shallow thinking about it. She wavered, considered returning to the Wainwright house and seeking shelter with the witches. Discarded the idea. Even if she could reach them, their protection would come at a price she didn't want to pay.

Before the fear could build, Rebekka broke from cover, running toward the bus stop.

A cry went up from one of the boys.

She didn't look back. Didn't slow as she pulled the dollar bills tucked away for emergencies from a pocket as she rounded a corner and saw the bus.

It slowed to a stop, disgorged its passengers.

She sped up, racing, knowing this was the last bus of the day and if it began moving, the driver wouldn't stop for her.

If not for an old woman who had to be helped down the stairs, Rebekka never would have made it in time. She clambered on before the driver could close the door and lock her out in his desire to finish work and get home before dark.

She paid and took a seat on the empty bus. Looked out the window.

All three of the boys were visible. One looked angry. He said something to the other two, then turned and ran.

Terror gripped Rebekka. Only days past, she and Levi had taken this same bus on their way to the Mission and found enemies waiting for them. If they hadn't gotten off at an earlier stop, they would have ended up in the maze or dead.

In escaping that fate she'd found herself a prisoner of the Iberás—though they'd labeled her a guest. And now, because of those events, she sought refuge with them.

Rebekka reached up and touched the amulet through her shirt. Was it wrong to put those at the Iberá estate at risk?

I have no choice, she told herself as the bus picked up speed.

She remained tensed, half expecting the silver car with the assailant from the night before to intercept the bus. If it happened the bus driver would hand her over without question, without reporting the incident if told not to by someone with authority or who offered money for his silence on behalf of a vice lord.

Outside the window the bus skirted the area where the wealthy and powerful lived. Downtown came into view along with her last memory of it, when her attention had been caught by a flag fluttering on the antenna of a black sedan—a red lion rampant centered on an elaborate shield design and set against a gold background—the heraldic crest of the Iberás, though she didn't know it at the time.

Fear returned in a rush. What if Enzo Iberá wasn't at the guard headquarters? Or if he was, what if he turned her away, refused to take her to his family's estate? Where would she find shelter for the night?

The stop closest to the building housing the guard drew near. Rebekka reached up and pulled the cable, signaling she wanted to get off.

When her feet touched the sidewalk she hurried forward. The hope for safety grew with each step, swelling and nearly edging out the fear of being turned out at dusk.

She entered the building, and after a brief phone call, the man on duty summoned another to take her to General Iberá's office.

Their footsteps echoed in a hallway lined with framed photographs of men in guardsmen uniforms. The pictures continued up the stairway and onto the next floor.

Rebekka forced steel in her spine and courage into each step forward. Both deserted her when her escort stopped in an open doorway and she saw the black-robed Father Ursu waiting there alongside Enzo Iberá.

Eight

REBEKKA turned, thinking only to escape. Her escort blocked her, fingers imprisoning her upper arms, forcing her forward and then turning her to face the priest and the general.

"There is no reason to fear," Enzo said.

Rebekka only barely smothered a hysterical laugh. In running from the man in the silver car, she'd fled right into the grasp of the person the witches claimed was responsible for her being hunted.

Terror beat at her, threatening to turn her into true prey, to replace the ability to think with only the need to fight if she couldn't flee.

Her breathing was ragged, her heart a wild pounding in her chest and ears.

The hands on her arms dropped away but the solid mass of the guardsman continued to block her escape.

Her fingers curled around the witches' token in her pocket. It was an unconscious gesture and yet the feel of it against her palm reminded her that she'd dared to use it, triggering a spell placed on it by the Wainwrights and summoning Aziel—a being from the ghostlands—in order to escape the Iberá estate.

Enzo had witnessed it. He'd heard Aziel's order to free her and his warning to cease searching for Tir or every man, woman, and child bearing the Iberá name would be killed. He'd heard Aziel tell the patriarch, "Your fate is now bound to the healer's."

Rebekka stiffened her spine and fought to make her voice sound confident as her gaze met Enzo's. "There is every reason to fear. The Church is still hunting me."

Standing next to Enzo, Father Ursu smoothed a hand over the material of his robes. "You are mistaken."

"I am not mistaken. Twice I've only barely managed to escape. Once last night. The other just a short while ago."

"What happened?" Enzo asked, his expression and sharp question making Rebekka believe he had no knowledge of her pursuers.

Rebekka told him about seeing the street boys and how both times it was followed almost immediately by the appearance of the man with the birthmark staining his face. She didn't mention Levi and the others, claimed instead that she'd managed to get away by finding a hiding place and waiting until it was safe to leave it.

By the end of her recitation, Enzo was frowning deeply. He turned to the priest.

Father Ursu opened his arms at waist height in a graceful sweeping motion. "I was drawn into this matter on behalf of the Iberás and by their request. The patriarch's dictate that the Church no longer concern itself with it has been honored."

The priest's gaze went to where the amulet lay hidden against Rebekka's skin. "There is more of the witches' evil on her than when I first encountered her. She is mistaken about the source of her troubles."

Doubt crept into Rebekka, allowed an opening by her desire to deny the matriarch's claim that her father was a demon. She hadn't told them about the memory and dream of the urchin, but the gift of the amulet hinted they knew of them.

They were the ones to tell her the Church was involved and to offer an intercession in exchange for a promised favor. But what if they were behind the attacks?

She released the token, her palms damp, her heart beating erratically. She didn't know who to trust. Not with her secrets. Not with her doubts and fears for her soul and her gift. But her purpose for coming here hadn't changed, despite the priest's presence. She couldn't go back to the brothel and risk calling disease-borne plague to her. She didn't dare go to either her homesteaded house or to the Wainwrights.

She needed shelter for the night. And if the patriarch, The Iberá, was willing to provide it, transportation to where the Barrens bordered the forests so she could go to the Fellowship of the Sign and speak to her mother.

"I need a safe place to stay tonight," she told Enzo. "Will you take me to the Iberá estate?"

More than once he'd argued with the patriarch in favor of turning her over to the Church. His voice was brusque as he said, "We need to leave now."

The drive to the Iberá estate was made in wary silence. Rebekka because there was nothing she would volunteer about her life to a general in the guard. Enzo because he remembered too well the rent in reality caused by her summoning and the shrouded figure who'd stepped through it, carrying a sigil-inscribed staff and bringing with him the promise of a retribution that meant the death of every man, woman, and child bearing the Iberá name.

Enzo's driver entered the estate through heavy gates bearing the heraldic crest of the Iberás, delivering them to the front entrance where the butler stood waiting to escort Rebekka to the room that had served as a luxurious prison only days ago.

Janita, the young maid who'd been assigned to Rebekka before, stood just inside the entrance, nervously twisting her hands. She smiled tentatively, seemingly caught between trepidation and happiness at seeing Rebekka again. "I've drawn your bath," she said. "The patriarch sent several dresses for you to choose from. You're expected at dinner."

Rebekka returned Janita's smile as she went to where the dresses were laid out on the bed. They were exquisitely crafted, made of the finest material and accompanied by matching jewelry.

"This one," she said, choosing a solid blue dress with a design allowing her to wear the amulet without revealing it.

"You will look beautiful in it," Janita said. "I will iron it then return."

There wasn't a wrinkle to be seen but Rebekka didn't protest. This was the pattern they'd worked out earlier.

Nakedness in others didn't bother Rebekka. Witnessing sexual acts had no power to shock or embarrasses her. But even if she hadn't required privacy because of the tattoo, the thought of someone assisting her with her bath, helping her bathe and washing her hair, was too intimate, too personal.

In the doorway Janita hesitated, half turning toward Rebekka long enough to say, "The patriarch has sworn me to secrecy about what I saw. I will never speak of it."

She left, closing the door firmly behind her. Rebekka took advantage of the hot water and scented soap.

It was impossible to hold on to either tension or fear in the comfort of the tub. She was safe, at least for the moment.

In the past she'd wondered what it would be like to live among those who didn't worry about food or shelter or even the law. To be surrounded by beauty and opportunity instead of horror and hopelessness. Now she knew.

You could choose to remain here, the voice of temptation whispered into her mind.

And those very words were echoed by the Iberá patriarch hours later after a formal dinner around a table laden with abundance.

She stood next to his motorized wheelchair on a walkway built on top of the estate's interior walls. Beneath them a pride of captive lions grew restless in anticipation of being fed.

The male lifted his head and roared. His challenge was answered by a male in a different enclosure.

Worry for Levi crept into Rebekka. She wondered if he and Cyrin and Canino had reached Lion lands yet.

"I spoke with Father Ursu after Enzo called to say he was bringing you to the estate," The Iberá said. "Derrick assures me the Church is respecting my wishes you be left alone. Without evidence to the contrary, I must accept what he says as true."

A door at the base of the wall opened. A small herd of deer bounded through it, their coats the same shade of brown as Feliss's furred back. When they saw the waiting predators they bolted.

The lions spread out, the females ranging ahead of the male, well versed in cornering and capturing prey in an environment they knew every inch of.

Rebekka turned away from the unfolding hunt. The patriarch said, "The deer are domestically raised, not wild caught."

The hum of the wheelchair preceded his repositioning it so he could address her directly. "What would it take to convince you to remain here, where your safety can be assured? I am prepared to offer anything within reason."

She saw him with the eyes of a healer. Beneath the expensive material of his trousers and shirt, the muscles in his legs and left arm were atrophied by what she thought was Lou Gehrig's disease. His limbs twitched involuntarily but his pride kept him upright, daring even disease to try to defeat his indomitable will.

Behind him was the estate. It would have been considered a mansion in the days before The Last War as well as in the present. There was beauty in every direction she looked. Well-tended lawns, elaborate gardens. Benches placed beneath perfectly balanced trees. Statues that would have seemed equally at home in an art museum.

"I can see that you're kept busy with work," The Iberá said, "if it's the thought of idleness that bothers you. My last offer stands. The quarters set aside for the veterinarian would be yours. Janita would also be assigned exclusively to you, or another, if you prefer a different servant. You would be free to build a clientele and travel to see them as you need to, escorted by my private guard, with all fees yours to keep. If there's something more you require, name your price."

It had been easy to turn away from the patriarch's offer the last time she was here. She'd had Levi to consider, and to a lesser extent Araña and Tir.

Tir and Araña were gone. Either dead in freeing Abijah, or, more likely, they'd taken Araña's boat and left Oakland.

With the maze destroyed and the Weres healed she'd kept her promise to Levi to help him liberate his brother. If she stayed here, she could use the money she earned to help him buy out Feliss's contract. She could do the same for the other Weres she considered her friends.

Behind her the lions made a kill. Rebekka flinched in reaction, not at the natural relationship between prey and predator, but with the knowledge that if she remained in the red zone, eventually she would lose her life there.

Allende's protection didn't extend beyond the brothels, and she knew too well how dangerous it was to be a female in the red zone, especially one bearing the tattoo of a prostitute. At sixteen she'd been dragged into an alley and nearly raped.

Only a stranger's intercession had saved her. He'd come out of nowhere, a sharp-faced Were outcast whose fingers ended in deadly talons and whose hair was plaited into a hundred braids adorned with black and red beads.

He'd eviscerated the two men holding her pinned and opened. Pulled the man lying on top of her away and castrated him, letting him scream for long moments before ending it in a spray of blood and ripped-out throat.

Shaking, nearly in shock despite having spent a lifetime witnessing the violence men were capable of doing to women—and to male prostitutes—Rebekka had allowed the stranger to help her to her feet and tug her clothing back into place.

Without thinking she'd healed a small cut on his arm, and the words he'd spoken afterward had changed her life. "Visit Dorrit. She's madam of one of Allende's brothels. Your gift is a strong one. She'll take you on as a healer."

Now even Allende's protection wasn't enough. Not unless the brothel became a self-imposed prison. Someone still hunted her.

As if sensing a weakening in Rebekka's resolve, the patriarch repeated himself. "Name your price."

Her price? The things she wanted most weren't his to buy.

Offering a dowry wasn't an uncommon practice. But a husband bought by money or a chance to gain an important position wouldn't be the kind of man who would love her and remain faithful. And beyond that, the dream catcher-like amulet against her chest served as a reminder. A warning.

She needed to know the truth about herself and her gift. About the father the matriarch claimed was a demon and the urchin whose breath tasted of disease and whose touch brought remembered nightmares of plague and death.

"I can't accept your offer," Rebekka said, her voice little more than a whisper.

The Iberá gave a barely perceptible shrug. "As long as I'm alive you may change your mind at any time. Will you accept a detail of guards to assure your safety?"

Rebekka nearly smiled at that, imagining men in pressed, black uniforms bearing the Iberá crest and trailing behind her as she went from brothel to brothel. "No. But I would accept transportation through the Barrens."

She paused, then decided to trust him with a truth few people knew. "My mother belongs to the Fellowship of the Sign. I need to visit her as soon as possible."

"I will arrange for you to be taken there tomorrow morning."

Addai

THE morning sun kissed Addai's back through the window as he was greeted by the sound of soft moans and the subtle slide of flesh against flesh, by the sight of a delicate feminine spine and the play of muscle underneath deeply tanned skin as the woman rose so the man she straddled followed in a desperate lift of hips off the mattress lest his cock be cast from the hot, wet heaven it was buried in.

Black wings spread across the bed, trembling in pleasure. Black hair spread across the pillow, a match to the woman's.

Another might have turned away. Another might have left and reappeared after moans gave way to the sharp cry of release.

Addai remained.

He waited for the hate that had once festered to come. For the rage that had been his daily companion to return. Remembered well the consuming fury that had led him to the Djinn Abijah and the betrayal of the brother he now watched taking pleasure.

Thousands of years of being enslaved and at the mercy of humans had seemed a fair price for Tir to pay for what he'd done. But as Addai saw Araña and his brother making love, it was anticipation that stirred inside him, not to join them on the bed but to have once again what they had now.

His cock hardened as another scene overlaid the one in front of him. As a different woman took Araña's place and black feathers became the snowy white of his own wings.

Soft, teasing laughter replaced murmurs and Addai's heart swelled, ached, as in his mind he looked into the face of a woman who had been dead before the birth of Jesus of Nazareth and Mohammed and a thousand other prophets and saints.

Sajia. A single instance of indecision had cost him the one whose soul completed his own.

He'd found her alone, drawing water from a village well in preparation of leaving as the rest of her family packed their trade goods onto camels. Djinn. Long-ago enemy. Sloe-eyed and gentle-spirited. He'd been hers from the instant she became aware of his presence.

Her fear had ripped through him. Shredding his sense of purpose as she backed away from him, water jugs shattering as they fell from trembling fingers.

How could he kill her? How could he see her enslaved, her will bent to that of the human priests who were given the captive Djinn?

He couldn't. Not when he wanted to possess her himself.

In the desert they'd become lovers. Husband and wife, mates, though his fear of becoming Fallen had kept him from saying the binding words, from tying his fate to hers and irrevocably making this world his own.

Addai's chest grew tight, his throat constricting against tears as he remembered the last time he'd seen her. The kiss they'd shared before he lifted her onto the back of a camel and watched her go, heat rising in shimmering waves off the sand as the caravan headed toward the distant mountains.

They went not to trade, but at the calling of the Djinn by The Prince who ruled them.

He'd fought the urge to go after her, not yet ready to say the necessary words so the gathered Djinn would accept him among them as ally and not enemy. He'd turned away, but even so, some part of her spirit already lived in him.

He'd felt the moment of her death. It was a searing blaze of pain across his soul. A chasm of emptiness that filled with terrible rage and hate when he went to the place where her body lay among others in a scene of devastation.

Tents burned and goats bleated in terror.

Camels ran through the encampment, freed from hobbles and ropes.

Angels bound captured Djinn in sigil-inscribed shackles or urns.

And amidst the carnage Tir stood with blood on his hands, thinking himself righteous. Glorious in victory.

A flash of movement, the rush of power over his skin brought Addai back to the present. To the sight of Tir in front of him, sword held ready, Araña only a step behind him with her knives.

"What brings you here?" Tir asked.

Addai's smile was as sharp as the weapon in his brother's hand. "The priest, Ursu. He continues to hunt for the healer in the hopes she will lead him to you. It's time you paid him a visit to show him you are now beyond his reach, and to make him cease his attempts to have Rebekka found and brought to the Church."

"Kill him?" The question held the anticipation of pure pleasure.

"No. His life still serves us."

The sword in Tir's hand disappeared, returned to the cold pocket of light and air that was its sheath. "I'll ask again in the future."

Addai looked to Araña, his gaze lingering on the spider-shaped mark riding her shoulder, proclaiming the nature of her Djinn soul and the House she was called to. "Neither you nor Tir may directly help the healer now. But she might have need of your boat. Will you leave it in Oakland for a while?"

"It can remain there for as long as it's needed."

Addai bowed slightly in acknowledgment, his attention returning to Tir. "Speak with Ursu."

"Should I strike a deal with Rimmon for Rebekka's protection while she's on the *Constellation*?"

"No. Let your previous bargain stand. Only the boat is to be guarded. When the time is right, the healer can learn she has access to it, and that the threat presented by the Church is over. I'll let you know when that time arrives. You can serve as messenger since you are familiar to her and to the werelion Levi."

"I'll leave now."

Addai's gaze dropped to the tattoolike spider above Tir's heart, the mark he'd gained by having the courage to speak the forbidden incantation and willingly bind himself to Araña. For an instant the past reached into the present, bringing with it memories of a different mark, a different choice. But the festering hate, the rage that had once accompanied those memories didn't come. Only anticipation filled Addai, and a desire hot enough to burn through eternity.

Iyar en Batrael, the most powerful of the Raven House, had gone to the fiery birthplace of the Djinn and called Sajia's name. After thousands of years she was reborn. And though she would hold no memories of their life together, soon she would be returned to him. His to love and possess.

"It is good to have you back among us, brother," Addai said, clasping Tir to him before letting go of his corporeal form, along with the past.

Closure

OAKLAND. There'd been nothing to explain the sense of anticipation, the exhilaration and hope that filled him when he first heard mention of this city.

Shackled, sold like an animal, he couldn't have predicted he would find freedom here—love—and with it redemption, a purpose other than vengeance and retribution.

Araña. Her name was a joyous shout in his soul, her body sweet pleasure and carnal torment.

Thinking about her made him harden. Being away from her was a scraping of sharp edges against his skin, a piercing of his heart, though with the binding of their spirits and the sharing of breath, Tir knew she lived and was safe.

He stood in front of the church. It was a huge, elaborate affair, a testament to wealth and power as much as to faith.

With his memory restored he could remember the very beginnings of it, all the iterations and deviations it had taken. The different directions it had gone off in. Splitting and splitting again in seemingly endless repetitions.

There'd never been only one belief, one interpretation of the creator's words and signs. The being they called God was unknowable to the creatures he'd fashioned from mud and breathed his spirit into. Just as he was often unknowable to his first sons and daughters, angels created from light and divine essence.

Tir climbed the steps. He passed through an arched doorway carved with images of his kind and entered the sanctuary. Even the Fallen could get this far, though their pleas for forgiveness weren't answered.

Inside, the air was cool and scented by candles. A handful of old men and women knelt on velvet-lined benches, heads bowed in prayer.

He walked by them, closing his mind to their entreaties and emotions though he felt the sudden race of their hearts as, deep within, they recognized him despite the human appearance he wore.

At the doorway leading into the private part of the church there were wards in place. Ancient protections against demons. Against Satan— The Usurper—the tester of human souls. And though the humans no longer remembered what the sigils meant, there were symbols carved there to protect against the wrath of the Djinn. Tir passed through the doorway without resistance or fear, moving farther into the church.

A young priest emerged from an office. He startled at the sight of Tir, started to frown but paled instead with the realization that the strap across Tir's bare chest held a sheath with a machete in it.

The papers in the priest's hand shook but he found his courage. "You can't be in this part of the church unaccompanied. I'll show you to the main office unless you'd prefer to return to the chapel."

Tir let a portion of his humanity fall away, used the voice that had once commanded legions and caused men to prostrate themselves before him. "I am here to see Father Ursu. You will take me to him."

The priest complied, his heartbeat thunder in Tir's mind. He turned and led the way, escorting Tir first through the areas set aside for the everyday work of the church and then into the domain of those who ruled it.

Utilitarian furniture gave way to antiques. Pastoral art gave way to glorious paintings done by masters dead long before The Last War.

"This is his office," the young priest said, stopping before a closed door, licking his lips and nervously backing away.

Tir read the priest's intention to call the guards. It mattered little. By the time they arrived the business with Ursu would be done.

In the interest of creating as little a ripple as possible for any of his kind to discover and question, Tir spoke in soothing tones, stripping away the priest's worry by saying, "Father Ursu will come to no harm at my hands this day. Leave in peace."

Calmness settled over the young priest. He turned from Tir, his attention going to the papers in his hands as he retraced his steps.

Tir waited only a moment before entering the suite Ursu commanded. Two men turned, one with a port-wine stain marking his face, the other wearing black robes woven of the finest material.

Ursu stopped in midsentence, his gaze going immediately to Tir's bared arms, searching for and not finding the tattoos that had once covered them. "If you could excuse me for a moment, Graham," he said, dismissing his companion.

"I'll wait out in the hallway."

The man slipped from the room, seemingly unbothered by the sight of Tir and the machete he carried.

Fear poured off the priest, measuring both his devotion and the heavy weight of the deeds he carried on his soul in serving his faith. His spirit trembled like a living thing trying to escape the presence of one who could see and judge it unworthy.

Tir had thought the priest would cower, praying for mercy and pleading his case. Instead Ursu remained standing, waiting, stirring memories to life of the thousands of years Tir had spent in the hands of men like this one.

The desire for vengeance rose inside him, a dark, cold temptation that had Tir lifting his hand to call his sword.

Don't, Araña said, a part of her with him always. *Finish the task Addai set before you and come back to me.*

Images accompanied her command, a carnal tangle of male and female, of wings and flesh, that came on a hot desert wind of desire and burned away thoughts of the past.

Tir met the priest's eyes. "My hand is stayed from striking you down. But see that I am now beyond your reach. Know that if you continue to search for the healer Rebekka or cause any harm to befall her, nothing will save you from my wrath, and it will not be a paradise your soul is delivered to."

Nine

REBEKKA entered The Iberá's study and saw the book she'd stolen the pages from pushed to the corner of his desk. Guilt threatened to seep in with the sight of it.

She suppressed it. Just as she resisted the urge to touch the amulet she'd received in payment for them. The last time she was in this room she was a prisoner soon to be turned over to the Church.

The Iberá looked up from his work. "You've had a chance to rest and consider my offer. Is your answer the same?"

"Yes."

"Very well. As promised, I have arranged for a driver and escort to take you across the Barrens. Should I have them wait and bring you back before sunset?"

A shiver passed through her with memories of the urchin and the rat. Until she was sure the amulet would protect her, she couldn't go back to the brothel.

Once there she wouldn't dare leave again. Twice now there'd been an attempt to capture her.

"No, they can return as soon as they leave me at the trailhead. I'm not sure how long I'll remain at my mother's house. As part of their religious duties, the men and women of the Fellowship come to Oakland. I can accompany them across the Barrens."

"Very well." His gaze shifted to her right as Enzo entered the room with another man, both of them wearing the uniform of a guardsman.

The Iberá said, "Captain Orst, this is Rebekka. She's a gifted healer. Should you ever be in a position to offer aid to her, I hope you will do so."

"Consider it done."

The guard captain studied Rebekka as if committing her features to memory. She did the same to him.

"Is transportation still required?" Enzo asked the patriarch.

"Yes. Please see Rebekka off. Captain Orst and I will wait until you return before discussing anything of importance."

Enzo gestured for Rebekka to precede him through the door. She went.

They left the main house and entered the section of the estate reserved for the private militia. One sedan and two jeeps stood ready.

Flags with the Iberá crest fluttered on the antennas. Drivers and armed men waited next to the vehicles. They straightened, standing at attention with Enzo's approach.

Rebekka opened the front passenger door before she could be placed in the back, and got into the car. After a brief word from Enzo, the driver slid in as the other men took their positions on the jeeps, machine guns gripped in their hands.

Engines roared to life. The gates of the estate swung open and as they passed through them, a small, internal voice whispered to Rebekka, telling her this could be part of her everyday world if she accepted The Iberá's offer.

She gave in to the fantasy. Instead of thinking about going to the Fellowship in order to find out whether or not her father was a demon, she imagined a life where she was making rounds, visiting clients.

It was sweet temptation, a balm of comfort. But it couldn't stand against reality when a short time later they encountered a blockade manned by guardsmen.

The three vehicles slowed to a stop. Rebekka's heart pounded and her palms grew damp. In her mind's eye she saw herself ordered from the sedan and taken into custody, then turned over to the man bearing the birthmark on his face.

With the guard in turmoil, there had to be factions supported by the vice lords, just as there were other factions being supported by the Church. She couldn't be sure whether or not the vice lords who'd profited from the maze were hunting her. She wasn't prepared to believe the threat the Church presented was over, regardless of Father Ursu's claim to Enzo. The priest had been willing to go to great lengths to capture Tir, and not just in order to see the Iberá patriarch healed.

One of the guardsmen positioned at the blockade approached the sedan. Rebekka fought the urge to bolt from the vehicle and run for her life.

Next to her the driver rolled down his window. "What's going on?" he asked when the guardsman reached them.

"A pocket of plague was discovered by a patrol."

Dread filled Rebekka in a cold wave of horror. She couldn't suppress a small cry as her hand went to the amulet.

The guardsman glanced at her and offered a reassuring smile. "No need to be alarmed, ma'am. We come across these from time to time. There are men in the guard trained to handle it. The threat has already been isolated and contained."

He turned his attention back to the driver. "It's safe enough if you stay on this road and don't turn into the affected area. I'd recommend you detour though. What's up ahead isn't a sight for a civilian. The men are in the cleanup stage."

More than anything Rebekka wanted to take the detour. The descriptions from the healer's journal had already lent themselves to nightmares containing vivid images of plague.

She wanted to believe what lay ahead had nothing to do with her. To pretend it would *never* have anything to do with her.

She couldn't.

She needed to see for herself. She needed to know. "Was the plague carried by rats?"

"I don't know, ma'am. But like I said, there's no reason for you to be alarmed. It's been taken care of."

"We'll go straight through then," Rebekka said, half hoping the driver wouldn't have to do as she directed.

The guardsman looked to the driver for confirmation. The driver nodded.

"All right," the guardsman said, stepping back and indicating with a wave to the other men stationed at the barricade that the Iberá vehicles could pass through.

The lead jeep moved forward. The sedan followed, and, in its wake, the second jeep.

The ruins of several skyscrapers blocked their view until they reached the end of them. Then Rebekka saw smoke billowing upward and another blockade, this one at the mouth of a street to the left.

A guardsman motioned them to keep moving, though he didn't protest when the jeep slowed to a crawl to allow the militiamen to see what was going on. The sedan followed suit.

Rebekka's hand pressed hard to the hidden amulet as they reached the barricade. She looked, her eyes going immediately to the pallets where corpses burned.

There might be five bodies, or seven. There was no way to count them or to know if they'd been dead when they were discovered, or killed by the guard to prevent the spread of disease.

Smoke escaped through the windows and cracks of a partially collapsed building near the pallets. A man stepped from it.

He was covered from head to foot in an enclosed hazard suit and carrying something Rebekka thought of as a modified flamethrower. Backing out behind him was another man, this one sweeping fire back and forth, burning every square inch.

Other men were visible doing the same. While still others stood with rifles at the ready, prepared to shoot anything trying to escape.

Rebekka's fingers curled around the amulet. Her chest tightened as she remembered the rat in the alleyway between the brothels.

If she took the witches' protection off, would she know the plague here had truly been eradicated? Or would animals carrying disease begin coming to her and be slaughtered by the guardsmen?

The sedan sped up as they reached another cluster of buildings, cutting off the view. Her relief at knowing the amulet protected her was equaled by the lingering fear of plague, and her guilt at not being able to use her gift to alleviate and prevent further suffering.

We couldn't stop, she told herself, though a part of her, a small part, whispered she was a coward, said even if they could have stopped, she wouldn't have ordered the driver to do so for fear of being killed when it became obvious the diseased were being drawn to her.

"Coward," she called herself again as she stood in front of the door to her mother's house, looking around, delaying the moment of truth.

The settlement was laid out like a spoked wheel, with the community building at its hub and long, enclosed passageways extending from it and leading to individual log houses, so even during the night, the members of the Fellowship could gather. Off some of the houses were additional passageways, linking freshly built cabins to those of the original community and ensuring no member was isolated.

Drifting through open windows came the smell of wood fires, roasted pork, and baked bread. It was accompanied by the sound of hymns sung in praise of God as women and children applied themselves to their chores.

Rebekka wanted to deny the matriarch's claim and Abijah's words. She hated to bring the past here, to this place of peace that was her mother's refuge. And yet she had no true choice. Her mother was the only one she trusted to answer her questions.

Growing up it had always been Chloe. Never Mom or Mother, the way it could be now, because what man who visited a prostitute wanted to be reminded of the consequences of sex or worry that a bastard child who looked just like him would one day arrive at his doorstep for his wife and his legitimate children to see?

Mouth dry, hand trembling slightly, she finally knocked. A man's voice bid her to enter. She did so and heard her mother's soft gasp before three small girls threw themselves at her with a squealed "Bekka!"

Immediately her heart lodged in her throat. She hadn't thought her mother's adopted children would remember her.

Rebekka knelt, hugging the girls to her. They were dressed in long skirts, the material soft from repeated washings.

Fierce longing swept through her. She wanted this, a home, a family.

"Have you come to join the Fellowship?" her mother's husband asked.

Boden was older than Chloe. Bearded and wiry. Devout in the faith that had redeemed him from drug use and a thief's life.

His welcome was contingent on her answer. Grim tolerance of a sinner in his home if she said no. Joyous celebration if she'd found God and was ready to embrace the Fellowship as he had.

"I can't," Rebekka said, looking at her mother over the heads of the girls. "I came here to ask Chloe something."

"I'll take the girls to work in the gardens," Boden said, ushering them ahead of him despite their protests.

A toddler remained, a sturdy boy who'd been hiding behind Chloe and was revealed when Rebekka crossed to her mother. He peeked up at her, one hand clinging to her mother's skirt, the other a spit-wet fist as he gummed his knuckles.

"This is little Boden," Chloe said, brushing her fingers across wisps of soft, white-blond hair. "He just came to us."

Rebekka knelt once again but the boy retreated, wrapping the material of the skirt around him and turning it into a concealing blanket. "From the Mission?"

The Fellowship took in orphaned children as often as their resources allowed it. And like many prostitutes, years of being used had left Chloe scarred inside, no longer able to conceive.

"Yes," Chloe said, brushing her fingers across Rebekka's hair in the same way as she'd done to the boy.

Rebekka rose from her crouch. Face-to-face, she and her mother were the same height.

Chloe caressed Rebekka's cheek with her fingertips, her eyes meeting Rebekka's, searching for something. "You've gotten more beautiful since the last time I saw you."

"I look like you."

Her mother's smile held more sadness than happiness. They were so close in appearance it was obvious they were mother and daughter. Not sisters, but only because Chloe's early life had aged her.

"I saw the expression on your face when you greeted the girls," Chloe said, her voice soft. "You could have the same thing I've found here. There are single men in the Fellowship who would make good husbands, good fathers. You could live with us until you settled on one of them and married. Your house could be attached to ours. The girls would love having a big sister. I would love having my oldest daughter here, where her soul would no longer be in peril."

Rebekka took her mother's hands in hers. She rubbed her thumb against the crosses branded into her mother's skin—self-inflicted in the ecstasy of worship. Her gaze flickered over the deep wooden boxes running along one wall, their tops covered in mesh to prevent the rattlesnakes they contained from escaping and curious children from getting bitten.

The Fellowship took the teachings of Mark 16, starting with the fifteenth verse, literally. For them, signs followed those who believed and were saved, confirming the *Word*. They could speak in tongues, cast out devils, and lay hands upon the sick. They could drink deadly things and take up the handling of serpents and no harm would come to them.

"I can't," Rebekka said. It wasn't just a matter of not accepting her mother's faith, but of not being willing to turn her back on the Weres.

The Fellowship would limit the use of her gift to the healing of their livestock and pets. Should she be in Oakland, fulfilling the mission to go out and preach, her talent might be bartered for things the community needed—but it would be used only on animals, not on Weres.

She touched the plain gold circle of her mother's wedding band.

The pressure to remain faithful and uphold God's laws, along with the long days of working together in groups often segregated by gender, made infidelity rare in the Fellowship. But while women and children weren't a man's property, they still came under his authority.

Rebekka looked up from her study of her mother's hands. There was no gentle way to ask the questions she'd come here to ask. "Tell me how I came to be born."

Her mother pulled away, flinching from memories of the past. She picked up the toddler, hugging him to her chest as if he were a shield against the pain.

"I knew this day would come. He said it would, when you were an adult. He told me I was to answer your question then, *only* then, or I would be sorry for breaking our agreement." Her arms tightened, making the toddler squirm and try to get out of them.

"I've dreaded it. Feared it. I've prayed it would never happen because if it did, it could only mean he intends to use you for some purpose."

"*He*, meaning my father?"

"Yes."

"What was his name?"

Chloe gave a harsh laugh. "John. They were all named John."

She set the toddler down among wooden blocks, then crossed to a worktable where handmade patterns were pinned to pieces of dark material. She took up a pair of scissors and began cutting.

Rebekka followed, remaining quiet as the stiffness slowly left her mother's posture. The scissors were laid down, though Chloe continued to stare at the fabric.

In a quiet voice Chloe said, "I grew up in a poor settlement near Sacramento. There were five children in the family. Two boys and three girls. The land my parents worked would support the boys when they took wives and started families, but not the girls. I was the second girl, not favored as my older sister was. My parents contracted me to a brothel owner in exchange for enough money to provide a dowry for my sister so she could marry well."

Chloe picked up the scissors. Put them down again.

"The settlement I grew up in was on a caravan route. Four times a year the traveling brothel stopped there. The year you were born, my father came to where we were camped. He didn't acknowledge me as his daughter. Instead he acted as though I was something dirty, beneath contempt, as if I'd chosen to become a prostitute."

There was pain in Chloe's voice, angry bitterness. "He came to offer my younger sister to the brothel master so he could buy livestock as a christening gift for my brother's first son. We didn't have room for another prostitute. But another caravan would come. And another, and eventually my sister would be made a whore. She was only two years younger than me, my closest friend when we were growing up. The one person in my family who loved me back."

Chloe turned then, facing Rebekka. "A man approached me the day after my father came to the campsite. He wanted me to become pregnant with his child. Abortions were mandatory for the prostitutes in the caravan. But he'd made arrangements with the brothel master—the older brother of the one you might remember—so I'd carry to term and be allowed to keep the baby. He offered enough money so my younger sister would be able to pick her own husband and never have to fear for her future.

"I accepted his offer, though he was in no hurry to consummate the deal. He delivered the payment to my sister, even waited until her engagement was announced before leading me away from the caravan.

"He gave me something to drink and impregnated me. I was only with him the one night. Most of what happened is blurry, except afterward, before he took me back to camp. He told me you were to be kept safe and taught to read, and if I failed to protect you while you were in my care, he would learn of it and kill me."

Her gaze dropped to the place where the mark of a prostitute had been forcibly inked onto Rebekka's skin. A hard shiver went through her, as if she was still frightened after so many years.

Rebekka thought of the dream-restored memory and the stark terror on her mother's face after the tattooing. They'd begun living in Oakland shortly after it happened.

She took Chloe's hands again. Squeezed them in reassurance. "Was he human?"

Wariness entered her mother's expression. "None of the amulets reacted in his presence. Most of those traveling in the caravan thought he was a gifted human, a sorcerer or a warlock."

"And you? What did you think?"

Chloe's shoulders slumped as if to allow a heavy burden to finally slide off them. "When he was on top of me, there was something inhuman in his eyes. It was almost as if he despised doing the very thing he'd paid to do."

"One last question," Rebekka said, wanting to free her mother from the torment of the past and not sure how much more she herself could bear knowing. "What did he look like?"

"He reminded me of a bird of prey. Sharp featured. His hair done up in hundreds of braids, each one of them with black and red beads woven in."

Light-headedness would have dropped Rebekka to her knees except for her grip on her mother's hands. She'd thought him a Were outcast the day he'd come out of nowhere and saved her from being raped, eviscerating her attackers and painting the alleyway red with their blood before telling her to seek out Dorrit.

Now the image of his fingers ending in deadly talons was overlaid by another, different only in color, a dark hand wrapping around her throat, a razor-sharp claw digging into her flesh, slicing through it with ease. Pulling away so a forked tongue could lap at blood-covered fingers. *Your father's involvement is a surprise. He had no love for humans when I was last among my kind.*

"I promise, just one more question," Rebekka said, her voice a whisper. "The day I was tattooed, did a rabid dog come into camp?"

With the change of topic her mother smiled. "Yes. I thought it would cause more nightmares but instead it seemed to chase them away."

Rebekka couldn't stop herself from asking, "Was there a boy there too? With a rat on his shoulder?"

"No. Maybe he was part of the terrifying dreams you'd had the night before. Do you remember having to be drugged because of it?"

"Yes."

Chloe pulled her hands from Rebekka's and used them to push Rebekka's hair back from her face, tucking it behind her ears. "It's all in the past now. The Lord is a forgiving god. I've repented and been saved. His spirit moved on me and brought with it a peace I wouldn't have believed possible."

She picked up the crucifix that lay against her chest and pressed it into Rebekka's hands, holding them to it. When Rebekka didn't flinch away, relief shone in Chloe's eyes, as though she'd feared, had secretly guessed, she'd lain with a demon to create a child.

Rebekka wouldn't tell her otherwise, not when her mother had found happiness and peace.

"Whatever the truth is about your father," Chloe said, her voice burning with faith, "you're human in all the ways that count. Stay here with us. Be baptized into the Fellowship."

Twice in as many days Rebekka had been offered sanctuary. Her answer to her mother was no different than the one she'd given the Iberá patriarch. "I can't."

"Think about it," Chloe said, pressing Rebekka's hands hard against the crucifix. "Regardless of how you came to be born, I love you."

Frustrated at having been ignored for so long, the toddler threw one of his blocks. It struck the wooden boxes, filling the room with the sound of rattlesnakes issuing a warning.

Chloe stepped away then, taking the sign of her faith with her. "We'd better go help the girls in the garden. They'll be mad if I keep you all to myself."

Messenger

THEY made the task easy, Tir thought, studying the Weres. Had they traveled steadily, they could have been deep in Were territory by now, but he could understand Levi lingering, delaying in order to spend time with his brother. Cyrin and the Tiger would be welcomed among the Lions, but for Levi, it would be a glimpse of all that he'd lost followed by expulsion and a forced return to life in the human world.

Cyrin and the Tiger worked on what was left of a carcass. The crunch and gnawing of bone by one was matched by the slurp and tearing of muscle by the other.

Smoke from a small fire and the smell of cooking marked the place where Levi prepared his meal, accentuating the difference between the Lion brothers. One trapped in a beast's form. The other in a man's.

Levi turned the slab of meat over and filled the air with the scent and sizzle of fat hitting flames. Tir's nostrils flared, not in hunger but with the memory of Levi leaving him shackled for the guardsmen to find the last time they were in the woods together.

He understood Levi's choice. He would have made an identical one. But forgiveness didn't come easily to Tir.

Enough, already, Araña spoke into his mind, her presence so natural he no longer noticed her arriving and departing. *Let it go or I'll have to punish you.*

The warning came with the image of her holding a thin leather belt. He hardened immediately, not at the prospect of feeling it against his skin, but of using it on her, whipping them both into a frenzy of desire. *Don't make threats you can't back up with action.*

She laughed in response. Sent him another image, this one of her sprawled on their bed, naked, ready for him. *Hurry. Give Levi the message meant for him and come home.*

Despite the husky words and the desire they held, she couldn't hide her worry over Rebekka's fate. Araña knew too well what it meant to be tested by the Djinn, and how readily they accepted death as the price of failure.

Tir glanced in the direction Levi would soon head, and where he would cross paths with the Were meant to be the healer's mate. Addai hadn't provided the details, though Tir could easily guess the end objective. In a battle for control of the Earth, the Weres would make formidable soldiers.

I'll be there in a matter of minutes, he sent Araña. *Be ready.*

Tir stepped from the shelter of the trees, and the Tiger and Cyrin both charged. He watched them bound toward him, a coldness filling his chest along with a willingness to call his sword into existence and slay them even though he'd taken part in freeing them from the maze.

Levi's shouted *no* had little effect in slowing either large cat. But at the last moment, both Lion and Tiger swerved, recognizing his scent from the maze, or, if not that, then the danger of carrying through with their attack.

They padded back to the carcass as Levi approached warily. His glance took in Tir's lack of collar and tattoos, then went to the forest, searching, finally saying, "We saw what the demon did to the maze. What happened to Araña?"

The concern in Levi's voice eradicated the last of Tir's ill will. "She is safe and well away from Oakland."

"Good. Someone is hunting Rebekka."

Tir's smile was menacing. "No longer. I took care of it personally. I've been told Rebekka shelters with her mother. When you see her next, tell her she no longer has to fear returning home. The *Constellation* remains in Oakland should there be a need to stay there for any reason. Rimmon's protection extends only to the boat itself."

Before Levi could ask questions, Tir retreated into the woods, forging deep enough to maintain the illusion of being human. A thought fed by will and he no longer wore flesh. Another, driven by desire, and he moved through an unseen corridor of reality, re-formed in a different place, black wings and body manifesting to Araña's welcome of heated kisses and hot flesh.

Ten

OAKLAND loomed in the distance. Tall buildings rising in defiance like human fists lifted in challenge.

Aryck's lips pulled back in a snarl, answering the symbolic threat, though he was surrounded by far more imminent ones. Silent, running on two legs because a man's form was better suited for traveling long distances at a faster pace, he was alert to every movement, every scent.

Melina paced at his side, making his snarl deepen. He knew why his father had insisted she accompany him. Koren hoped proximity would lead to a successful coupling, so in the event of Aryck's death, their line would continue with an unborn child. And in the event Aryck survived this journey to collect the healer, he would return with Melina as his mate.

Aryck's fingers flexed in frustration. For parts of their trip they'd worn fur, and the scent of a female deeply in heat had very nearly driven him to cover her. He'd resisted only by fierce determination and a concentration of purpose.

The route they traveled was one his father had shared with him mentally. In the time since Koren was an enforcer, the scenery had changed very little.

They were now in territory inhabited primarily by ferals and rogues, those whose human and animal souls had separated, one battling the other for dominance to the extent they could no longer live within pack society or follow pack law.

Ferals ended up wearing fur. Their beast ruled, reverting to animal instincts but drawing on human cunning without also feeling bound to the pack. It made them a danger that had to be driven from Were lands. Rogues shifted back and forth in a continuing fight. Most fled Were lands voluntarily. They left before they broke pack law and ended up being made outcast or killed by their own kind.

The scent of hyenas hit Aryck. There were pure animals and Were, though he couldn't tell if they were one pack or several.

Among Weres who were prey animals, mixing with herds containing pure animals was like donning camouflage. But among predators, a willingness to pack and mate with beasts was the mark of a feral or rogue.

He'd expected to find a heavy concentration of them here. Like other supernaturals, ferals and rogues were drawn to human settlements and cities, because despite the risk, prey was plentiful.

They were close to what the humans called the Barrens. It was a blackened, burned-out place where the dregs of human society took refuge, the insane and hunted, those so reviled they didn't dare live in the red zone as the healer he sought did.

Distaste shuddered through Aryck, that she'd make her home among outcast prostitutes. It didn't surprise him the ancestors knew of the healer's existence. It was in their power to restore those they'd judged unfavorably, though it happened so rarely he'd never seen evidence of it.

Aryck spared a glance at Melina as the scent of hyena grew heavier. He hated the necessity of it, but knew it would be safer to have the jaguar's strength.

"We change before going any farther," he said, stopping and immediately removing his pants and supple moccasins, ensuring the pouch containing payment for the healer, gold coins unearthed in ruins on Jaguar lands, was well secured.

For once Melina stripped and stood naked without the conscious offering of her body. Like Aryck, she quickly rolled her footwear into her clothing, then knotted it to make a loose fabric collar that could be worn while in jaguar form.

Aryck shifted first, the collar of clothing already around his neck. Melina did the same.

Low to the ground the scent was even more intense. It carried not only traces of hyena but wolf and coyote, feral dogs as well as deer and rabbit.

This deep in the forest there was no trace of humans, but that wasn't surprising. Even with their guns they would be nothing but prey here.

Aryck moved on, with Melina traveling farther from his side than before. He was anxious to get to the red zone and find the healer. Willing or not, she would accompany him back to the Jaguar's summer campsite.

The trees thinned as they neared the Barrens. Rubble and debris turned the path they were on into a winding trail full of blind spots.

Aryck slowed, sensing danger an instant before three spotted hyenas scrambled over hills of vine-covered ruin while two others blocked the path in either direction, creating a vicious cage. Their excited whooping added to the adrenaline spiking through his blood and he lunged, using his weight to his advantage to knock a small male to the ground as it leapt from the piled rubble.

There was no time for finesse. Aryck buried his canines into the animal's throat, clamped, and ripped, severing the jugular.

Searing agony whipped through his side and flank as his skin was pierced by two attackers. Behind him Melina screamed in fury and pain.

He turned, raking his claws over the animal trying to eviscerate him, blinding it in one eye. It retreated, giving Aryck a chance to spin around and savage the animal whose bite had torn through muscle to crush leg bone.

Fury, pain, the will to survive burned away any vestige of thought. He attacked with teeth and claws, not content just to drive his attacker away.

Aryck killed his opponent, then focused on those circling Melina. She was bleeding from a tear in her side but had held them off.

He launched himself, nearly blacking out as he used his hind leg, but somehow managing to land on his target and bite, severing the spine so the animal went down underneath him.

Melina pounced on a large female. Aryck felt the rip of muscle and tendon, the crack of bone in his other back leg as the beast he'd blinded in one eye overcame its injuries, forgetting them in the frenzy of fighting, and with the whooping calls announcing the rapid approach of another pack. He turned, driving the hyena off him as Melina killed her attacker.

Strength bled out of Aryck with the loss of blood and the severity of his injuries. He knew he was a dead man, the ancestors' prophecy coming to pass, though not in the way he'd envisioned it.

His legs were both broken, too badly damaged to hold his weight. He was injured beyond what could be healed by shifting form, even if he had the strength to manage it.

The whooping calls were closer now, moments away given the speed of hunting hyenas. He would die where he lay, fighting until they ripped out his internal organs.

Aryck growled at Melina, using a sound that meant *retreat*, *climb*, *hide*. She showed her teeth and growled in response but was already scanning, looking for a route, a tree, the instinct for self-preservation greater than any other and beginning to override all else.

She'd taken only a few steps before the first of the new pack appeared, coming from the direction of the forest instead of the Barrens. A feral led it, the scent different from the pure hyenas in the first attack. It was followed by a second feral and then a third, their rolling gait and obvious intelligence enough to send terror out in front of them.

Aryck pulled himself into a crouch, half expecting the hyena he'd injured to attack from behind. Instead he heard it yelling, the roaring scream of an animal trying to escape.

An instant later he saw the reason for it. A male Lion charged past him, closely paced by a Tiger. In front of Aryck the lead feral dropped as a bullet smashed into its skull.

Before the first two of its companions could escape, the big cats were on them, taking them down like prey.

The remaining pack members fled, laughing, filling the forest with the high-pitched sounds of their intense fear.

Melina wheeled and snarled, prepared to launch herself at a new threat. Aryck turned his head just as a man holding a gun said, "I don't, want to shoot you but I will if you attack."

The voice and face were vaguely familiar but Aryck couldn't concentrate. With the hyenas gone and the need to fight no longer present, adrenaline flowed out of him, leaving him hollowed out, nauseous until pain descended and shock started to settle in.

He fought against blacking out and was only vaguely aware of Melina giving up the jaguar's shape for a human one, of the Lion and Tiger padding over, sitting, their heads cocked as they listened while she and the man talked.

Aryck struggled to full consciousness with the mention of the healer Rebekka. Despite the futility of it, he tried to change shape, failed even as the conversation ended and the man moved to his side and crouched next to him.

Were, Aryck had time to think. *Lion.* And then darkness descended in a wave of agony as he was lifted off the ground.

IT was backbreaking work, bending over each plant, not just to harvest but to check for disease and insects. Rebekka ached from it.

A few plants in front of her a girl pulled a bug from a leaf and tossed it a short distance away. A bold mockingbird snatched the bug up before it could crawl away.

The mockingbird wasn't the only bird brought to the garden by the prospect of an easy meal. Robins dotted the aisles, waiting for a chance to dart in and snag an earthworm as children harvested small potatoes for the evening meal.

Finches and sparrows of various types were equally plentiful, varying from shades of brown to gold. A lone male cardinal sat on a low tree branch, while higher up, two scrub jays began squawking and quarreling, the sound of it making the cardinal fly away.

Rebekka stood to stretch the muscles of her back and take a moment to look over at where the younger children played on blankets or took naps, watched over by older girls and women on break. She'd taken her turn underneath the trees and out of the sun several times since coming to the garden with her mother to work.

At midday everyone stopped for a lunch of bread, cheese, and fruit. She'd had a chance to play with the girls, to hold her mother's new son.

A different ache filled Rebekka as she thought about the children. When she was at the brothel she rarely allowed herself to dream of a husband or children. They had no place there. But here . . .

She rubbed her chest, wished. But the feel of the amulet hidden by her shirt was a sharp reminder of the horror she could call to her and the answers she still needed if she was ever to be able to use her gift to free the Weres from life in the brothels.

In the row next to Rebekka, her mother straightened, facing her. Chloe lifted her hand, shading her eyes.

Around them, other women also stopped working. Several of those looking in the same direction as Chloe murmured to their neighbors, causing them to turn.

Curious, Rebekka did the same and immediately knew what had caused the women's reaction. They might be devout, married for the most part, but they weren't blind.

The man accompanying the Fellowship's leader was physically beautiful. His presence reached across the distance and held them all spellbound.

He wore homespun clothing, dark and somber, plain like Edom's. But where a carved, wooden crucifix hung from a leather strap around the Fellowship leader's neck, this man wore gold crosses in his earlobes. And instead of short hair, his was long and black, reminding her of Tir.

"This is Brother Caphriel," Edom said, the introduction carrying through the garden in a warm, powerful tone. "He is also *Of The Sign*, though his fellowship is far from here."

"Thank you for welcoming me among you," Brother Caphriel said.

His voice had an even more profound effect on the women and children than Edom's had. They left their places, gathering like a flock to a shepherd.

Rebekka didn't fight when her mother's hand closed around her upper arm, drawing her forward. *Human*, she thought as they neared Caphriel, maybe gifted in the same way as Edom was, with the innate ability to attract followers and hold them to him.

The women and children murmured greetings. And as Caphriel offered each a personal smile, *saw* them individually, it was as if he were the sun and they were flowers soaking in his warmth.

Rebekka was unnerved by what she witnessed, yet not quite unaffected by it. When his attention was finally on her she wanted to step away in equal measure to the desire to step forward.

His eyes seemed to blaze when he looked to the spot where the hidden amulet touched her skin. "Speak with me, sister. I see you carry a heavy burden. Let me offer you a chance to be rid of it. Let me shine the light where darkness claims a part of your soul."

Next to him, Edom said, "God is a living god. He doesn't have a body. Except us. We're his hands and his mouth. We're his way into this world."

"Amen," the gathered said in refrain.

"Let Brother Caphriel share The Word with you, Rebekka! Let him pray, so The Spirit might move on you!"

Hands pushed Rebekka forward with an "Amen." Bodies formed a wall, blocking any possibility of retreat.

"Come, let us speak privately," Caphriel said, turning away, separating himself from the crowd.

Rebekka followed, not sure whether it was hope or fear, free will or hidden command, making her place herself in front of him.

His eyes bored into her as though he could see the desires of her heart. "Brother Edom tells me you have a powerful gift for healing.

But it's not enough. Is it? You long for a family, a husband to love and be loved by. Children. A place to call home that is free of horror and full of peace."

Rebekka wet suddenly dry lips. "Yes."

"You can have those things. Brother Edom spoke to me about your mother as we came to the garden. I can sense she bears a tattoo, and you a similar one. I can guess the shameful nature of it.

"There are those who embrace the scripture proclaiming the creator a gracious god, slow to anger and abounding in love. Forgiving wickedness, rebellion, and sin, though he doesn't leave the guilty unpunished. For the sins of the parents, the children are punished to the third and fourth generation."

Goose bumps broke out on Rebekka's skin as she remembered the policeman quoting similar words as justification for holding a child down and forcibly, painfully, leaving a mark that destroyed hope and possibility.

Caphriel's face warmed with compassion. "Forgive those who trespassed against you. They do not understand the nature of the Father. The god of the early days needed to be harsh to ensure his children were not led astray."

"And the god of the end days? Is he any less harsh?" Rebekka said, the words escaping unbidden, forced from her subconscious as a result of her encounters with Father Ursu and the witches, by the terrible fear resulting from the memories and dreams of the urchin. "I looked and there before me was a pale horse, and its rider was given power to kill by sword, famine, and plague, and by the wild beasts of the earth."

Caphriel threw back his head and his laughter was a burst of sunshine. "The end days aren't yet upon us. There is no reason you can't find what your mother has. Peace. Acceptance. Love to create and sustain a family."

His smile was glorious temptation. "I myself have a small gift for healing. I can remove the tattoo with a touch if you accept all that I offer. You will never have to worry about disrobing in the presence of others. You'll never have to fear revealing your body to the man who claims your heart and being repudiated or turned away from in disgust."

Caphriel's eyelids lowered. "The darkness I see in you is tied to your gift. Unless you rid yourself of it, death will follow in your wake."

The icy fear Rebekka had kept at bay since realizing the amulet offered some protection returned in cold waves. She couldn't have spoken if she wanted to.

Caphriel leaned forward, offered his hands. "You don't have to live with such a burden. Pray with me, sister. Ask that your gift be made pure so you can go forward with peace in your soul and the knowledge you serve only a higher cause."

His voice held promise and conviction. His words tasted of happiness, sweet and infinitely tempting.

Rebekka believed without question. Any prayer made in his presence would be answered. Her gift would be changed so she no longer had to fear calling sickness and plague to her.

She lifted her hands toward his, only to hesitate. She was a child of the brothels, an inhabitant of a world where everything came at a cost.

Brother Caphriel had seen some of what lay in her heart, but not all of it. If Edom spoke of her gift, then he also confided how and where she used it.

"What about the outcast Weres? Will I still be able to heal them?"

There was a subtle hardening of Caphriel's face. "You can't serve the light and the dark at the same time. If you want your soul and your body cleansed of the things setting you apart and causing you fear, then you must turn away from those who are damned. You must separate yourself completely from the path that being able to heal the Were outcasts places you on."

Levi's image came to Rebekka's mind. It was followed by Feliss's, and Dorrit's, and so many others'.

Some of them were still in her life. Some gone, dead or their contracts sold, or their debt to the vice lord paid.

She couldn't turn her back on those she'd come to care about, even if in coming here she'd learned the truth of her father, and knew he was the one who'd sent her to the Were brothels.

The amulet bought her time to figure out who she could trust. Until then she had to trust herself to make the right choice, to do the right thing.

"No," she said, her hands falling back to her sides.

Caphriel straightened and suddenly there was something terrifying about being in his presence. "So be it," he said.

The words rang with icy, unnerving finality. And the dread stirred to life by them remained with Rebekka through the return to her mother's home and the evening meal. Lasted up until she saw Levi appear at the edge of the forest, beckoning for her to join him.

Eleven

REBEKKA blinked, hardly daring to believe it was Levi and not some apparition. How could he know she was here?

Yet as she continued to stare, he didn't disappear. If anything his gestures became more frantic.

When he risked taking a step away from what little protection the trees provided, Rebekka signaled she was coming, sudden fear shoving aside her doubts and questions. The members of the Fellowship weren't prone to violence but they weren't avowed pacifists either.

Levi was too close to their homes, too close to the women and children. A flaring of an amulet warning a Were was near would bring men with pitchforks and hoes, perhaps even with rifles.

Chloe turned from the cabinet where she was putting away a dish she'd finished drying. Her gaze went immediately to the window.

All semblance of peace left her expression. She'd met Levi once, the first time he'd escorted Rebekka across the Barrens. She knew what he was.

A hasty glance over her shoulder, to where her husband was supervising the children as they helped him tend the snakes, conveyed Chloe's nervousness, not for their safety, but at what Boden's reaction would be if he caught Rebekka exposing his children to evil and wickedness.

Rebekka knew they'd fought over her before. Boden allowed her visits only because he hoped to save her soul.

Unlike Chloe and her, he had never lived in the red zone where contact with Weres was common. Until drug use made him a thief, and a criminal's tattoo caused his parents to cut him out of their lives and business, he'd had a comfortable life among what served as a merchant middle class.

He didn't know what it was to survive as her mother had, as the Were prostitutes were forced to. Before Boden experienced the worst of humanity, he'd been saved by Edom and joined the Fellowship.

"Don't go," Chloe whispered. "The first step toward salvation is the hardest."

"I have to." Only something bad would bring Levi here. "Tell the girls I'm sorry I didn't say good-bye. Tell them I needed to leave quickly because of an emergency."

"I won't lie to Boden if he questions me. He may not allow you in our home afterward. He may forbid you from seeing the girls again."

Rebekka's throat tightened. She saw them rarely but she still cared for them.

"I have to go," she repeated, eyes pleading with her mother not to allow Boden to have the final say.

"Wait a minute," Chloe whispered, moving away from Rebekka to pick up a blanket lying neatly folded on a chair. She returned, pressing it into Rebekka's hands. "Be careful."

Tears wet Rebekka's eyes. She had the fleeting fear she would never see her mother or the girls again.

"I love you," she said, hugging Chloe before slipping out of the cabin.

Rebekka's chest ached. As she hurried toward the woods she imagined the worst, Cyrin or Canino stumbling into a trap or being riddled with bullets. When she reached Levi, she asked, "What's happened?"

He pulled her into a hug, then released her. "A Jaguar is badly injured. The bones in his back legs are broken, possibly crushed in a fight with hyenas. We got the bleeding stopped but he was fading in and out of consciousness when I left. He's in a place we can defend during the night. It's in the Barrens."

Rebekka didn't need to glance up at the sky to know there'd be no time to return to the Fellowship, even if an offer of shelter and safety was assured. The forest was already dark with the onset of dusk.

"I can leave now."

Levi indicated a path. "Run in front of me."

She ran, turning when he directed her to.

Questions pounded through her with each footfall but she had no breath to spare for conversation.

At the edge of the Barrens they stopped and she doubled over, sucking in air, her sides and legs burning. It was nearly full dark and though the night didn't hold as much terror for her as it did for the majority of humans, she was still scared, more than she would have been if they remained in the forest.

"It's not far," Levi said, speaking close to her ear. "Ready?"

Rebekka nodded and straightened. Saw the gun in one of his hands and the knife in the other. This time he led, treading lightly, the pace slower than it had been, more cautious, though it was brighter, easier to see among the ruins than it had been in the woods.

Bats dipped and fluttered, making a meal of insects. Moonlight caught on the eyes of creatures crouched among vine and rubble. The faint smell of burning wood reached Rebekka, brought on a breeze that also carried the fragrant scent of night-blooming flowers.

Levi finally stopped in front of what had once been towering apartment buildings. Now they were a forbidding structure of narrow passageways formed by twisting, rusting steel.

From within came the rustling of hidden creatures, the scurrying of rats. Rebekka shivered, remembering the diseased animal in the brothel alleyway.

Nausea threatened as she thought about the pocket of plague elsewhere in the Barrens. She feared she'd made a terrible mistake in coming here, in turning away from Brother Caphriel's offer. She might just as readily be used as a weapon against the Weres as come to be the healer who could make the outcasts whole.

They climbed, careful of jagged edges. There were traces of smoke now.

Levi gave a soft whistle. It was answered by Cyrin's chuffing and a low rumble, most likely from Canino.

The rough stairway ended, leveling out into what remained of a hallway between apartments. Behind half-fallen walls was a living room complete with furniture long ago destroyed by rodents and rot.

Light came in through an opening above, adding to that provided by a small fire. Rebekka processed it all as she sought the injured Jaguar and found him unconscious on the floor.

She moved forward carefully. The female Jaguar was unexpected but there was no doubt in Rebekka's mind that the woman crouched next to the prone figure was a Were, and most likely the male's mate.

The Jaguar female was exotically beautiful and equally deadly. Her eyes glowed catlike and every line of her body screamed possessiveness, advertised her willingness to defend and attack.

Levi positioned himself at Rebekka's side. He sheathed the knife but the gun remained in his hand.

"Step back, Melina," he told the Jaguar. "Give Rebekka room to work."

Melina snarled. Her eyes held distrust and dislike. Her body telegraphed unwillingness but she obeyed Levi's order.

Rebekka dismissed Melina's behavior. She was well used to seeing those same emotions along with hate for all humans, including her, in some of the brothel prostitutes.

She knelt next to the male. His breathing was shallow, rapid.

There was a rip in his side, long enough, deep enough, he'd only barely escaped having his internal organs spill out. His fur was matted with blood, his legs and flank torn open.

Tendons and muscles were shredded. Bone glistened in the light provided by the fire.

Rebekka took a deep breath, calming and centering herself. She'd healed worse, much worse.

She refused to give in to the fear that had been with her since waking from the memory and dream of the urchin. Her fingers glanced over the hidden amulet. She had witch-provided protection. She trusted the Wainwrights that much at least.

Rebekka gathered her will to focus it, leaned forward, and placed her hands on either side of the broken bone, intending to concentrate her efforts there. But instead of a tingling in her fingertips, instead of the flowing warmth of her gift manifesting itself, there was only the feel of blood-caked fur and a body lacking heat.

Fear returned, swallowing Rebekka as Brother Caphriel's image flashed into her mind, his hands outstretched, her own lifting in that instant when she was tempted by his voice, by the promise his words held.

Before utter panic could take her, another image forced the one in the Fellowship garden away. Of skeletal, bone-white hands offering the amulet, calling it protection for one with her gift.

Rebekka trembled so violently that Levi crouched down next to her, asked urgently, "What's wrong?"

She couldn't tell him, wasn't sure she ever would. Her heart thundered and she knew all of them would hear it, just as they would all scent the terror gripping her. First that she'd lost her ability to heal Weres, and then, that she hadn't, but to use her gift meant she would have to remove the amulet and risk calling the diseased to her.

Her breathing was little more than short pants. She felt as if she was running again from the maze, from the demon Abijah's words, from the Church spies positioned outside the witches' house. But there was no outrunning this nightmare. No escaping it. And watching the Jaguar die as a result of her cowardice would only add to it.

Rebekka lifted her hands away from his matted fur and took off the necklace, shaking so badly the beads woven into it clacked. She set it on the ground next to her, gasped as an ice flower bloomed immediately in her chest, while at the same time her fingers felt as though fire streaked through them.

It was similar, yet different than it had been before. But there was no time to consider it and give it meaning.

She gathered her will. Gripped the Jaguar's legs again on either side of the crushed bone and torn skin.

Rather than come as a tingling sensation followed by a gentle blending of purpose and desire to heal, her gift came as a taking. As if she were nothing more than a tool, a conduit for a power rooted in the earth, something raw needing eyes and intelligence to focus it, and a soul to judge who was worthy of being touched by it.

Pain screamed through Rebekka, originating in her legs, her side and abdomen, the locations mirroring the Jaguar's injuries. The shock of it made her try to jerk her hands away, to stop using her gift. But it was too late for that.

It was like standing against the flow of molten lava. And in her mind's eye she saw her blood seeping into the amulet.

Red like the beads that were a part of it.

Red like those her father wore in his hair.

Perhaps not a power rooted in earth after all, but in the flames of a fiery hell.

It didn't matter. Of one thing she was sure—her gift was meant to be used on the Were.

Rebekka stopped fighting and felt the rightness of the choice deep within. Her will flowed into the Jaguar, walling off enough of the pain so she could concentrate on healing him, recognizing as she did so that while her gift had come without any cost except for exhaustion before, that was changed now.

Pain sliced through icy numbness. The intensity of it overwhelmed Aryck, turning human and Jaguar souls away from the steady, strong pounding of the ancestors' drums.

Heat followed. Flowing in and forming a wall. Blocking the shimmering pathway to the shadowlands and trapping his two earthly souls to the faint beat of a heart housed in flesh, denying them the possibility of joining the eternal soul in triumphant unity.

Slowly he grew more aware, Jaguar and man rolling and tumbling in the warmth, bathing in it as though it were a pool of water. For long moments both were content to remain submerged.

Strength came with the heat, a feeling of wholeness, rightness. Rich scent pervaded, lush and feminine and totally unfamiliar.

The Jaguar mentally sprawled on its back, playfully exposing its belly, making the man, the enforcer, struggle away from pure sensation and toward conscious thought.

Memory returned in bits and pieces, with the concentration of burn in his leg, the slow mending of bone and flesh.

Healer. The word came into sharp focus and Aryck forced jaguar eyes open. His beast soul purred in approval at the first sight of the woman kneeling next to him.

Mate. Not a word but a recognition by the Jaguar, a claiming that had Aryck snarling in denial, rejecting the possibility of it.

"Stay calm," a man's voice said, accompanying the command by positioning the barrel of a gun in front of Aryck's face.

Behind him Aryck heard Melina's hiss of fury, sensed movement, but it was halted by low, rumbling growls. Tiger and Lion. He remembered them now, racing ahead to attack the feral hyenas.

Aryck subsided, heart beating even faster when he realized the Jaguar was very content to lie still beneath the healer's hands, to luxuriate in the heat spiraling into its body with her touch, connecting the two of them in a way that had the man anxious to shift form so he could heal the rest of his injuries and break away from her.

For the first time in memory Aryck felt a separation of self, his two earthly souls diverging rather than integrating, preparing to battle against each other for dominance instead of existing in seamless harmony.

Even now the Jaguar was noticing the Lion who smelled too human hovering protectively at the healer's side. It wanted to warn him away from her, to press between them, crowding her into a corner where she could be kept apart from other males.

A low growl threatened to erupt, this time the Jaguar's instead of the man's. Aryck suppressed it, as alarmed by the Jaguar's desire to guard a human female as he was by the unraveling of self. He forced rational thought to prevail over instinct, ruthlessly overpowering the Jaguar soul when animal possessiveness bled into human images of coupling.

The healer's hands moved to his other leg. It was less badly damaged, the bone more broken than crushed.

Additional strength poured into Aryck. He focused inward, as if watching an unseen gauge slowly rise until it finally reached the place where he was well enough to shift.

Pain returned in a heartbeat, marking the transition between beast and man. It was a price Aryck paid willingly, thinking he could more easily repudiate the Jaguar's claim of having settled on a mate. But the moment he saw the healer through human eyes, desire raked through his belly. She was beautiful with her dark brown hair and blue eyes, with her gentle features and body created for pleasure.

No, he silently snarled, denying his physical reaction to her. Denying the Jaguar's need to assure itself she was okay when it noticed her trembling as she reached for a necklace on the ground next to her.

Aryck turned away and found the collar of clothing. He untied it and dressed with uncharacteristic haste for a Were who found no shame in nakedness or the evidence of desire.

He'd barely fastened his pants before Melina was there, her clothed body pressed to his, rubbing against his erection as though claiming it for herself and publicly marking her territory. The Jaguar threatened to rise inside of Aryck and drive her away if the man didn't do it.

At least in this his two souls were still in agreement. Aryck pulled her arms from around his neck and met her gaze with one ordering her back.

Her eyes flashed and her lips tightened. She obeyed, her face taking on an expression of disgust as she turned her attention to the healer and the man with her.

Had the healer not come, Aryck knew he would be dead and any hope for the cubs dead along with him. He'd heard the drums calling him and seen a pathway shimmer into existence. He'd felt the tug of the eternal soul anchored in the shadowlands, holding his place among the ancestors until his two Earth-bound souls joined with it there.

A thank-you was due before he spoke to the healer about the cubs. Aryck steeled himself against feeling the claw-sharp rake of lust as he turned to go to her.

Despite the Jaguar's claim, she was *not* his mate. To want a human in that way was an invitation to become rogue and ultimately be made outcast.

He would rather die than have that fate befall him. He would never willingly live outside of a pack and away from Jaguar lands.

Twelve

TINY tremors continued to go through Rebekka but she was too exhausted to hang on to the terror that had flashed into her when the Jaguar sprang away. As soon as he'd ended their physical contact, the terrible coldness in her chest returned with swift vengeance, as if once freed from concentrating on healing the Were, her gift reached out, calling for the sick and injured to come and be healed.

She suppressed a whimper. More than anything she wanted to lie down and sink into a dreamless sleep. But she was afraid that small measure of peace would be denied her. She was afraid to sleep. To dream.

Levi's silence bristled with worry. It radiated from him, shouting at her for an explanation about the amulet.

There'd be no avoiding conversation, though even if she wanted to confide everything, she couldn't, not among strangers, nor even Cyrin and Canino. She wasn't sure she would tell Levi at all. He carried enough burdens without her adding to them, especially now, when he was escorting his brother home.

From the day she'd found Levi nearly dead in the woods and healed him, then talked Dorrit into hiring him as a bouncer and guard so he could remain near the maze in the hopes of one day rescuing Cyrin, he'd sworn to protect her. He would put aside his chance to visit Lion lands if he thought she needed him.

"The Wainwright matriarch gave it to me for protection," she said, answering Levi's unspoken question as she looked up from spreading the blanket onto the floor.

His nostrils flared. He wanted to ask *Against what* and *Why do you need it*. She could see what it cost him to let it go.

"What did they require in exchange?"

He was careful, as she'd been, not to speak of witches.

"Nothing. I offered the pages I took from the Iberá estate first, hoping . . ."

She let her voice trail off, knowing Levi would finish the sentence by assuming a bad night at the brothel had driven her to the witches in an effort to learn how she could deepen her gift.

He relaxed. She expected him to scold her for leaving the safety of the brothel before he returned. He surprised her by saying, "You were right about Tir. He looks and smells fully human but he can't be. He found us earlier in the day, before we encountered the Jaguars. The tattoos were gone. So was the collar around his neck. He told me you were with your mother."

Rebekka's breath caught as she thought of Brother Caphriel and how he'd reminded her of Tir. "How did he know I was there?"

Levi shrugged. "I don't know. He wanted me to pass on a message. You no longer have to fear returning home, but in the event you need to stay on Araña's boat, it's available, though Rimmon's protection covers only the *Constellation*."

"And Araña?"

"Safe and away from Oakland."

Rebekka sagged with relief. "It's over then?"

Levi hesitated for only an instant. "I think so. Tir said he'd taken care of the threat to you personally. I believe him."

Rebekka caught herself lifting her hand to touch the amulet but aborted the movement, not wanting to draw Levi's attention to it. Her chest became tight with renewed uncertainty about the future.

She forced calm on herself. She could go home, or at least to the house she'd homesteaded in the gifted area. She had money to pay for food, enough to last until she better understood the change to her gift and whether she could safely return to the brothels—or if she dared trust the witches enough to tell them about the urchin's visitation and ask for their help.

The Jaguar male joined them, crouching next to Rebekka. His posture was stiff, making her wonder if he felt beholden, or worried how to pay her. Before she could tell him she'd come at Levi's request so there was no debt, he tossed several gold coins onto the blanket.

"For healing me," he said. "Thank you."

The timbre of his voice sent unexpected heat into her belly. Rebekka turned her head slightly, truly seeing his features for the first time.

He was dark, strong. Silky black hair framed a face that was breathtakingly masculine. Green eyes blazed with confidence and the underlying wildness that came with being purely Were.

A flutter went through her chest, an edgy awareness that had her hastily dropping her gaze in sudden confusion, then keeping it there in dismay at recognizing the signs of physical attraction. When he'd shifted form she'd barely noticed his nakedness before the icy chill exploded in her chest and she'd turned her attention to putting the amulet back on.

Rebekka hesitated, then reached out to scoop the coins up. They'd buy her time. They'd help buy Feliss's freedom. The Jaguar stopped her with a hand around her wrist, sending her heart racing and an unwelcome blush to her cheeks.

Levi growled a warning. It was met by an answering one.

The Jaguar's fingers tightened on her wrist. He pressed close enough for his body heat to envelope her and arrow downward to settle between her thighs.

"Please release me," she said, pressing her legs together and wanting to deny his impact on her. He was pure Were. Worse, he had a mate.

The sound of her voice seemed to shake the Jaguar out of his instinctive predatory behavior. He freed her wrist and moved away, out of arm's reach. "The coins are a token payment. I'm Aryck, the enforcer for my pack. You are Rebekka, the healer who works in the outcast brothels?"

She dared to look at the Jaguar again, embarrassed by the blush staining her cheeks from having reacted physically to him. "Yes."

"I came to Oakland for you. Five of our cubs will die without your care."

"Then they die," Levi said, his cold words making Rebekka turn toward him in disbelief.

His expression was closed off. "I'll escort you back to the red zone at first light. Cyrin and Canino can go on without me. To get to Jaguar lands you have to pass through Wolf territory. They'll kill you on sight. No human is allowed there."

He challenged Aryck with a stare. "Or can you guarantee her safety both coming and going?"

"There are no guarantees. Only the promise of more coins."

Rebekka wavered, knowing there was often little difference between courage and foolishness. But to turn away from helping cubs—children—and let them die. "What's wrong with the cubs?"

"It doesn't matter, Rebekka," Levi said, taking her hand, squeezing. "Say no without hearing the details. They'll only haunt you. Think of all those in the brothels who rely on you."

"Outcasts," the female Jaguar spat. The derision contained in the single utterance said the cubs' lives were more valuable than a city full of those shunned by the pure Were.

Aryck's fingers curled around Rebekka's upper arm. Possessive. Commanding. Sending heat spreading through her belly and shame into her heart. Without her noticing it he'd moved next to her again, so close his scent and presence seemed to wrap around her like a blanket.

She tried to pull away but his grip only tightened. "They're being eaten alive by something humans created, a weapon left over from the days of The Last War. Even if our healer could find a way to stop the spread of whatever is consuming the cubs, infection will take them or they'll survive so scarred they'll wish they'd been allowed to die."

Aryck's voice was little more than a growl yet Rebekka heard horror in it, as well as a pain so acute it had turned to fury. The journal she'd taken from the witches in payment became a heavy weight in her pocket. There were accounts of such weapons in it.

The Were healer had called it bio-nanite technology, writing about organisms bound to programmable machines that locked onto their targets genetically. Hundreds of those in his care had died before he found a way to counter it with a combination of plant extracts that could be made into a wash to halt the spread of destruction. Hundreds more had died afterward from infection—or suicide when they rose from makeshift hospital beds and saw what they'd become.

Choices, Rebekka thought. Had the witches somehow known she'd be presented with this one? Was it a test to see if she would turn her back on the outcasts in favor of going to aid the pure Weres? And the price she would pay if she did—her own death?

It was safe to go home. Tir had seen to it. She could heal those in the brothels with the greatest need, taking off the amulet long enough to do it. She could give the recipe for the wash to Aryck. But if the damage was already too extensive, the infection too pervasive . . .

The thought of children suffering and dying tormented Rebekka, stirred her compassion and her conscience, touched the place inside her that longed for a family of her own. She healed the prostitutes so they could be abused and injured again, but with the cubs, she could make a real difference in their lives.

"I'll go with you," she told Aryck.

"I'll accompany you," Levi said.

"Not into Jaguar lands," Aryck said, a deep growl in his voice. "Not unless you can shift to lion form and prove you're not outcast. You smell almost completely human."

Rebekka jerked her arm, trying to pull away again, hating the enforcer for the prejudice he represented and for the pain she knew his words caused Levi. "If you want me to heal the cubs, then Levi—"

"Only the pack leader can grant permission for him to enter our lands. If it's your safety he's worried about, then I promise to personally see to your protection from the time we enter Jaguar lands until you meet him where our border touches Lion territory. If he fears sending you alone, without an ally, then the Tiger can remain with us. We'll leave at first light and travel through the night once we're in Were lands."

Rebekka turned toward Levi, her hand squeezing his, asking for reassurance—acceptance of her choice and Aryck's terms. "This will allow you time with your family." *To say your good-byes.*

Levi gave a small, reluctant nod. "Promise to send Canino for me when you start home. I'll come back to Oakland with you."

Aryck's fingers tightened on her arm as if in protest. Rebekka refused to acknowledge him in any way. "I promise."

Satisfied, Aryck released the healer and moved away, passing through the doorway and into what remained of a hallway. He looked down the twisting wreck of stairway and longed to descend, to escape the confining space and nearness to the human female.

He'd touched her twice without wanting any contact at all, been unable to suppress either the Jaguar need to be at her side or the possessiveness that rose at seeing the obvious closeness between the healer and the Lion outcast.

Levi. The Lion had seemed vaguely familiar before, but injured, dying, Aryck hadn't been able to place him until after the healing. Now he had brief memories of seeing Levi and Cyrin among the Lion pride when he'd gone there on pack business.

Alliance was rare among the Were groups, but because the Wolf and Hyena packs in the territories near theirs were so large, Lion and Jaguar maintained a cautious association. He remembered being told Levi and Cyrin had left to explore, as many males who were considering forming their own packs or prides did, then hearing later they hadn't returned and were presumed dead.

Better dead than outcast, Aryck thought, and the Jaguar agreed even as it snarled and chafed at hearing the low murmurs of Levi and the healer talking.

Aryck could have mentally spoken with his father when they neared Jaguar lands. He could have secured permission for Levi to enter their lands. With the healer so close and the cubs in such dire need no one would have challenged the decision. But almost as quickly as the thought had come, he'd discarded it, acting on instinct and not after giving it rational consideration. The idea of Levi accompanying them, remaining at the healer's side—

The Jaguar screamed in protest at the sound of rustling as Levi lay down next to the healer, serving as her protector. Aryck's fingers flexed involuntarily. The muscles in his arms stood out. He was nearly over-taken by the urge to drop onto his hands and knees to accommodate the shift between forms as Jaguar soul separated further from human one.

His earlier fear returned in a heartbeat, edged once again toward horror. The unraveling of self was the first step on the rogue, outcast path. He stiffened with resolve, refusing to bend and change until rea-son dictated it.

Behind him the fire slowly died, no longer needed to ward off shock and provide light for the healer—

Claws raked through Aryck's belly at his continued effort to hold her at a distance by refusing to use her name. *Rebekka*, the Jaguar purred, filling human nostrils and coating the man's tongue with her scent. Flooding their shared senses with the sublime pleasure that had come from her touch. Enforcing the absolute belief of having found a mate with the hardening of Aryck's cock and images of covering her in human form, thrusting into her as he bit her shoulder and marked her with his teeth.

Sweat coated Aryck's skin as heat scorched through him. His hands opened and closed as he fought to suppress both desire and the morph-ing of one erotic scene into another.

For long moments he struggled, man and Jaguar souls at odds with each other, fighting for dominance, not in form but in will, as they had never done before.

The sound of engines drawing steadily closer halted the battle. Aryck spared a glance over his shoulder. Melina had already shifted form. The Tiger, Canino, and Cyrin were on their feet, ready to meet any threat posed by humans.

Levi was sitting, gun on the ground next to him. The hea—

Sharp pain raked Aryck's gut, making him gasp and bend over as the Jaguar returned to the fight with a vengeance. He said, "I'm okay, Rebekka," when she sat up, obviously ready to come to his aid.

The use of her name sheathed the unseen claws tearing through him. But the sight of the unbound hair framing her face and emphasizing how very feminine she was had his stomach muscles quivering as he imagined her placing her palm against his abdomen, soothing him with heat and touch before moving lower. Stroking him. Taking his cock in hand.

The Jaguar purred in satisfaction at having accomplished its purpose. It retreated so thoroughly that all sense of separateness disappeared, leaving Aryck's heart beating erratically in defeat.

Gunfire erupted nearby, jerking Aryck's attention away from Rebekka. He shed his clothing and shifted form.

His black coat made him invisible as he prowled down the twisted metal staircase and into the dark. Melina and the other two big cats followed him.

They spread out, remaining close to the building and readying themselves for attack. The vehicles drew near enough for the conversation of the humans occupying them to be heard, but turned away without coming into sight.

Sporadic gunfire sliced through the night until eventually the drone of the engines lessened and disappeared completely. A wary calm settled, a thin cloak draped over a world filled with silent predators and equally silent prey.

Canino sharpened his claws on a tree growing out of rubble. Cyrin watched him for a moment, then claimed another tree, shredding its bark and making it bleed sap.

A female cat yowled its desire to mate into the night and the entreaty brought Melina prowling to Aryck. She positioned herself in front of him, presenting her swollen vulva.

She was heavily in season. Riper than she'd been the night before when, despite his resolve, the genetic imperative to breed had nearly driven him to cover her.

There was no temptation now, no stirring of desire. Aryck knew the reason, though he refused to contemplate it, to risk undoing the seamless integration of Jaguar and human souls by thinking about Rebekka and vehemently denying he'd already found his mate.

He turned away, noting both Tiger and Lion were now watching. Spectators rather than competitors.

Melina persisted. Purring and crouching.

He rebuffed her yet again, annoyed by her continued overtures. Only his conscience over inadvertently encouraging her as they traveled made him hesitate to embarrass her further in front of an audience.

As if incensed by his continued rejection, or subconsciously aware of the threat Rebekka posed, Melina became more aggressive. She rubbed, marked him with the scent of her heat.

In a heartbeat Aryck reacted, his patience and restraint at an end. He snarled and pinned her underneath him, not the rough play before big cats mate, but the warning of an enforcer.

Sharp teeth slid through fur and skin and he tasted blood. A low, rumbled growl deep in his throat promised an attack that would leave her scarred in both forms if she persisted in trying to entice him into covering her.

Melina became completely submissive, acknowledging her acceptance of his will, and in an instant she was forgotten, her behavior triggering images of Rebekka doing the same, her hair caught up in his fists, her thighs splayed and her body joined to his.

Need flashed through Aryck, human lust and Jaguar possessiveness, a scorching heat commanding him back into the building.

He took his human form and dressed. The man impatient for dawn, telling himself he cared only about getting Rebekka to the cubs, the Jaguar intent on reaching lands the Lion outcast at her side couldn't enter.

Thirteen

ARYCK steadied Rebekka as her foot caught on an exposed root. Exhaustion clung to her, and this time he didn't fight the urge to keep his hand wrapped around her arm.

Her opposite shoulder sagged under the weight of the blanket now serving as a satchel. It was laden with what she claimed to need save for one ingredient, a root he was unfamiliar with.

"Thanks," she mumbled, not attempting to pull away from him as she had the other times, her jerky movement accompanied by an elusive hint of sexual interest rather than distaste at being touched by a Were.

Though Levi and his brother had left them miles earlier, peeling away to go to the pride's summer gathering place, his scent still clung to Rebekka. It mixed in with that of woman, of sweat and dirt and the plants Rebekka carried.

Aryck's lips lifted in a silent snarl at smelling the outcast, at remembering Levi embracing Rebekka and making her renew her promise to send Canino when she was ready to go back to Oakland. Not for the first time he wondered if Levi had been made outcast by the ancestors *because* of her, if she was Levi's downfall as well as Cyrin's and Canino's.

Their smell was nearly pure cat and neither of them had changed into human form. It made him think the ancestors had been merciful, allowing them to retain their beast form.

They could live their lives in Were lands, could even take mates and breed there as long as they didn't go feral. And if they were willing to risk it, they could enter the bone cave in a Petitioner's Rite and perhaps regain their human forms with an ancestor's intercession.

Aryck took his hand from Rebekka's arm as he considered the possibility she might carry a witch-charm that worked on male Weres, making those around her feel protective.

As they'd traveled directly through Wolf territory rather than staying to the border routes where there was some neutrality, he'd felt watched. Yet no one had emerged from hiding to challenge or attack.

Then again, it could be word had spread of what happened to the cubs, and the Wolves had decided to let a human pass through their lands without openly acknowledging it. They might be waiting on the outcome, concerned there were similar weapons buried among the ruins on their lands.

Aryck glanced at Rebekka, seeing fatigue on her face. They'd traveled with little rest and been forced to push hard to make up time when the plants she needed required detour or delay.

More than once he'd seen her touch the journal in her pocket, rubbing over it as she worried her bottom lip. Her concern for the cubs was easy to read, though he didn't need to see it in her expression; her actions told him as much.

Despite the pace he set she hadn't uttered a sound of complaint or protest. Each time he'd thought she would falter and demand they slow down or stop, she'd draw from a well of internal strength and find additional stamina.

Mile by mile his resistance to the Jaguar's claim weakened, though he hadn't fully accepted it and didn't intend to. Nor would he allow himself to act on the desire continuing to simmer in his bloodstream.

In jaguar form Melina ranged ahead, moving farther away and faster in the relative safety of Lion territory. Canino prowled at Rebekka's other side, streaks of tree-shadow merging with the stripes on his orange coat.

Each time he brushed against Rebekka, whether the act was unintentional or by design, the Jaguar made its presence known to Aryck. Suddenly waking like a separate entity to growl in protest.

Resisting the Jaguar set a battle for dominance into motion. After the first one, Aryck acquiesced, maneuvering Rebekka away from Canino while telling himself the sooner he got her to camp, the better.

A day to heal, perhaps another to rest and get her strength back, and then she would be gone from their lands, her safety entrusted to Levi. With her absence he would no longer have to fear the unraveling of his earthly souls into two separate entities.

Another mile passed. Twice Aryck reached out to keep Rebekka upright.

Each time it was more difficult to end the physical contact. The Jaguar grew edgy. Or he did. Aryck couldn't discern where the emotion came from, only that thoughts of stopping so Rebekka could rest warred with the need to get to the cubs.

Close to the border of Jaguar lands he reached mentally for his father. The alpha's relief swept into Aryck. *Hurry. Three of them are close to death. The other two are not far behind. Nahuatl holds their souls to this world.*

Koren didn't ask if the healer accompanied them. To do so would be to doubt Nahuatl's vision from the ancestors.

Aryck updated his father with a stream of images. Starting at the place where he and Melina had encountered the first of the hyenas. Ending with their current location.

Show me the root she seeks.

"Stop for a moment," Aryck said, his hand on Rebekka's arm halting her as he spoke. "Let me see the picture of the root you need."

She pulled the journal from her pocket and opened it. He bent lower, and though he couldn't read the words describing where the plant came from, they were locked in his memory from having detoured numerous times only to meet with failure.

It grows near springs where the water tastes of iron, he said, eyes traveling slowly over the drawing as he made himself look at every detail, from the shape of the leaves all the way down to the root.

Come directly to camp. I'll describe this plant to Phaedra, then Nahuatl and the elders if she doesn't recognize it.

What happens with the human encampment?

Quiet. There was the briefest hesitation, marking Koren's distrust and suspicion. *Tracks from one of the heavily armored vehicles went into Wolf territory near where it borders Bear.*

You think the Wolves are dealing with the humans?

It was a distasteful idea to Aryck. But in the histories the elders passed down through their stories, there were tales of Wolves being rewarded for attacking other Were groups for the benefit of humans.

Aryck could follow his father's line of thought, his suspicion that perhaps the Wolves wanted to expand their territory. Guns could be found in the rubble and salvaged. But without ammunition, they were useless, and ammunition was difficult to acquire. It required a trip into the human world and could wipe out a pack's store of recovered coins and gems.

Coyotes preferred flight over fight. Their land was ruin-filled, more suited to hiding than hunting. They held it unchallenged because it served as a buffer of sorts between stronger, larger predatory groups.

After a long moment of silence, Koren answered, *I don't know if the Wolves are dealing with the humans. The sudden quiet bothers me as much as the gunfire did. For now, we wait. We watch. We try to make sense of what the humans are looking for on Coyote land so we can assess the danger of them moving into our territory.*

The link with his father fell away. Aryck offered the book to Rebekka, unconsciously holding it in a way that forced her fingers to brush against his. Only to release it and walk away when his cock responded instantly to her touch, and his mind filled with fantasies of pulling her more firmly against him.

Rebekka placed the journal in her pocket with shaky hands. The sudden race of her heart edged out exhaustion and cleared the fuzziness from her mind.

Why now? she wondered, trying to ignore the fluttering through her chest and the lingering heat where their hands had touched. *Why him?*

It was obvious from the way Aryck stalked off that he wasn't any happier about the physical attraction than she was. So why did he find excuses to touch her? In a day, maybe two, she'd be on her way to Oakland.

She closed her eyes but couldn't escape the sight of him. He was there in a hundred images. In both of his forms.

It wasn't just his physical beauty affecting her; it was his determination. His relentless resolve to save the cubs that caused a melting sensation in the region of her heart and a traitorous internal voice to whisper, *And he doesn't have a mate.*

Despite what she'd thought when she first saw Melina crouched next to Aryck's jaguar form, they weren't paired. There was no bond-scent, Levi said, so they weren't permanently mated.

She felt a blush rising to her face as she remembered the awkward conversation she'd had with Levi before he left with Cyrin. It was a talk spawned by her embarrassment at not being able to hide her physical reaction or the shame she felt at desiring someone she thought was already claimed by another.

Despite Levi's warning her against getting involved with a pure Were, one who might play with her but who would never take her as a mate or leave his world for a human one, a fantasy crept into her thoughts. Of touching her hands to Aryck's chest, exploring with her fingertips. Tracing the smooth flow of muscle and circling tiny nipples.

The melting heat in her chest slid downward, through her belly and into her labia. Her channel spasmed.

She opened her eyes, banishing the images. Levi was right.

Getting involved with a pure Were, especially one who lived outside the red zone, would be a mistake. It would only lead to heartbreak.

The crushing weight of exhaustion returned and Rebekka wanted to close her eyes again and sink to the ground. She doubted landing on hidden rocks would matter at this point. Sleep would claim her before she touched the bed of leaves on the forest floor.

Imagining it increased the pull of gravity. Her knees bent in preparation for yielding.

Canino rumbled and rubbed against her, jolting her to wakefulness. She placed a hand on his shoulder as ahead of her Aryck turned, his lips pulling back in an instant snarl and his eyes going fierce.

As silently as he'd stalked away, he returned, his movements holding the dangerous grace of a jaguar going after prey. His hand gripped her wrist like an iron manacle, the impact of it forcing her to take a step away from Canino.

Canino snorted before yawning widely. His emotions brushed against Rebekka's empathetic senses, amusement coupled with satisfaction at having delivered a barbed taunt to another big cat.

"There's no time to waste," Aryck said, his voice gravelly, harsh. "Three of the cubs barely remain in this world. The other two are not far behind them."

His words were a club Rebekka used to beat back exhaustion and keep it behind a barricade of determination. "Let's hurry then."

She refused to fail the cubs. Even without the root she needed for the wash she could use her gift to battle infection and to restore skin and muscle.

It wouldn't be permanent, not until the nanites were destroyed. But she could stabilize the cubs, keep them alive until a true healing was possible.

A mile passed in bristling silence with Aryck shackling her to his side and ignoring her. The longer it continued, the angrier she got.

Rebekka tugged, attempting to break Aryck's hold on her wrist. His fingers tightened in reaction. She pulled again. Harder. And when he didn't let her wrist go, she halted, digging in her heels so there was a sharp jerk down the length of their arms.

He turned, and she felt her lips pulling back in a snarl of her own. "Release me."

Surprise probably accounted for him doing just that. It was there in his eyes, glinting along with something else. Appreciation maybe.

Rebekka refused to contemplate it. She shook out her arm like a prisoner freed from a chain, then, without a word, continued in the direction they were headed with fast, purposeful strides.

He caught up easily, striding close enough so every other step it seemed as though his arm brushed against hers, sending a jolt of awareness through her. To take her mind off his effect on her, she asked, "Will your pack have found the root by the time we reach the cubs?"

Aryck faltered, recovering with cat quickness so there was barely a change in the smoothness of his movements. She added, "I know you were showing someone the picture of the plant."

"How?"

Her eyebrows drew together. She wondered why he would ask such thing when the answer should be obvious. "I live and work among Weres."

"Outcasts."

She drew away from him then, a step, all the trail allowed but enough so there would be no casual touch of his skin against hers. "You say it as if they were all guilty of crimes."

His nostrils flared. She braced for an argument. Instead he answered her original question. "My father is speaking with our healer, Phaedra, about the root. If she's not familiar with it, he'll ask others."

"And the cubs? Can you describe their current condition?"

"No. He didn't show me images of them."

The tightness in Aryck's voice revealed his fear they would be too late. Rebekka returned to his side, unable to stop herself from taking his hand in a silent offer of comfort. "I can run for a while."

He brushed his thumb against her knuckles in a soft caress, then slipped into an easy lope. She fell behind within steps and found a pace she could sustain.

They slowed and sped up as needed. Stopped when absolutely necessary.

Rebekka drew on strength beyond any she thought to possess. She endured because she couldn't accept the price of failure. Pushed on, fueled by optimism when she drew abreast of Aryck and he said, "The plant has been found and the roots harvested. Phaedra assumes you'll need boiling water to create the wash. It should be ready by the time we reach camp. We're close now, less than a mile."

"Good," Rebekka said, the pain in her sides making it difficult to say more.

They arrived a short time later, finally stopping in front of a house well hidden by trees. From inside the small building came the steady beat of drums and songlike chanting.

Rebekka forced herself to remain upright though she trembled with physical exhaustion. The gathered Jaguars would view it as a sign of weakness, but at least they wouldn't scent fear on her at being in their presence. She'd come too far, endured too much, to feel anything but a driving need to get to the cubs and heal them so she could finally rest.

An old woman stepped through those gathered. She was cool-eyed and assessing. "The water boils," she said, thrusting a wooden cup into Rebekka's hands. "Drink this. It will revive you so we can make the wash for the cubs. They grow worse, but I believe there is still time to heal them if we hurry."

Phaedra, the healer, Rebekka thought, drinking the bitter brew and recognizing it as a stimulant some of the brothel prostitutes used when they wanted to work longer hours to pay off their debt more quickly.

She handed the cup back to the old woman. "This way," Phaedra said, leading Rebekka to the back of the house where other Jaguars waited.

It was easy to pick out the parents of the cubs. They stood in pairs, desperate hope shining in their eyes as well as the promise of death if a human caused further harm.

Several copper pots hung over small fires, the water in them boiling. On a nearby table lay the roots she needed, along with bowls, knives, and stone pestles.

Aryck took the blanket-made satchel from her shoulder before she could slide it off. He unknotted it, gently dumping the contents on the table. Rebekka pulled the journal from her pocket, opening it to the page describing how to make the wash.

Phaedra emitted a low, threatening growl and instantly Rebekka found herself behind Aryck. Canino crowded in, trapping her against the table and answering Phaedra with a growl of his own.

Several men shed loose clothing, shifting form. They crouched in readiness for attack.

A knife appeared in Aryck's hand, pulled from a sheath he wore on his thigh.

Fourteen

THE back door opened, freeing the stench of infection and making the sound of the drums beating within throb through the air. A man stood in the entryway.

"Enough," he said, his voice holding such command Rebekka knew instantly he was the alpha, and most likely Aryck's father given how closely they resembled each other.

His gaze fell on Canino. "This is no place for you. Melina will take you to my home until the cubs have been healed. The enforcer has promised Rebekka safety while she is among us. No harm will come to her on Jaguar lands."

Rebekka touched Canino's shoulder, using her gift to communicate calmness and acceptance. He rubbed against her, eliciting a growl from Aryck, before padding away to follow Melina.

One by one the male Jaguars reclaimed their human shapes and pulled on their clothing. The pack leader sent a hard stare at Phaedra. She bowed her head slightly. "I am too old to have reacted without thinking. The book smells of Jaguar, but its origins and how it came to be in human hands aren't as important as its contents. My apologies to Rebekka. If she will read what has been written, we will set to work."

Aryck stepped back and Rebekka reclaimed her spot next to Phaedra. The Jaguar healer made no attempt to see the words written on the pages as Rebekka described what needed to be done.

Phaedra listened. She assigned tasks to those gathered, halting Rebekka only once and asking to see a picture of a familiar plant bearing an unfamiliar name.

Compared to the length of the journey, creating the wash took very little time. Yet by the time it was done, the concentrated solution mixed with cold water so it could be safely applied, Rebekka's worry was profound.

"The parents will apply it to their cubs," Phaedra said, though she lifted one of the basins containing the wash and carried it into the house herself.

Rebekka stood aside, allowing the others to precede her. Four couples passed by, the male in each pair stopping to pick up a basin before following his mate inside.

Aryck motioned Rebekka ahead of him. She entered the house, barely noting the old men with their drums or the caped figure with his back to her.

It was obvious every effort had been made to keep the sickroom sanitary, but the stench was overwhelming. She sought out the cubs with her eyes, a soft sound of distress escaping with the first sight of them.

Horror filled Rebekka, though she'd known what to expect. They were nearly unrecognizable as something living instead of slabs of skinned meat.

Pallets were positioned to allow family members to gather around them. Only the shape of their limbs told her four of them were in animal form while the fifth was a boy of about eight.

Unlike the cubs in jaguar form, there was only one parent present at the pallet the boy lay on. Tears streamed down the woman's gaunt face, and she rocked, so lost in grief she seemed unaware of the activity going on around her.

Phaedra tended the cub. Rebekka went to her side, taking up a small cup and dipping it into the basin.

Aryck joined them, crouching next to Rebekka. "This is Caius. His mother is Deidre. She recently returned to the pack after losing her Tiger mate. Caius is like his father."

Rebekka spared a glance at Caius's mother. Pitying her at the same time she wished she could deliver a slap to turn Deidre's attention to the child who needed her.

The neglect hadn't just started. By Deidre's rail-thin body and face, she hadn't bothered to hunt or eat for weeks, if not longer.

Rebekka looked down at Caius. Aryck said, "If not for him, the others would be dead. Rubble gave way, creating a pit. They fell on an undetonated weapon. He went to their aid, first helping them to stable ground, then coming to camp. It was an amazing feat for one so young and badly injured."

"I won't let him die," Rebekka promised, pouring the wash onto Caius's legs.

Before she could use her hand to smooth it over the raw mess of exposed muscle and cartilage, Aryck's was there, gently spreading it. This close to death or healing, there was little point in worrying about contamination.

She refilled the cup then emptied it, falling into an easy rhythm with Aryck as behind them the drums beat steadily, insistently.

The alpha joined them, taking a position next to Caius's mother. He watched, remaining silent, his expression harsh. When they were nearly done bathing Caius's front, he spoke directly to Rebekka, asked, "Does the wash work? Does it kill the thing eating him alive?"

A chill swept over her, the forerunner of a fear she refused to let take her, though it still revealed itself in fingers that fumbled, trembled slightly at the back of her neck as they removed the necklace.

Rebekka anticipated the icy bloom in her chest, but perhaps because she was surrounded by so many in desperate need of healing, it didn't come when she handed the amulet to Aryck for safekeeping rather than risk it being stepped on or lost as she gave herself over to her gift.

She placed her hand on the cub's raw torso, holding back her will to heal. The area beneath her fingers was streaked with infection, but compared to the hungry, buzzing energy coming from the cub's back, it felt calm.

"Turn him," she said, not wanting to tell them the wash was working until she could be sure.

Aryck and Phaedra repositioned Caius, exposing a back nearly as ravaged as his front. Rebekka placed only her fingertips on his skin.

There was no mistaking the source of the buzzing energy. Despite the lightness of her touch it felt as though she'd placed her hand in a swarm numbering in the millions.

Without her saying anything, Aryck took up the cup, dipping it in the wash and pouring it on the area around her fingers. Calm claimed the area instantly and it remained that way.

"It's working," she said, spreading the wash.

Caius began whimpering. His mother reacted to it, making low keening sounds until the alpha silenced her with a slap that brought her from her grief long enough to obey his command of silence.

When there was no trace of the hungry buzzing, Rebekka said, "It's gone. I can begin now."

Phaedra rose to her feet. "We check the others first, to make sure the things eating them are no longer present."

Rebekka stood, appreciative of the older healer's wisdom. The alpha accompanied them as they stopped next to each pallet and Rebekka touched the cub lying on it.

When they'd checked all of them, Rebekka turned, intending to go back to Caius. A man carrying a staff made of bones and wearing a Jaguar headdress that flowed into a furred, rosette-covered cape blocked her path.

Shaman, she thought as black eyes bored into her as if he tried to see into the depths of her soul.

He pointed to a cub lying on a pallet near Caius. "He is closest to death."

Rebekka accepted the shaman's judgment. She went to the cub and knelt next to him.

Phaedra joined her. "They are all weak and heavily drugged. They won't be able to shift to speed the healing process."

Rebekka had expected as much. She placed her hands on the cub, closed her eyes, and brought her will to bear.

Her gift manifested in the same way it had when she healed Aryck, in a taking, as if she was nothing more than a tool, a conduit for a power that burned through her like fire, demanding a price for using it, pain that had her gasping, crying, as it felt as though her skin was being ripped from her body at the same time bones in her chest shattered.

There was no gentle guiding, no concentrated effort to eradicate infection and repair places where bone and soft tissue had been eaten away, no conscious choice to cover exposed muscle and sinew with skin and fur. But the pain lessened as those things happened. And as the pain diminished she became aware of drums beating, those in the small room seeming to echo elsewhere, in a place beyond her physical ability to hear them.

The phantom beats faded completely as the end of pain signaled the end of the healing. Exhaustion swept in. Rebekka managed to open her eyes in time to witness the joy on the faces of the cub's parents as they pulled him in jaguar form onto their laps and held him to them in a hug.

Tears streamed down the mother's face. The father swallowed several times and yet his voice was still clogged with emotion when he asked, "Can we take him home?"

"Yes," Phaedra said, standing, helping Rebekka to her feet.

Even with the healer steadying her, Rebekka swayed. She had no sense of how much time had elapsed, only that her clothes clung to her, drenched in sweat.

It took tremendous effort to take up a position next to another cub. A cup was pressed into her hand. She drank the bitter stimulant, but its effects barely registered this time. When the cup was empty, Rebekka braced herself for the pain to come, then leaned forward, willing herself to somehow find enough strength to heal the remaining cubs.

Aryck forced himself to stay at Caius's side as Rebekka was led from pallet to pallet. He kept his back to her, not wanting to see her pain, not wanting to see her exhaustion or the way her shirt clung to her, stirring possessive, protective instincts he was no longer positive belonged solely to the Jaguar.

He'd wanted to view her as a human using her gift only for the promise of wealth. He'd thought to use her physical weakness when compared to his kind to counter the Jaguar claim of mate. But those defenses had crumbled during their push to arrive in time, and disappeared completely when he'd seen what it cost her to heal. She was no less dedicated than Phaedra.

Caius's whimpers signaled greater and greater pain. "Stay with us," he murmured, afraid the cub's Earth-bound souls would give up this world and join the eternal one despite Nahuatl's chants and the beat of the pack's drums.

Koren crouched beside Aryck, placing a hand on Caius's forehead, as if he too felt the cub's tenuous hold on life and was offering his strength, his will, to the boy's. Eyelids opened, holding fear and pain, an unspoken plea for release.

"Fight the call of the ancestors," Koren said. "The others have been healed, you will be as well."

Rebekka joined them, so weak her eyes were barely open as Phaedra helped her take up a position next to Caius. The Jaguar soul rose in Aryck, demanding the human form act, using arms the beast didn't have to lift Rebekka and take her to the cabin that was also Jaguar den.

When Aryck refused to act, claws raked through his chest. He ground his teeth together, that and the clenching of his hands into fists the only external sign of the battle being waged inside him.

A sharp glance from his father made him redouble his efforts to suppress the Jaguar. The Jaguar fought back when Rebekka began the healing with a soft cry of pain, her continuous trembling sending it into a frenzy.

The only escape was to stand and walk to the other side of the room. Leaving Phaedra's home would be better. Aryck knew it, and yet he couldn't force himself through the doorway.

He concentrated instead on the beat of the drums. Watched from a distance as inch by inch Caius was healed, his skin slowly reappearing to cover exposed muscle and bone until no trace of the destruction was left.

Rebekka collapsed and Aryck was by her side instantly, lifting her into his arms without it being a conscious decision. Phaedra motioned toward a small room. "Put her on my bed. I will make her comfortable."

The Jaguar growled in denial, so loud in Aryck's mind that when he felt his father's eyes boring into him he was afraid the sound had escaped. He braced, expecting to hear a sharp mental command along with a private snarl of displeasure and warning.

Help came from an unexpected source. Nahuatl said, "I made the house behind mine ready for the healer, as the ancestors bid me to do when they showed me her face and gave me her name."

Daivat's house. The son made outcast.

Aryck's sweat chilled on his skin. The threat held in the reminder of Daivat's fate helped drive the Jaguar's desires back, caging them in bars of ice, though it didn't force the two Earth-bound souls into a harmonious weave.

"Take her there," Koren said. *And come to my home immediately afterward.* "Phaedra will accompany you so she can make the healer comfortable."

Aryck didn't dare respond mentally for fear the Jaguar would choose that moment to issue a challenge. He gave a slight nod, accepting his father's spoken command as well as the one sent privately.

He left with Rebekka in his arms. Phaedra joined him, carrying a basin and a soft rag.

Daivat's home was similar to his own. One room with a large bed made of piled woven blankets and bison pelts, a place used more to experience the sensual pleasures that came with coupling in human form than to sleep in.

The Jaguar's growl rumbled through Aryck as he placed Rebekka on the bedding. There would have been a fight for dominance had the blankets and pelts smelled of another male. But Nahuatl had seen to them. They smelled of sunshine and rye grass.

Phaedra set the basin down after filling it with water from a bucket left ready. "I'll tend her now," she said, her hands going to the front of Rebekka's shirt, efficiently undoing the first several buttons.

Aryck couldn't look away as the material of the shirt parted in a small revelation of flesh. The sight of it was enough to make his cock harden, and in his mind he continued freeing the buttons, peeling the sweat-soaked fabric away and stripping Rebekka of it completely so his hands could take over the task of bathing her, turning it from impersonal service to sensual exploration.

Phaedra glanced up then, spearing him with knowing eyes. He turned and left, as much to keep from exposing the battle he was waging with himself as to avoid her ordering him to go.

Outside a flash of red drew his eye to a cardinal taking flight. He smiled at seeing it. The bright color of its feathers reminded him of the beads on Rebekka's necklace.

The amulet was a barely discernable weight in his pocket, yet the satisfaction that purred through him with the feel of it there was immense.

The Jaguar's—at having something of hers while they were separated, at having a reason to return to her side as soon as possible.

The man's—at having been entrusted with the necklace in the first place.

Aryck took the first step toward the alpha's home. Reluctant in a way he hadn't experienced since he was a child summoned for a misdeed.

The smell of cooking meat greeted him. *Pork*, Aryck thought, following the scent of it to the fire pit in back of the cabin.

His stomach rumbled and his mouth watered, both reminding him of how long he'd gone without food. Koren gestured to a log carved vaguely into the shape of a chair. "Sit."

It wasn't quite a command and yet it wasn't an invitation either. Aryck sat as his father turned a slab of meat over on a salvaged piece of metal grate.

Grease hit the fire underneath and sizzled. Hunger pangs, a much less painful version of the Jaguar's clawed insistence, raked through Aryck's belly.

"The healer?" Koren asked.

Aryck tensed despite himself, silently cursed at reacting when he realized his father had been surreptitiously watching for it. "She sleeps. Phaedra bathes her."

He put indifference into his voice, though heat throbbed through his cock as he imagined Rebekka naked on the furs, her eyes beckoning him to join her. Her body a temptation he couldn't resist when she rolled to her hands and knees, calling him to her with a sultry glance over her shoulder.

Aryck nearly rose to pace. Would have if not for his father.

This time there was no mistaking the origin of desire. The fantasy of Rebekka wanting him to cover her wasn't an image forced on him by the Jaguar.

Koren prodded the meat, letting the silence build between them. Aryck clenched his jaw to keep from filling the space between them with words, grateful his father intended to hold this conversation orally instead of mentally, where suppressing the Jaguar might become impossible.

Koren transferred slabs of pork to metal plates, handing one of them, along with a knife and fork, to Aryck. They ate, the silence continuing, moving into a comfortable lull until all the meat had disappeared and the plates were set aside.

"The healer is not what I expected," Koren finally said, leaning forward and placing his forearms on his thighs in a relaxed pose, though the air between them was laced with edges. "For all her human frailty there is strength at her core."

Aryck acknowledged the comment with a shrug, as if neither the strength nor the weakness mattered to him. By the narrowing of his father's eyes, he knew it was the wrong gesture to make.

Koren stood, abruptly shedding the feign of casualness. He paced, as Aryck had wanted to earlier. Ten steps forward, then back again to reclaim his seat and shock Aryck by saying, "She reminds me of your mother."

Their eyes met. His father's expression hardened. "I understand the attraction of a female who needs a strong male to keep her safe. Your mother preferred the human form but even when she wore fur, she was no fighter. Her nature was too gentle. If she'd been pure animal instead of Were, she would never have survived to breeding age."

He rose again. Paced. Ten steps forward, then back to his seat.

"I knew I should stay away from her. I knew she was not the right mate for an alpha. But dominance is bred into our line and submission attracts us. One coupling and no other female could hold my interest."

His shrug mimicked Aryck's earlier one, as if the past wasn't unimportant. But the seriousness in his voice and the fact he'd never taken another mate gave lie to it.

"In the end my lack of control and my choice cost me. The man might desire a soft mate, but the Jaguar needs a strong one, an equal in both will and form."

Aryck nearly laughed at his father's erroneous assumption. But he had no desire to reveal the battle that had raged since the Jaguar encountered Rebekka.

The silence descended once again. It grew heavier when Aryck didn't rush to reassure his father that he understood the warning and planned to stay away from the healer.

Koren's eyes darkened and his mouth firmed. Aryck braced himself for the strike of his father's verbal claws. "As soon as the cubs have successfully shifted between forms, and the healer has rested and eaten, I will assign others to escort her to the Lion camp so she can return to Oakland and the outcast brothels."

The Jaguar screamed denial, animal soul unraveling into a nearly separate entity and trying to take its true shape in order to offer a direct challenge to the alpha. Aryck turned his head quickly, hoping his father hadn't seen the beast looking through human eyes.

He wrestled to remain in control, a small part of his rational mind welcoming his father's plan. If he could hold out until she was gone, then the threat she represented would lessen immediately and, over time, fade completely.

His earlier fantasy flashed through his mind, of her naked and welcoming him. He pushed it away. Another female, a Jaguar, would come along and—

Searing pain raked through him, the kind preceding a change of form.

His father rose and shed his clothes in preparation for shifting.

It was enough warning for Aryck to accept a truth he still didn't want. It wasn't just the Jaguar who saw Rebekka as a potential mate, who needed to spend time in her company. "I promised to personally see to her protection while she was on our lands."

The words settled the Jaguar enough so Aryck dared to look at his father. Koren's face showed nothing of what he was thinking, but his voice was little more than a growl. "Guard the cabin if you wish, but stay away from her until she wakes."

Caphriel's Pawn

RADEK rolled off the prostitute and stared at the ceiling as she slid the used condom off his semiflaccid cock. He spared her a glance as she padded naked across the room to drop it into a twisted piece of salvaged metal serving as a trash can.

The sight of her swaying breasts and round buttocks didn't hold his interest. His mind raced, and despite the release of sex he could feel the restless tension building in his chest, the uncertainty gnawing at him.

By now there should have been some evidence the smart-virus he'd poured into the pond was working. There hadn't been, and because of it irritation sizzled through him.

His leaving the compound several times a day was drawing too much attention from his brother's lapdog, Nagy. But he could hardly send men out and order them to look for signs of dead wolves or elk.

Having to handle this himself was wasting valuable time. Time better spent analyzing the recovered files and determining which of them could be turned into the wealth that was now only part of his nightly dream.

Radek closed his eyes for a moment, hoping the imagined cheering of the crowds would soothe him. It didn't. If anything it increased his restlessness, made him feel as though he were in a race against some unseen opponent and victory was far from assured.

The bed dipped as the whore returned. She took his cock into her mouth.

Radek kept his eyes closed. He shifted his concentration to the feel of the prostitute's lips and tongue, hoping to use physical pleasure to recapture the golden glory he experienced in his dreams. It didn't work.

His frustration grew, taking on an ugly edge as his penis softened further and the whore released him to ask, "Should I leave now?"

Radek's eyes snapped opened. *Worthless slut!* To imply with her tone that her failure to provide a distraction was somehow his fault and she'd just as soon go service the convicts and dregs of society.

He rolled off the bed and stalked to his desk, opening a drawer with a jerk. He'd intended to retrieve the bottle of brandy he kept there, to soothe himself with a glass of it, but the sight of the canister with the picture of a hyena scratched into its surface turned frustration and irritation into giddy exhilaration.

Epiphany struck, explaining his uncharacteristic desire for one of the camp whores. He turned slightly, eyes flicking to the prostitute's tattoo, the garish black circle with a red *P* in its center.

He'd nearly sent her away when he saw it, not wanting to think about the terrorist-created disease that had led to prostitutes being marked during The Last War. He was glad now he hadn't. It had given birth to divine inspiration, a call to action that replaced his worries of failure.

There were hyenas nearby. Their whooping calls and laughs made the hair rise on his arms each time he heard them.

Radek smiled as a plan took form. He could hardly ask someone to deliver the carcass of a goat or cow to a hyena's den, but the corpse of a whore was a different matter.

He knew just the man to do what needed to be done. One who frequented the red zone brothels and had more than once been required to pay for extensive damages to the prostitutes there.

A comment to Gregor, something to the effect that this particular whore was a spy and he, Radek, wouldn't mind paying the penalty if she disappeared while he held her contract. Another, about hyenas leaving no trace of their prey—

Delicious. Too bad he couldn't invite Captain Orst to his quarters for a drink. Now there was a whore of a totally different kind, a true spy, though Radek doubted he'd ever be able to prove the guardsman was owned by the Iberás.

Radek suppressed a giggle as he imagined Orst meeting with an unfortunate accident and becoming a feast for hyenas, animals that would spread the smart-virus to Weres of the same form. If only—

First things first, Radek thought, interrupting his fantasy and pouring two glasses of brandy, filling one to the top and the other halfway.

If he'd truly thought ahead, he would have diluted the contents of the canister, but . . . He shrugged it off. Inspiration *had* struck when he was in the perfect position to act on it.

Careful to keep his back to the bed and the waiting prostitute, he matched the level of liquid in the second glass by adding the concentrated solution of smart-virus.

The whore was sitting at the edge of the bed when he closed the drawer and turned. Boredom changed to interest at the sight of the two glasses in his hand.

Radek nearly laughed when she licked her lips. "I see I don't have to ask if you'll share a drink with me before you leave."

She sent him a coquettish look, repositioning herself so she was once again fully on the bed. "I won't leave at all unless you send me away," she said, thrusting her chest forward, her fingers playing with a pale pink nipple as she spread her thighs to give him a good look.

Radek suppressed a shudder, hoping she didn't notice his cock had softened further at the prospect of intimate contact with a virus-ridden slut.

She took the glass he offered and tossed it back quickly, as if she hoped doing it would lead to a hasty refill.

Good. She won't notice the taste of the concentrate if there is one.

Her hand slid down to her cunt, playing there as she held out her arm in a silent request for more.

He tipped his hand, pouring a portion of brandy into her empty glass. Why not? He could afford to be generous.

Her smile held the promise of a sexual romp he had no intention of participating in. She drew her arm back, raised the drink toward her mouth.

Liquid sloshed onto her chest as the glass touched her lips. She had time for a tiny gasp before a seizure took her and she went over backward, heels drumming, pounding the mattress violently.

Shock held Radek motionless, clearing his mind of all thought until the smell of urine and released bowels brought him back to himself.

Terror threatened to grip him. He combatted it by turning away and going to his computer, passing through the multitude of password-protected gates before reaching the information left by the scientists along with the canisters.

Rereading it calmed him. The smart-virus wasn't keyed to a particular delivery host—that, he'd remembered when inspiration struck. What he'd failed to remember was that it was designed to weaken prey, making them natural targets for predators and scavengers like hyenas.

Properly mixed it wouldn't have killed the prostitute outright. The whore would have met her end in a different manner, in Gregor's hands.

Radek shrugged. It was done now.

He closed the file, having gotten what he needed from it. Already a new plan was forming, a modification of his original one. It would be distasteful to have his father's militiaman think the two of them shared the same sick passion, but it couldn't be helped.

Radek picked up a pair of work gloves before moving to the hook where his formal clothing hung, the dark suit and pristine white shirt his father insisted be worn in his presence. With a tug he freed the silk tie.

He snapped it between his hands, testing its strength. *It will do*, he thought, and the Ivanov family crest embroidered onto it would serve as a reminder to Gregor of who owned his loyalties.

Radek returned to the side of the bed. The worst of the seizure had passed.

The whore no longer drummed the mattress with her heels but she continued to flail weakly, her mouth opening and closing, her eyes rolling around, reminding him of a fish.

Foam flecked her lips. He shuddered and slipped his gloves on, not wanting any contact with her bodily fluids despite what he'd read in the file.

He looped the tie around her neck before grabbing one of her wrists and securing an end there with a knot. He did the same at the other wrist.

Deviant sex held no interest for him, though so many of those he'd grown up among seemed drawn to it, a reflection of their boredom as much as a flexing of their power. The thought of actually playing with death in the pursuit of pleasure, of risking it with erotic asphyxia, was revolting.

Radek shuddered again as he grasped the silken tie on either side of the whore's neck. *I do what I must*, he told himself, grateful she'd finally stopped moving and was already well on her way to expiring.

He pulled, tightening the loop wrapped around her throat in order to leave telltale marks, the illusion of sex play gone wrong. She struggled at the very last, so weakly it was barely noticeable.

Radek used the sheet to wipe the foam from her mouth, then stepped back, gauging the position of her body. Not optimal. But acceptable. *Good enough*.

He turned away from the scene, shedding the gloves and dropping them on a rarely used chair. He'd deal with them, and the mattress, later. The soiled sheets and the whore's clothing could be burned in the trash barrel at the back of his quarters.

Radek took a few minutes for a sponge bath, being sure to dampen the edges of his hair. He dressed—Gregor would hardly expect to find him standing naked and wringing his hands while waiting for help to arrive—then stepped out of his quarters long enough to flag down a worker and send for the militiaman.

Gregor arrived moments later. He took in the scene and turned sly eyes toward Radek.

Radek's mouth soured. "There are hyenas nearby. Find where they gather and dump the body. Remain within sight of it until you see them start feeding."

"It could take a while, especially if I stay long enough to make certain there's nothing left for the guardsmen to find if they decide to go looking for a missing prostitute. Probably be good if someone saw her leave your quarters and slip into the one housing the convicts."

"You're right on both counts."

Gregor's smile turned as hard as his eyes. "After doing a stretch in Were-infested woods, I'd sure like to unwind by having the same kind of fun you had here. I wouldn't have guessed you enjoyed it like this, not with your reputation, but now I can see for myself you do. Coming up with the cash to pay the penalty money has always been a stretch for me. Maybe you could help me out there, since you own all the contracts."

Radek's stomach churned, both at the blackmail demand and Gregor's likening the two of them. He glanced in the direction of the bed but instead of a corpse he saw himself riding in an open-topped jeep through the wealthiest section of Oakland, his father next to him, witnessing the adulation.

"You'll have your fun," Radek said. "But you'll wait until I tell you another whore can go missing."

Fifteen

THE sound of chattering teeth dragged Rebekka from the depths of sleep. *My teeth*, she realized vaguely, still caught in the fog left by utter exhaustion.

She shivered, slowly becoming aware of how cold she was. Tasted the bitterness then. It coated her tongue and instinctively her mind sought to identify it, to link it to the reason she was so cold.

Memory flickered, of repeatedly accepting the wooden cup from Phaedra, drinking the stimulant. *Foolish*. She was lucky it hadn't killed her, shutting down her nervous system or causing her heart to fail.

She reached out, finding fur-soft pelts and pulling them over her, snuggling into the warmth they promised as she breathed in the scent of sunshine and rye grass. A hint of fear edged in when the cold deepened and her teeth continued to chatter, but exhaustion was a heavy weight, clouding her mind. Her body's need for sleep was an anchor she willingly followed, expecting oblivion and gaining it for a time, until images from the healer's journal came to life, lifting from the pages and becoming real.

Battlefields littered with corpses.

Cities filled with bodies.

At first they were human strangers. But slowly they morphed into Weres.

The prostitutes.

Dorrit.

Levi and Cyrin.

Canino.

Then the cubs and Aryck.

Rebekka woke screaming, panicked, her hands burning and her chest frozen.

Awareness slashed through her, intermingling with the memory of the flamethrowers and men in protective suits. She was calling the diseased from the Barrens to her. Whatever carried it was distant still, but coming.

Blindly she sought the amulet, tossing furs and blankets aside in desperation. She stood as she remembered giving it to Aryck for safekeeping, only realizing she was naked except for her panties when the door crashed open and he entered the cabin.

The alpha and Melina came in after him, then an older man carrying a lantern. By then Rebekka was shaking uncontrollably, her breathing fast and loud. She grabbed a fur and covered herself.

Melina's derisive laugh was followed by equally cutting words. "All that screaming over an owl?"

The words sent Rebekka's gaze to the bird fluttering helplessly beneath the open window. It provided the focus she desperately needed for her gift.

The Jaguars might think her frightened in the dark, but she preferred it to their knowing the truth, guessing at the importance of the amulet. They'd kill her if they knew. Or destroy the witch's protection and chase her back to Oakland like a bomb set to explode in the midst of the human world.

Rebekka eased toward the small owl. She reached with her mind, sending waves of calm. It stopped fluttering, though its breathing was as rapid as hers.

As soon as she touched it the coldness in her chest disappeared, burned away by the flow of healing warmth. It wasn't as hot or intense as it had been when she touched Aryck or the cubs, but it didn't need to be.

Her arm hurt, as if bones were shattered there. She knitted the damaged material back together with quick, deft mental strokes, noting it was easier, her thoughts more sharply focused, further proof her gift had been changed when the witches bound the amulet to her with blood.

Rebekka's pulse raced with thoughts of the red beads, so very much like the ones her demon father wore in his hair. Her hands trembled slightly as she removed them from the owl and it took flight, escaping into the night through the open window.

Cold exploded in Rebekka's chest. Because she expected it, she didn't react outwardly to the terror it brought with it.

The threat was still distant, but closer than it had been moments earlier. There was no hiding the scent of fear from the Jaguars.

This far away from human civilization, deep in Were territory, they had no reason to worry about supernatural predators, no reason to close or bar the windows. But they would assume it wasn't the same for her.

Somehow she managed to keep her voice steady as she turned toward them and said, "I'm sorry I disturbed you with my screams."

They'd stopped just inside the doorway, not wanting to panic the owl and cause it to further injure itself. Rebekka tightened her grip on the fur and crossed to them, her apparent discomfort over being nearly naked gaining another derisive laugh from Melina.

Rebekka ignored it and reached out, saying to Aryck, "I'd like my necklace back."

He removed it from his pocket, but instead of handing it to her, he stepped behind her and placed it around her neck. She was acutely aware of heat and scent, of the rub of fur against her skin, not his, but it was suddenly very easy to imagine—

She cut the thought off only to have it return when his fingers lingered at the nape of her neck, stroked, making her tremble in a way that had nothing to do with the faded nightmare images or the icy cold no longer filling her chest.

Heat coursed through her, originating at the place his skin touched hers. It was reminiscent of what had happened when she healed him, flowing like a power rooted in the earth, molten lava capable of burning away the protective shield a lifetime spent in brothels had erected.

She'd seen Aryck naked, but that wasn't what made her vulnerable where he was concerned. It was his obvious care for the Tiger cub, the gentleness with which he'd bathed Caius in the wash while the boy's mother rocked, locked in a world of grief.

Rebekka stepped forward, breaking the contact, but not before there was a crack in her defenses. Her nipples hardened and breasts ached. Need pooled in her belly, bringing with it a hastily suppressed fantasy of Aryck's hand stroking over her abdomen, sliding between her thighs to cup her mound.

She tightened her grip on the fur, created a wall around her emotions. There was no way to hide even the tiniest hint of arousal from Weres.

It wasn't something she had to worry about at the brothels. Nothing of what she witnessed there stirred anything to life except revulsion and hate and pity.

She made herself face the Jaguars boldly. Melina's lips twisted in disgust and loathing, while next to her, the lantern in his hands, the older man's dark eyes captured Rebekka's. Without the snarling headdress she hadn't recognized the shaman. But now, just as she had before, she felt as though he was trying to see into the depths of her soul.

"I'm fine," she said. "It's okay to leave me."

Aryck met his father's gaze and tried to keep any hint of challenge from surfacing. He had no desire to revisit their earlier discussion or his near loss of control. "I'll remain with Rebekka until she falls asleep."

Koren's expression didn't change, but Aryck still felt his father's displeasure and worry. *If you mate with her, you risk the part of your soul residing with the ancestors.*

She's not in season.

He couldn't leave her. He didn't need to look down and see the length of his erection pressed against the front of his pants to know he had already lost part of the battle with himself.

Desiring Rebekka should be impossible for him. She was human, a woman who lived among outcasts. Either should have been enough to cool his blood and keep him away from her. But he'd no more been able to stop his fingers from caressing her neck than he'd been able to stop the fantasies of mounting her, of thrusting into wet heat and clinging welcome and marking her with his teeth as he did it.

He was rock hard. And though he had no intention of acting on it, not yet, he also had no choice but to remain in her presence.

He wouldn't be able to overcome the Jaguar's protective need to guard its mate after hearing her screams of terror. If he attempted to leave, the Jaguar would fight him—and win.

His father ushered the others out, closing the door behind them and leaving the cabin in darkness broken only by a hint of moonlight.

Aryck's reality shrank to the woman standing only inches away from him. Heat and scent swallowed him up, urging him to take the small step that would bring his body into contact with hers.

She moved away, saving him from himself. "You don't have to stay," she said, turning her back to him. Adding on a whisper, "It would be better if you didn't."

He didn't need to ask her why. She couldn't hide her physical reaction from him any more than he could hide his from her.

It would be better if he didn't stay. He knew it, believed it still on some level. But, perversely, having her fight the attraction only made it all the harder to let her escape.

Male instinct, Jaguar and human both, told him to close the distance, press his suit. Rebekka's turning her back to him and wrapping the fur around her like a shield only intensified the need.

The silence stretched between them, growing taut with the call of their bodies to each other. He took a step before he could stop himself, inhaled deeply. His arms lifted to pull her against him. His lips parted on a soft pant, his tongue ready to tease over the skin at the nape of her neck, to taste and stroke before the bite that would mark her as belonging to him.

The Jaguar quivered in eagerness, anticipating victory. Or maybe the man did. He was no longer certain they held separate desires.

Heat pulsed through him, a hard, steady throb, like the beat of the drums summoning the ancestors. Some small sliver of sanity whispered this was a mistake, told him he was on the path to becoming outcast. But against the roar of desire it didn't stand a chance.

It was safe. There was no risk of impregnating her.

She tensed when his arms encircled her, but didn't pull away. The intimate contact made him light-headed, hinted at how thoroughly he'd lose himself when flesh pressed to flesh.

A soft whimper escaped when his lips found her neck. His tongue darted out in a wet caress.

She melted against him. But her resistance lingered, offering both challenge and warning.

Drawing sounds of pleasure from her became his mission. Having her soften and willingly drop the fur to the floor to reveal her body became his resolve.

His hands pushed their way under her arms, settled over her breasts, cupping, kneading their fullness, turning the fur separating his palms from her nipples into sensual torment instead of modest protection.

He trailed kisses along her shoulder, sucking the petal-soft skin as her pulse beat wildly in her throat. Her scent intensified, a lush, intoxicating fragrance that made him want to bury first his fingers in her wet slit, and then his tongue.

His hands drifted downward, and she tensed as if struck by an icy arrow. Her resistance returned with a jerk that freed her from his arms. "I can't," she mumbled, moving away from him.

She didn't turn to face him until she reached the door, as if she'd risk the night to escape him. It held him at bay, clearing the lust long enough for a silent, rational voice inside him to question the wisdom of giving in to desire, to remind him of what his father had said. *One coupling and no other female could hold my interest.*

"I can't," she repeated, tongue darting out, wetting her lips and sending a hot spike of need through his cock.

He knew it wasn't revulsion or shame that had driven her out of his arms. Her scent didn't lie, and even now she trembled, fighting to keep herself distanced from him.

It was enough to help him maintain control, to satisfy the Jaguar and the man so they remained smoothly integrated. He retreated to the open window, perching in it and gaining a measure of relief when the night air cooled his skin and filled his nostrils with the smell of pine and dirt and leaves.

Leaving wasn't an option. Not yet.

Rebekka let out a soft sigh. She calmed, at least outwardly. Inside, turmoil reigned.

Aryck's touch made her feel things she'd never experienced before, even when she'd imagined herself attracted to Levi. A part of her wanted to give in, to live in this moment only, without thought of the future. Temptation whispered through her, telling her that denying herself what pleasure she could find in this life was foolish.

Looking at Aryck, desire curled in her belly and slid down into her woman's folds. She wanted to feel his arms around her, to lose herself in the wonder of sexual exploration his kisses promised. But those desires warred with the knowledge of what doing it might ultimately cost her.

She thought of the tattoo inked into her skin. She'd be gone soon, a forgotten interlude in his life. The mark might not mean anything to him, but her virginity was the only thing she had that might offer proof she was no prostitute.

Rebekka crossed to the mound of blankets and furs and lay down. She didn't know why Aryck stayed, but she couldn't bring herself to tell him to leave.

A flutter went through her belly as she looked at him outlined by moonlight in the open window. Everything about him spoke of strength and contained power, of sensuous promise and carnal acts.

Her clit stiffened and she had to fight to keep from touching it, from sliding her fingers between slick folds and imagining it was him. From changing her mind about denying him.

Fantasies slipped into her mind, images made explicit by a lifetime of witnessing sexual encounters. She turned her face away in an attempt to rid herself of them, to once again silence the voice of temptation.

"Are the humans in Oakland so ignorant they don't appreciate your gift?" he asked, drawing her attention back to him. "Surely there is a demand for your services among them."

Her thoughts went to The Iberá's offer, to the luxury and protection that would come if she accepted it. "There is."

Aryck slid off the windowsill and padded over, stopping at the very edge of the huge sleeping area and sprawling, a huge cat in a human form. "Then why do you work in the brothels? Why do you live among outcasts?"

Always before there was derision in his tone, harsh judgment when he spoke the word *outcast*. There was a hint of it in his question but it was overridden by curiosity.

"They need me."

"You waste yourself on them. They serve a punishment meted out to them by the ancestors."

Her eyebrows drew together in puzzlement. "What do you mean?"

He hesitated a moment, then answered, "Each of us possesses three intertwined souls. Human. Animal. And an eternal one residing with our ancestors in the shadowlands. Losing the ability to shift into beast form or being of mixed form in this world is a sign of judgment. It's a way of marking an outcast so others know immediately that the eternal soul has been cast out of the shadowlands."

"I don't believe that can be true of all outcasts."

"You don't believe because you're not one of us. What you know of our world and our kind you've learned from the worst of us."

"Only because you turn your back on anyone caught between forms or who can't shift into a purely animal one. Do your ancestors demand it? Or is it fear and prejudice?"

He stirred restlessly, angrily. "You question things you have no right to."

It would have been easy to let it drop but she couldn't. "I live among outcasts. I see their suffering every day. I witness the degradation and pain and horror that come with selling their bodies so they can survive. What do you know of life in the red zone? Of being powerless because you have no pack, no family, no place in Were society?

"You're so certain they all deserve to be where they are. Some of them do. I can accept that. But tell me how a child born with a mixed form because her Were mother is held prisoner and raped by a human hunter is guilty of a crime and should be forced to live an outcast's life."

Aryck stood, unable to remain still as Rebekka assaulted him with questions that weren't his to answer. He was an enforcer, not a shaman. Pack law was pack law, and when it came to outcasts and humans, it had remained unchanged by generations of Jaguar alphas.

Almost against his will he found himself saying, "Weres born in a mixed form are killed by their mothers or left to die."

"And if they're not? Then is it okay to kill the child at three years old, or four, or ten, or twenty? Did you ever stop to consider how The Last War and what followed created millions of orphans with no knowledge of their heritage? People whose descendents carry Were genes that lie dormant, who think they're human until physical trauma triggers a healing response and leaves them trapped between forms."

"Impossible."

"I've seen it for myself. Are you calling me a liar?"

Aryck clenched his jaw, paced to the door, and told himself he should open it and leave. Instead he turned, only to feel the sharp blade of another question.

"What if Caius can't shift into tiger form after all he's been through? Would you drive him away? Send him to the city to become a victim and claim he deserved it? Kill him if he refused to leave?"

Aryck stalked over and crouched next to her, a growl forming in his chest, in his mind. "Enough."

She sat up, clutching the fur to her naked chest and sending a roar of heat through him to rival the anger. In that moment she seemed every bit as fierce as a female Jaguar defending something of value.

Bare shoulders and cascading hair, strength welded with femininity.

The sight of her aroused him, making him want to rip the fur away and silence her with the thrust of his tongue into her mouth, the thrust of his cock into her slick sheath, despite the danger of one day becoming the very thing they argued about because of it.

Her eyes met his boldly, challenging him. Telling him she was his equal in every way despite having only one form.

"Enough," he repeated, raw need twisting in his gut. His testicles heavy and full and his cock throbbing.

She licked her lips, nearly shredding his control. Her scent changed subtly, with the beginnings of desire.

Naked, stretched beneath him on the furs, she wouldn't say no to him again. He would make sure of it.

One coupling and no other female could hold my interest.

His father's words slipped into Aryck's thoughts again. He wanted to deny them, to ignore them, to shake them off and tell himself he was not his father.

He couldn't. Worse, Rebekka was making him question his beliefs, the rigid framework of his world.

Aryck stood, afraid to risk remaining in her presence.

A turn. A step.

The Jaguar came to life with a vengeance, beast soul riving away from the whole. Refusing to leave Rebekka.

Aryck embraced the pain, willingly accepted the escape from conversation and questions his furred form allowed. He pushed his pants off his hips, not able to deny the pleasure at feeling her eyes on him, traveling down his body.

It was all he could do not to turn, to display the hard length of his cock jutting upward, spasming against his abdomen and wetting his skin with escaped arousal.

Her scent deepened. Her breathing became erratic.

The rustle of furs had him imagining her naked. Made him realize man and beast were once again fully united in their desire to claim this woman.

With a thought Aryck commanded the change, knowing if he turned back toward Rebekka in a human form, he would take her, without care for the consequences.

Rebekka was torn between relief and disappointment as Aryck became Jaguar. It was for the best, she reminded herself, lying back down but unable to suppress the small thrill that came when he padded over and settled next to her.

Heat poured off him, so much of it she wanted to kick off the covers and lie naked in the cool night air. A flush spread over her skin at the erotic image.

He began purring, a low rumble that felt like a rough tongue lapping over her swollen folds and hardened nipples. She shouldn't, she knew she shouldn't, and yet she couldn't stop herself from reaching over and running her hand down his neck and over his shoulders.

Both his forms were magnificent. Beautiful.

For the first time in her life she wished she'd been born something other than a gifted healer. If she were a Jaguar—

But she wasn't, and only pain would come of imagining otherwise, of dreaming there could be a future here with him. She was human, fathered by a demon, her gift altered by a supernatural being who'd turned it into something that would bring death to those she lived among if she wasn't careful.

Aryck's purrs deepened, drawing her away from her troubled thoughts. Stroking his fur eased her, quieted her mind and her body, finally allowing sleep to reclaim her.

Sixteen

REBEKKA woke to a strong male body covering hers. Warm skin touching warm skin. Making her feel safe, protected, desirable.

Muscles rippled beneath her hands as they glided over a naked back. The hard throb of an erection pressed against her belly and ground against her stiffened clit. Lips nuzzled her ear. A cheek rubbed against hers, bringing a scent that had come to represent temptation. *Aryck*.

Her nipples were tight, aching points stabbing a smooth chest. She let herself pretend, keeping her eyes closed, not wanting the fantasy to end as her fingers lingered at the base of his spine, then dared to go lower.

His moan was a rumbled purr as her hands smoothed over firm, muscled buttocks. He lifted onto his elbows enough to allow him to trail kisses to the edge of her mouth.

Like a cat, his tongue darted out, licked along the seam of her lips. Enticed.

She opened for him. Her lower lips did the same. Unfurling, making her want to spread her legs wider and cant her hips. To tear away the barrier of her panties so he could find her opening and join their bodies with the thrust of his cock deep inside her.

His tongue slid into her mouth, rubbed against hers as his body rocked, each movement striking her clit. She opened her eyes, unable to deny herself the sight of him above her.

He growled in satisfaction. Shifted his weight onto a single elbow, freeing his hand to cup her bare breast.

Desire rushed through her. A whimper escaped and she arched her back.

His face tightened, nostrils flaring as his fingers rubbed over her nipple, clamped onto it and tugged, eyes more jaguar than human. Daring her to deny him. Promising exquisite pleasure with her acceptance.

She licked her lips and his hips jerked, thrust his rigid cock against her clit and made her cry out. Lust flashed through her and she clamped her legs against his.

He lowered his head. Lapped at her nipple. Took it between his lips and suckled.

Need made her forget everything else. She tangled her fingers in his hair, writhed under him as gentle sucks gave way to the feel of teeth, to pain that only fed the pleasure.

With a growl he released her nipple, laved and kissed her breast, burying his face in her cleavage before once again covering her mouth with his. His tongue thrust aggressively as his hand went to her panties, fingers curling around them at her hip in preparation of ripping them away from her. Enough sanity remained for her to cover his hand with hers, stopping him.

Before he could renew his sensual assault, the door opened with a crash, and Aryck rolled to his feet, ready to defend against attack. Rebekka sat and grabbed a blanket, pulling it up to her chest.

The sight of Melina and Phaedra cleared the haze of passion from Rebekka's mind with the effectiveness of stepping out into the rain during the winter season. But it did nothing to eradicate the lust pooled in her belly and between her thighs.

Her breathing remained harsh, as did Aryck's. A blush stole over her at seeing him standing naked, perfectly at ease. Uncaring and unconcerned about the hardened length of cock on display.

The Jaguar healer came farther into the room. Rebekka noticed the bundle in Phaedra's arms then, recognized her own clothing, clean and folded, the journal lying on top.

"Leave us," Phaedra said to Aryck, including Melina with a glance.

Aryck bent over, retrieving the pants he'd dropped to the floor the night before. The action afforded Rebekka a view of sculpted muscle, of graceful power and sheer masculinity.

Her channel clenched, wetting her inner thighs with arousal and sending a spike of need through her clit. He looked back at her, eyes holding heat and knowledge. If they hadn't been interrupted, he would be inside her now.

She shook her head in silent denial but knew it was a lie. He stepped into his pants, drawing them up with excruciating slowness. Behaving like a cat wanting adoration and smiling as he got it when she licked her lips.

Rebekka turned her head. A fist tightened around her heart. She'd be gone soon, probably after she'd eaten.

Phaedra handed Rebekka the bundle as Aryck and Melina left. Rebekka set the journal aside and dressed quickly, needing the armor of clothing to cover the awkwardness of what had happened—or nearly happened—with Aryck.

"Your breakfast should be almost ready," Phaedra said, turning and walking toward the door.

Rebekka saw her shoes next to it. She picked them up rather than stop to put them on.

A young girl tended a fire at the back of the cabin. Rebekka's mouth watered at the smell of spiced sausage and fried potatoes.

"Sit," Phaedra said, gesturing to a heavy log as she took over the chore of cooking.

Rebekka sat, dropping the shoes to the ground rather than put them on. The rich loam was cool against her feet, fertile where much of the land they'd passed through to arrive at the Jaguar camp had been red dirt and sandstone.

The girl lingered, obviously curious. Rebekka sent her a tentative smile and had it returned.

Phaedra glanced over her shoulder at the girl. "You have roots and berries to gather if you hope to continue your lessons today."

The girl slipped into the woods, quickly disappearing from sight.

Rebekka looked around. Like the healer's cabin, this one was well hidden and seemingly isolated. It was a concession to the jaguar in their natures, she guessed, since the big cats were solitary creatures.

Levi had told her Lion prides lived in family groups, several generations of females with their mates and offspring sharing the same dwelling. Wolf packs were the same, though an alpha pair ruled and membership depended more on mutual agreement than blood ties.

A plate thrust against her hand scattered Rebekka's thoughts and made her stomach rumble. She set the journal on the log. Phaedra sat so it was between them.

With the first bite of food it became impossible for Rebekka to do anything but eat. She was ravenous, starved. Thinking back on it, the last meal leaving her feeling full had been at the Iberá estate.

When she finally finished eating there was nothing left, on either the plate or the skillet. "How are the cubs?" she asked.

Phaedra's smile held the answer. "They shift between forms and already chafe at being told they can't stray far from their homes. I suspect their parents will soon grow tired of having energetic and rambunctious boys underfoot."

"Caius included?"

The healer's smile faded. "He is well, but his mother remains the same. Our kind mate for life. Some do not survive the loss of the bond."

There were herbs and potions to combat depression. During The Last War shock and grief had driven many to turn inward and lose touch with the world of the living.

By Allende's order, Rebekka didn't make or dispense mood-altering drugs to those who worked in the brothel. That was a business for a vice lord. But like the stimulants some of the prostitutes took, drugs to lift a user out of depression were available.

"Can you give her something?"

"It's not our way."

Rebekka looked around, taking in the beauty of the dark woods only a few steps beyond the fire pit. She breathed in the pine and cedar scent, the smell of earth. Listened to the birds and sought them out: quail pecking and rattling through scrub, a crow sitting high in a tree, a cardinal a few branches beneath it, a red-tailed hawk flying above, crying out in a harsh, prolonged *kee-ahrrr*.

She understood why Phaedra wouldn't interfere. Here nature would take its course. It held the capacity to soothe and restore, but it was also ruled by a law dictating survival of the fittest.

Rebekka set the empty plate aside and picked up the journal. She traced the edges with her fingertips, remembering Phaedra's threatening growl when she'd first seen it. "This belonged to a man who was alive during The Last War. He treated anyone brought to him, human or Were. I received it in payment for a healing. The person who gave it to me knew it had once belonged to a Were. I'm not sure if they knew he was Jaguar, and I don't know how it came to be in their possession."

"I reacted badly. I've had few dealings with humans and none of them good. You are not what any of us expected." Phaedra laughed softly. "Save for Nahuatl, the shaman, perhaps. But that's the way of those who visit the ancestors, to dole out information only as it's deemed necessary."

Curiosity led Rebekka to risk getting into an argument with Phaedra as she had with Aryck. "The Weres in the brothels don't mention the ancestors."

"The ancestors aren't to be spoken about lightly. Their reach is long, even for those who've had their eternal soul cast out of the shadowlands."

Rebekka wondered if Phaedra ever questioned whether *all* those trapped between forms had been judged by the ancestors. She considered challenging the healer's beliefs as she'd done Aryck's, then shrugged the thought away. She wouldn't be here long enough to change the way they saw those they considered outcast.

"Do I leave today for Oakland?"

"I hoped to convince you to stay and share the knowledge contained in the journal. Koren, our alpha, hasn't granted permission, but I believe he will once he learns Nahuatl spoke to the ancestors and your continued presence in Jaguar lands won't anger them."

A flash of need hit Rebekka, having everything to do with Aryck and nothing to do with remaining in order to discuss healing. Heat crept up her neck and into her cheeks as her body readied itself for him. There was no way to hide what it meant from Phaedra, who'd witnessed evidence of the attraction already.

Rebekka expected Phaedra to warn against any involvement with Aryck; instead the healer said, "In our pack knowledge is passed down orally. Our history is learned sitting at the feet of our elders. The stories we tell are created and embellished at the fireside. The best of them are committed to memory and become favorites.

"There are marks we use to leave messages behind. We don't put ink to paper, or know how to read what others have recorded. Until you came, bringing the journal, I thought there was little that hadn't been passed down, healer to healer. I was wrong. Now I know much has been lost. I hope you will stay and share what was once known by one of my kind."

Rebekka rubbed her palm against the material of her pants. Her pulse sped up when she felt the Wainwright token in the pocket, then slowed with the realization Phaedra must have found it and decided that possessing something connected to witches wasn't important and didn't make Rebekka a threat to the Jaguars.

Unbidden the image of Annalise came to mind, leaning forward, talking of a coming war between supernaturals, of there being choices that might ultimately lead to the deepening of Rebekka's gift so she could fully heal the Were outcasts, allowing them to shift between forms.

This was one of those choices. Rebekka felt certain of it.

Her hand strayed to the amulet. Her mind went to the past, to the demon father who'd saved her from rape and sent her to the brothels.

This world was far removed from that one. And whatever his reason for fathering her, she didn't think she'd serve his purpose here.

But here offered a measure of safety, of peace, as long as she kept the amulet on.

And temptation, a small voice whispered in her mind, her body tingling with pleasure at the memory of Aryck on top of her, his cock thrusting against her stiffened clit as his tongue fucked in and out of her mouth. If they hadn't been interrupted . . .

She wet her lips. Her heart pounded in her chest as she realized even though the answers she needed were in Oakland, and remaining near Aryck would only lead to pain, she couldn't leave, not when she had an excuse to remain. "I'll stay and share what's in the journal with you."

"Good." Phaedra rose to her feet. "I need to speak with Koren."

Rebekka remained seated. She clamped her thighs together, but instead of easing the throbbing in her clit and swollen labia, it seemed to intensify her awareness of them. Until Aryck she'd never viewed herself as a sexual being. She'd suppressed all desire, not wanting to be turned on by witnessing carnal acts she knew degraded and slowly killed something inside those she loved and considered her friends.

She touched the place where the tattoo was hidden beneath her clothing. She'd thought to save herself, to use her virginity as a way of proving she was no prostitute. But that assumed she would find a man she could trust with both her heart and her body, someone she could share her life with—her secrets.

How could she think she'd find that now? Who would want a demon's child? A healer whose gift could also bring death on an unimaginable scale?

Need rippled through her at remembering the hungry look in Aryck's eyes. Why not take the pleasure he offered?

Because I don't think I can keep my feelings separated from my body, she admitted, a chill invading as she imagined Aryck seeing the tattoo and knowing what it meant, then turning away from her in disgust because of it.

A small hand holding a bouquet of purple flowers appeared in front of Rebekka's face, jerking her from her thoughts. She turned her head slightly and saw the Tiger cub standing on the other side of the log she sat on.

"For making me better," Caius said.

Rebekka took the flowers, holding them close to her nose and inhaling. "Thank you." She patted the log next to her. "Would you like to sit?"

He looked down, shifting from one foot to the other before finally mumbling, "I have a favor to ask."

She reached over and took his hand. His nervousness crept up her arm and settled into her chest. "Ask."

Blue eyes looked at her through shaggy, white-blond bangs. "Will you go with me to meet the Tiger?"

Her heart turned over in her chest. Of course Caius would want to meet Canino, someone who was like him.

"Do you know where he is?" She hadn't thought about Canino since arriving at the Jaguar camp.

"Yes."

"Let me put the flowers in the cabin and my shoes on and we'll go."

They found Canino sunning himself on a huge flat-topped boulder next to a small pond. He yawned widely, revealing his canines. A roar followed when Caius ducked behind Rebekka.

"Can you ask him to shift?" Caius whispered, trying to keep his voice low enough so it wouldn't carry to the Tiger.

Sudden guilt burdened Rebekka's heart, casting doubt and making her question whether or not she'd done the right thing in agreeing to stay here longer instead of returning to Oakland and the Weres who needed her there. "He can't change form."

"Oh." Caius edged out from behind her. "It doesn't matter."

Canino stood, body rigid, lips pulling back in a silent snarl.

Caius retreated behind her again.

Despite the show, Canino's emotions didn't register against Rebekka's senses as a threat. They were more like those of a cranky, solitary male whose nap had been interrupted and who intended to go back to sleep unless his unexpected visitors were committed to staying.

There was a tingling of curiosity directed at Caius as well. A touch of sadness that made her wonder how Canino had come to be held in the maze, and if he'd lost a mate and offspring in the process.

Rebekka turned long enough to put an arm around Caius and maneuver him so he stood in front of her. Anxiety and the desperate desire to be accepted vibrated through his small body.

She leaned down and placed a kiss on the top of his head, sending the same waves of calm she used with injured wildlife to soothe him. "Aryck told me if it weren't for you, the other cubs would be dead."

Caius's chest swelled and he stood a bit taller. "He did?"

"Yes. You were amazingly courageous to do what you did for them. Now introduce yourself to Canino. He won't hurt you."

The Tiger chose that moment to charge.

He came at them fast and Rebekka jumped, her pulse skittering despite her belief he wouldn't attack her.

Caius froze in place, making only the tiniest of sounds.

At the last moment Canino veered, nearly knocking Caius and her over with the rub of his side before padding back to the rocks and stretching out again, tail twitching and curling against the stone like a striped question mark, as if asking, *Well, what are you waiting for?*

"Go on," Rebekka said, cupping Caius's chin and tilting his face upward so she could place a kiss on his forehead.

The cub pressed against her, soaking in the affection. Rebekka's thoughts strayed to his mother, locked in her grief over the loss of her mate and failing the son she'd created with him.

It took several moments for Caius to gather his courage and determination. Finally he stepped away from her and shed his clothing with the same unconcern over nakedness she was used to in the brothels.

His change wasn't as fast or graceful as Aryck's had been. It was accompanied by mews of pain before it was done.

Joy filled Rebekka at having the white Tiger cub with blue eyes brush against her legs and purr like a giant kitten. She knelt, scratching his neck and behind his ears. "Go. I'll stay for a while."

Rather than invade Canino's space, Caius padded over to the edge of the pond. He swiped at the water. Pounced on fish or shadows or nothing at all, making Rebekka smile.

Curiosity got the better of Canino. He leapt from his resting place and landed with a giant splash, then swam over to stand in the shallow water and shake next to Caius.

With a laugh Rebekka picked up the cub's discarded pants. She folded them as she walked over and claimed Canino's place in the sun.

Contentment came with the feel of the sun's rays against her skin, lowering her guard so a daydream crept in. Of Aryck and a little boy who looked just like him.

The Watcher

TORQUEL en Sahon took flight as Rebekka drowsed in the sun. This daughter pleased him greatly.

Her strength lay not only in her gift but in her compassion for others. She was a survivor, and yet it hadn't hardened her.

There was worse to come now. Death that couldn't be prevented.

For the first time he wished he could call a halt to her testing and reveal himself to her. He wanted to acknowledge her with the writing of her name in the Book of the Djinn.

He couldn't. Despite his standing in the House of the Cardinal.

This test of value to the Djinn wasn't Rebekka's alone.

Torquel landed on a branch close to where the shaman, healer, and pack alpha stood near the challenge circle. He ruffled red and black feathers as he settled to listen.

"It won't anger the ancestors if she remains on our lands," Nahuatl said, and Torquel smiled inwardly.

There were ties to the Djinn among the Were ancestors, just as Djinn blood ran through many of the alpha lines. It had been diluted over time, but it still manifested in the ability to speak mentally to those sharing a family bond, to shift form quickly and have greater endurance.

Addai had done his work well in convincing the shaman to listen and accept what must have seemed like the words of malicious spirits. Death didn't necessarily change the nature of those who crossed over to live in the Were shadowlands. Troublemakers existed, those who took delight in meddling.

The alpha's expression didn't change but Torquel could read Koren's tension. He worried for his son's fate yet he was trapped by duty to the pack. "How long do you need?"

Phaedra pursed her lips. "A day, perhaps two, to memorize what's in the journal. That assumes she won't be called away to heal or her voice doesn't fail her from reading the passages."

A muscle twitched in Koren's cheek. "Two days. She leaves our lands sooner if you finish before then. She remains longer only if it's absolutely necessary."

Wolf howls drifted into the clearing from nearby, a song of woe and entreaty that rose and fell without cessation to become a haunting melody.

It brought Aryck to his father's side. "Go," Koren said. "Choose two others and take them with you."

Torquel let his physical form dissolve in a swirl of air that made the oak leaves rustle softly. *So Caphriel's moves in this game begin to play out.*

Seventeen

ARYCK couldn't stop thinking about Rebekka. Her scent, her heat, her soft, lush body as it lay beneath him.

He'd intended to wake in his furred form to avoid temptation and another argument about the outcast. But whether it was beast or man that initiated the change as he slept, the moment he'd awakened and felt her against him he'd wanted her more than he'd ever wanted another female. He'd felt whole, his two Earth-bound souls in perfect harmony.

It broke no laws to couple with her. The trouble lay in what could happen afterward, what lengths he might go to to keep her, and how quickly he would be made outcast because of his actions.

His stomach knotted at the prospect of facing his father or a new enforcer in the challenge circle. Of being brought to the ancestors' attention for judgment, though he could be cast from the pack by the alpha's word alone.

What made worry congeal in his gut was suspecting the Jaguar might not care. It hated being away from Rebekka, had raged and clawed and fought to dominate until the wolf song brought unity to human and Jaguar souls. And still Aryck felt edgy. Out of sorts.

He wanted to finish what they'd begun. He could no longer deny the need driving him, leaving him constantly hard and aching. Nor could he pretend he would be able to give her care over to Levi, not without paying the price and becoming rogue, the separation between human and Jaguar souls nearly irreparable.

When he wasn't thinking about tearing away the barrier of her panties and thrusting into her, he was remembering her words and questioning his beliefs about outcasts. What if not all of them had been judged by the ancestors? What if sometimes they were simply the product of genetics, as Rebekka claimed?

Fear expanded in his chest at the image of her heavy with his child. That was what the Jaguar's choosing of a mate meant. But what if their offspring weren't pure of form?

Aryck pushed himself to go faster, trying to outrun the questions and the implications. Instead new ones found him.

Was he being tested by the ancestors? Or did they want to bind Rebekka to the Jaguars?

The pack knew of her existence only because of the ancestors. And while there were others who had the strength and ability to retrieve her, they'd ensured he was the one sent.

Deep inside his psyche the Jaguar purred in approval at the thought, absolutely convinced she was meant to be its mate. Fear lost its grip on Aryck's heart, though there was no time for further contemplation.

The wolves came into view. Five of them paced in their furred forms while their leader stood, legs apart in buckskin trousers with knives strapped to his thighs.

They were trespassing well within Jaguar lands. It was a challenge that wouldn't have gone unanswered previously. But coming on the heels of what happened to the cubs, their song containing such heartfelt entreaty allowed an opening for peace rather than violence.

"You dare much," Aryck said, meeting the Wolf's gaze and holding it.

The Wolf's lips tilted upward in a slight smile. "As did you when you crossed our lands with a human. Had it been left to me, you wouldn't have been allowed to pass without losing fur, blood, and possibly your life. But wiser heads prevailed. Or so it would seem. We have need of the healer."

So I was right, Aryck thought. Crossing Wolf lands he'd felt watched. He'd wondered at the ease of doing it. "Why do you need Rebekka?"

"A family group became suddenly ill. Seven of them in all, a mated pair with three of their adult offspring and two young pups. They returned to the village and began convulsing, then quickly lapsed into unconsciousness."

"Poison? Humans from the encampment have driven into Wolf lands."

"Our healer can find no trace of poison. And like your alpha, ours has decided to play a waiting game in the hopes the humans will leave after they've finished their salvage operation. We followed the tracks left by their vehicles but found no evidence they'd done anything but look for ruins to excavate."

The Wolf's answer felt and smelled like the truth to Aryck. He sought his father out mentally, replaying the conversation.

Turn the healer over to them if they will agree to two conditions. She must be returned to us after she is finished seeing to their sick. And both she and the Lion outcast must be safely escorted through Wolf territory when it is time for them to return to Oakland.

Three conditions, Aryck said, fighting to keep the growl from his mental voice. *I will accompany her when she goes to heal the Wolves.*

A long pause filled with disapproval followed. *Three*, his father agreed, voice terse.

Aryck conveyed his father's terms. The Wolf didn't hesitate to agree to them.

"Remain here," Aryck said. "I'll go get Rebekka."

He returned to the cabin given to Rebekka. Entering after a knock, a smile formed at encountering Caius's scent mixed with that of flowers.

Delicate purple blossoms drew him to the makeshift vase on the small table. He touched a petal with his fingertip, stroked its softness, and thought of Rebekka's skin before turning away and leaving the cabin.

Around back the fire in the pit no longer held heat, though the smell of sausage grease lingered. His smile faded when instead of heading in the direction of Phaedra's house or the small clearing serving as both formal and informal gathering place, Rebekka and the Tiger cub's scents went into the woods.

It wasn't dangerous, not this close to camp, but he didn't like her wandering with only the cub for protection. He followed, his frown turning into a pulling back of lips accompanied by a low growl when he realized their destination.

Canino. He should have anticipated Caius would seek Rebekka out and ask about the Tiger male.

Remembering all the times Canino had bumped and rubbed against Rebekka as they traveled set Aryck's teeth on edge. The Jaguar stirred, its desire to reach Rebekka melding with the man's.

Aryck slipped into a lope. With no human form, Canino had been settled temporarily near a small pond.

The path opened up and Aryck saw Rebekka. She was sitting with her face lifted to the sun and her eyes closed. Caius was draped over her lap in tiger form, biting and batting Canino's tail as it flicked back and forth.

A furious tide of emotion roared through Aryck. A swirling mix starting with the desire to mate but settling into jealousy as Jaguar and man both seethed.

He didn't dare give in to the urge to shift forms, though he couldn't stop himself from stalking toward her. On some level he knew it was perverse to want her to startle in guilt and jump to her feet, to hurriedly put distance between her and the Tiger. Without a human form, Canino wasn't competition.

But knowing it didn't change anything. Didn't erase the image of her lounging next to another male, a cub with them as though they were a mated pair.

It did nothing to calm him when she opened her eyes, offering a smile in greeting even as Canino rolled to his back and she casually scratched the big cat's chest. If not for Caius lying across her lap, Aryck would have picked her up bodily and hauled her off. He had to settle for a terse, "You're needed. Seven Wolves lie unconscious after suffering from convulsions."

Caius scrambled off her lap and Rebekka rose to her feet, hand going to the pocket of her pants to touch the journal in a gesture Aryck was well familiar with. "I'm ready," she said.

Two steps and she was within his reach. His fingers closed around her wrist and touching her, taking possession, soothed him, though not enough to keep him from meeting the Tiger's gaze and baring his teeth in warning.

Canino yawned.

Aryck nearly shifted.

"We need to hurry," Rebekka said, snapping his attention back to her.

The amusement lurking in her eyes broke the leash of his control. If she hadn't hurried to keep up with him, he would have dragged her onto the path and out of the Tigers' view. He managed a little more distance, so sound wouldn't carry and bring Canino and Caius running to investigate. Then he trapped her against a tree, his hand pinning hers above her head, holding her in an open, defenseless position as his mouth slammed down on hers.

He'd agonized since Phaedra ordered him away from the cabin. But instead of pining for him, seeking him out, Rebekka had sought the companionship of other males. It was infuriating, challenging—

It was an excuse to do the very things he'd been fantasizing about.

His tongue battled hers. His arm snaked around her waist, pulling her lower body tightly against his.

He ground into her. Rubbing his cock against her mound, her clit, until she smelled of pure, feminine arousal. Until she softened, whimpered, grew compliant and submissive.

The Jaguar urged him to take her to the ground. To use human fingers to rip and shred her clothing so it would never again be a barrier to mounting her, mating her.

The man was more than willing. Since Phaedra sent him away he'd relived those moments of having Rebekka beneath him, her thighs spread and her body receptive, needy.

He growled low in his throat, frustrated, not wanting to free her hands or to remove his arm from her waist. His mouth left hers and the growl deepened when she whispered, "The Wolves."

A flash of guilt made him bare his teeth. He remembered the urgency he'd felt, the fear he wouldn't get her to Jaguar lands in time to save the cubs.

"We'll finish this later," he said, nostrils flaring at her shiver of erotic fear and the look in her eyes that said she still needed to be convinced.

He stepped back but couldn't bring himself to release her completely, not when they would soon be in the presence of other males. Wolves. Enemies.

Rebekka allowed Aryck to lead her to where the Wolves waited. Her thoughts and emotions were in too much chaos to protest the hand shackling her wrist as though she were a prisoner—or a prized possession.

Her channel spasmed. No man had ever reacted to her the way Aryck did, as if she belonged to him and it was all he could do not to take her.

She shouldn't let it go further. Couldn't. She knew it, but the minute he touched her, her mind shut down and her body ruled.

They were wrong for each other. He was pure Were and she was a healer who lived in the outcast brothels. They had no future together.

You don't know that, a small internal voice claimed. *You're gaining allies. Phaedra. The parents of the Jaguar cubs. Aryck, whose father is alpha. Perhaps even the shaman and the Were ancestors.*

Hope fluttered through Rebekka's chest with the memory of Phaedra's words. *Nahuatl has spoken to the ancestors and your continued presence on Jaguar lands won't anger them.*

There'd been no talk of a time limit when she agreed to stay and share knowledge. And now, she was proving herself useful, an ambassador of sorts. What if—

A cold weight settled in her chest. There were other considerations besides giving in to lust or chasing the dream of having a husband and children, a true home.

"What do you know about the sick Wolves?" she asked.

"Little more than I already told you. A mated pair with three grown and two young pups returned to the Wolves' village and began convulsing. They quickly lapsed into unconsciousness. Poison was suspected but the Wolf healer found no trace of it. Their trespassing so boldly onto our lands means the healer can't save them and the alpha worries for his pack."

They reached the gathered Wolves a short time later and, despite their coming in peace and asking for her help, Rebekka couldn't suppress a small shiver at the sight of those in their furred form. Too many times she'd witnessed ferals running in packs and ripping humans apart in the red zone.

"You have nothing to fear," the man with them said, stepping forward. "I am Jael, the pack's enforcer. Your safety is guaranteed."

A smile played at the corners of his mouth as his gaze flicked between her and Aryck, glancing down to the possessive hold on her wrist. His nostrils flared, taking in the scent of desire that no doubt still clung to them. But his expression quickly grew somber. "We need to hurry. I'm not sure even now we will make it back in time."

Eighteen

AT least thirty Wolves milled around a home constructed of hides. All of them were in animal form. They bristled with hostility and suspicion, circled, some of the braver ones showing their teeth.

A glance from Jael sent them backing away. He opened the flap and stepped aside to allow Rebekka and Aryck to precede him.

It was roomy inside, large enough to house the family it belonged to. They lay clustered together. A man and a woman in human form, and from the looks of them Rebekka thought they were two of the adult offspring instead of the mated pair. The rest were furred.

The Wolf healer was there, along with a shaman. Both were crouched on the opposite side of the unconscious family.

The shaman wore a cape made of wolf hide. His hair was braided with beads made of bone. Scars marked his chest, as if a giant eagle had dug its talons through flesh and muscle and risen in flight with him, leaving him hanging, suspended in the air.

The drum he held between his knees was stretched hide trimmed with wolf fur and decorated with bone beads. He struck it with his fingertips, pounding out the steady rhythm of a heartbeat as the Jaguar elders had done in the presence of the dying cubs.

With matching yellow eyes, the Wolf shaman's face so closely resembled that of the healer next to him that Rebekka thought they must be brother and sister. Neither spoke as she knelt beside the female who'd been in human form when she slipped into unconsciousness.

The scent of urine and released bowels was strong, clinging to the sick, though they'd been washed by the healer.

Aryck crouched to Rebekka's right, Jael to her left.

"The family returned to their home in wolf form after being gone several days," Jael said. "If they were showing signs of illness, no one noticed. They weren't here long before the pups began convulsing. By the time our healer answered the call for help, only one of the adult offspring remained standing, and he wasn't able to shift to human form to answer her questions. He appeared disoriented. Within minutes he seized, then lapsed into unconsciousness. Since then there have been other seizures, milder than the first one."

Rebekka moved closer to the two pups. They were the same size. Twins. She had no experience with Were young other than the Jaguars, but based on their appearance she guessed they weren't much older than Caius when in human form.

The only hint they were alive came with the slight rise and fall of their chests. As she watched she saw pausing in their breathing, as if their bodies forgot it was necessary to sustain life.

A glance showed the same thing happening in the five adults, regardless of their form. *Something toxic*, she thought, *something affecting their nervous system*.

She was grateful for Aryck's presence next to her, for the heat radiating off his body as she lifted her hands, removing the amulet and handing it to him for safekeeping. Even braced for the frigid iciness, its blast was so intense she gasped.

This was plague. Virulent. Infectious. And despite the depth of their unconsciousness, the Wolves stirred, as if they would come to her, as if the virus itself knew her.

Horror and dread and gut-knotting guilt nearly overwhelmed her. The taste of disease filled her mouth.

She remembered the urchin's breath. His ice-cold lips against hers. *I've given you a piece of myself.*

Rebekka forced herself to touch the pup's torso. There was a sense of invasion, of hunger. It pulsed, built, grew more intense as she slid her hand upward, stopping when her palm rested on his forehead.

This was where the disease struck, attacking the brain, shutting down bodily functions. It was encephalitis, or something like it.

She slid her hand down, along the muzzle. The sense of being connected to the virus intensified, as if it was concentrated there in the saliva, pooled to spread to other entities instead of throughout the body.

Rebekka closed her eyes. Gathered her will and gave herself over to her gift.

She was spared the pain that had accompanied healing the Jaguar cubs and Aryck because the Wolf pup felt no pain. But she experienced the same sensation of being a tool, a conduit. Heat poured through her unchecked and uncontrolled, filling her chest and eradicating the numbing cold before traveling down her arm and through her hand.

This time the rush of power came with a greater awareness. She heard the shaman's drums, and in the distance an echo of them that made her think of the Were ancestors, of the eternal soul Aryck claimed lived among them. She *felt* as though a part of her slid into the pup, her gift and will only names she'd used to define a piece of her own soul.

Infection burned away in its path. Damaged tissue was repaired and restored.

The pup roused, fully healed. Jumped away from Rebekka and barked in alarm at finding her there.

The break in physical contact was like a dousing in frigid water. She turned her attention to the pup's twin, healing him then moving on to their adult siblings and parents.

If not for Jael's presence, the roused Wolves would have attacked. That was always the risk when healing the unconscious. A command from their enforcer and they took a human form.

Worry and guilt made Rebekka feel like vomiting. She shook, not just in the aftermath of using her gift, but with knowledge that there was sickness nearby. It stretched like an ethereal string across the distance. She could tell its direction by the cold spear lodged in her chest like a pointer set in a compass, the density of it warning there had to be a number of those infected by the virus.

Desperate, not wanting to believe she'd brought plague with her, Rebekka latched onto the hope this was just a random pocket of infectious disease, as the guardsman in the Barrens claimed happened from time to time. The diseased were east and north, instead of west, where Oakland was.

Tremors wracked her as she turned to Aryck. Her fingers clumsy in her haste to take the necklace from him.

Once it was in her possession the chill dissipated and the sense of disease disappeared. But their absence granted only a small measure of relief.

"What was wrong with them?" Jael asked.

"A virus attacked the brain. It was concentrated in their saliva. That's how it spreads."

In wolf form pups licked their parents' lips to elicit attention or food. Submissives did the same to more dominant animals.

They greeted and groomed one another. Shared prey and water. All of it having the potential to spread the virus.

If instead of going directly to their home, this family had stopped and interacted with others when they returned to their village, the entire pack would have died.

Rebekka's stomach cramped with nausea. She couldn't admit to knowing there were others who were sick, didn't dare risk letting them know there was a connection—even a tenuous one—between her and a plague. And yet she couldn't ignore it, letting it spread.

As much as she wished it was otherwise, there were no cures for this contained in the journal. Her mouth went dry as she scrambled to find the right words and the best way to convey the danger. She was spared by the Wolf healer, who also realized a risk to the pack remained.

The healer spoke to the oldest of the family members, a man with silver streaked through his hair. "Did you return because you felt the beginnings of illness, Gaetan?"

"No." Gaetan indicated one of the twin boys. "Until Jakob began convulsing, there was no warning anything was wrong."

"Your family became ill within minutes of each other. It makes me think you were exposed at the same time. And also that the incubation period doesn't vary, despite differences in weight or age."

The Wolf healer met Rebekka's eyes as if seeking her agreement. When Rebekka nodded, the healer asked Gaetan where the family had been.

"We hunted to the east, in the meadow near Bear lands," Gaetan said, naming the direction Rebekka felt the sickness coming from. "We ate rabbits as we caught them. At dawn yesterday we took down an elk cow while wearing our fur."

Gaetan frowned. "She was easy prey. Not something a Wolf questions. We fed and slept and fed, none of us changing forms. When little of the carcass remained, I decided to return home, thinking it had been a good outing for the pups."

Rebekka's throat grew tight with the remembered scene from the Barrens. "In the city, those in power burn the bodies of anyone or anything they believe might carry an infectious disease."

"A wise precaution," Jael said. "How many were in the elk herd, Gaetan?"

"Ten."

"It's likely they are all infected. If there's a chance they carry something that might wipe out the pack, then we have no choice but to kill them all and burn the bodies."

"Let me try to heal them first," Rebekka said.

Jael turned toward her. "You and Aryck may accompany us, but I make no promises. I won't put the pack or its members at risk."

THERE was little left of the elk carcass Gaetan and his family had feasted on. Jael ordered it burned where it lay at the edge of the meadow, leaving two Wolves behind to carry out the task.

None of the Wolves was in animal form. Like Jael, each carried knives at their thighs. The blades were augmented by other weapons: crossbows, regular bows, wrist-braced slingshots, long spears with barbed steel points, and several rifles.

An hour after leaving the kill carcass, they found another dead elk. Scavengers were already busy at work.

Meat bees and flies buzzed around and on it. Two turkey buzzards hopped away, not taking flight until the Wolves were close enough to make them prey.

It was impossible to tell how the animal died, but there was a single set of wolf tracks leading away from it. Jael's eyes met those of a man who looked several years younger than him and shared a family resemblance.

Brother, Rebekka thought, seeing something pass between the two of them. She turned her head and caught Aryck watching the exchange with interest, guessed, like he and his father, the Wolves communicated telepathically.

A signal from Jael resumed the hunt. They moved steadily upward, toward a ridge.

Away from the meadow the land grew increasingly dry and hot. Unlike the dense pockets of forest surrounding the Jaguar and Wolf homes, the soil beneath Rebekka's feet was fragile, supporting the growth of scrub and manzanita and very little else.

As they crested the ridge she saw a copse of trees in the canyon below, its location indicating a spring. They climbed downward, traveling on narrow, well-worn paths.

Rebekka was fairly certain they were moving east and north. She felt sick with the knowledge that if she removed the amulet, they wouldn't need to travel at all; the elk would come.

Guilt tried to work its way into her consciousness. She beat it back. *I'm doing what I can*, she told herself. Nothing good would come of revealing her secret.

Her memories circled repeatedly. From urchin visits to the encounter with her father, to the things the Wainwright witches had told her and given in payment, to what her mother had revealed. Her father might be demon, but the urchin was clearly his enemy, and an enemy to the Weres as well.

The journal in her pocket was a weight against her thigh, making her think of the Jaguar cubs, who would have died without the knowledge contained in it. Just as her father had once saved her from rape and sent her to the Were brothels, he'd been responsible for the protection offered by the amulet and the deepening of her gift because of it. He was allied with the Wainwright witches. He had to be. Was it such a stretch to believe he meant for her to be here now?

A glance at Aryck and a flutter went through Rebekka's chest. Or was she only looking for a reason to give in to the feelings she'd experienced since the first time she truly saw him as a man?

He turned his head then, meeting her eyes. Heat came. Instantly. Flushing through her with memories of waking beneath him, of the promise in his eyes when he'd pinned her against the tree.

She dropped her gaze. His hand stroked down the length of her spine in a silent message. *Later.*

Prints in the mud around a spring indicated the herd had been there. No one drank.

They kept going, coming to what was little more than a watering hole. There were additional tracks, including those made by a heavy vehicle.

Aryck knelt down to study a partial human shoeprint at the edge of the water, glanced up to the spot where dirt and crushed scrub told a tale of vehicles stopping and turning around. "The humans from the encampment were here."

"Several times," Jael said. "They've explored other areas as well. This is the deepest they've come into our lands."

Aryck considered his father's suspicions when it came to the Wolves and the human interlopers. There had long been distrust between the various predatory groups. Some of it was rooted in history, and in the case of the Lions and Hyenas, by genetics, but much of the pressure came from territorial disputes.

Pure animals were held in check naturally. Their numbers rose and fell according to what the land could sustain.

They starved when there was not enough food. Females didn't go into heat, or the offspring they gave birth to were so weak they didn't survive into adulthood.

It was not the same for Weres, especially those belonging to the dominant groups. Having the ability to reason put them at an advantage. Being able to shift form gave them an edge. It also meant their numbers could increase radically, and often did when females got pregnant while in their animal forms.

Wolves could give birth to upward of fourteen pups. It was perhaps one reason werewolves had starred in so many human stories well before the supernaturals made their presence known.

The predatory Weres controlled the size of their packs by splitting and taking over new territory, driving away those in possession of the land they wanted or—if necessary—fighting, reducing their numbers in the way humans had always done, through warfare.

For the same reasons predatory Weres did not associate with those who became prey in their animal forms, they did not intermingle much with other predators. Doing so increased the risk of interbreeding and, with it, of family alliances being formed that would lead to divisiveness in the pack should the two groups go to war. It was easier to kill a stranger than someone you'd shared food with or seen with their children and mate. And with prey, better not to realize after the fact that you'd eaten a friend.

Aryck glanced at Rebekka. He could still feel the imprint of her body against his, could still taste the kiss they'd shared. It took only the thought of her to make his cock start to harden.

Days ago he would not have believed such a thing was possible. Days ago he'd recoiled when the Jaguar called her mate.

A question slid into his consciousness, similar to the one that had risen as he ran to intercept the trespassing Wolves. Had the ancestors revealed Rebekka's existence and sent him to her for a greater reason than just the healing of the cubs?

The Wolves had let her pass through their lands. Such a thing would only happen if the alpha allowed it.

Their alpha might have given permission on the off chance there were old weapons on Wolf land. But considering it now, Aryck realized it was far more likely the alpha had allowed them to cross because the shaman advised it.

Without Rebekka's presence the Wolf pack would have been eradicated. And because of her, he was here, among them, sharing a hunt with their enforcer and contemplating alliance.

Not just alliance, Aryck admitted to himself, but claiming Rebekka as his mate. He was rapidly coming to believe the ancestors favored it. Or maybe the fear of being made outcast stood no chance against his desire to couple with her.

He rose from where he was crouched at the edge of the waterhole. Coming on the heels of what had happened to the Jaguar cubs, and the way the virus acted, striking all the members of Gaetan's family without regard to age or body mass, it was hard not to be suspicious of the humans in the encampment, who'd suddenly gone quiet after making their presence known by filling the night with the sound of gunfire.

"So far the only sick or dead have been Wolves and elk," Aryck said. "I would have expected to find deer carcasses as well, possibly coyote and fox."

Jael caressed the knife hilt against his thigh. "I've been thinking the same."

With a minute wave of his hand, Aryck indicated the footprint at the edge of the water. "There's no proof the humans in the encampment are behind this but it seems foolish to ignore the possibility. This incursion into Were lands might just be the beginning of their plans for our territory.

"Without knowing who is behind the foray and what kind of power they wield in the human world, all of us are at a disadvantage. Not sharing what we learn or uniting against the threat adds to our disadvantage. What we do, or don't do, will ultimately affect all of us. One group of us attacking might well be answered by declaring open season on all of us. Yet if the humans are somehow behind this virus . . ."

"Your analysis is a good one." Jael glanced at Rebekka. "The healer could be sent to Coyote lands. She could visit with the humans and gather information. They'd allow her into the encampment."

Aryck bared his teeth. "No."

Jael's lips quirked up in a small smile but then he stilled, eyes growing distant for an instant before saying, "My brother has found a dead Wolf."

The mental communication confirmed Aryck's suspicions about Jael. Like him, the Wolf was an enforcer of the alpha's line.

"A pack member?" Rebekka asked.

"Once," Jael said, his voice not inviting further questioning, though it was unneeded between Wolf and Jaguar.

Jael pulled one of the knives from its sheath and leaned over, using the blade to sever a thin manzanita branch. He stripped it and carved something on it in several places before stepping closer to Aryck and allowing him to see the symbols. "These warn against drinking the water here."

The gesture spoke louder than words. Rarely did different groups share what counted as their written language.

Jael tossed the marker to one of the other Wolves. "Make several more and place them around the watering hole, then catch up to us." To Aryck he said, "Let's continue on. After the elk herd is located and dealt with I will speak to the alpha about the possibility of a formal alliance. In the past I wouldn't have considered approaching him with such a suggestion, but I think perhaps he will be more receptive now, especially given he has let both a human and a Jaguar come among us."

Miles later they found the remains of two Elk. Aryck's hand curled around Rebekka's arm at the sight of them.

The bodies were fresh. Their tracks and faces pointed in the direction of the Wolf village, as if they were retracing their earlier route. There was no obvious cause of death, but the urine-soaked ground and scattered feces hinted at convulsions.

He'd known from the outset they were tracking a mixed herd, a small family of Were traveling with pure animals for added safety. He hadn't wanted to upset Rebekka by talking about it, not when there was every possibility the Wolves would be forced to kill all those in the herd rather than let any of them escape to spread the virus. He'd hoped they carried the virus without being affected by it in the same way as the Wolves. The dead in front of him said otherwise.

Jael left men to burn the bodies. And though no one spoke openly about them being Were, the Wolves bristled with emotion. Fear and rage and worry.

Aryck allowed another mile of steep climb to pass before he left Rebekka's side and moved alongside Jael's. Keeping his voice low, he asked, "How far until we reach the Elk village?"

"Close, I think"—there was a brief hesitation—"given the smell."

Aryck nodded. The breeze carried the scent of death.

They approached a place where the trail forked. Left went toward Bear territory. Right toward Jaguar, passing through Coyote lands to get there.

Protectiveness rose in Aryck, the desire to shield Rebekka from what most likely lay ahead of them, not just the dead but the disposal of them. The Wolves would have to burn the bodies of entire families, including children, some of them in human form, all of them infected when those traveling with the herd of animals returned home.

Steps away from the branching trail, Aryck said, "Rebekka and I will wait here."

"I'll send someone to tell you what we find."

Aryck stopped as the Wolves continued on. He took Rebekka's wrist as she reached him, forcing her to a halt. "Jael will let us know if you're needed. We'll wait here."

"No," she said, fighting his grip. Jerking and pulling. Finally trying to peel his fingers away.

He countered by wrapping his arms around her and holding her tightly against him. She stiffened, resisting still. Her heart thundering, pounding like fists against his chest.

"Let me go. Please. It could be too late by the time someone comes back to get me."

Aryck gave her the truth with lips touched to her forehead. "It's already too late."

Her hands maneuvered between them, pushing against his chest in a continued effort to escape. "You don't know that."

He rubbed his cheek against hers. "Think how quickly the virus affected the Wolves. They succumbed at almost the same time and were all near death. If not for the shaman's drum holding them to the living world, they would probably have crossed to the shadowlands before we got there."

She stilled with understanding, making the very connection he'd meant to spare her from. "The last two dead Elk were Were."

"Yes."

A tremor went through her, a soul-deep shudder. Her hands slid down and around his waist, arms hugging him, drawing comfort as she softened against him.

Mine, he thought, accepting it fully, completely. Determining to act on it as soon as they were back on Jaguar lands.

It didn't take long for the smell of smoke and burning flesh to reach him. He set Rebekka away from him just before a Wolf arrived, one whose scent was close enough to Jael and his brother's to mark him as a sibling or cousin.

"There is no need for a healer," the Wolf said. "Fire will bring Bears, if they're not already watching. Jael said to tell you he believes the Bear enforcer will also see the wisdom of approaching his alpha about forming an alliance."

It's a first step, Aryck thought. He couldn't ask for more or even guarantee his father would support the idea. "I'll speak to the alpha when I return to camp."

The Wolf focused on Rebekka. "The pack owes you a great debt. We will not forget it."

Nineteen

DUTY and desire warred inside Aryck as soon as he stepped foot on Jaguar lands. He should go directly to camp to discuss the possibility of alliance with his father. Even now he should be reaching out mentally to the alpha and sharing all that had happened since going to the Wolves' village. But rather than doing either, he detoured, taking a path leading to a dried-up spring.

Anticipation grew with each step, desire rebuilding. His heart beat fast and hard in his chest, like drums around the fire, building to a crescendo. Beside him Rebekka was quiet, somber, lost in thoughts he could easily guess at. But for the Were, life went on. There was little use in grieving over the Elk.

She'd saved seven Wolves from death. That was all time allowed.

He led her to a place where sandstone had eroded to become a soft bed, then halted, drawing her into his arms. She trembled but didn't resist him, didn't turn her face away when he slowly lowered his.

Brushing his mouth against hers, he said, "If not for you, the entire pack would have died."

His words had the opposite effect of what he'd intended. She withdrew emotionally, stiffening in his arms and looking away.

Tenderness filled him. He understood. She was a healer and a human, far removed from the harsh truth of survival among pure Weres.

She couldn't know that if other groups had learned of sickness spreading through the Wolf pack, they would have acted, slaughtering the Wolves either to stop the spread of disease or to gain control of the territory. He didn't doubt she'd witnessed terrible things in the brothel, but nothing as horrible as genocide and war.

He pressed kisses to Rebekka's neck, pausing to suck, to take the tender skin between his teeth. The desire to mark her strengthened as his cock hardened.

Her ear drew him upward and he captured the lobe, teased it with his tongue. Sucked. He was rewarded by the softening of her body, a melting against him accompanied by the heated scent of awakening desire.

"Let your worries go," he murmured, sliding his hand up her side and over, taking possession of her breast as his tongue explored her ear.

Her moan and the jolt he felt go through her were all the encouragement he needed. He tightened the arm around her waist, pulled her against the thick ridge of his erection as his palm glided over her nipple until it hardened and she began grinding against his cock.

He abandoned her ear, needing to claim her mouth and thrust into the wet heat of it with his tongue in a prelude to doing the same to slick nether lips. He wanted to taste her passion, to mark himself with her scent before sheathing his cock inside her.

Satisfaction purred through him at the look of desire in her eyes, at the way her tongue darted out, wetting a mouth that parted in anticipation.

A spike of pure heat shot through his penis as he imagined those same lips on his shaft, caressing his length before wrapping around his cock head and slowly sucking him deep into her mouth.

With a rumbled growl he captured her lips, his hand leaving her breast long enough to jerk her shirt out of her pants, then slide upward, his palm against smooth skin until it encountered her bra.

He pushed under the unwelcome barrier, wondering why she would wear such a thing. She was so lush, so feminine, so utterly desirable. There was no reason to hide it with layers of clothing.

Their tongues twined, tangled, slid against each other, stoking the fires of lust. Pleasure whipped through him when her fingers glanced over the back of his neck before spearing through his hair, gripping him, holding him to her as if she never wanted the kiss to end.

Their breaths mingled, becoming one. Aryck closed his eyes, sinking into the moment, the pleasure of having her in his arms.

Pliant. Willing. Responding to him.

There was no doubt, only desire, a feeling of rightness. This was meant to be. He'd been a fool to fight the Jaguar's claim, to waste time fighting the attraction she held for him.

He captured Rebekka's nipple between his fingers, rolled and tugged and squeezed until her whimper brought the Jaguar to life, not in separation but in full integration, in a dominant demand to feel their mate's body naked beneath them.

Aryck forced himself to abandon her lips. "Undress for me," he whispered, ensuring her compliance by recapturing her earlobe, sucking, feeling her breast swell and nipple harden further.

Heat poured into Rebekka, engulfed her. She wanted him, shook with the need to accept the pleasure he offered.

But what would happen afterward? For there to be a future together, he had to know about the witches and their talk of a coming war that would change the world yet again. He needed to know about her demon father, and that she'd been created for a purpose. She had to tell him about the urchin. Reveal the full truth of her gift.

Desire ebbed with images of the burning pallets in Oakland and the dead Elk here. As if sensing her retreat, Aryck said, "Life goes on."

He renewed the sensual assault on her nipple. Tugging, squeezing, the rhythm sending flutter after flutter through her womb, making her grow swollen and wet with need, ready again as he repeated his command. "Undress for me."

The light filtered in through the trees, denying her the protection of the darkness. It was only a phantom sensation, she knew it wasn't real, and yet she felt the tattoo as if it were raised on her skin. It brought a more immediate fear, a vulnerability she'd lived with far longer than worries about her father or her gift.

What if Aryck saw it and knew what it meant? What if he turned away in disgust? Or even after she told him the truth, his eyes continued to hold doubt? Or what if it didn't matter to him for the same reason the prostitutes in the brothel sought one another out for pleasure or comfort without forming permanent ties?

He hadn't spoken of a future together. Hadn't indicated he wanted anything more than physical release.

"I'm not sure I can do this," she said, though her body seemed determined to make it a lie.

Her hands remained in his hair. Her pelvis continued to grind against his, each strike of her stiffened clit against his erection sending a jolt of pure ecstasy through her.

"I'll help you then," he murmured, making her womb clench with one final thrust of his tongue into her ear before he stepped back far enough that his hands could undo the buttons of her shirt.

He started at the top, eyes becoming molten as each button was freed to reveal another few inches of skin. It unnerved her at the same time it made her feel incredibly feminine, desirable in a way she'd never viewed herself as being.

She was a healer. That was how she'd defined herself for so long. It obliterated the label of prostitute's daughter and helped keep her own sexuality at bay.

But now she found she didn't want that any longer. She wanted to be more than a healer.

Aryck pushed her shirt off her shoulders and down. It fell away, leaving her standing in bra and pants. He'd seen her wearing nothing but her panties and yet there was something erotic in appearing before him like this, her nipples hard points against the thin material of the bra.

Nervousness made her lick her lips. The way he zeroed in on her mouth, his expression growing hungry as his hand moved to the front of his pants to grip his erection sent a thrill through her, a rush of feminine power.

It gave her the courage to take off her shoes and pants, then step forward to grasp his waistband. "Your turn," she said, arousal soaking her panties and wetting her inner thighs as she remembered him the night before in the moments between shifting, when he was a cat in human form, expecting admiration. "I want to see you again."

He captured her hand, replacing the one at the front of his pants with hers. She blushed despite being no stranger to nudity or the male form. In the brothels she'd undressed prostitutes when they couldn't do it for themselves, had handled their sexual organs with emotional detachment.

Aryck brushed the back of his hand against her heated cheek, a curious, speculative expression on his face. It lasted only until she traced the laces at the front of his pants.

His features went taut. She licked her lips again and felt his cock pulse beneath her fingertips.

Slowly, partly in nervousness and partly in anticipation, she loosened the leather strips holding the pants closed. Her labia grew more flushed and swollen, her clit harder. She was intensely aware of them, of the need centered there. Throbbing like a second heartbeat.

The laces gave, loosening the pants so they dropped to the ground, freeing Aryck's penis. Exposing it. Revealing a wet tip and pulled-back sheath, the heavy testicles beneath, framed by powerful thighs.

Everything about him was masculine perfection, a sensual beauty of sleek muscle and innate strength combined with the absolute confidence of a bold, dangerous predator.

His cock grew fuller under her perusal. Another drop of arousal beaded on its tip.

He took her hand once again, guiding it to his erection. His hand remained there, covering hers.

Without the material of his pants, she closed her fist around him, felt the thrill of his low moan all the way to her toes. He leaned in and recaptured her lips, grasped her hair and held her to him as he thrust his tongue into her mouth, the hand covering hers moving up and down on his shaft.

It was so decadent, something belonging to fantasies she barely acknowledged having. He was smooth steel and velvety softness combined.

On an upstroke she rubbed her thumb over the wet tip, reveled in the way his hips jerked. Then jerked again when she did it a second time.

His hand left her hair, sending pleasure through her as he caressed her back, seeming to pause at each vertebra. He lingered at the base of her spine, fingers sliding into her panties, dancing over the spot where the cleft between her buttocks began.

Her ass cheeks clamped together instinctively, and he ended their kiss with a soft laugh. "I don't want you that way, not for the first time, anyway."

He leaned in and flicked her earlobe with his tongue, whispered, "But in the end, I'll have you every way it's possible for a male to have his female."

Rebekka's heart stuttered as hope slammed into it, tripped into a racing beat until she realized the only promise inherent in his words was that he would do to her what a man could do to any female, whether she belonged to him or not. It wasn't a declaration of love or an acknowledgment of a shared future. It was a promise of carnal exploration and pleasure, nothing more.

A hint of pain snaked through her chest, and yet despite it she didn't want to stop what they were doing. She wanted more. She wanted to feel him deep inside her, his body joined with hers. But going that far risked her heart and she'd guarded it too long to casually expose it now.

She rubbed her cheek against his, glad she couldn't see his face as she said, "I'm not ready to couple with you." *Yet*. She heard the unspoken word as clearly as if she'd said it.

His tongue slid into her ear then retreated. "There's more to lovemaking than the act of fucking."

Her heart did a slow roll in her chest. Was it lovemaking for him?

She didn't have the courage to ask, or to face all the additional questions that would come after that one. There couldn't be talk of a future without a discussion of the past.

She didn't resist when he maneuvered them to the sand. Stripping her bra away before pressing her to the ground and positioning himself above her.

The heat of his cock burned through the thin barrier of her panties. Rebekka moaned at the feel of it sliding up and down along her clit. She shivered with the renewed thrust of his tongue against hers, answered each parry with one of her own.

Her hands roamed over smooth muscle and firm buttocks. Repeatedly returning to the silky strands of his hair and refusing to let the kisses end until he shifted his weight onto an elbow with a growl.

His hand went to his cock then, tightened at the base of his shaft as if fighting to keep from coming, and the knowledge she was responsible emboldened Rebekka. She became the aggressor, forcing his hand away from his heated penis so her fingers could curl around it.

She captured his tongue with her lips. Sucked hard and deep in a sensual battle she was determined to win.

Pleasure swept through her when he lost control. Arousal poured from her slit as he began thrusting, fucking through the tight clamp of her fist with steady, desperate movements.

She took his moans, swallowed them as his penis jerked, wet her belly and chest with his seed. He shuddered above her for long moments, finally breaking the seal of their lips, his breath coming in fast pants as he pulled from her grip and lay on his side next to her.

His eyes glittered as they traveled down to where he'd spent himself on her. His face was flushed, not with embarrassment but with satisfaction. "To steal your earlier words," he said. "Your turn."

Her toes curled as he leaned in, mouth latching onto a nipple. A whimper escaped when his hand cupped her mound, rubbing, pressing in time to the pull of his lips.

She lifted her hips with each of his sucks, didn't think to protest as his hand slid beneath the waistband of her panties. A shudder went through her when his fingers grazed her slit, collecting the moisture there before going to her clit. A cry followed as he stroked the tiny head, tormenting her as she'd tormented him.

Her channel clenched, sending more arousal to soak her panties. She felt the press of teeth against nipple, arched her back at the implied threat of a bite.

He clamped down harder, to the point pain and pleasure blended, his fingers concentrating on her engorged clit, finding all the ways she liked to be touched.

Her movements became frenzied. Her heart raced at a dizzying pace while her lungs struggled to get enough air.

She grew desperate for relief, to feel his fingers slide into her opening and find the spot deep inside her that would make her come.

Her moans turned into fevered pleas, and finally a breathless "Please."

His touches became more devastating, more demanding. He intended to make her as helpless in desire as she'd made him.

His mouth went to the breast he'd been neglecting. Biting and sucking the nipple, keeping her hovering on the edge of climax as he gave it the same attention as the first.

Her hands roamed his back. Without conscious thought her nails dug into his flesh, raked over his skin.

It inflamed him. His head jerked up. His eyes blazed. He brought his face inches away from hers as he fucked into her with his fingers, striking her clit with each thrust.

She gave herself over to sensation as he watched. His mouth covering hers at the moment of release, swallowing the sounds of her pleasure as she'd swallowed his.

Twenty

AS Rebekka dressed she felt shy, uncertain. Defenseless against physical desire and her growing feelings for Aryck.

She couldn't lie to herself. Only his need to return to camp and discuss forming an alliance kept them from doing more than they'd already done.

Despite her internal arguments against it, when he touched her intimately, her resolve not to give in weakened dangerously. They needed to talk.

She braved a glance at Aryck. He seemed aloof, withdrawn, his thoughts already on other things.

Aryck felt Rebekka's eyes on him and looked up. Uncertainty clung to her like a shroud, making him want to close the distance between them and rip it away.

Was she regretting what had happened between them? Already thinking about leaving him and returning to Oakland with Levi?

The Jaguar's silent snarl mirrored the man's. His scent coated her belly and chest in a primitive warning to all others that she belonged to him. Hers marked him as well, as did the shallow scratches on his back.

Unable to stop himself, he took the few steps needed to reach her. There was a hint of resistance when he pulled her into his arms.

The Jaguar reacted badly, thrashing to separate life with a desire for Rebekka's complete acceptance and submission, demanding Aryck take the skin at the base of her neck between his teeth and clamp down hard enough to leave visible proof of her claiming.

Aryck fought the urge, already thinking it would be best to bathe before going into camp rather than to openly acknowledge what had happened between them. He needed to speak with his father, to Nahuatl, and, if necessary, the elders, not just about the possibility of alliance among the Weres but allowing Rebekka to remain in their lands and belong to the pack as his mate.

It could be done. Perhaps it *had* been done deep in the past, in a story the elders held in their memories but chose not to share.

Frustration rumbled through him at not being able to speak openly about the future. To make promises. The Jaguar threatened to claw its way through his gut at the possibility the needs of the outcasts in the brothels might hold the greater power over her.

Aryck's arms tightened on her. If she thought to return to Oakland, then she was mistaken.

He nuzzled her ear and felt a shiver of renewed desire go through her. It soothed the Jaguar.

"We've got to get back to camp," he told her. "I need to speak to my father."

Her arms went around his waist and her body melded to his. She turned her head, pressing a soft kiss to his cheek. "I know."

He couldn't release her without taking her lips fully. Expressing his hopes and desires in the only way he could at the moment.

She softened further against him. Yielded to the thrust of his tongue. Answered the command of his two souls that she accept, submit.

Her response calmed the Jaguar's wild emotion even as she roused the man's desire to take her fully, hardening his cock in readiness for it. He ended the kiss, released all but her hand, unwilling to let her go completely as they headed toward camp.

"Jael said something about a human en—"

"No!" he said, stopping, tugging her into his arms again and touching his nose to hers. Letting her feel the full weight of an enforcer's stare. "It's not for you to worry about. The Wolf baited me. Nothing more. He'd no more allow you to go to the encampment than I would. You're too valuable to risk, and the humans there aren't to be trusted. Only caution on the part of the alphas has prevented us from attacking and driving them from our lands already."

"They're salvaging?"

"It appears so. We're playing a waiting game, hoping they'll leave when they've found what they came for or found nothing of value."

He tilted his head, giving in to the temptation to kiss her once, twice, a third time to reduce the sting of the words that had to follow. "This is Were business, Rebekka. Don't interfere in it."

She stiffened and pulled out of his arms, though she didn't try to take her hand from his. Jaguar and man both churned in discomfort, hating even the tiniest of her emotional retreats. In an effort to recapture the closeness, Aryck said, "Tell me about your life in Oakland."

Rebekka shot him a look, part disbelieving and part hopeful. But her voice contained pure challenge. "I live among Were outcasts."

The tightness in his chest was immediate. The subject of outcasts was not one a Were took lightly. He managed to keep any hint of it from his voice. "Tell me," he coaxed, squeezing her hand.

She did. Describing the various brothels and talking about the vice lord, Allende, who offered protection, but at a price. Speaking of the things that were an everyday part of her life, the injuries she healed. The red zone, the maze that no longer stood. Oakland itself.

Aryck found himself growing more worried. Not just at the horrors she saw daily and the danger inherent in her life among humans, but at how much she might believe she was needed by those the ancestors had judged. How difficult it might be for Rebekka to leave her world for his.

It was almost a relief when they neared camp and one of the more private bathing spots. He wanted a few minutes of additional pleasure with her before pack business claimed his attention, a few minutes to convince her body, if not her mind, of how much better a life spent with him would be over the one spent healing outcasts.

He stopped at where the trail split away, carried Rebekka's hand to his chest, and rubbed it against his nipple. "This path leads to a stream with a pool. We can bathe together before I leave you at your cabin."

She was instantly nervous, shy again despite the intimacy they'd already shared. "I don't have a towel. Unlike you, I can't change form to shake myself dry or walk around naked until the air does it for me."

Aryck laughed, taking her hand to his mouth and nibbling on it. "No one would object if you wore only skin. In fact, the males would enjoy it."

He would enjoy it. And while the Jaguar wouldn't tolerate another touching her, having others admire her lush form only added to the satisfaction that would come with claiming her fully. "If you insist on a towel, we can come back."

Her eyelashes lowered to hide her expression, but she didn't say no. They continued on, the trail ending at the clearing behind the alpha's cabin.

Guilt intruded at once again putting desire before duty, his subconscious choosing this route so he wouldn't fail his pack. If he slipped into the water naked with her, he wouldn't be able to leave until she was fully his.

He realized it would be better for her to bathe without him, for him to wash the most telling scents from his skin elsewhere, then find his father. Aryck stopped, reluctantly releasing her hand. At her questioning look, he said, "You tempt me to forget my responsibilities. I'll join you when I can."

He pointed to an opening several yards to the left. "Take that path, then the first right, followed by the third, and you'll end up just beyond the cooking pit of your cabin."

"If I return to the pool, will there be others bathing there at this time of day?"

"You'll know before you reach the deep portion of the stream. It's a place lovers go and, as you have reason to know, Jaguars aren't quiet in their passion."

She took a step away from him and he found he couldn't let her leave without one last kiss. He snagged her wrist, halting and turning her in a smooth movement, placing his mouth on hers just as the cabin door opened.

His father's dismay slammed into him through their mental link. Melina's low, savage growl reached his ears.

The Jaguar's hackles rose in reaction to the threat it contained. Aryck ended the kiss and released Rebekka, noting the discomfort in her eyes when they flicked to his father and Melina before she made her escape.

He hadn't wanted to so flagrantly defy his father's wishes when it came to Rebekka, but there was nothing to do about it now. The scent of sex clung to his skin. The scratches marking his back screamed she'd been lying beneath him.

"Leave us," Koren told Melina.

She glowered at Aryck, eyes burning with seething emotion, making him fear for Rebekka's safety. "Harm Rebekka and you'll meet me in the challenge circle."

"The healer's safety has been guaranteed while she's on Jaguar lands," Koren said, adding weight to Aryck's warning, though he tempered it by adding, "She'll be gone in a day or two, as soon as Phaedra gains the knowledge contained in the journal."

Melina gave a slight nod, acknowledging Koren's concession to her pride, and what Aryck thought was his father's continued support of her as the female who would bear his grandchildren.

Never. Aryck found it difficult to believe he'd once wanted Melina even as an outlet for physical release.

She stalked away, gone from his thoughts even before she disappeared from sight.

"You coupled with the healer," Koren said, dark anger seeping into his voice.

As enforcer, Aryck couldn't claim it was none of his father's business. And because Rebekka was human, it mattered all the more.

"Not yet."

"Not ever then. I didn't lose my mate to have you throw away your own life by ending up an outcast."

It was a low, ruthless blow. Guilt and fury rushed into Aryck with the reminder his mother had died giving birth to him. His fingers flexed, the Jaguar sheathing and unsheathing phantom claws at the savageness of the verbal attack. "It won't come to that."

"So you're a shaman now?" Koren asked, his expression unchanging, his body posture all but inviting Aryck to challenge him physically so he could demonstrate why he was alpha and his will was pack law.

"I believe the ancestors want her to remain here, as my mate."

Koren laughed. "You're thinking with your cock."

Aryck snarled, kicking off his shoes in unconscious preparation for a fight. "Without the ancestors' intervention we wouldn't have known of her existence. There were others who could have been sent to retrieve her, but it was me who had to go."

"You're rationalizing so you can fuck a female you know is wrong for you. In this you're my son."

"My choice is not the same as yours. Look at the value Rebekka has already brought to the pack. The cubs are healed. The Wolves acknowledge a debt to her. There is more."

"Things as enforcer you should have shared hours ago?" Koren said, his voice silky menace. "But instead you failed in your duties, became sidetracked by lush curves and soft skin, by a slick channel and an alluring scent."

Aryck bridled at the charge but couldn't deny it, not when moments ago he'd felt the sting of guilt in the wake of nearly giving in to the temptation to delay further. Only his pride had kept him from seducing Rebekka earlier, taking her with his cock instead of his fingers after she made him lose control and come with only her hand. Had she been willing initially, he would have coupled with her repeatedly, not returning to camp until they were both sated.

"I told you how it was with your mother. In the end my lack of control cost me. I'll protect you from yourself to the extent I can. From this moment on, I assume the mantle of responsibility for the healer and forbid you from going near her while she is on our lands."

The Jaguar screamed to life, flashing in Aryck's eyes. He didn't try to suppress it or hide the truth from his father, that man and beast were unified in their desire for Rebekka as a mate. "And when she leaves our territory?"

"Then you will have to decide how badly you want her. Whether you desire her enough to follow her to Oakland and lose your position as enforcer, and very likely your place in the pack."

The threat shocked Aryck, making it feel as though ice coursed through his bloodstream and settled in his core. His mind froze for an instant but thawed with the recognition of scent. His father's worry blended with the sharp tang of anger and frustration.

"I intend to speak to Nahuatl."

It couldn't be forbidden.

Koren shrugged, and his emotions fell away. "Do so. If the ancestors have plans for the healer, then they will make them known. Until then your first duty is as enforcer. Or do you wish to step aside and let another claim the position?"

"No."

"Then tell me what happened in Wolf territory."

They'd reached a place of both stalemate and compromise. Aryck accepted the opportunity to move past the issue of Rebekka—for now.

"It'll be easier to show you," he said, and, with the touch of his mind to his father's, condensed the important images and conveyed them in a brief stream of information.

When it was done Koren said, "You did well to take the initiative and suggest the possibility of alliance. I will speak to Nahuatl and Phaedra first, then to the elders individually, sharing this information with them and drawing on their memories. Take a few others and swear them to secrecy. Search our lands for signs disease has spread here, and for evidence the humans might be responsible for what happened in Wolf territory. Then see if you can draw the attention of the Hyena and Coyote enforcers, and if they, too, might support alliance."

It meant a delay in speaking with Nahuatl about Rebekka. It meant his father would speak to the shaman first.

Aryck pushed away his uneasiness that the ancestors would be influenced or change their minds before he could make his case to the shaman and ask for Nahuatl's intercession with them, or the guidance necessary for him to face them himself in a Petitioner's Rite.

He glanced in the direction Rebekka had gone. When he returned, he'd speak to Nahuatl and, if it was still necessary afterward, get word to her about his father ordering him to stay away from her. There was no time now. More was at stake here than his desire to take her as a mate. "I'll leave immediately."

Twenty-one

REBEKKA wrung her panties and bra out one last time before turning toward the place where the rest of her clothing hung draped over low branches. She glanced around, feeling self-conscious at the prospect of leaving the deep pool.

Her hand slid over her belly, trailing heat in its wake. Her channel clenched as she remembered the hot spray of semen jetting from Aryck's cock, the look of sublime pleasure on his face, and the heady feeling that had come from making him lose control.

Her clit stiffened with the memories and she played with it, stroking the underside and across the tip, imagining it was Aryck's fingers, Aryck's tongue.

A blush stole up her neck and across her cheeks as she pictured him between her thighs, black hair whispering across her skin, his mouth doing exquisite things and making her feel feminine and desirable.

Twice she'd told him no.

She wasn't sure she would give him the same answer the next time.

Was it love?

Or simply lust?

Was there any way to know for sure without risking her heart? Without yielding her body?

Her fingers left her clit and settled on the tattoo, tracing it without looking down at the ugly mark. Her heart thundered at the very prospect of revealing it and witnessing his reaction.

She'd half hoped Aryck would join her in the water, his arrival forcing her to let him see the tattoo. To tell him about the laws still upheld in places in the San Joaquin and about stepping out of the caravan bus when the settlement police were there to collect the sin tax. He'd listened as she told him about life in Oakland, though she'd only told him about her life among outcasts, not about her mother. Or her father.

Fear threaded through her heart. She had other secrets to reveal.

Soon, she promised herself. Once she was more certain of him.

Weres were physical, earthy beings. He might be acting on lust alone, with no thought beyond experiencing shared pleasure.

Rebekka left the water, grabbing up the towel on the bank and hurriedly drying herself. A few steps took her to her clothing.

She hung the wet panties and bra on a branch, then dressed. The weight of the journal against her thigh reminded her of the promise to Phaedra.

Was it only this morning she'd agreed to share the knowledge contained in it? So much had happened since then.

She pulled the book from her pocket, wondering if Phaedra had gained permission for her to remain with the Jaguars. Doubt crept in as Rebekka remembered Koren's expression when he'd stepped out of his cabin. The alpha didn't approve of Aryck being with her.

A chill swept through her. What if Koren sent her away this very night?

It wouldn't come to that, she realized. Ice replaced the chill as dread returned.

He wouldn't send her back to Oakland, not with disease threatening. She was needed here, more now than before—even if she'd brought the devastation with her.

"There's no proof I did," she whispered, speaking out loud to give the words the ring of truth.

The healer's journal documented the horrors of biological and germ warfare let loose during The Last War. The Jaguar cubs had already stumbled on one weapon; who was to say there weren't more on these lands?

The knots of fear and worry and dread loosened as Rebekka saw a different possibility. She was here when she was needed the most, with the journal and the amulet, both given to her by the Wainwrights—her father's allies.

If war was coming, as the witches claimed, then what side would the Weres stand on?

She couldn't suppress a shiver as she remembered those moments when she healed the Wolves, when she'd heard the drumbeats of the Were ancestors. Hope slipped in as she thought about her argument with Aryck and his claim that being made outcast was the result of having the eternal soul cast from the shadowlands.

If there was any truth in it, then shouldn't the ancestors be able to restore those in the brothels, so they could shift fully between forms? Shouldn't she be able to gain intercessions on the outcasts' behalf as a result of the healing she did *here*? If she could, then there would be no need for her to return to Oakland. A future with Aryck would be possible—assuming that was what he wanted.

Old insecurities resurfaced. She wasn't sure a man was capable of being faithful to only one woman over the course of a lifetime together. Wouldn't the temptation to stray grow more acute the longer a Were was with someone who had only one form? Was it even possible for the permanent bond both Phaedra and Levi spoke of to exist between a Were and a human?

Rebekka's elation tumbled away with the thought of Levi. If the Were ancestors could restore those viewed as outcasts, wouldn't the Lion shaman have already approached the ancestors on Levi's behalf?

He couldn't be blamed for being twisted into a monstrous shape by a human using witch-charmed silver. Instead of being exiled from the pride, Levi should be rewarded for choosing a human shape so he could work to keep others from ending up in the maze as he waited for the chance to free Cyrin.

Rebekka put the book in her pocket, deciding to seek out Phaedra. While she shared the information in the journal, she could ask about Were ancestors and outcasts.

She found Caius and Canino at the cabin. The Tiger was sprawled underneath a tree while the boy was practicing with a slingshot.

Caius hugged her in greeting, rubbing his cheek against her shirt. She leaned down and kissed the top of his head.

"Phaedra sent me here to wait for you. I'm supposed to show you the way to her cabin. She's cooking a meal."

Rebekka's stomach rumbled with the reminder of how long it'd been since she'd eaten. "I'll be right out," she said, going into the cabin long enough to leave the damp clothing in a place where it could dry.

She laughed at her modesty. The Weres stripped in the blink of an eye. If her panties and bra gained any attention at all, it would be because they were a novelty.

When she stepped outside Canino was up and standing a short distance away. Caius took her hand, grinning as he led her to the Tiger.

"Watch this," he said, vaulting onto Canino's back. "I'm going to ride instead of walk."

Canino grumbled but didn't shake the cub off. They walked, Caius talking excitedly about how he'd spent the day, only going quiet as they neared Phaedra's cabin.

Rebekka's mouth watered with the scent of cooking meat. After the stench of the corpse fires burning the Elk she hadn't thought it would be possible to eat meat again.

Life goes on. Aryck's voice whispered through her mind, her nipples tightening with the remembered feel of his fingers and mouth on them.

Caius squeezed her hand, drawing her attention to him. "Somebody cooks a meal for me every night. In exchange I do chores, like gather wood." He puffed up his chest. "I also give them the rabbits I catch in my snares."

Her empathetic senses felt his happiness dim an instant before his chest sank and his voice dropped. "Mostly everyone cooks me stew because I'm still growing and stew can be taken home and eaten later."

And shared with a mother lost in grief, Rebekka thought. One who couldn't be helped directly but who could be kept alive until she found the strength to live and be the mother her son needed.

Rebekka wanted to take away Caius's pain, but anything she said would be a platitude. She remained silent.

He traced one of Canino's stripes then glanced sideways at her, partially hiding behind his bangs. "Do you think it would be okay if I took Canino to my cabin?"

The hope underneath the words made Rebekka's throat tighten with unshed tears. She didn't know how to answer his question except to say, "Let's ask Phaedra what she thinks."

"Okay," Caius said in a small voice.

They stepped into the clearing behind the healer's house. Instead of kettles boiling water for making the wash, a stew was on.

Phaedra looked up from her stirring. "This needs a little longer on the fire before it'll be ready. You've got permission to stay on Jaguar lands for two days in order to share the knowledge in the journal with me. If you're willing, this is a good time to start. You can read to me while I make the pan bread."

Two days. An ache settled in Rebekka's heart. She wondered if that explained why Aryck didn't join her at the bathing hole, because a couple of days of physical pleasure weren't worth creating a rift with his father over.

With fingers that trembled slightly Rebekka retrieved the journal from her pocket and sat on a smooth log. Caius slipped off Canino's back and sat next to her.

She willed herself not to think of Aryck or anything that had happened after leaving Wolf lands. "Do Were healers discuss treatments and help one another?"

Phaedra's lips turned up in a tiny smile. "For healers and shamans the territorial lines are not as sharply defined as they are for the other members of our pack."

"So anything useful in the journal, you'll pass on?"

"Where I can."

Rebekka opened the journal and began reading about poisons. When she noticed Caius's rapt focus on the pages of the book, she used her finger to note the words as she spoke them.

She read through the sound of bread frying and stew being dished up, only stopping and setting the journal aside when Phaedra handed her a bowl.

Caius got his own meal and returned to his seat next to her. "Will you teach me how to read?"

He dipped his bread into the stew before offering it to Canino. It disappeared in a single bite, making Rebekka laugh despite the ball of sadness that formed around her heart at how little time she had left on Jaguar lands.

It wasn't just thoughts of Aryck that made her ache. She would miss this. Joining Phaedra for meals and having another healer to share information with. Watching Caius with Canino. Sleeping with the windows open and no fear of the night.

"I only have two days; less now, I imagine," she told Caius.

His small chest puffed up. "I'm a fast learner."

"You have to know your letters first."

"I can learn them now." He grabbed two twigs and handed one of them to her.

Rebekka leaned over and drew an *A* in the soft dirt, then proceeded to tell him everything she could remember about the letter as he practiced drawing it.

They were at *M* by the time they'd finished eating and Phaedra had poured stew into a small kettle for Caius to take home with him. His ability to focus drifted from the wonder of letters, his hope to read eclipsed by a much deeper one.

He looked down at his feet then sideways at Rebekka. She took his hand and squeezed, offering her silent support.

"Phaedra," he said, voice hesitant. "Do you think it would hurt if I showed Canino where I live?"

The healer contemplated the question, finally saying, "No. I don't think it would hurt."

"I guess I better go then."

Caius gave Rebekka a hug before lifting the small kettle and leaving. She picked up the journal as Phaedra used stored water to clean up after the meal. "I can continue reading to you if you want."

"I would like that."

Rebekka opened the book to the page where she'd left off but didn't start reading. It seemed like the perfect time to ask, "Do the ancestors have the power to change an outcast back into a pure Were?"

Phaedra looked up from her washing, her eyes going to the book, contemplating, perhaps, the rightness of information being shared in both directions instead of one. She gave a small nod, more to herself than to Rebekka.

"Yes. They have the power, but there is always a price to be paid where they are concerned. In the case of outcasts there is a rite they can submit themselves to, providing they are not under a pack death sentence. It is a direct test by the ancestors. Few survive it."

"Can a shaman intercede on an outcast's behalf?"

"It would be a rare undertaking. The ancestors see more than we see. A shaman is never quick to question their judgment when it comes to the outcast." Phaedra's expression held compassion. "You're thinking of the Lion?"

"Yes. And those in the brothels."

"I'm sorry I can't offer you hope."

In that moment the beaded leather holding the amulet around Rebekka's neck felt like a collar, a reminder that her desire to heal the Weres and her gift were leashed to her demon father, and whatever plans he had for her. She opened the journal and resumed reading it to Phaedra. Tried not to think about Aryck, and why he hadn't sought her out.

The Watcher

TORQUEL en Sahon flew from tree to tree, changing forms as he followed the alpha from elder to elder. Cardinal to jay to thrush to woodpecker to mourning dove.

He took a wren's form in the clearing where a couple of elders supervised young boys as they lay twigs and sticks in the fire pit in preparation for the evening storytelling.

If he'd had human lips, he would have smiled. The paths laid centuries upon centuries ago were joining, becoming entwined, with this daughter serving as both catalyst for change and knot binding the threads of the weave together.

As it was becoming in the shadowlands, so would it become in this world of the living, with Weres mingling freely, irrespective of type.

It had to be so.

What good was an army constantly at risk of being at war with itself?

The irony of it wasn't lost on Torquel. The outcasts these Weres shunned so thoroughly already mixed freely in brothels and hidden cities.

Koren's progress toward the elders was halted by the Jaguar female Melina. Torquel took flight at the sight of her, landing on a low branch close to where they stood.

Melina pulled her hand from her pocket. Opened it to reveal the Wainwright token. "She uses witchcraft on Aryck. This is why he's become enthralled with a human. I took it from her pocket while she was bathing."

Koren took the blackened pentacle from Melina's palm. "Where is the healer now?"

"I don't know."

"Find her. Keep an eye on her without her being aware of you."

He closed his fist around the token. "Don't speak to anyone else about this."

Melina gave a solemn nod but as she turned away to do as the alpha ordered, a satisfied smile emerged.

She bears watching, Torquel thought, but followed Koren to the shaman's house, becoming a small breeze passing through the doorway as Nahuatl ushered the alpha inside. Then a mouse whose black fur blended perfectly with the dark shadow of descending dusk.

Without prelude Koren passed the token to Nahuatl. "The human healer carries this."

Nahuatl showed no surprise at the sight of it. "Phaedra found it when she washed Rebekka's clothing. She brought it to me then. It is nothing. A sign of alliance, no more."

"An alliance with witches. They are our enemies."

"Some of them. Not the ones who gave the healer this token. Or at least they are not our enemies at the moment. You have been out among humans. Their world is painted in shades of gray, not the black and white of ours."

"You approached the ancestors after Phaedra brought you the token?"

"Yes."

When the shaman didn't say more, Koren turned his back as if hiding the shame of what he said next. "She's bewitched Aryck. I assumed responsibility for her protection while she's in our lands and ordered him to stay away from her before he ends up outcast because of her. He believes the ancestors want her among us, as his mate. He intends to speak to you about it."

Nahuatl stepped forward and placed a hand on Koren's shoulder. "When he comes, I will tell him the ancestors have already spoken to me on this matter. If she survives an outcast's trial, then the pack can claim her as one of their own."

Koren turned to face the shaman. "Do you think she will survive it?"

Nahuatl shrugged. "I know only that years ago one of the ancestors showed me the witches' token and told me the day would come when a human arrived in Jaguar lands bearing it. And should the pack wish it, the human could be tested for worthiness and made one of us."

Koren's hand clenched and unclenched. "In this moment it seems like our way of life is under assault. The humans invade Coyote lands. Disease struck the Elk and they carried it to the Wolves. Aryck argues for an alliance among the Weres and the Wolf enforcer favors it as well."

"This is news." Nahuatl indicated chairs covered in bison fur. "Let me hear it in detail and with your permission share it with the Lion shaman. We are to meet later at the edge of the shadowlands. The pride's grand matriarch wishes to speak with Rebekka. If you allow it, the Lion outcast and several others will come here tomorrow and take her back with them if she's willing."

"I'll tell those on patrol to meet the Lions and escort them to camp."

Good, Torquel thought, abandoning the mouse form in a swirl of air.

Outside the shaman's cabin he became an owl lifting in flight, leaving the Jaguar camp in search of the grim evidence left behind in Caphriel's game.

Caphriel's Pawn

I'VE gone too far to stop now, Radek thought. Not that he wanted to, not when the dreams of the previous night had been filled with images of inglorious failure and servitude, of Weres overrunning the human world and subjugating mankind.

Time was nearly out. He didn't know how he knew it, but he did. It felt as though some internal clock had suddenly sped up, making his pulse race and intensifying the urge to look over his shoulder.

He was hyperaware of Gregor's eyes boring into his back. Watching, taking note. Not to carry information back to Viktor or the Ivanov patriarch, but to increase his leverage so Radek would forever be footing the bill for his sexual perversions.

Ultimately he'd have to do something about Gregor, but not now. Not now.

Radek stirred the super-virus into the bucket of feed. With no evidence of dead elk, wolves, or hyenas, he'd split the encampment's herd of meat goats, taken those he intended to use as a weapon against the Weres, and had them placed in a separate, enclosed building.

Gregor had become necessary, at least for the moment. Someone needed to take care of the goats. They were rank creatures and *he* certainly couldn't be expected to muck out their paddock area or see to their water and all their feeding requirements. Someone needed to guard them so they didn't end up in the human food supply.

A shudder went through Radek as he slipped the empty liquor flask he'd smuggled the virus into the building with into his pants pocket. Sudden sweat made his shirt cling to his sides. According to the documentation he'd found with the canisters, of the three super-viruses, this one was the most volatile, the most likely to mutate. It was a trade-off the scientists accepted, greater risk offset with the benefit of being able to kill a wide range of Weres having a cat form.

Cats were survivors. They were consummate predators. According to the data chip accompanying the canister, of all the Were groups, the scientists considered jaguar, leopard, and cougar shapeshifters the most likely to be able to survive prolonged human warfare on this continent and rise to power.

Radek picked up the bucket of feed. He'd already made a show of taking measurements of the goats when he arrived earlier, then of pouring in some of the fictional growth formula kept in a bottle near the feed.

The make-believe recipe supposedly came from the safe uncovered by the workers. His stated desire to test it served well enough as an excuse for taking charge of the goats and having Gregor assigned to them.

Radek turned around and took the several steps required to reach the paddock fence. The goats crowded forward, already anticipating the feast his presence had come to represent. He lifted the bucket and poured its contents into troughs made from metal barrels.

Three more days, he thought, holding his breath to keep from inhaling the acrid stink of goat piss as the herd consumed his offerings. In three more days they'd all be ripe, virulent, and ready to be struck down like piñatas at a party.

Releasing them wouldn't be a problem. He'd make up some excuse, perhaps something along the lines of them needing to graze naturally as part of their accelerated growth regime. And while the herd was out of sight of the encampment, they'd escape.

The last of the feed disappeared, leaving the metal barrels licked clean. Radek looked up and saw Gregor, eyes narrowed and hard, his hand rubbing the bulge at the front of his pants in a not-so-subtle reminder he hadn't yet been paid for disposing of the whore.

Radek suppressed a smile. Yes, he could easily see how the animals would manage to escape, how the story would be spun—of noble Gregor growing concerned and leaving them unattended while he searched for the prostitute who'd gotten lost after accompanying him in his capacity as goat herder.

She'd stay lost of course. Gregor would make sure her corpse wasn't found.

It was a simple plan. Effective and efficient. More important, it felt *right*.

He'd give it more thought before setting it into motion, but there was no reason not to whet Gregor's appetite, to prime the pump, so to speak.

"Three more days of waiting should do it," Radek said. "Considering the long hours you've been putting in and the degrading nature of the work for an Ivanov militiaman, I don't think anyone would question your need of a whore and a break from the confines of the encampment. As a caveat, I do reserve the right to veto your choice of female companion. Their contracts vary in terms of their worth."

Gregor's hand curled around his cloth-covered cock. He wet his lips in anticipation. "Three days sounds good. It's been too long since I had the kind of fun I like."

Twenty-two

REBEKKA woke lying in twisted bedding and covered in a light sheen of sweat, her hand in her panties, fingers wet against her stiffened clit. She looked around, disoriented by the fevered intensity of carnal dreams, half expecting to find Aryck in the cabin, directly responsible for the wicked images and decadent sensations.

She found only quiet emptiness and realization. A validation of her fears from the evening before.

Aryck wasn't going to seek her out. Not when she'd be gone from Jaguar lands tomorrow. Not when it would mean discord between his father and him.

She sat, crossing her arms over her bare breasts and rubbing her upper arms. Goose bumps chased away the lingering heat of dreams and remembered touch. But the cool, early-morning air only partially accounted for the chill invading her.

In the cool light of dawn she faced a hard truth. Aryck regretted what happened after they left Wolf lands.

Falling asleep Jaguar and waking up in human form, lying on top of a willing female, could be explained as a momentary lapse, a healthy male responding to physical stimuli without it being a conscious choice. But willfully engaging in such activity with a human, to smell like sex and have his father—his alpha—catch them kissing and see the shallow scars she'd raked across Aryck's back, was different.

From the time she was a child old enough to understand what her mother and the others did to survive, she'd noticed how many of the visitors crept in and slunk away, not wanting anyone to know they'd been with a prostitute.

"It's for the best," Rebekka whispered, hoping that speaking the lie would make her believe it.

She rose from the bed made of fur and blankets and dressed quickly, as anxious to escape her thoughts as the unwelcome solitude of the cabin.

Phaedra was at the fire pit behind her own cabin. She smiled as Rebekka stepped from the path and into the small clearing.

"You're up early. I thought you might sleep in this morning after reading so late into the night. I'll start breakfast in a few minutes."

Spread out along the length of a log was a collection of leaves, berries, roots, and bark. Rebekka studied the combination then said, "You're making a painkiller from the journal?"

"Yes, though as a healer I can't hope the opportunity will arise to test this particular potion."

Rebekka laughed, understanding exactly what Phaedra meant as she'd experienced it herself more than once in the course of learning new things as a healer. She took the journal from her pocket and flipped to the page with the recipe, watched as Phaedra accurately dealt with the various ingredients.

Despite coming to understand how the oral sharing of knowledge began almost at birth among pure Weres, Rebekka was still amazed by how quickly Phaedra was able to memorize information.

"You got it exactly right," she said.

"You doubted?" Phaedra made a clucking sound and muttered, "Youngsters."

Rebekka felt her heart swell with affection, with a sense of belonging. She closed the journal and slipped it back in her pocket so she could help Phaedra with the last step, pouring the painkiller into clay pots then sealing it in with hot wax.

Afterward it seemed perfectly natural to work together in preparing breakfast. Rebekka took charge of the fried potatoes and sausage, Phaedra the eggs.

The scent of cooking food soon filled the clearing. As Rebekka nudged a sausage link and turned the potatoes, she thought of the Tiger cub.

"Caius said someone cooks him dinner each evening. What about breakfast? Will he come by for it?"

Phaedra tsked. "A cub whose belly is always full won't be motivated to become a better hunter. Breakfast is for those of us whose duties keep us close to camp and not lingering for days in the forest as we feast on a fat deer while wearing our fur."

Rebekka startled. Shock coursed through her until she realized that of course it would be different for Phaedra. She was Were, a healer by calling and desire, rather than possessing a gift in the way humans did. It made sense Phaedra could hunt and kill without turning her talent into a thing of evil.

With thoughts of evil, the image of her demon father rose in Rebekka's mind. She was saved from contemplations of him, from the confusion that came in painting him with the brush of sin when his actions seemed to speak otherwise, by Phaedra flipping an egg neatly onto a plate and handing it to her.

"I imagine Caius will track you here when he doesn't find you at your cabin," Phaedra said. "You restored more than his health. Between the attention he's gotten from you and from the Tiger, he's been a different child, happy and extroverted instead of withdrawn and timid."

Rebekka served the potatoes and sausages before sitting on the fireside log. "Do you know what happened when he took Canino home with him?"

Phaedra chuckled. "Yes. It went better than I thought it might."

"Caius came here first thing this morning. His mother changed into Jaguar form and chased Canino away from their cabin last night. It's the first intense reaction Deidre has shown since returning to the pack.

"She's slipped back into her despair since then. Caius was worried, but I assured him that what happened was a step toward healing and

Canino would surely recognize it for what it was and not avoid him because of it.

"The cub went off to check his snares. I'm sure he also intends to visit Canino to reassure himself that he's still accepted by the Tiger."

"He will be," Rebekka said, scooping up a forkful of eggs. "I think Canino needs Caius as much as Caius needs him."

"I suspect you're right."

They finished their breakfast and were washing dishes when Caius rushed into the small clearing, yelling, "Rebekka! I was riding Canino and he took off running with me on his back! He crashed into a Lion to say hello and I went flying through the air and landed right at Koren's feet! The Lions want you to come for a visit. That's why they're here. The alpha told me to look for you and bring you to where they're waiting."

Caius's voice lowered to a whisper. "There was an outcast with the Lions. He smelled almost completely human."

Rebekka's heart leapt at the prospect of seeing Levi again even as dread became a leaden weight in her gut. "Is someone sick?"

"Nobody said so. They don't smell like they've been around someone who's sick. They don't smell worried about anything and they don't seem anxious to get back home. Maybe they just want you to read the book to their healer too."

Caius wrapped his arms around her in a tight hug. Rebekka dried her hands on a cloth then returned the hug, leaning down to rub her cheek against his soft white-blond hair.

He squeezed once more then wriggled out of her arms. "We better go. The alpha is waiting."

She said good-bye to Phaedra and followed Caius into the woods. Several yards down the path her thoughts went to Aryck.

Memories crowded in, of how often he'd glowered at Levi as they traveled, especially when she and Levi were sitting or walking together and talking quietly. At how adamant he'd been that Levi wouldn't enter Jaguar territory.

Looking back at it, she could almost attribute Aryck's behavior to jealousy. Or maybe she just wanted to believe there'd been something more than sexual curiosity or desire brought on by close proximity and shared horror.

Aryck hadn't sought her out but she wanted to tell him where she was going, and with who, rather than have him find out later. Though maybe he already knew Levi was here. Maybe he was glad because it saved him from uncomfortable explanations or obvious avoidance.

"Was Aryck with the alpha?" she asked, pleased at how normal her voice sounded.

"No. He might be at his cabin. Do you want to go there first? The alpha didn't say I had to bring you to him straightaway."

Nearly painful flutters went through Rebekka's chest. It was an excuse to see him. She recognized it for what it was, and yet despite everything she knew about men and about pure Weres, a tiny spark of hope still lingered inside her.

"Yes, I'd like to tell him I'm leaving."

A flock of quail took flight in a roar of wings and shaken leaves. Caius cocked his head in a very catlike gesture but didn't leave the path to explore what had startled the birds.

It was impossible for Rebekka to gauge the size of the Jaguar camp or how many cabins were hidden away in the woods. It was equally impossible to tell how far or close Aryck's home was from Phaedra's since they didn't travel in a straight line.

Aryck's cabin looked like all the others she'd seen. It was small, set in a dense pocket of trees and surrounded by a clearing to allow for cooking in a fire pit and for seeing anyone who might approach it.

Standing at the very edge of the forest Rebekka felt her confidence waiver and her nerve desert her. She rubbed damp palms against her pants.

It's foolish to seek him out, she thought, and might have turned away except for Caius saying, "You want me to go with you to the door? Or stay here and wait for you?"

She gathered her courage and straightened her spine. *I broke into the maze and lived to tell about it. I met the demon Abijah and survived it. I can do this.*

"I'll be right back," she told Caius, afraid of what he might witness if he stood next to her at Aryck's door.

Rebekka forced herself to breathe deeply as she crossed the clearing, but it didn't slow the wild race of her heart. She knocked, though she imagined scent and sound had already carried news of her arrival.

Melina opened the door. Naked and looking sated with her hair unbound and her eyes slumberous.

Pain slid into Rebekka like a knife, tearing through her in a single slash that left agony in its wake and no way to hide it.

"If you're looking for Aryck, he's bathing in the stream," Melina said. "If you hurry you might catch him."

The Jaguar female stretched, emphasizing bruised, well-attended nipples. "I hope you *do* find him. Making me jealous got him what he wanted and he *knows* what coming back with your scent on him will do to me."

Rebekka turned away, sickened, her throat tight and eyes burning as she fought not to give in to tears.

"What's wrong?" Caius asked, his gaze darting back and forth between the cabin and her.

"Nothing," she managed, taking his hand in a desperate need for the comfort of touch. "Let's go to where the alpha and the Lions are waiting."

Rebekka held the tears back until she reached Levi. But as soon as he pulled her into a fierce hug, her control broke.

She wrapped her arms around his waist and wet the front of his shirt, managing to suppress choking sobs but not the trembling that came with the pain of betrayal and the death of a dream she'd only just allowed herself to believe possible.

He didn't ask what was wrong, though she felt his anger in the tension bristling along the length of his body. Heard it in the low growl of his voice when he asked, "You'll come with us?"

"Yes." Rebekka stepped back, keeping her face turned away from the Jaguar alpha. "Is someone ill or injured?"

"No. The grand matriarch wants to speak with you."

Caius recaptured Rebekka's hand in a fierce squeeze. "Can I go with you, so I can keep learning my letters? And you can start teaching me to read?"

Canino rumbled his approval of the question and signaled his willingness to visit the Lion pride by sitting next to Caius and leaning into him with such force the cub curled his arm around the Tiger's neck.

"The boy is welcome in our territory," one of the Lions said. "We'll see to his safety."

"He may go then," Koren said, accompanying them to the border of Jaguar lands and officially handing off responsibility for both Caius and Rebekka to the Lion who seemed to be in charge.

Levi's hand tightened on Rebekka's arm as soon as they were out of Jaguar hearing. "What happened?" he asked.

Cyrin echoed his brother's concern by pushing between them and snarling with such fury Rebekka touched the thick ruff of his mane and sent soothing waves of calm.

"Nothing happened," Rebekka lied, glad she'd bathed the night before so they wouldn't scent Aryck and the smell of passion on her skin.

Her emotions were too raw, the pain too new and too deep to talk about. She wasn't sure she would ever be able to confide the truth to Levi. How could she, when he didn't settle on one female either?

"Melina said something to her," Caius volunteered. "Rebekka was fine until that happened."

"I'm still fine," she said, making an attempt to sound as she usually did. "How could I be anything but fine when I'm seeing and learning things humans are rarely allowed to?"

Levi's narrowed eyes and taut features said she wasn't successful in fooling him. But he let the subject drop, and Caius filled the silence.

He told the others about her reading the journal to Phaedra. Recited the alphabet and shared what he knew about each letter. And after they'd stopped long enough for Rebekka to introduce a few new letters and draw them in the dirt, he went on to tell them about what he and Canino had already done together, and the things he wanted them to do.

His enthusiasm lifted Rebekka's spirits even as it made her think about those in Oakland who needed her. She glanced at Levi, remembering the early days, when she'd taught him how to read. And how he, in turn, had offered to teach Feliss.

Worry for those in the brothels edged into Rebekka's thoughts. It was time to go back, perhaps pay a visit to the Wainwright witches.

The weight of the journal in her pocket reminded her of her promise. There was very little of it left to share with Phaedra.

Her time on Jaguar lands was nearly done anyway, and Phaedra had said territorial lines weren't as sharply defined for healers. She'd said she would pass on the information contained in the journal to others.

Rebekka slid her hand into her pocket and touched smooth leather. If she read what remained to the Lion healer, then she and Levi could leave from there. She could return to Oakland without having to see Aryck again.

It should have sent relief spiraling through her. Instead it felt as though a heavy weight of sorrow encased her heart.

It's better this way, she told herself, hoping if she repeated the words enough, she'd truly believe them.

She willed herself to wall off all thoughts of Aryck—without success.

Images crowded in.

Of Aryck injured, risking death to come to Oakland and find a healer for the cubs.

Of Aryck with Caius, gently smoothing the wash over ravaged flesh and muscle.

Of Aryck standing with the Wolf enforcer and suggesting alliance.

And though she tried to suppress it—of the look in Aryck's eyes. The heat of his hands on her, making her feel beautiful, feminine, wanted.

Remembering it made her skin flush and her breasts swell with the phantom touch of his lips and fingers on her nipples. It made desire pool in her belly and threaten to slide lower, between her legs.

Knowing her companions would scent her arousal gave Rebekka

the strength to push the memories back. Coming into sight of the pride's home helped erect a barrier against their return.

It's better this way, she silently repeated, forcing herself to give this world she would most likely never visit again her full attention.

Where the Jaguars lived in cabins and the Wolves lived in a tentlike village made of animal hides, the Lions lived in low adobe buildings built against sloping canyon walls. None of them had wooden doors or shutters, but all had roofs laden with rubble and supporting the growth of scrub, so from above it wouldn't be obvious they were dwellings.

Lions lounged on the roofs, sunning themselves and watching with interest. More than one cub crouched above a doorway as if preparing to spring on an unwitting playmate or sibling when curiosity drew them outside.

Eucalyptus trees added shelter without eliminating the openness of the area in front of and between the dwellings. The scent of the trees filled the air.

"This way," Levi said, guiding her toward a building where at least thirty Lions gathered, almost all of them in animal form.

She felt his tension where his palm touched her shirt. It pulsed from him to her in a steady beat echoing with pain. And as they reached the pride members, Rebekka knew its source.

Levi didn't exist for them. They looked through him, their movements orchestrated so even as they cleared a pathway to the doorway, there was no acknowledgment of his presence.

Her heart ached and guilt washed over her. She'd been so consumed with her own pain as they traveled, she hadn't noticed that of the Lions, only Cyrin interacted with Levi.

Two men stepped to the doorway opening, blocking it with wide-leg stances and crossed arms. The Lion to the left radiated curiosity while his companion seethed with distrust and disapproval. It was the latter who said, "Only the healer may enter."

Twenty-three

LEVI'S hand fell away from her back. "I'll wait for you here."

She glanced down at Caius. He crowded against her side, unconsciously seeking security. His attention focused on several cubs.

They tussled in lion form, engaged in a mock battle for possession of a dead rabbit. As she watched, one of them snatched it up and bounded close to where they stood, dropping the carcass with a quick look to Caius before grabbing it back and leaping away, only to be tackled by his companions.

Rebekka laughed and ruffled Caius's hair. "That looked like an invitation. Go play."

He clung for a moment longer before shimmying out of his clothing and shifting, then cautiously approached the Lions. After some hissing and puffed fur, he was soon rolling and leaping and tumbling.

With a last look at Levi, Rebekka entered the dwelling. There was no furniture, though there were several thick piles of fur scattered around the small room. Given how few of the Lions she'd seen in human form, and considering the open nature of the dwellings, Rebekka guessed that unlike the Wolves and Jaguars, the pride spent most of its time wearing fur.

A young woman appeared and motioned Rebekka forward, leading her deeper into the building. The lighting grew more diffused, coming from the rooms with window and door openings and filtering into those farther away from the outside.

Though they weren't lit, Rebekka noted squat candles placed on metal sconces set high in the walls. The woman signaled they'd reached their destination by repositioning the furs, pulling them so there were three abreast facing a lone pile, then gesturing to the isolated seat and saying, "Sit. The grand matriarch comes."

Rebekka removed the journal from her pocket and sat cross-legged with it on her lap. The young Lion female left.

Several minutes passed before Rebekka heard the sound of slow, shuffling footsteps. Instinct and the tenets of courtesy demanded she stand, but her rational mind urged her to remain in a nonthreatening position and not inadvertently issue a challenge.

The grand matriarch entered, a stooped, white-haired elder flanked by a woman of Phaedra's age and a man Rebekka immediately guessed was a shaman. His hair was worn in dreads, resembling a mane around a face bearing swirling designs branded deeply into it, so even when he shifted form he would be recognizable.

Like Caius, his eyes were blue. But unlike the Tiger cub's, the shaman's were sightless.

All three Lions were draped in loose deer hides of varying lengths, giving Rebekka the impression they'd covered their nakedness at the last minute and as an afterthought.

Slowly the grand matriarch lowered herself to the pile of furs in the center. When she was settled, the shaman and older female took up positions on either side of her.

"Word of your deeds has spread throughout the Were lands," the grand matriarch said. "It stirred my interest and since I had cause to invite you here, I indulged my curiosity. You deserve Pride thanks for returning Cyrin to us. I have heard it said you showed great courage and risked your life on his account."

It took only the memory of Levi's pain pulsing through her as he was shunned to make Rebekka speak out on his behalf. "If anyone deserves thanks, it's Levi. Cyrin would be dead if Levi hadn't chosen a human form so he could stay in Oakland and work to free his brother."

The grand matriarch waved the words aside with a pale hand. "Since you are owed Pride thanks, I will speak to you on this matter. We mourn the loss of the one you praise. But we no longer say his name out loud for fear of drawing evil fortune to ourselves. He is dead to all except his pride family, and in two days' time, after they have performed certain rites, even they will no longer see him.

"If he lingers among us beyond that time, he will be seen as a malevolent spirit bent on causing harm to the Pride. He will be hunted, and the physical body holding him to the land killed by those who have apprenticed themselves to Hotah, our shaman. The world of the dead is Hotah's to navigate. Upon Cyrin's return, he approached the ancestors, hoping because of the way Cyrin's brother lost his life among us, it could be restored through purification and judgment. They spoke plainly on the matter."

The grand matriarch paused and, with a slight tilt of her head, indicated the woman next to her. "The ancestors said that for Magena's grandson, whose soul has already been sundered and cast from the shadowlands, only death of the body will come if he presents himself to them."

Even though Rebekka expected as much, hearing the words added to the sense of inevitability she felt bearing down on her. If Levi was to be made whole, she had to become a healer like the ones Annalise Wainwright spoke of, which, in the end, meant she would have to do her demon father's bidding.

Her hands tightened on the journal, and feeling the leather beneath her palms reminded her of earlier thoughts, and her plan to return to Oakland without going back to the Jaguar lands or seeing Aryck again. It took only moments to tell the Lions of her promise to Phaedra and to convey the value of the information contained in the long-dead Jaguar's recordings. The grand matriarch was nodding her approval even before Rebekka asked if she could remain long enough to speak to the healer and pass on what she hadn't yet shared with Phaedra.

"Magena is our healer," the grand matriarch said, naming Levi's grandmother. "Go with her. You will be welcome in her pride home."

Rebekka relaxed her grip on the journal. At least for the next two days, Levi would be welcome as well.

ARYCK returned to camp chafing under his father's edict to stay away from Rebekka. His insides felt raw, shredded by Jaguar clawing and his own frustration.

Not for the first time, he worried about what she might be thinking. He'd been gone much longer than he intended.

No sign of disease or proof of human involvement had been found. He'd managed to draw out both Coyote and Hyena enforcers, and both had held off attacking in favor of listening to his thoughts on the wisdom of alliance. But had he known so much time would pass, he would have paused long enough to get word to Rebekka before leaving camp.

Now the delay stretched longer out of necessity. It couldn't be helped.

Aryck rubbed his hand over his bare chest, trying to smooth away the misgiving building there. He turned onto the trail that would take him to Nahuatl's cabin.

The shaman was outside, pulling a deer hide from a soaking barrel and placing it flesh side up on a flat table. "You wish to speak to me about the healer," Nahuatl said, choosing a knife and putting the back edge against the skin, skudding away the dirt and fatty tissue that still remained after the initial scraping.

Aryck bridled, though he'd expected his father's interference. "The alpha told you I believe the ancestors want her to remain here, as my mate?"

"He told me."

Aryck's heart tripped into a fast, pounding beat. Even the Jaguar, for all its confidence, felt nervous about stepping into a realm where allies and enemies could be neither embraced nor fought. There was risk involved in approaching the ancestors directly, which was why most sought out the shaman rather than chance being made outcast, or gain an answer but at the cost of taking on a task named by the ancestors.

For Rebekka he would take the risk. "I wish to go through a Petitioner's Rite."

Nahuatl looked up from the hide. "It will gain you nothing. Because it suited them, the ancestors have spoken on the matter."

Aryck's uneasiness heightened. "And their answer?"

"If you wish to make her your mate and have her remain here, they will judge her as they would an outcast, through Rite of Trial. If they find her worthy, then they will mark her as pack."

"My father knows this?"

Nahuatl laid the knife aside and picked up the hide, taking the few steps necessary to submerge it in a barrel of water warmed over a low fire. "Yes."

Aryck turned away, his thoughts in turmoil, his chest tightening as he imagined Rebekka going through the ritual preparation that included three days of fasting in seclusion followed by a full day of purification in a sweat lodge built near the entrance to the cave where the bones of the dead were placed.

There were stories told of Weres who survived the trial, but in Aryck's lifetime he'd stood witness once as a child and once as pack enforcer, watching as an outcast emerged naked from the sweat lodge at sunset and willingly entered the cave to withstand the torment of the ancestors until the sun rose.

One of the outcasts never left the cave. His body rotted and his bones joined those of the pack dead.

The other met his death underneath the night sky. Killed by those gathered as witnesses when he fled the cave in terror.

Aryck rubbed at the ache centered in his chest, fought against the fear whispering through him, that he was doomed to lose her—to Oakland and the outcasts or to death.

The thought of leaving his father's pack and starting his own flickered in his mind but found nothing to hold it there. Without the sanction of the ancestors, who would follow a Were with a human mate? And without a pack, there was no way to carve out territory and defend it.

Aryck came to a place where the paths crossed. The instinct to return to his cabin until he'd found a solution, something to offer Rebekka beyond a message saying he was forbidden to be in her presence, was strong. But worry over what she might be thinking in his continued absence was stronger.

He couldn't risk going directly to Phaedra's cabin. In all likelihood Rebekka would be there.

Aryck headed toward the clearing where pack members gathered as a community. Melina was there among several suitors.

As soon as she saw him she left the other males, coming to him smelling of sex and satisfaction, though he doubted she'd let any of the other males penetrate her vaginally and fill her channel with seed. This deeply into heat, she wouldn't risk being mated to a beta male.

When she would have rubbed against him, the Jaguar rose in Aryck's eyes, reminding her of the promise made in the Barrens. Anger joined the other scents pouring off her. Aryck wondered what it would take for her to move on and hunt for a mate among the males of a different pack.

A smirk marred features he'd once thought beautiful but that no longer held any interest for him. "I don't know why I still want you after you've been with that whore. Fucking a human is revolting, though I guess you're not alone in that perversion. She was quick enough to go to the Lion outcast when he came sniffing around for her."

The Jaguar erupted in possessive fury, becoming a distinct entity and trying to force the change so it could savage Melina and then hunt down the outcast and slay him.

Aryck's emotions matched the outraged jealousy of the beast, melding human and Jaguar souls together a heartbeat after they'd separated.

He retreated to the forest, recognizing he was too dangerous, too volatile, to question Melina or anyone else about Rebekka.

He seethed. Cursed. Snarled in rage and defiance and frustration, only barely aware of his surroundings as he walked.

Images superimposed themselves one over another. The closeness he'd witnessed between Rebekka and the Lion in the Barrens and as they'd traveled. Their quiet conversations and easy touches.

On the heels of reality came tormented imaginings, of Rebekka and Levi together, their bodies joined, slick with sweat as they strained toward release.

Aryck's fingers flexed, phantom claws emerging. She was his and he wouldn't let her go without a fight.

The resolve cooled the rage boiling through him, allowing him to glimpse the pain underneath before he brought his emotions under control.

With a start he realized he was well on his way to Lion territory. He kept moving forward, his father's command replaying in his mind, providing an opening for him to do as he pleased and go to Rebekka.

The alpha had forbidden contact while on Jaguar lands. He'd warned against loss of pack and position if Aryck followed her to Oakland.

There was nothing to prevent him from going to Lion lands. And given the need to speak to their enforcer about alliance among the Weres, he had every reason to go there.

Those thoughts blocked all others for a mile. But slowly, with each step, truth chiseled away at them, exposing them as rationalizations and sickening Aryck so his skin crawled and became clammy.

He stopped, touching his forehead to the smooth maroon-colored bark of a madrone tree and closing his eyes. A breeze swept over him, emphasizing the chill at his core.

This was the path to being made outcast. Not the desire for a human mate, but the slippery twisting of words so he could justify his actions even as he knew deep down he was violating a trust.

The alpha's will was pack law, and though his father hadn't specifically forbidden him from being with Rebekka on Lion lands, the intent behind Koren's edict was clear.

Frustration and longing and the sharp-edged threat of returning jealousy made Aryck push away from the tree. He turned back toward Jaguar lands and a second confrontation with his father.

Koren was waiting for him in the same place they'd argued the day before. His arms hung loosely at his side, his expression grim and his feet bare.

"Rebekka is in Lion lands," Aryck said, more statement than question.

"Yes." An image came with the answer, the outcast's arms enfolding her while tiny tremors wracked her body as though she cried in joy at being reunited with him.

Aryck's control over his emotions nearly slipped. To keep the Jaguar from capitalizing on the weakness and taking over to challenge the alpha, Aryck launched a verbal argument.

"I spoke with Nahuatl. If the ancestors are willing to allow Rebekka to come before them, then there is no justification for banning me from her presence. Without a chance to speak together, how can she make a decision about undergoing the trial so she can join the pack and become my mate?"

Koren's hands opened and closed as if he fought himself. The father whose love and fear had put the edict in place versus the alpha, who knew there were no stories told by the Jaguar elders of another human being allowed the chance to go through the rite.

To stand in the way of whatever destiny waited for Rebekka and, because of her, Aryck, was to risk offending and enraging the ancestors.

A muscle spasmed in Koren's cheek like a final protest before he said, "Follow her into Lion lands if you must. Ensure whatever knowledge she hasn't shared with Phaedra is passed on to the Lion healer. But unless she is willing to turn herself over to Nahuatl and begin the three-day fast, she is not to step foot in Jaguar territory again. She can remain with the Lions if they allow it or return to Oakland with the outcast. The Wolves can see her safely through their lands as they've already agreed to do."

Twenty-four

THE Jaguar seethed and writhed in fury, barely controllable by the time Aryck tracked Rebekka to a building that smelled of the outcast and those related to him. Phantom claws raked through his belly and chest. If he found them together, limbs entwined, there would be no stopping a shift in form and an attack.

Cyrin roared from his lounging place above the doorway of the dwelling, as much of a greeting as a warning. He jumped down, barring Aryck's path for an instant before turning and serving as a guide through the maze of rooms.

Aryck's fingers flexed and unflexed as he heard low murmurs coming from deeper in the pride home. Jealousy built with each step as over and over again the image his father had shown him played through his mind, Rebekka in Levi's arms, crying in joy at being reunited with the outcast.

He reached a doorway and saw her sitting cross-legged, the journal in her hands, her head bent as she studied it. The Jaguar stilled as it drank in the sight of its mate. The man grew more furious when she refused to look up, refused to acknowledge his presence even after Caius, who sat at her side with Canino serving as a backrest, yelled, "Aryck!"

He managed a smile for the cub. A polite nod to the older woman also sitting in the cozy circle. Growled, "We need to talk," to Rebekka, the Jaguar's calm ebbing in equal measure to the man's rising temper at being ignored.

It was all he could do not to stalk over and jerk Rebekka to her feet, to make her look at him before he carried her out of the dwelling if she refused to go willingly.

Neither he nor the Jaguar liked the way the Lion outcast was sitting close to her. It was almost too much when Levi leaned into her and murmured, "If you want to speak privately with him, you can use my room. If you don't, I'll see him out."

"Try it," Aryck said. He'd take great satisfaction in beating Levi in a fight and clearly demonstrating to Rebekka who was the better choice.

He bared his teeth in warning and fury when she reached over and touched the outcast's forearm. Managed not to attack only because she said, "I'll talk to him. Between what I've already read to Phaedra and your grandmother, there's not much of the journal left to share. Will you finish reading the last of it? And help Caius with his letters and words?"

Lion gold eyes sent their own challenge to Aryck. "You're sure?"

"I'm sure," she said, handing him the journal and ruffling the cub's hair before standing.

Rebekka glanced at Aryck then, and the pain in her eyes was like a lance through his heart. She turned her back and walked away without a word to him, bringing a renewed surge of anger, only this time it joined a churning mass of confusion and worry and doubt.

He had only one cure for it. The moment she stopped, signaling they'd reached their destination, his hand curled around her arm, forcing her to face him.

His lips slammed onto hers in a fierce claiming. And when she went rigid, refusing to open her mouth, he didn't relent, didn't let her deny the heat between them.

His hands swept over her back, her sides. Around to cup her breasts.

His tongue battered at the seam of her lips, demanding entry until they parted willingly and she softened against him.

No! Rebekka screamed silently, but her body betrayed her with the desperation of a junkie getting a fix.

Despite the pain he'd caused her she grew flushed and ready, felt need coiling in her belly and sliding downward, desire filling her breasts so they thrust in invitation against his palms, chafed at the clothing separating them from the feel of his skin against hers.

When he started unbuttoning her shirt, she dredged up the image of Melina standing in the doorway of his cabin, forced herself to remember the Jaguar female's hateful words.

"No!" Rebekka said, jerking out of Aryck's arms and stumbling backward, away from him.

He snarled and came after her, trapping her against the smooth adobe wall. His body vibrated fury. "Forget him, Rebekka. If the Lion outcast was right for you, then the two of you would already be a mated pair. You're mine. The Jaguar chose you the day you healed me and I agree with the choice."

His declaration cleared Rebekka's mind. She searched his face and saw possessiveness there.

A part of her wanted to believe it meant something, but she steeled herself against false hopes and additional betrayal. No doubt the married men who frequented the brothels looked at their wives the same way, expecting them to remain faithful even as they broke their vows.

"And Melina?" Rebekka spat, putting her hands against Aryck's chest and pushing with all her might.

He didn't budge.

"What about her? She means nothing to me."

He lied. Or maybe he told the truth. Maybe he cared only about having what seemed unattainable.

The misery she'd experienced since he left her the day before returned in a rush. She battled it with a fury matching his earlier anger.

"I won't be used by you or made part of some game of jealousy you play with Melina. She wanted me to find you bathing in the stream after you'd been with her. She—"

"What are you talking about?" Aryck interrupted, voice harsh with demand.

Fury blazed in his eyes, and his body was rigid with it. "It's been years since I touched Melina other than to warn her away from me. I regret ever having been with her in the first place. Even then it was casual between us. If she told you otherwise, she lied."

His hands curled around her upper arms, yet despite the iron in his grip he wasn't hurting her. "Now tell me what you're talking about," he demanded again, outrage battering against her empathetic senses. Confusion. Frustration.

Was she a fool to think his emotions were genuine? To give him a chance to convince her that what she'd seen and heard was a lie?

Part of her wanted to cringe away from anything that would cause additional pain. She refused to allow it. She hadn't cowered when Abijah caught up to her. She hadn't taken up her mother's faith when she learned her father was a demon.

"I went to your cabin to tell you I was leaving with the Lions. Melina was there, naked and looking like . . ."

Aryck's eyes darkened with deadly savagery. "She must have known you were on your way there and set out to drive a wedge between us. She's my father's choice of a mate for me, not mine. I haven't been to my cabin since you left me outside the alpha's home. I've been gone from camp on pack business."

Aryck leaned in, searing her with the brushing of his lips against hers. Burning away her anger and distrust by saying, "There's been no other female for me since the moment in the Barrens when the Jaguar saw you for the first time. I tried to fight it. But now I believe we're meant to be together. I want you as my mate."

"Is it even possible for us to have the same bond two Weres can have?"

"Yes. On my word as a pack enforcer, it's possible."

His hands went to the front of her shirt, his thumbs caressing hardened nipples and sending a bolt of heat through her belly and into her woman's folds. "Let me love you. Let me join with you."

A lifetime of restraint fell away. She wanted to take a chance on him. On them.

"Yes," she whispered.

Aryck covered her mouth with his before she could take back the words. He hungered, needed to make her completely and forever his.

His cock pulsed when she parted her lips without requiring persuasion this time. It strained against his soft trousers, anxious for its own greeting as her tongue rushed to rub against his in sensual welcome.

One kiss slid into another, until the need to feel skin to skin became too great to ignore. He stripped her shirt away, hands returning to her breasts and creating a different kind of hunger.

One day his children would nurse there, their creation forever binding him to Rebekka. But for now her lush feminine curves and dark, dark nipples belonged only to him.

He left the wet heat of her mouth, kissed downward to take an areola between his lips and suckle. He purred in satisfaction at her sounds of pleasure, at the feel of her hands in his hair, holding him to her.

More. All. He wanted to lick and kiss every inch of her. To mark her skin with his teeth in passion as well as in a warning to other males to stay away from her.

She trembled against him, the scent of her arousal filling his nostrils and luring him in a siren call he was powerless to resist. She tensed when he unbuttoned her pants, uncertainty and fear mingling with the heady smell of lust.

He wouldn't let her retreat this time as she had after they left Wolf lands. This time she'd know the feel of his mouth on her, the swirl of his tongue over her clit and the thrust of it in her slit.

With a jerk he pulled her pants to her ankles. Went motionless at the sight before him.

Rebekka froze. The heat that had let her pretend everything would be all right disappearing in a flash, leaving her shaking and trying to shore up her defenses.

He knew what the tattoo meant. It was there in his sudden stillness, in the rigidness of his body.

I won't cry, she told herself. *I won't beg him to believe me.*

She couldn't stop herself from flinching when he touched the red *P*. From trying to move away from him.

He stopped her with hands on her hips. Looked up at her, a feral expression on his face instead of one filled with disgust and loathing.

"No other male will ever have you again," he said, deadly promise in his eyes. "I'll kill anyone who attempts it."

Her heart pounded against the wall of her chest as if attempting to break free and escape the risk of further pain. "There's never been anyone. You're the first I've ever been intimate with. The tattoo was forced on me when I was eight. Because I was in a brothel caravan in the San Joaquin and my mother was a prostitute."

He inhaled deeply, as if he would smell the truth on her. His eyelids lowered and there was the distinct sound of masculine satisfaction in his voice as he said, "I'll be your first. And your last."

She was lost with the words. With his belief and acceptance. Left defenseless against the heat from his mouth as he pressed his lips to her mound, overwhelming her, making her cry tears of happiness as well as ecstasy.

She held nothing back as he lapped at her wet, swollen folds. Went willingly when he rid them both of clothing and shoes, then urged her onto the pile of furs serving as bedding. She spread her thighs for him, anxious for him to kneel between them and continue tormenting her with carnal kisses and the hot, decadent touch of his tongue.

Aryck couldn't get enough of her. His cock was hard, slick in its readiness to be inside her. Never had a female overwhelmed his senses the way Rebekka did.

He wallowed in the scent of her, in the luscious heat between her thighs, in the wet evidence of her desire. He wanted to rub every inch of his skin against her mound so all of him smelled of her.

She was so responsive. Her cries alone were enough to have him gripping his penis to keep from spewing his seed outside of her as he had the last time they were together.

The Jaguar screamed, wanting her on her hands and knees. Demanding he cover her that way, thrust inside her with teeth clamped to the back of her neck while in human form since she had no furred one.

Aryck kissed up her body, knowing he was too close to losing control. She deserved tenderness, adoration. He should deny the Jaguar and take her first in the way a human male most often takes the woman he considers his future wife.

He couldn't. Beast and man were too closely aligned in their desires, their needs, his two Earth-bound souls united as they'd always been until disagreement over Rebekka set them against each other.

That foolishness was done with. She was meant to be his mate. He knew it. Accepted it. Rejoiced in it.

He rose above her, rubbing his throat over her lips, growled, "Bite. Leave your mark." And very nearly came when he felt her teeth on him.

Fever raced through him. A wildness that had him snarling and writhing, a cat caught in a sexual trap he had no desire to escape.

She released him with the lick of her tongue against his flesh and he knew only urgency. Only the primal, undeniable urge to mate.

He forced her to her hands and knees, a part of him noting her willingness, purring in pleasure at the way she readily went to her elbows and spread her thighs, presenting him with her wet, swollen vulva.

Another time he'd stop to nuzzle, to lick in approval. This time he came over her, found her opening.

In deference to her virginity, he worked his way in, one torturous inch at a time. Each one of them a test of his endurance.

She was so wet. So hot and slick.

Her channel clung to him. Tightened on him mercilessly. Resisted even as it enticed him to surge forward.

He was panting, shaking by the time he was fully seated.

And underneath him she was whimpering, trembling.

Not in pain, but with the same ecstasy rippling through him.

She rocked backward, urging him to begin moving, and he was help-less against the feminine command. His fingers found her clit, rubbed over it as his hips thrust. Thrust again. And again. Not giving in to the Jaguar's need to mark her until after she screamed in release and he followed, pumping through the hot, wet evidence of her pleasure and filling her with his seed.

Shivers of pleasure ran the length of Rebekka's body in the after-math of lovemaking. Her channel clenched in protest as Aryck's cock left it, but her emotions soared when he repositioned them on the furs so they lay facing each other, limbs entangled.

She traced the flow of muscles along his upper arm. It felt so good to be held by him, to feel the press of his chest against her breasts and the warmth of his penis nestled in the juncture of her thighs.

Her clit pulsed like a softened heartbeat where it touched smooth foreskin, and his subtle rubbing against it sent sparks of renewed desire through her. She understood now the lure of sex, what brought men and women to the brothels even if their money didn't buy them true intimacy.

A blush slid upward and blossomed across her cheeks as she became aware of voices. Unlike the Jaguar camp, there was no privacy to be found among Lions. The open windows and doorways meant the sounds of passion carried throughout the dwelling as well as beyond it.

Aryck's rumbled laugh made her blush deepen. He stroked her cheek, his teeth flashing white in amusement. "Embarrassed? How can you be after growing up among prostitutes?"

"This is not the same. This matters."

"I'm glad," he said, taking her mouth in a series of slow kisses that filled her with pleasure, making her labia swell and part in readiness for him.

Her hand slid down his side, then between their bodies. Seeking him out. Finding him. Her fingers curling around his hardening cock.

This time his laugh held rising desire and purring anticipation. He nibbled at her lips, whispered against them, "Coupling is not something cats feel any shame in doing, or in being *seen* doing. But I'll admit, I don't have the necessary control at the moment to allow any other male to watch us together and fantasize about having you."

She brushed her thumb over the head of his penis. His buttocks flexed and his hips gave a quick thrust. Levity gave way to intensity of expression as he rolled, flattening her back against the soft fur.

Her thighs splayed voluntarily, hips canting to make it easier for him to fill her. But when she would have guided him to her opening, he stilled and gave a low, threatening growl.

It took an instant to hear what he heard. She guessed whoever approached was purposely making enough noise to alert a human.

The footfalls stopped just beyond the doorway. Levi said, "There's a sick Lion, Rebekka. My grandmother would like you to accompany her to the boy's home. After what happened to the Wolves, the pride is wary."

With lithe grace Aryck got to his feet. Rebekka followed, blushing again when his semen escaped her slit and further marked the insides of her thighs with his scent.

He leaned in, teeth clamping down on her shoulder. Biting her then soothing the tiny pain with the caress of his tongue.

He collected his pants and stepped into them. She gathered her clothing and quickly dressed, toeing on her shoes at the doorway, then stepping out of the room.

Levi's expression was neutral, but she knew him too well not to see his worry, feel it. Some of her happiness fell away with the realization that in two days he would have to return to Oakland. With or without her.

Aryck's hand curled possessively around her arm. Her eyes met his and a pang went through her heart as she wondered what lay ahead for them.

Magena waited near the dwelling entranceway. "It's best you remain inside," she told Levi.

He handed the journal to Rebekka. She slid it into her pocket and followed the Lion healer outside.

In tiger form, Caius bounded over to Rebekka. He stood on hind

legs, powerful front limbs wrapping around her waist and nearly knocking her over with the exuberance of his greeting. She gave him a quick
hug and he dropped to all four paws, padding back to Canino.

"This way," Magena said, turning to the left.

Rebekka had thought there were a lot of Lions present when she
arrived; now it looked as though their numbers had tripled in the time
she'd been there. A great number of them were agitated.

They paced, filling the late afternoon with the sounds of their roars.
What cubs she saw were gathered and contained in circles of adult
females who made it clear with teeth and claws they wouldn't let even
the most energetic of their charges leave.

All but Magena wore fur. Rebekka understood why Levi's grandmother had directed him to remain in his family's home.

From somewhere in the mistletoe-laden oak forest that started
where the eucalyptus grove ended, a burst of giggling came, high-
pitched and eerie. It was followed by grunted laughter and the telltale
whooping of hyenas.

It made the hair stand on the back of Rebekka's neck. Her heart
raced in trepidation and dread built with each step.

Several Lions charged in the direction of the noise, more for show
than with the intent of entering the forest. They stopped after going
little more than a hundred feet, paced and roared in warning, gouged
the trees with the rake of their claws before turning and padding back
to the clustered dwellings.

"It's a pack of pure animals," Magena said. Her voice held concern
over the proximity of the hyenas, and their unnatural behavior at ven-
turing so close to territory claimed by a huge pride of Lions.

Twenty-five

A Lion in human form ushered them into the end dwelling. The front rooms were crowded with others. "Everyone having contact with Kerr has been quarantined here," he told Magena.

"Good. How is your son now?"

"Weak, sweating. Only marginally worse than when I sought you out."

"Has he convulsed?" Rebekka asked.

"No."

"Is he conscious?"

"Yes. Come. I'll take you to him."

They passed through several vacant rooms before reaching an opening covered by a heavy elk pelt. The man pulled it aside to reveal a candlelit room, and a boy in his late teens curled into a fetal ball in the center of it.

The window was also covered, as if to minimize the possibility of disease being spread in an airborne manner. It muted the sound of the Lions and hyenas, but in such close proximity, the wild laughter and roars still seemed loud.

Both she and Magena knelt next to Kerr. Aryck crouched at her side.

The boy's father took up a position opposite them. "He's emptied the contents of his stomach and his bowels."

Kerr began trembling. Shivering violently. His teeth chattering.

Magena touched a hand to his forehead. "Fever."

She glanced at Rebekka. "He took down a young buck the hyenas injured but didn't kill. The pack outside came upon him as he gorged himself. They chased him off the carcass and pursued him. He was already ill by the time he returned home."

"Can he change forms?"

"Not again. He did once, to tell his father he felt sick and try to heal through shifting, but he couldn't retake his lion form. There are cures, preparations I would normally make and dispense for these symptoms, but given what happened on Wolf lands . . .

"The pride has gold they can pay you with. Please use your gift so we can know if there are others who will soon fall ill."

High-pitched, eerie giggles pierced the hide covering the window and stabbed into Rebekka. Sweat broke out on her skin.

A shudder passed through her, so noticeable Aryck placed his hand on her back. He stroked her spine in a calming gesture, murmured soothingly, "You're safe. Whatever has stirred them up and brought them this close to the Lions won't bring them any closer."

Rebekka fought to keep from shaking. If Kerr carried disease then it was already among the Lions. If the hyenas were sick then she would call them to their deaths and possibly expose those outside to virus-borne plague. And if she refused to use her gift, she would have to reveal a secret that in all likelihood would lead to her being blamed for what happened on Wolf lands as well as what happened here.

They would kill her. Perhaps they would kill Levi and Aryck as well.

She was damned by any choice she made.

The hide covering the doorway pushed to the side. A white Lion with pale blue eyes entered.

Rebekka knew the shaman by the swirling brands on his face. He sat, allowing the hide to fall back into place and once again serve as a door.

Despite his sightless eyes, she felt as though he'd come to serve as witness to the proceedings. A last glance at the fur-covered window and she made her decision. The risk of doing nothing was too great.

She removed the amulet. As Aryck took it from her, it felt as though ice shattered and splintered in her chest, the blast of it so sharp and intense it doubled her over.

In self-defense and instinctive reaction she placed her hands on the Lion teen. Warmth flowed into her, but it was mild, tepid, and she knew immediately that unlike the Wolves and Jaguars she'd healed, the Lion was nowhere near death.

The knowledge came to her not just because there was no battle between shaman and ancestors, no drums beating in either this world or the place Aryck called the shadowlands, but because the boy's need didn't absorb her gift. Touching him didn't stop the frigid emptiness from spreading, as if some unseen cavity was opening up inside her.

She remembered thinking as she healed the Wolves that her will and gift were just another name for a part of her soul. So she concentrated, consciously gathering what she'd always called her will, and it was like reeling in a part of her that traveled outside of her body and *was* her gift.

Heat replaced the icy emptiness until the only reality was the sick Lion. Then, as she'd done with the Wolves, she looked for the source of illness and its cause.

She touched the teen's lips and jaw and throat for infection pooled in saliva. His forehead for the encephalitis-like inflammation. She found neither.

Her hand moved lower and he moaned in pain when she reached his abdomen. There was infection there. By the amount of it she thought it had been building for some time, perhaps ignored while he was in lion form, or perhaps—

A memory clicked into place. She recognized the ailment as a burst appendix. It was rare among Weres but she'd encountered it once before, soon after moving to the brothel Dorrit managed.

Rebekka drew on the power that had first come to her after accepting the amulet, pulling heat from the core of the Earth—or perhaps the fires of a demon-filled hell—to burn away the mass of infection rather than call on the boy's own body to fight it.

Time lost all meaning. Nothing existed outside of healing until the boy rolled away, breaking the physical contact.

Reality returned in a rush of frigid cold and horror. Outside the dwelling came a hyena's scream abruptly ended.

The feeling of ice in Rebekka's chest grew muted, diminished as though the danger close by had melted away, the intensity fading with the deaths of the hosts carrying it. What remained felt like a single shard driven through her heart, leaving her with a sense of it well beyond the eucalyptus grove, somewhere deeper in the forest. It winked out completely when she took the amulet from Aryck.

Rebekka started to rise to her feet. Magena stopped her with a touch to her arm. "What was wrong with the cub?"

"A burst appendix causing a large pocket of infection."

"Good," Magena said but didn't relax. "Will you accompany me outside to examine the dead and injured?"

Rebekka's skin felt clammy, coated with guilt. The image from the Barrens rose in her mind, human bodies burning on wooden pallets, and, following it, the Elk she'd seen in Wolf lands.

She didn't want to see evidence of the urchin's horrible gift. She'd known when she elected to heal Kerr that any choice she made damned her.

But like that one, there was no denying Magena's request. "I'll go with you."

Aryck helped her to her feet. She found comfort in the feel of his warmth at her side, in the way he threaded his fingers through hers.

Some of the guilt and fear lessened when they emerged from the dwelling and learned none of the Lions had been killed. But the horror remained at the sight of the hyenas who'd been slain when they left the forest and were attacked by the pride.

"Touch the dead first," Magena advised. "So you'll know the disease if it's present in the Lions. I'll order anyone who had contact with the hyenas to gather in one place, regardless of whether they have injuries needing a healer's attention."

Rebekka nodded her acceptance of the suggestion. She went to where the closest hyena lay on ground saturated with body fluids.

She crouched at the head. Aryck crouched with her, holding out his hand in an offer to take possession of her necklace.

Rebekka steeled herself for the awareness of plague that would strike when she gave it to him. Suppressed both gasp and shiver as it came.

This time relief was mixed in with awareness. She couldn't be certain, but it seemed as though what she'd felt earlier was the same, as if the pocket of disease remained in the same place.

The thought gave her pause and made her palms dampen. If she had the courage, could she find the source and either heal the carriers or see them destroyed by the Weres?

Magena joined them at the side of the dead hyena. Rebekka let the question go, forcing herself instead to lay a hand on the animal's forehead.

Like the Wolves, there was massive inflammation of the brain. But unlike them, it had manifested differently, into something like rabies and yet *not* rabies, even if the hyena's unnatural behavior mimicked it.

Rebekka placed her fingertips on the hyena's muzzle. Immediately there was the same horrifying sense of connection she'd experienced when she touched the Wolf pup, the same sense of recognition, as if the virus massed in the saliva and tried to come to her hand so she might carry it to another host.

The taste of disease filled her mouth. Thick and viscous.

She scrambled to her feet, managing only a few steps before bending over and retching.

Clamminess returned to coat her skin. She knew in that instant she couldn't go on carrying the full burden of the secret.

Aryck enfolded her in his arms, nuzzling her cheek and whispering kisses across her ear. "What can I do to help you?"

"You're doing it," she said, pressing against him, hugging him tightly as his strength bolstered her own until she could move away and kneel next to a second corpse.

Magena and Aryck both joined her. She was conscious of the Lions milling, gathered and held in groups. Most of them remained in their animal forms, though the grand matriarch and shaman weren't.

Fires had already been lit in preparation for burning the bodies. Rebekka touched the hyena's forehead and muzzle before removing her hand and saying to Magena, "I needed to be sure. They both carry the same virus. It's like rabies but not quite the same. Their saliva is full of it."

"Do you wish to touch more of them?"

Rebekka couldn't suppress a shudder. "No."

She stood and looked down. But instead of seeing spotted fur and the distinctive shape of a hyena, she saw the slick black fur of a dog killed by settlement police years ago in the San Joaquin.

You brought the rabid dog here, little healer.

Forget now, until it's time for you to join the game.

It was as if she'd come full circle, except this time she wasn't the little girl told to forget or the adult who up until days ago didn't know who her father was. She might be a pawn still, but even pawns had choices.

She glanced at Aryck, her eyes lingering on the amulet in his hand. She'd given him her body, taken the risk he'd turn away from her in disgust and call her a liar when he saw the tattoo.

He'd done neither. Now she had to trust he'd accept her once he knew she was fathered by a demon and gifted with something terrible by her father's enemy.

In the distance she could feel plague, still seemingly where it had been before. It was only a matter of time before it spread.

"I'm ready to check the Lions now," she told Magena. "One with an open wound would be best."

"All but the most seriously injured healed themselves by shifting before I could tell them not to," Magena said, worry in her voice as she led Rebekka to a tight knot of Lions surrounding a fallen pride member.

The young male was too weak to lift his head but his eyes followed Rebekka as she came to his side. Broken bones protruded from both front legs and blood pooled beneath his torn flanks and chest.

Despite his injuries, he was calm, trusting. She touched the places where teeth had ripped into his hide and found nothing but stinging pain. It was the same where the bones had been crushed and broken by powerful jaws.

Cautiously she said, "I'll check others after I heal him, but I don't sense any of the virus in his wounds."

This is the same as what occurred on Wolf lands, Aryck thought as he surveyed the scene around him, the ground littered with dead and the pyres burning with those now being thrown to the fire.

This was the end result of weapons targeted at individual species. Only instead of Elk and Wolf, this disease was meant for Hyenas. There could be no other explanation.

The hyenas had stood no chance against a Lion group swollen to three or four times its normal number as the individual family prides gathered as they did each year at this time. And yet they'd come— infected by something like rabies but not contagious across species lines as rabies was—attacked, and been slaughtered because of it.

He didn't believe it could be coincidence that two previously un-known diseases had struck so soon after the humans trespassed and began salvaging in Coyote lands. It was clear to him they were meant for the Weres.

A glance around and he knew it was clear to the Lions as well. Several males climbed to high perches in the eucalyptus trees. They wore skin instead of fur, and each carried a drum strapped to his back.

Their hair was in dreads, marking them as the shaman's apprentices. And though Aryck had never witnessed it, the Jaguar elders occasionally told stories of days long gone, when humans from Europe arrived and brought with them diseases that wiped out clans and packs and tribes. When drums beat, not in a summoning of the ancestors but in a shaman call for others to enter the shadowlands and share news of the danger threatening all of them.

War with the humans now seemed inevitable. Those in the encampment would die and eventually someone would come in search of them.

The Weres could ensure there was no trace of their involvement, but they couldn't hide the truth. Not when there were gifted humans who could enter the spiritlands and speak with those killed, and necromancers who could summon any souls that lingered and hear their testimonies.

He sought Rebekka with his eyes and found her a distance away. Pride filled him as he watched her healing the last of the Lions who'd been too severely injured to change forms.

She would survive the ancestors' trial. He didn't doubt it, not after all she'd done for the Weres.

He'd expected to have more time with her before he told her what Nahuatl and his father said. He'd thought after a night of lovemaking his confidence would be hers and she'd want to stay and be his mate.

There was no delaying it now. Duty to the pack required him to accompany the Lions as they followed the hyenas' trail and sought evidence it had crossed a human's.

He felt sure they would find it, and when they did, he would need to return to Jaguar lands. After the human encampment was destroyed, except for those left behind to patrol, the Jaguars would move to their winter camp.

For Rebekka to accompany him, she would have to agree to go through the rite. It could be done in their winter territory. There was a sacred grove of trees and a cave where the bones of the Jaguar dead were placed.

Worry crept in as she finished her task and came to him. He'd wanted more time, but even as he pulled Rebekka into his arms, Chátima, the Lion enforcer, was at his side, saying, "We leave now to see what we can learn by following the hyenas' trail. You'll accompany us?"

"I'll catch up to you. I need to speak with Rebekka first."

Aryck led Rebekka to a place where they could speak privately if they were careful to keep their voices low. After fastening the amulet around her neck he took her hands in his. They trembled as if she feared what he might say, and her eyes held a worried, haunted look.

Every instinct demanded he soothe and reassure. Comfort and drive all fear from her life.

He leaned in, touched his mouth to hers. Licked the seam of her lips.

She opened for him on a low moan. Her tongue greeting his, sliding, twining, making him begin to harden.

He deepened the kiss. Extended it. Drew it out and never wanted it to end, though he knew it had to. Others depended on him for their safety, their lives.

His lips clung to hers. He couldn't seem to pull away and so he said what he had to against the sweet softness and carnal temptation of her mouth. "If we find evidence the humans are responsible for the disease on Were lands, we will destroy the encampment. If that happens, the Jaguars will retreat to the most remote and inaccessible portion of our territory. I want you with me. I want you to be my mate."

In anticipation of her reaction, he freed her hands and imprisoned her in his arms. "But you must agree to go through the Rite of Trial before you can return to Jaguar lands."

She stiffened, her hands going to his chest, pushing. "Haven't I already proven myself to the Jaguars?"

"Yes, but without the approval of the ancestors you can't be made part of the pack."

"The same ancestors you claim are responsible for making outcasts? You speak of them as though they're divine beings who have the right to judge. As if in death they're somehow more infallible than in life."

Fear of losing her filled Aryck. He was handling this badly. Desperation seized him and made him speak without thinking. "Will you still wish to be my mate if I'm made outcast by the ancestors? Do you want to one day offer me the same choice you gave Levi?"

As soon as the words were out he knew it'd been a mistake to say them. He slammed his mouth down on hers to prevent her from answering, to keep their argument from escalating as it had the first night she was in Jaguar lands.

He kissed her with all the raw emotion churning inside him. Knowing he had to leave, not just to see to his duty, but before he made things between them worse. Before she gave him an answer he didn't want to hear.

Against her lips, he said, "The ancestors had a hand in your being brought to Were lands. It was because of them *I* went to Oakland instead of another male from our pack. It can't be coincidence you're here, at this time when your gift is desperately needed. They will judge you worthy. I'm sure of it. Think on it while I'm gone."

With one last kiss he released her. "You are the only female I've ever considered taking as a mate," he said, then turned and loped away, telling himself he hurried to follow the hunting Lions, and not because he was afraid to stay longer.

Is Aryck right? Rebekka wondered, watching him move with easy grace through the eucalyptus grove. Did the ancestors who played such an important role in the lives of the pure Weres mean for her to be Aryck's mate? She'd had a similar thought. Only instead of the Were ancestors, she'd been thinking of her father.

Rebekka became aware of the stench of burning flesh. She thought back to the bodies in the Barrens on her way to the Fellowship, and the moment in the garden when Brother Caphriel had offered to change the nature of her gift. But at a cost.

The Were ancestors were no different. Phaedra had admitted as much. *There is always a price to be paid where they are concerned.*

Would standing before them lead to her becoming a healer who could make those Weres trapped between forms whole, as Annalise Wainwright prophesied? Or would it only take her farther away from being able to help them, just as going with Aryck would take her farther from Oakland?

Or would it lead to nothing but her death?

"Choices," Rebekka murmured. At least she remained certain about one of them. She could do something about the threat she felt in the distance. She could prevent another slaughter while she came to a decision about Aryck and the rite.

She wasn't afraid of going alone. The Weres knew she was in their lands and Aryck's scent would identify her. She was far more frightened of what she'd find and that it might be virulent and fast acting, delivering death to anyone with her before she could prevent it.

Her hand dropped to the journal in her pocket. It was too valuable a thing to take with her as she sought out the plague. Levi already carried the coins she'd gotten from Aryck in the Barrens. The trick would be in giving him the book without rousing his suspicions. If he knew what she intended, he would accompany her.

The answer came to her when she saw Caius and, nearby, Canino. She hurried to the Tiger, pulling the journal from her pocket as she did.

Canino rumbled a greeting. She held the book out, asked, "Will you take this to Levi for me?"

The Tiger got to his feet and gently took the journal between his teeth. His tail flicked in the direction of the cub like a lure as he trotted off.

Caius bumped against Rebekka's leg then bounded after Canino. Rebekka left, doing her best not to draw attention to herself as she headed toward the nearest place where eucalyptus trees gave way to denser forest.

She expected to hear the pounding of footsteps or Levi's voice yelling for her to stop. But somehow she made it, slipping among mistletoe-laden oak and startling a cardinal from its perch.

Rebekka dared to look back. There was no sign of pursuit.

Her hands lifted to the amulet. She took it off, holding it up, studying it.

The black feather anchored on either side by red beads swirled and fluttered in a tiny breeze, shimmering in a spectrum of light and color. She hesitated, gathering her courage and her resolve.

Don't be a coward, she told herself. If she was to do this thing, then she needed to be fully committed.

She hung it from a tree branch. As soon as her fingers left it, awareness came like a frigid arrow pointing her in the direction she must go.

The first step away from the witches' protection that had come to symbolize her father's as well was the hardest. And the ones that followed weren't much easier.

She refused to look back, even when the drums began beating behind her.

Twenty-six

ARYCK knelt near the abandoned den area. The smell of hyena was strong, and in the concentration of urine marking their territory, so was the stench of disease.

The irony of it being *this* pack wasn't lost on him. Not so many days ago he'd stood on the rise above and tossed the bodies of Daivat's victims to the hyenas.

Today there were other victims. Pups and those already weakened by age, along with several of the males he'd thought were new to the pack.

Disease had taken some of them. Violence had taken others.

This was Jaguar land and the moment he'd stepped onto it he'd touched his mind to his father's. With a thought, he let Koren see the scene before him.

Though it was their land, neither protested when Chátima rose from his position next to Aryck, saying, "I'll leave men behind to burn the bodies. The rest of us can spread out, tracking the individual pack members."

It was a good plan. And it quickly yielded results. Within minutes a Lion roared in discovery, bringing the hunters to the place where a human's scent lay heavily around a tree.

Aryck undressed and shifted to jaguar form. A leap, claws digging into bark, and he was climbing, following the scent upward into the concealing branches, then out onto a limb where the man had lain, masturbating and leaving semen on the leaves, making Aryck spit in distaste.

Below him several of the Lions had changed as well, their lips pulled back and noses close to the ground to read the story they found there. Aryck backed up, retracing his movements until he could jump.

He landed near his pants and shed his fur in favor of being able to speak. "A man watched from above."

One of the Lions also took a human form. "There are footprints in the dirt here. The impressions are deeper arriving than leaving. He carried food and left it for the hyenas, then waited to make sure they took the bait. The smell of hyena and lack of remains makes it impossible for me to be sure what he fed them. Perhaps it was a woman's corpse, or possibly she handled the meat and cut herself while doing it. There was a trace of her scent, that's all."

Aryck met the eyes of the Lion enforcer. "The humans either came to Were lands with the intent of killing us or they found something in the ruins they excavate that allowed them to do it."

"Agreed," Chátima said. "Waiting them out is no longer an option."

Aryck conveyed what they'd discovered to his father. Koren said, *It's good you have already made overtures toward alliance. Nahuatl answered the drums of the Lion shaman and found Wolf, Bear, Hyena, and Coyote gathered in the shadowlands. We will meet tonight, shaman, alpha, and enforcer, each trio accompanied by fifteen armed warriors. With safe passage granted directly through each other's lands, we can react quickly to the threat the humans pose.*

An image of the place accompanied Koren's words, along with the position of the moon to fix the time. *I will speak in favor of attacking immediately. The elders are in agreement. I think the other alphas will come to the meeting with the same intent.*

I will see you there, Aryck said, glad he had time to return to the Lion dwelling place and speak with Rebekka again before joining his father and the others.

IT took Rebekka miles to figure it out. At first her own fears blocked her ability to do anything more than put one foot in front of the other. But slowly, when there seemed to be no change in the place harboring whatever carried the plague, she was able to think.

She wondered then if she'd needed to come to Were lands to fully make the connection, to understand the amulet didn't block the diseased from coming to her; it kept the part of her spirit that *was* her gift from seeking them out and drawing them to her.

In a way, it was similar to a human shaman spirit-walking in the ghostlands or a Were visiting ancestors in the shadowlands. The difference was that before the urchin had appeared and restored her memories, unleashing the part of him he'd given her by the stream when she was a child, her soul traveled only as far as those she touched.

What had taken her a while to understand was that regardless of what he'd done, it was still *her* spirit, and just as a shaman was able to choose where he or she went in the ghostlands, or whether they entered them at all, she could now do the same.

It took conscious thought, a willful leashing of the part of her that fled, causing the cold to blossom in her chest, but she could do it. She didn't *need* the amulet any longer, though having it would serve as a safeguard until control was second nature.

But if she'd gained surety in one regard, in another, doubt had crept in. Was the urchin figure her father's enemy, or his ally?

She'd had to mentally block that line of inquiry time and time again. It would only spiral into an endless circle without beginning or end.

A war was coming between supernaturals. Her role in preparing for it had been scripted by beings she couldn't understand and whose realities she couldn't fathom. In the end, she had only her heart to guide her, her sense of right and wrong.

So what does it mean when it comes to a future with Aryck?

An ache formed in her chest, so intense it equaled the icy pull drawing her inexorably to her destination. She was no closer to an answer to that question than she had been when she watched him leave.

ARYCK hadn't yet reached the eucalyptus grove marking the heart of Lion territory when he caught Rebekka's scent along with that of both Tigers. He smelled Lions too, which was to be expected, but it was the odor of frequent travel and not a recent passing.

Missing was Levi's scent. And his brother Cyrin's. They'd both been with Rebekka and the Tigers when she came from Jaguar lands to these.

A tightness formed in Aryck's chest. This was not a direct route from the Jaguar camp to the Lion dwelling places.

He crouched. Inhaled deeply. Studied what he could see of the partial prints left in the thin layer of dust that would remain until the rains came.

Rebekka traveled away from the Lion homes. And though he couldn't be certain, not without examining more of the track, Caius and Canino followed rather than accompanied her.

Their paw prints left impressions on top of hers, never the reverse. And still there was no sign of Levi.

Aryck stood and turned toward Chátima. Despite what his eyes and nose told him, he asked, "Did you bring Rebekka through here?"

There was suspicion in the enforcer's expression, along with a measure of pity that had Aryck fighting to keep his lips from pulling back in a snarl.

"No. This is not the path we traveled. You spoke to her about what would happen if we found evidence the humans were responsible for the hyenas' sickness?"

It was no less than what his father would ask in front of the others when they gathered. "Yes."

Chátima looked in the direction she'd gone. They both knew this valley ultimately fed into the one the Coyotes claimed.

The Jaguar rose in Aryck, flexing its claws through human fingers. The man had no intention of letting anything happen to Rebekka. "I'm going after her. The meeting place is close to the encampment. I will collect Rebekka and bring her with me."

"When the vote is taken, it will be in favor of killing everyone in the encampment and letting their god sort them out. We can't risk that even one of them will escape with whatever knowledge has allowed them to wage war on us with disease."

"I know."

The Lion enforcer sighed heavily. "Your female is a healer, soft-hearted by nature. And human. She can't be blamed for wanting to prevent the deaths of the innocent. I will speak to the grand matriarch and then follow you to make sure Rebekka is stopped from warning the humans of our intentions. As you say, the meeting place is in the same direction."

Aryck spared only an instant to bare his teeth at the implied threat. Then he turned and ran, racing to get to Rebekka before harm came to her, his guilt building with each step at having handled their last parting so badly.

Haven't I already proven myself to the Jaguars? she'd asked, the words haunting him now.

She had. He was the one who hadn't yet proven himself, hadn't been willing to seriously consider starting a pack of his own. There'd be no need for her to stand before the ancestors then.

He still believed he had their blessing when it came to making her his mate. If she agreed but wanted further assurance, *he* would be the one to stand before them in a Petitioner's Rite.

DUSK descended in the valley Rebekka had entered a short while earlier. The air cooled with the growing darkness and she knew she would have to take shelter for the night soon.

Ruins stretched out before her. Foliage-covered mounds of concrete forming an intricate, forbidding maze.

A distant ridgeline looked familiar. She wasn't sure whose territory she was in but she thought perhaps it was Wolf.

Nocturnal animals had already begun stirring. They rustled as they moved around in burrows dug out of rubble and nests built in dense foliage. The sound of an owl hooting seemed like an ominous omen.

She nearly lost her nerve, almost gave in to the temptation to save this task for the morning. The taste of disease now coated her tongue regardless of how often she tried to banish it by chewing on bay leaves or sipping from honeysuckle flowers. The knowledge she was close, very close, kept her moving forward.

"Just a little bit farther," she told herself, jumping when her words were punctuated by a gun firing close by.

It was a single shot, a rifle or pistol rather than a machine gun. A few of the Wolves had carried them, though she hadn't seen them among the Lions or Jaguars.

Despite the sense of urgency pressing her, she stopped. Listened. Heard nothing unusual until a breeze brought the faint sound of bleating.

Goats. Penned animals would explain why her destination seemed fixed.

Was she near the encampment then? It was horrifying to think the Weres could be right about humans purposely letting disease loose.

Indecision held her. Go forward or turn back?

She'd seen no evidence of animal husbandry among the Weres. But what if it existed? What if plague had been unknowingly introduced to their flocks and herds?

Just a little farther, she decided. Just far enough to know one way or the other, so she could either heal the sick or hide and wait for help to come.

Aryck would come for her if he returned to the Lion pride homes and found her missing. Levi would say something to his grandmother when he realized she was gone.

Rebekka moved forward cautiously. Once again the breeze brought the sound of goats.

They bleated continuously. Sounds of agitation and distress.

The taste of sickness coated her tongue more heavily. It slid down her throat until she bent over and retched.

She forced herself forward. The rustling of animals hidden in the ruins grew louder.

An involuntary cry escaped when a burrowing owl launched itself upward in front of her like a warning to stop.

Her nerves stretched tauter. Just a little bit farther, she told herself again. Just until she reached the corner ahead.

Thick, wild grapevines began to dominate. They formed curtains in what might once have been windows and trailed across the path, making it treacherous.

As she drew near the corner she thought she caught the whiff of a campfire. She relaxed a tiny bit. The Jaguars cooked over fire pits. Surely any humans in the area would have eaten their meals earlier and doused their fires so they could take shelter.

Rebekka reached the corner and discovered just how badly she erred.

Men approached on another path, from the direction the earlier gunfire had come from.

In a glance she took in the black-and-white-striped uniforms that work-gang convicts wore in Oakland.

The deer carcass carried on a pole between two of them.

The militiamen accompanying them.

Before she could dart out of sight, a convict ranging ahead of the others noticed her. She turned and ran. Hoped they wouldn't dare follow this close to full dark.

A shout told her otherwise.

Then racing footsteps.

A rifle fired a moment later, sending a bullet crashing into the rubble to her right.

She tripped on grapevines and fell. Scrambled to her feet but the delay had cost her.

She managed another few yards before one of the men tackled her, driving her into the ground.

Two others joined the first. Flipping her. Pinning her arms and legs. Tugging at her clothing. Rape on their minds and in their expressions.

Out of the corner of her eye there was a flash of white. She fought to escape even harder when she realized it was Caius barreling toward her.

Canino followed, and in an instant she was freed, though she didn't dare rise to her feet. Machine gun bullets sprayed above and around her, shredding vines and ricocheting off stone.

The three convicts lay dead, killed by Tigers or the militiamen. She couldn't tell without examining them, and didn't care to. Her heart thundered and fear gripped her as she visually searched the ground near where Canino and Caius had disappeared into the mazelike ruins, desperate to see no evidence either of them had been hit.

"Grab her," the militiaman holding the machine gun said, his eyes and body making a continuous sweep, his finger never leaving the gun's trigger. "She goes back with us. She needs to pay for the trouble we're going to be in because of her."

"I like the way you think, Gregor," the man carrying the rifle said, drawing close enough for Rebekka to recognize the Ivanov crest embroidered into his collar.

She scrambled backward. Desperate hope flaring to life. If only she could escape and take the information back to The Iberá . . .

He stepped between her and his companion, providing an instant of protection against the spray of machine gun bullets. When he jerked an amulet from beneath his shirt and glanced down to see if she was Were, Rebekka rolled to her feet and tried to dart away.

She made it only a few steps before pain splintered through her head. Unconsciousness followed.

Twenty-seven

THE closer Aryck got to the encampment, the more he feared for Rebekka. What did she hope to accomplish by making this trip?

Humans who would unleash the horrors she'd seen in Wolf and Lion territory wouldn't be open to reason. She had to know that.

Suspicion tried to invade his thoughts as it had many times since it became obvious she was heading directly to the encampment. How did she know the way?

Aryck refused to contemplate she might betray the Weres. But the Lion enforcer who'd caught up and now easily paced him grew grimmer with each mile.

Full dark had arrived, a time when natural predators hunted, and Rebekka was defenseless against them save for the calm her gift allowed her to project. Above them the moon inched higher, slowly moving closer to when the Weres were to meet.

They'd already passed the turnoff leading to the ridge path and the place where the encampment would be visible. Aryck pushed on, determined they would find her safe and unharmed.

Hope surged through him at the sound of something coming their way and making no attempt at stealth. Caution dictated he take cover.

A glance to the side and Chátima pointed to where he intended to veer off the trail. Aryck chose a place opposite, in case ambush became necessary.

Both remained human. Both drew knives from sheaths worn at their thighs. Both readied themselves to attack.

What had sounded like one entity became two. Aryck cocked his head, interpreting the footfalls. Two and four, with the four-footed animal the heavier and both of those approaching close enough to hear them panting.

Aryck was already standing and hurrying forward when the Tigers came into view, Caius holding his side, the smell of human blood and sweat preceding them.

"What happened?" Aryck asked, reaching them a moment before Chátima did.

Tears rolled down the cub's cheeks. A sob escaped. "We didn't know the humans were so close until it was too late. They caught Rebekka when she tried to run away from them. They were holding her down and pulling at her clothes. Canino and I stopped them. But then the two with guns started shooting and we couldn't get close again. One of them hit Rebekka so hard she didn't get up. They left the dead humans but they took her with them to the encampment."

Despite the pain stabbing through Aryck's heart he knelt and pulled Caius into a hug. "You and Canino showed great courage to do what you did, and even greater sense to retreat and seek help rather than throw your lives away. Rebekka wouldn't have wanted you to do that. We'll get her back. *I'll* get her back."

"We should have caught up to her right after she left. She asked Canino to take the journal to Levi. Then we found her necklace hanging from a tree." There was confusion and hurt in Caius's voice, the pain of a boy who knew the sting of abandonment and loss.

"I'm sure she had a reason," Aryck said. "We'll ask her about it when she's back with us, then warn her against going off alone again."

He set Caius away from him and said to Chátima, "The Tigers will accompany us to the meeting place."

"Agreed."

They backtracked. Then took the trail that climbed out of the Coyotes' ruin-filled valley, finally reaching the ridge where the other Weres waited.

The mental link with his father allowed for the easy transfer of information. What surprised Aryck was arriving to find his father had openly revealed their ability to communicate by sharing what Caius had said with the others.

"I intend to go after her as soon as my duty here is finished," Aryck said, keeping his voice from offering a challenge, though inside the Jaguar seethed at the delay even as the man knew it was necessary.

The Wolf alpha was the first to respond. "We owe the healer a debt. If we decide to eradicate the settlement tonight, then our attack can begin after you've freed her. If necessary, the Wolves will provide a distraction."

Koren folded his arms across his chest as if to bar the part of him that was father instead of alpha from expressing itself. "We, too, owe the healer a debt. We will also allow enough time for her to be recovered."

"We will as well," the female Lion who acted on behalf of the grand matriarch said, sparing the Hyena, Coyote, and Bear alphas a quick glance before pointedly turning her attention to the encampment. "Unless there is an objection, let us agree to the Jaguar enforcer going first, and then to seeing this thing done tonight. There is no advantage in waiting and every reason to eliminate the threat to us immediately."

It took less than five minutes for the alphas to reach agreement, and only another twenty for the enforcers and the men who would go with them to settle on a strategy for attack.

As Aryck started toward the path that would take him to Rebekka, Nahuatl stopped him. "Perhaps she went to the encampment to meet someone but was intercepted by others unaware of her purpose. Are you so sure you know her heart?"

A knot of pain formed in Aryck's chest as he flashed back to his last conversation with her. He wasn't sure of her heart when it came to him. But for the Weres, especially the outcasts, he had an answer. "Yes."

REBEKKA swam upward to consciousness with nausea and panic pressing in on her. She fought back the urge to vomit, terrified of dying with it filling her throat, blocked from escaping by the gag tied brutally around her head.

She was bound, wrists to ankles, and lying on her side. Frantic sound, a sense of urgency, pounded into her, slicing through the pain in her head and bringing her fully awake.

The pungent scent of goat surrounded her. Their frantic bleating and repeated battering at the fence separating them from her brought horrifying knowledge racing with it.

Plague. They were ripe to deliver it.

Voices expanded her awareness beyond the goats and their desperate, instinctive desire to get to her. This close to them it was harder to call back the part of her soul that was her gift. She managed it, but her control wouldn't last.

The animals quieted. A black mouse decided to change hiding places. It darted past her, its fur brushing her forehead, the soft feel of it taking away the stabbing pain that remained from the blow.

Rebekka sought out the voices through slitted eyes, careful not to let the two men who argued a short distance away know she was conscious. One of them was the militiaman who'd carried the machine gun. The other wore a rich man's clothing, though she didn't recognize him.

She closed her eyes again, listened as the stranger said, "I told you not to leave the herd unattended."

"And I got tired of listening to them. I got tired of smelling goat piss and stinking like it. I wanted to do some hunting, and I padlocked the door shut to keep your precious herd safe. You should be grateful I went after deer and bagged something better. It saves you the cost of a prostitute. For now anyway. Down the road I'll expect you to let me have one of them—call it hazardous duty pay, a little bonus to compensate me for the shit I've had to deal with."

"I'm the one who decides what your services are worth."

An ugly laugh met the comment. "Are you, Radek? The Ivanov patriarch pays my salary. Your brother Viktor gives the orders I say 'yes Sir' to, not you. If you and I didn't share a common interest when it comes to liking women dead at the end of our fun, I wouldn't be standing in this shit hole. I'd be in my nice bunk fantasizing about killing the whore underneath me while I pounded into her with my cock."

Someone banging on the door jerked Rebekka's eyes open. A voice from the other side yelled, "Get out here, Gregor. Now. Captain Orst wants to see you. He wants to hear what you've got to say about letting three convicts die and why you and Morse left their bodies behind. I want to know the same."

Hope surged to life inside Rebekka at the mention of the guardsman she'd met in The Iberá's study. It had to be the same man. He must have accompanied the convict work-gang. It wasn't unheard of when their labor was contracted out.

She struggled into a sitting position, grateful her hands were bound to her ankles in front of her instead of behind. She tried desperately to get the gag out of her mouth, and, finding it impossible, to wriggle to a place where the man at the door would see her when it opened.

Her control of her gift slipped. The goats resumed bleating frantically and trying to escape their pen. The taste of disease filled her mouth and clung to her nostrils, bringing with it another nearly overwhelming urge to vomit.

"Get out here, Gregor!"

"Go," Radek said, moving the short distance to Rebekka and using his foot to send her sprawling backward. "I don't want to deal with that prick Orst tonight, or my brother's lapdog Nagy. Take care of your mess or you won't get to have fun with your prize."

The militiaman left.

Radek bolted the door after him then paced in agitation back and forth between Rebekka and the pen.

He cursed Gregor and Orst and Nagy. Muttered about changing his plan, about the goats not being completely ready, about the wisdom of freeing a couple of them since there were tigers in the area.

Desperation seized Rebekka. Somehow she had to escape and get to Captain Orst. She had to tell him Radek was purposely letting plague loose. She had to stop the Weres from attacking the encampment and slaughtering innocent people for something only Radek was responsible for.

His head whipped around suddenly, catching her looking at him.

Fear entered his expression. It scared him that she'd overheard his mutterings. That she might have guessed what he was doing.

Radek came over to her. He drew the pistol from a holster at his side and pressed the barrel to her forehead.

Her heart thundered in her chest. The bleating of the goats was so loud she wasn't sure anyone would hear the sound of gunfire over it.

His finger tightened on the trigger then released it. Tightened and released again as if he was working himself up to pulling it.

Pounding on the door made his hand jerk. Rebekka whimpered, knowing she would be dead if the knock had come an instant earlier, when his finger touched the trigger.

"Who is it?" he yelled.

"Gregor."

Radek let him in, the pistol still in his hand.

"Enjoying a little foreplay?" Gregor asked, his smile sickening Rebekka, sending dread crawling through her. She'd seen the same look on other faces after they'd picked a prostitute and made their bargain with the madam.

Radek moved into the doorway. "No one else comes in here tonight. And you don't leave."

"Morse is owed a little fun with her. He's the one who hauled her back."

Radek cast a glance at Rebekka, visibly calculating the risk. "Just him. Have your fun tonight. Dead or alive, she leaves the encampment tomorrow."

Gregor laughed. "She'll be gone. I think we both know which way it'll be."

He locked the door after Radek left, unzipped his pants, and pulled out his flaccid cock as he walked toward her.

Her terror projected onto the goats. They hurtled themselves at their pen with renewed agitation.

"Shut up!" Gregor screamed, his penis remaining limp in his hand.

Twenty-eight

ARYCK dropped soundlessly to the ground. Blood seeped from small cuts on his chest and arms where spikes of metal from the concertina wire on top of the encampment walls had pierced the thick leather hides he'd laid on top of them.

Light blazed around only a few buildings, powered by generators that would be easy to disable. Lanterns bobbed in the darkness, marking the places where men patrolled and making them easy targets.

When the first of them fell, the others would riddle the night with machine gun fire. If they weren't already doing it after seeing amulets blaze to life in the presence of Weres.

There would be dead on both sides before this was over. *Rebekka won't be one of them.* She would be safe outside the fence before the attack started.

A short distance away the goats continued to panic at having picked up the scent of so many predators closing in on them. He'd heard them from the place Rebekka was taken to the ground, smelled them on one of the men who'd been there and left alive.

Aryck's lips pulled back in a feral promise of retribution. It was the same man who'd hidden in the tree and masturbated as the hyenas ate the deadly gift he'd left for them.

Aryck pulled the knife from its leg sheath and moved toward the goats. His progress was slowed by the need to stay clear of amulets set throughout the encampment, as well as those worn by the men patrolling in groups of three and four.

He was within sight of the building housing the goats when Rebekka's scent reached him, wafting through slits in the boards and laced with pain and fear.

Man and Jaguar screamed in silent fury, but hurried footsteps kept Aryck from racing forward.

He ducked behind a pile of dirt left next to a hole leading into a room once buried but now cleared. A human passed close enough for him to know the man had been one of the two responsible for bringing Rebekka to the encampment.

Aryck launched himself, as silent in his two-legged form as he was in his animal one. An amulet at the front of the man's shirt flashed red, but before he could sound a warning, the blade in Aryck's hand sliced through flesh and muscle and blood supply as easily as a jaguar claw through hide.

Sheathing the knife, Aryck took up the dead human's gun. He checked to make sure it was ready to fire, delayed only long enough to drag the body to the excavated hole and tumble it in, hoping to delay discovery long enough to set Rebekka free.

Anticipating the door would be locked, he ran the remaining distance, used momentum to force his way into the building and Jaguar agility to get out of the doorway. A glance was all Aryck needed to take in the scene. To see Rebekka's bruised face and the cloth keeping her screams silenced, her shirt hanging open after she had been chased and knocked to the ground, a man reaching for a machine gun, his zipper down and his tiny cock hanging limp.

Fury engulfed Aryck. Rage overwhelmed reason and eradicated any thought of remaining undetected. He aimed and pulled the trigger, the bullets making the man dance backward until the gun was empty.

Aryck tossed it aside and hurried to Rebekka. She was standing, tugging off the gag, hastily putting her shirt to rights.

Koren's mind touched Aryck's in instant communication. *We'll divert their attention elsewhere.*

"Let's go," Aryck said, wanting to shake her, kiss her, punish and cherish her all at the same time.

Rebekka resisted when he tried to hurry her toward the door. "The goats are diseased," she said, halting him in his tracks. "They carry something that will kill Tigers, maybe other things. There's a man here I trust. A captain in the guard. He promised The Iberá if I ever needed his aid, he'd give it. Leave. I'll find him. I'll—"

The Jaguar snarled at the very idea. The man growled, "I'm not leaving you."

There was no time to argue. No time to deal with the threat the goats presented except one way.

Lanterns lit the small area. Barrels of fuel were stored against one wall like a private hoard.

Aryck picked up the dead man's machine gun. Despite what he felt for Rebekka he had a duty to the pack.

He jerked her to his chest, clamping her there.

"Forgive me," he said, doubting in his heart it would be possible for her to do, but pulling the trigger anyway, and killing the goats with the sweep of his arm.

She stood stock-still when he released her. Didn't move again until fire raged in the pen, consuming straw and eating at corpses alike. Then she ran for the door.

He followed, grabbing her arm and dragging her into the darkness, away from the building that rapidly became engulfed in flames.

In the distance arrows tipped with fire rained down on the encampment. Wolves howled and Hyenas laughed. Lion and Jaguar roared while Coyotes sang and humans yelled.

He feared she'd curse him, revile him for what he'd done; instead Rebekka turned into him, pleaded with her eyes and voice. "Let me find Captain Orst. I can stop this. I can make sure there's no more virus and the person responsible is punished. There's no need to kill innocent humans and start a war that will lead to Weres being legally hunted. Please, Aryck. Leave. Trust me to do this."

Every instinct demanded he get her away from the encampment. Both Jaguar and man bridled at the ease in which she seemed to think she could send them to safety while remaining in danger herself.

He should say no. But he found he couldn't.

"We'll look for this Captain Orst," he said, sending a message to his father to have those outside continue providing a distraction instead of attacking in earnest.

Rebekka closed her mind to the carnage they left behind. There was nothing she could do for the goats. Nothing she could change.

Despite the horror of what Aryck had done, she understood his actions. She accepted the necessity of it. Leaving the animals alive was too great a risk.

She had no time to heal them if Radek was to be stopped and war against the Weres avoided. And yet her heart wept all the same. She could have healed them. If not for their trying to get to her, Gregor would have raped her.

They found Captain Orst shouting orders to men in black-striped clothing. He turned when Rebekka called his name, shocked recognition coming to his face as he saw her step into the light.

Immediately he strode toward her. The amulet lying against his chest flaring when he was steps away.

He started to draw his weapon but stopped when Rebekka said, "Radek is responsible for the trouble with the Weres. He let plague lose on their lands. Elk, Wolves, and Hyenas have been affected so far."

"You have proof?"

There was no hiding the truth, no need to now that she'd gained a measure of control when it came to bringing the sick to her. "My gift drew me here. The goats being guarded by Gregor were diseased. I'm the reason the three convicts he was with earlier are dead. They caught me in the woods. The Were protected me against being raped but couldn't stop Gregor and his friend from bringing me here. I was in the building when Radek was there. I heard him mumbling to himself."

"Remain here," Orst said, turning and walking away, disappearing from sight for moments that seemed to drag even as they made Rebekka's heart race and her mouth grow dry.

He returned accompanied by six men wearing the uniform of the Ivanov militia, including one wearing a captain's stripes. Radek was with them.

Aryck forced her behind him, keeping the machine gun aimed at the approaching men. "Do you continue to trust him?"

"Yes."

The men stopped before the amulets they wore recognized Aryck. Orst continued on, into striking distance.

"Captain Nagy is prepared to search Radek's quarters for proof of Rebekka's claim," he said to Aryck. "You're free to keep the knife. But you need to surrender the gun before the two of you can accompany us."

Rebekka touched Aryck's back. It vibrated with tension, with reluctance, with the struggle to trust others for protection instead of relying on himself.

"Please, Aryck," she whispered, leaning forward and placing a kiss between his shoulder blades, uncaring if Captain Orst and the others knew she'd taken a Were for a lover.

Aryck let the butt of the machine gun swing so the barrel was pointing at a star-filled sky. With a low growl he said, "Take it."

Orst took the weapon, and they joined the others. He handed it to one of the militiamen.

"Put the amulets under your shirts," Captain Nagy said.

After his men had complied, he forced Radek forward with a pistol pressed to his back. The other five militiamen fanned out, two of them flanking Rebekka and Aryck, rifles held across their arms in a casual pose, but barrels aimed and fingers resting on the triggers.

The terror in the encampment was palpable. Outside the walls the night was filled with the sounds of Weres in their animal forms. Inside them men shouted orders to move the barrels containing fuel and get the trucks away from wooden buildings, concentrating on salvaging and slowing the spread of fire rather than wasting water in an attempt to put it out.

Men wearing work-gang clothing and others bearing the tattoos of lawbreakers worked side by side with guardsmen, militiamen, and prostitutes in various stages of undress.

Radek's agitation increased as they neared the building that must be their destination. He looked around frantically for an ally but whether it was because they were caught up in their tasks or because they didn't want to become involved, backs remained turned in his direction.

"He stinks of fear," Aryck murmured. "It grows stronger with each step he takes."

Radek bolted, only to be immediately dropped to the ground by Captain Nagy.

The militiaman holstered his weapon and freed handcuffs from a pouch attached to his belt. He wrenched Radek's arms behind his back, securing them with a snick and slide of metal on metal, before fishing a key ring out of Radek's pocket and tossing it to Captain Orst.

Captain Nagy stood, hauling Radek to his feet.

"This betrayal will cost you," Radek said, expanding his threat to include all of the militiamen. "My family will make it impossible for any of you to find work. You'll be lucky if you can eke out a living in the red zone."

Orst unlocked and opened the door. Light poured out, a luxury created by the generator steps away.

With a shove Captain Nagy forced Radek forward toward Orst. "Take charge of him."

"In," Orst said, the look on his face revealing how much he would enjoy a challenge from Radek.

Radek entered. When a militiaman would have followed, Captain Nagy lifted a hand. "You men stay out here."

He pointed to where the generator stood, its steady throb at odds with the noise and confusion coming from behind them. To the man closest to it, he said. "Get the can of gasoline. Put it next to the door."

As the militiaman complied, Nagy unholstered his pistol. A glance at Rebekka and Aryck, accompanied by the flick of his wrist, indicated they were to enter the building next.

Aryck tensed. Rebekka's heart pounded. If she was wrong—

I'm not. Radek's increased agitation and doomed escape attempt had to mean something inside the building would incriminate him. She stepped through the doorway, knowing Aryck would follow her.

A low growl rumbled in his throat as soon as he did. "Something died in here," he said, using his body to position her between him and the wall.

Captain Nagy entered. The door closed behind him, trapping air and scent inside.

Rebekka could smell a hint of urine and voided bowels. She remembered the conversation she'd overheard. "Gregor said he and Radek shared a common interest. They both like to kill women at the end of their fun."

Captain Orst frowned, directed his words at Nagy. "The Were smells death in here. Two prostitutes have gone missing. The last one left the brothel building with Radek but never returned. He claimed he finished with her early and sent her away. Gregor provided an alibi, saying he saw her later going off with someone else."

Captain Nagy shrugged. "While I find the murder of a prostitute personally distasteful, it's not what brings us here. Do what you can to prove the healer's allegations against Radek before this night ends in slaughter."

Still standing protectively between her and Captain Nagy, Aryck flexed and unflexed his fingers, as though he was close to shifting forms and attacking.

Rebekka touched his back. Stroked. Her stomach knotting in nervous anticipation as Captain Orst went to the desk.

One of the keys slid smoothly into the top drawer. Orst pulled it open and reached in, removing a green canister whose design and appearance made Rebekka think of something left over from the days of war.

Setting it on the desk, he said, "It's got an image of a wolf engraved into the metal."

A second canister joined the first. "Hyena."

A third followed. "This one appears more generic. I presume it's meant for big cats of all types, certainly the image could mean mountain lion or jaguar."

The muscles against Rebekka's hand bunched in a prelude to attack. She wrapped her arms around Aryck's waist. "Wait," she whispered, hugging him tightly.

Twenty-nine

ORST'S expression held nothing but loathing as he looked at Radek. "Death is too good for a man willing to unleash plague. Tell me where the information files relating to these canisters are."

Radek sneered, his earlier fear falling away. "Find them yourself. If you can. You have no evidence against me. All you have is the accusation of a woman who is willing to sleep with an animal. Even if you did have proof, I'd take my chances with a jury of my peers. They'd see me as a hero! A visionary! Someone with the courage to act and get rid of the Weres."

"They'd see you for what you are, the worst of what humans are capable of."

Orst placed his hands on the keyboard and began typing. Rebekka's only experience with computers was at the library. She didn't know how to do more than perform searches for information on what the librarian called an internet, a network of huge private computers all storing massive amounts of data and connected together by cables running underground.

The captain knew quite a bit more. It didn't take long before the sound of typing stopped and the movement of his eyes indicated he was reading.

When he looked up he said, "I found his notes. The super-virus targeting werewolves was placed in a small pond. It degrades fast outside of a host. It should be inert, and any wolves or elk infected by it dead at this point. Bait of some type was used to infect the hyenas. Radek didn't have time to distribute it to more than a single pack. I'm sure Captain Nagy would be willing to order his men to hunt—"

"The hyenas have been dealt with," Aryck said, his voice harsh.

"Then that leaves only the third super-virus. It was being fed to the goats. I can attest that none of them have left the encampment."

Captain Orst straightened and directed his attention to Radek. "Radek Ivanov, I am placing you under arrest. You have the right—"

Gunfire silenced him, its thunder throbbing through the room as Radek toppled backward with a hole in his forehead.

Aryck surged forward, knife drawn but halting almost instantly as Nagy's weapon lowered. The militia captain said, "I think you'll agree, Captain Orst, it is in the best interest of all the Founding Families that there be no mention of plague and no mention of what was found at this site. As far as my men and I are concerned, Radek died in a fire started most likely by drunken carelessness and which spread quickly, creating chaos and panic and also drawing predators to the area. Pardons and a payment of coin will erase any memory of flaming arrows."

Captain Nagy holstered the pistol and walked to the door. He opened it long enough to retrieve the gas can he'd ordered put there.

Uncapping it, he moved to the desk and upended it so gas spilled over the computer and canisters and into the drawer. Radek's body was next.

"We will evacuate at dawn," Nagy said. "Considering the likelihood there are other caches of bioweapons here, I suspect the Weres will have no objection to us planting ordnances and detonating this excavation site."

He shook the empty can and tossed it aside. A small smile played at his lips as he turned and faced Orst. "I suspect the Ivanov and Iberá patriarchs together wield enough power to have these lands declared off-limits to humans seeking to run salvage operations in them."

Rebekka couldn't read Orst's expression. She didn't know how he felt about Nagy's approach to justice. His voice was without inflection as he asked Aryck, "Is this solution acceptable to the shapeshifters?"

Aryck hardly dared to believe the threat to the Weres could be over and they could resume living as they—

A glance at Rebekka halted the thought. No, not as they always had.

He touched his mind to his father's, getting the same answer he would have given had he been alpha. "It is acceptable to us. We'll remain to witness your departure and will follow you to the border of the lands we claim. As long as no one offers us a threat, safe passage is granted."

"Fair enough," Orst said.

Captain Nagy pulled a pack of matches from his pocket. Lit one and dropped it into a pool of gasoline on the desk.

It ignited in a whoosh of flame and heat, making the Jaguar snarl and demand retreat. Aryck took Rebekka by the arm and guided her toward the door, but neither of them left until after Nagy set multiple fires and both he and Orst exited ahead of them.

Orst departed to spread news of the evacuation and an agreement with the Weres for safe passage. Nagy gave the same order to the five militiamen but remained with Aryck and Rebekka, escorting them out of the encampment only after the building Radek had occupied had been reduced to smoldering ash and pieces of charred wood.

Aryck led Rebekka away from the gathered Weres, taking her to a small pond surrounded by oak trees draped in Spanish moss. He desperately needed to be alone with her, to celebrate their survival with the touch of flesh to flesh, to lovingly chastise her for scaring him so badly.

Rebekka undressed with the unselfconsciousness of a Were, discarding her clothes and wading into a pond shallow enough to hold some of the day's heat at its edges, and pockets of warmth a little deeper. Aryck halted her with a hand on her hip, stopping and turning her.

The water settled into smooth calm around them at waist height.

Cicadas and crickets and frogs renewed their songs. In the distance, an owl hooted.

"You're hurt," Rebekka said, smoothing her fingers over the cuts he'd gotten when he crossed over the concertina wire, then leaning in, taking his breath away as she touched her mouth to his chest and arms, healed him with the brush of her lips and the sensuous wet glide of her tongue.

He'd thought she would revile him for slaughtering the goats. Instead, she'd changed the course of the night and the fate of both Weres and humans. And now she tended to him, treated him as a Jaguar female wearing fur would treat its injured mate.

"I'm sorry—"

Rebekka stopped him by lifting her arms and putting them around his neck. By touching her mouth to his, preferring a different kind of conversation.

Words seemed unnecessary, an intrusion that would shatter the peace of the setting and the time they had together before they had to face questions about their future.

Aryck responded like a man in the grip of a desperate hunger, taking control of the kiss and pulling her against him so tightly their bodies touched in an unbroken connection. Heat poured into her, filling her breasts and turning her nipples into hard, aching knots before sliding into her belly. Her clit. Her labia.

He grew hard and it was impossible not to rub against the smooth, heated length of his cock. Her nether lips became swollen, parting in readiness.

She captured his tongue. Sucked. Reveling in the way his hips jerked and a low moan joined the night sounds.

His hands roamed. Settled again on her hips. Lifting then lowering her onto his cock.

She moaned. Wrapped her legs around his waist.

His mouth never left hers as he took her in fast, hard thrusts. Not coming until she'd cried out in release.

They were both breathing fast when he freed her mouth. He bit her shoulder then, a sharp rebuke instantly soothed with the swipe of his tongue. "I've never known fear like I did today, when I crossed your trail and realized you were heading in the direction of the encampment."

Her heart dropped to her stomach. She'd hoped to delay reality, to delay the truth. But she didn't shy away from it. "My gift doesn't just allow me to heal. What I said to Captain Orst, about the goats drawing me to the encampment because they were diseased, is true. But there's more to it. If they'd been free instead of penned, I could have drawn them to me, though I wouldn't have done it intentionally. By the time I got to them, I'd learned how to control that part of my gift."

Speaking the words out loud, she realized somewhere along the way she'd stopped thinking of the urchin's gift as something terrible. It made her a weapon, but one that could prevent those, like Radek, from using plague to kill the Weres.

"It's a dangerous gift to have," Aryck said, no censure in his tone. He touched his mouth to hers, nibbled on her bottom lip. "And a secret best shared only between mates unless there's need for others to know."

Her heart soared, and she decided to give him the rest of the truth. "My father isn't human. I've seen him only once, when he saved my life and told me I'd find work and protection in the Were brothels. I think he's a demon."

Aryck buried his face where her neck met her shoulder. Inhaled deeply and said, "Whatever your father might be, you smell fully human to me."

A small growl followed. "And you smell of other males. If they weren't already dead, I'd have to leave so I could attend to the matter."

Without warning he went over backward, submerging them both before letting her go and becoming a jaguar. As a playful cat he swam in circles around her, brushed against her, repeatedly requiring her touch until finally nudging her back to shallow water.

When he shifted to human form and stood before her in the moonlight, the water sluicing down his body, Rebekka could see why ancient civilizations had once formed cults around his kind. He was a primal, powerful male meant to be worshiped. Legs apart, the heavy globes of his testicles and hardened cock were a symbol of potent masculinity.

Rebekka rose up on her knees. His sharp intake of breath brought a smile to her lips, as did the way his cock became more engorged, straining away from his body as if begging her to take it into her mouth.

She placed her palms on his thighs and felt the slight trembling of a man waiting for pleasure to be given freely rather than demanding it. She rewarded him for his restraint by touching him, sliding a hand between his thighs to cup his testicles as the other took him, thumb brushing against his exposed cock head.

His moan sounded loud in the quiet hush surrounding them. His hips bucked, driving his penis through her fist and sending a rush of feminine satisfaction all the way down to her toes.

She leaned forward, heard his breathing become harsh even as he tried to close the distance between his cock and her mouth with another thrust.

A dart of her tongue, a quick swipe, and she shattered his control. His fingers tangled in her wet hair to prevent escape. His body curled over hers, and his voice was little more than a growl when he said, "Now, Rebekka."

Her channel spasmed at the rough command. Arousal escaped her slit to join the water wetting her inner thighs.

She waited for his hands to tighten in her hair before she yielded. But even then she denied him. Her tongue laved instead of darted, the slow swirl offering torment instead of relief, the warning press of her teeth keeping him from simply taking.

Waves of lust forced the air from Aryck's lungs with each slick glide of her tongue over his cock, leaving him panting, nearly mindless with the urge to push through kiss-swollen lips and into the hot cavern of her mouth.

White-hot need defined him. Much more of her torment and he would be the one on his knees, begging her to take him. Suck him. *Please.*

Already the word trembled on his lips. He said her name instead, putting an edge of threat into it, a promise of retribution.

She took more of him. Because *she needed, she wanted*, and not because he'd commanded it.

It didn't matter. It didn't diminish the roar of pleasure rushing from his cock to his head. It didn't slow the quick, shallow thrusting of his hips.

On a moan he gave himself over to her ministrations, lost himself in a release he couldn't hold back.

As he'd thought would happen, she brought him to his knees. Only rather than making him beg, she pushed him over to lie in the water, muscles lax and heart thundering, a smile on his face and a contented purr rumbling though him.

Aryck welcomed her when she settled on top of him, a sensual, feminine blanket that covered him nicely. He trailed a finger down her spine, looked deeply into her eyes.

She was aroused. As needy as he'd been.

Her nipples were pebbled points pressed to his chest. Her vulva swollen and hot against his cock, her thighs splayed and resting on either side of his in unconscious pleading for him.

A human male couldn't have answered her silent call, but for a Jaguar—especially one who'd nearly lost the female he wanted as a mate—it was easy. He hardened at smelling himself on her, at brushing his lips across hers and tasting himself there.

It was darkly carnal—to want to imprint himself on every one of her senses—but all aspects of his soul demanded it.

He rolled so she was underneath him, hands supporting her upper body so she was only partially in the water. He cut off her surprised laugh and turned it into a sigh of pleasure by filling her with his cock.

"That feels so good," Rebekka said, the throbbing ache between her thighs soothed by having him inside her. She wrapped her legs around his waist, touched her lips to his.

Each of his thrusts sent her spiraling upward. And with every rub of her nipples and clit against his wet skin, she surrendered to sensation— and ultimately to an ecstasy that sent her soul flying as his penis pulsed in long, hot surges of release.

Only reluctantly did she let her arms and legs fall away so he could move to his side. She sat, content to stay in the warm water rather than sit naked on the ground out of it.

He sat as well, pulling her onto his lap. "You've proven yourself to the pack and to the ancestors. The Were owe you a debt they can't repay. Stay with me. Be my mate. If my father still insists you go through the Rite of Trial, then I'll leave his pack and form my own."

He pressed a kiss to the place where her neck and shoulder met, sucked on the mark he'd left there. "I wouldn't have considered it possible, or even wise before, but with you as my mate, Lions, Wolves, even Hyenas might be drawn into the same pack. We could include them, furthering the idea of alliance and cooperation."

Rebekka's chest expanded with hope. Her lips trembled, and the words, when she could speak them, were barely more than a whisper. "And the outcasts trapped in the brothels, those not condemned by pack law?"

The instant tension in his body and tightening of his arms around her answered before he did. "If they are willing to go through the rite, they will be allowed onto our lands. Those the ancestors judge as worthy will have a home with us and be protected against recapture or retribution as a result of their life among humans."

Her heart slowed to a painful throb. "Very few survive the rite." *And Levi wouldn't be one of them.*

"They could be given time before the rite, instruction, a chance to do things that would gain favor in the eyes of the ancestors."

A breeze picked up, coming from the direction of the encampment, and as if speaking about the ancestors drew their attention, Rebekka thought she heard the beat of drums.

Aryck nuzzled her ear. "You hear them?"

"Yes."

"Those belong to the shamans. There are six of them. If the elders possess stories of hearing so many shamans representing different Were groups calling upon the ancestors as one, they've never shared them with the pack. This is a time of great change, perhaps with the possibility of redemption for the outcasts you care so much about."

He kissed her shoulder. "If you're one of us, an alpha's mate and a pack's healer, a human whose presence in Were lands has already spawned a legend to be passed down for generations to come, then surely you are also fated to help the outcasts find a way to come home."

Annalise Wainwright's words whispered into Rebekka's mind, speaking of war and alliances being forged, of healers who would emerge so those Weres trapped in an abomination of form would be made whole.

Hope returned in a crawl, too tentative to give voice to. Desire followed as Aryck's tongue traced the shell of her ear and he murmured, "We'll talk again about our future after the encampment is gone. Until we return to witness the departure of the humans, I intend to show you what it means to be claimed by a male Jaguar."

AT dawn a plume of dust marked the convoy of trucks on their way to Oakland. Only two jeeps remained, positioned well away from the encampment, their drivers waiting for the command to leave.

Captain Orst leaned against the back of one vehicle. Captain Nagy stood several steps away from the other.

As Rebekka watched, a man wearing the Ivanov uniform exited the encampment. Two others came afterward, followed by a fourth and a fifth.

The last of them to leave stopped in front of the militia captain for a conversation. Captain Nagy gave a brief shake of his head, accompanying it with a gesture toward the jeep closest to them.

The man walked over to it, spending a minute doing something Rebekka couldn't see. When he turned back toward the site, she guessed he must have a control unit in his hand, given the antenna jutting from it.

He seemed to do a count of the men gathered around the vehicles. Then satisfied, he looked forward, at the site, and yelled, "Clear!"

The word rang through the abandoned valley and was followed seconds later by the thunder of explosives. Concrete shattered and dirt erupted, reaching skyward as if a volcano spewed its unheated contents in one mighty heave.

Clouds of debris billowed outward for a short distance. And from the swirling mass, a figure emerged, an urchin dressed in gray rags with a rat sitting on his shoulder.

Fear tore through Rebekka at the sight of him, and, sensing it, Aryck's arms tightened around her. He nuzzled her ear, murmured, "We'll face my father and Nahuatl together."

Out of the corner of her eye she saw movement, guessed the alpha and shaman were approaching, and knew by Aryck's reassurance that he didn't see the apparition standing amidst the destruction.

The urchin reached up and stroked the rat. "Game over," he said, his image blurring into the dust created by a second explosion. "For now, Healer."

Addai

LIGHT coalesced in front of where the urchin stood with debris billowing through his noncorporeal form. It bent and twisted into a human shape silhouetted by glorious white wings. Gained presence without becoming flesh by drawing color through it while remaining diffuse, transparent to eyes seeing only what had a physical reality.

You always did have a touch for the dramatic, Caphriel, Addai said, the words spoken on a plane unheard by the mortal.

And you weren't always a fool for lost causes. Does this form suit you better, brother?

The grubby child with the rat perched on his shoulder transformed into a man astride a horse. He spread his arms wide and lifted his face to the sky. *And death sat upon a pale horse, given power to kill with sword and plague and pestilence and disease, and with the wild beasts of the earth.*

Addai shook his head. *The quote grows tiresome. As does this often-repeated conversation. But I'll say my lines so we can move beyond them. You won't go unchallenged. You won't succeed in the task assigned you.*

Caphriel morphed again, from a horseman of the Apocalypse to an angel whose resemblance to Tir was unmistakable. *Ah, brother, even if I've yet to discover the source of your motivation, I'm glad you continue to cling to your delusions. You and those you call allies won't wrest this world away from our father, but the game between us helps pass the time.*

He looked at the place where Rebekka and Aryck stood, the alpha and shaman approaching them. *I concede. This victory is yours, Addai. But there are other cities and other game pieces. In the end your efforts will come to nothing. Those living here will be gathered and judged, and I will finally be free of this world.*

A stretching of black wings and Caphriel was gone, leaving parting words whispering through Addai's mind. Echoing Addai's own.

Until we meet again, brother.

Until we meet again.

Thirty

REBEKKA remained in Aryck's arms when Nahuatl and Koren reached them. His openness about their relationship chased away some of the chill caused by the urchin.

"We heard the drums last night," Aryck said.

For the first time Rebekka saw acceptance in Koren's expression when he looked at her. "There is no need for you to stand before the ancestors and be judged. They have heard of your deeds and spoken. Jaguar. Wolf. Lion. Coyote. Hyena. Bear. You may move freely in those territories as one who belongs there."

She wet her lips, preparing to ask the same question she'd put to Aryck when he spoke of forming his own pack. Aryck beat her to it. "I told Rebekka if she would agree to be my mate, I would see to it those outcasts not condemned by pack law would be allowed to enter our lands. I promised they would be given time and instruction before undergoing the Rite of Trial, a chance to redeem themselves so they would face the ancestors and hope to survive it."

"The ancestors spoke on this," Nahuatl said. "As well as on the subject of the healer becoming your mate."

Against her back Rebekka could feel Aryck's heart speed up to match the quick race of hers. Hope curled in her belly, warm and sweet with the possibility her dream of a husband and children could become a reality. But as Nahuatl's dark eyes met hers, a chilly tendril of foreboding wound its way through the hope, arriving with the knowledge that nothing came without price.

"What Aryck has promised you is acceptable to the ancestors," the shaman said, "as is your becoming his mate. If you remain on Were lands. To return to the human world is to risk the corruption of your soul."

Nahuatl turned and walked away. Koren hesitated, as if he would say something; then he too left without a word.

Aryck's lips touched Rebekka's neck, brushed over her ear. "Stay. Be my mate."

She squeezed her eyes shut against tears. The fast race of her heart only a moment ago now a slow, painful beat, bringing with it images from her life in Oakland.

The heavy weight of choice settled on her shoulders. She could have a mate, children, friendships extending beyond a single group of Weres. Safety unlike anything she'd ever known and a life full of love and happiness. But at a cost.

With the threat posed by the encampment gone, there would be little need of her gift among the pure Were. Most of their injuries could be cured by a shift in form. What little sickness befell them naturally could be treated with remedies.

To accept this life was to be defined as mate and mother instead of healer. Her heart craved it, yet at the same time, it seemed wrong to abandon those in need, and care only about her own happiness.

Rebekka turned in Aryck's arms, looked up into the face of the man she wanted to spend a lifetime with. How could she leave him? But what if staying meant her gift would never deepen so she could heal the Weres trapped between forms? What if staying meant their only hope lay in escaping the red zone and surviving the ancestors' Rite of Trial?

What about those who weren't Jaguar or Lion, Bear or Wolf, Coyote or Hyena? What about Levi, who would die if he stood before the ancestors? And Cyrin and Canino, trapped in their animal form, not outcast but not whole either?

Tears gathered at the corners of her eyes. "I need time alone, to think," she whispered, touching her lips to Aryck's in a silent plea for him to understand the struggle keeping her from giving him the answer he wanted.

He crushed her to him, mouth claiming hers in desperation. She responded with like emotion. Opened for him, her tongue rubbing and tangling with his. Their breaths mingling, bodies pressed tightly together, both of them afraid of what would happen once they separated.

Rebekka felt torn apart, bereft when he released her and stepped back. Cold replaced the heat of his body, the burden of conscience leaving no room for passion.

"I'll meet you back at the Lion dwelling place."

His expression became that of a protector. "No Were would dare attack you, but I don't like leaving you unguarded."

She laid her hand on his chest. "If I'm to live in these lands, I have to be able to survive without a personal bodyguard."

A muscled twitched in his cheek. Conflict was written in taut muscles and rigid posture.

Aryck covered her hand where it rested on his chest, pressed as though he wanted to anchor her to him. "Be careful."

Rebekka felt the loss with each step away from Aryck. She knew it was nothing compared to the agony she'd experience if she returned to Oakland.

Why contemplate it at all? a small voice whispered in her mind. Hadn't she wondered if working in the brothels only perpetuated the misery? Hadn't she done enough for others?

Memories of lovemaking contrasted against the loneliness she'd known before. Images of teaching Caius his letters brought fantasies of other children learning to read, small boys who looked like Aryck. Didn't she deserve happiness, too?

Arguments and counterarguments chased themselves around in her thoughts as she walked through the woods until, weary of the battle between her heart and her mind, Rebekka sat on a log beside a dry creek bed.

A male cardinal landed a few feet away from her, a bright splash of color against yellowed grass. Seeing it reminded her of those moments standing in front of the Wainwright house after the dream and the rat in the alley sent her running to them.

The blood red of the cardinal sitting in a nearby tree had seemed like an omen waiting for interpretation. It seemed like a second omen to have the cardinal appear now, at another crossroad in her life.

The thought sent uneasiness rushing through Rebekka. She rose to her feet, only to realize the true source of her sudden nervousness.

A Jaguar watched. It remained crouching just long enough for its fury to reach her, and for Rebekka to recognize Melina before she charged.

There was no time to scream. No time to react.

No need to as the cardinal morphed into a tiger and launched itself at Melina, its weight and unexpected appearance giving it the advantage.

They collided then hit the ground, the tiger landing on top, driving its canines into Melina's exposed throat and clamping down savagely, cutting off air and sound and delivering a killing bite.

He turned toward Rebekka, and in her mind's eye she saw him even before the tiger became the man who'd saved her from rape when she was sixteen and sent her to Dorrit.

Her mother's voice rang through her mind. *John. They're all named John.*

Rebekka's eyes went to his hands, expecting to see wickedly curved black talons. Instead his fingernails were short and clear. Human, not demon.

His sharp features were the same, as was his hair. He wore it in a hundred braids, all of them with black and red beads woven in—a cardinal's coloration to go with the image of it on his bare chest.

She felt foolish for having missed the connection, for not having questioned how often she noticed a bird not commonly seen.

The fear-spiked adrenaline caused by Melina's sudden appearance and attack washed away, leaving Rebekka nauseous. Or maybe it was the knowledge that whatever plans her father had for her were about to be revealed.

She studied him as he studied her, was reminded of the raven outside the Wainwright house who'd sat in the same tree as the cardinal before shifting into a supernatural being so powerful at masking his nature not even Levi could see beyond the human facade, of Zurael, the shamaness Aisling's mate, who had the same otherworld feel.

"What are you?" she asked, hesitating on a breath before acknowledging the relationship between them. "Besides my father."

"My race is ancient, existing before the birth of mankind. We ruled here once and will do so again."

"Demon."

"That name was given to us by our enemy, when the oldest and most powerful of us was twisted into a terrifying shape in an effort to subdue us. Since then we have hidden behind the label and been forgotten by humans even as time and the power of their belief has given birth to a legion of true demons."

Dread clawed through her but it didn't stop her from saying, "Abijah said you had no love for humans. What do you want from me?"

Not for the first time since the testing began, Torquel felt regret. Were it in his power, he would prevent his daughter from suffering further. He'd found it unbearable to see her bound and gagged, at the mercy of human trash.

It had been a small transgression on his part to take a mouse's form and heal her with a quick touch of fur to forehead. A small interference he'd present himself to be punished for should The Prince demand it.

He wished he could reveal the things she needed to know. Bestow the gifts he could on her. But he was as trapped in these proceedings as she was.

"What do you want from me?" she asked for a second time, her courage swelling his heart with such pride that he wanted to embrace her, to become a true father to her, a teacher and confidant.

There wasn't much time. The enforcer would soon come looking for her.

Torquel asked, "Do you love the Were?"

She stiffened, looking for the trap in his question and, after a long moment, springing it closed by answering, "Yes."

"Then I've come to give you a choice. Remain here and make a life for yourself, or accept my gift and return to Oakland as a healer who can heal not only those Weres caught between forms, but those trapped in only one form."

Rebekka knew with absolute certainty he could bestow such a gift on her. Deep down, a part of her had guessed it would come to this the moment Aryck spoke openly about her becoming his mate.

"And if Aryck is willing to come with me to Oakland?" she asked, churning with uncertainty, wondering if he loved her enough to enter her world, if he would be willing to risk becoming outcast—

But how could he be trapped between forms if she could heal him?

"The Jaguar can't know unless he chooses to accompany you or to follow afterward. It's one of the conditions. Until you leave Were lands, you can't reveal the change to your gift, nor can you heal the outcast here. Those coming to these lands must seek out the shamans and survive the Rite of Trial or, if they are in animal form, present themselves in Petitioner's Rite, as they have always been able to do, and have their penance named."

"And the cost to me of making a Were whole?"

Approval shone in her father's eyes. "No more than you can bear. Nothing the life you've led hasn't prepared you for. Great gifts always come with great responsibility.

"The choice is yours to make of your own free will. It will be offered only this once, and your answer required after I've told you the last condition associated with it, and that is, you can tell no one about my presence here and what we spoke of."

Her gaze slid to Melina's lifeless body then back to him.

"The Weres will see no evidence except that left behind by an unknown tiger."

"What do I call you?" she asked, putting off the moment of choice.

He cupped her chin, his hand sun-baked and warm. "One day,

daughter, I hope to give you my name. But that day is not this one. Now tell me your answer."

Her heart did a slow, painful roll in her chest. There was only one she could give. She couldn't deny the calling of her gift. "I'll return to Oakland."

"My spirit to yours," her father said, touching his mouth to hers, his breath passing to her through lips parted in surprise.

He stepped away and tossed something in the air. Reflexively she caught it, looking down to find the blackened Wainwright token in her hand. A touch to her pocket confirmed it was missing, lost somewhere on Were lands and now returned by her father, perhaps as a renewed sign of alliance with the witches.

Before she could ask anything further, his shape changed to a tiger's. He padded over to the dead Jaguar, roaring repeatedly as if to draw attention to his presence, then with a final glance in her direction escaped into the forest.

ARYCK started running at the sound of a tiger roaring. It wasn't Canino. The voice was too deep, and he was fairly certain the Tiger and Caius were with the Lions, if not on their way back to Jaguar lands.

With each step he cursed himself for ever agreeing to allow Rebekka to wander the woods unprotected. He'd been certain no Were would dare risk the wrath of both ancestors and pack, and the purely animal would remain in hiding or leave until things returned to normal in the area.

He caught Melina's scent and felt an icy foreboding. A primal scream built inside him, a Jaguar sound of fury and a man's of fierce denial. It welled up, the emotion like a balloon expanding in his chest, putting pressure on his heart, swelling to squeeze his lungs and make it nearly impossible to breathe.

His surroundings passed in a blur. He was only barely aware of others crashing through the brush, rushing to confront the intruder without knowing Rebekka was there as well.

Branches slashed at his arms and face and bare chest as he ran. Inside him the Jaguar was crouched, ready for a swift change of form and a fight to the death if necessary.

He stepped into the dry creek bed, feet barely touching the smooth stone and cracked soil. Fear gripping him at what he would find ahead.

Relief and shock whipped through him when he saw Rebekka standing several feet away from Melina and unharmed. He didn't stop running until she was in his arms, held tight against his body, both of them shaking.

Aryck pressed kisses to her mouth, her neck, her ear. His hands roamed feverishly as he assured himself she was truly alive and uninjured. Questions assailed him but he couldn't keep his lips from returning to hers long enough to ask them.

Wolves and Coyotes, Lions and Jaguars arrived. Some continued on, following the scent of tiger that remained thick in the air. Others lingered, Nahuatl and his father among them.

What happened here? Koren asked.

His father's use of their mental pathway helped force Aryck's mind back into reasoned thought. He couldn't bring himself to release Rebekka but he managed to contain his emotions so conversation was possible.

"What happened?" he asked her.

Rebekka's shudder was followed by trembling, the tightening of her arms around him. "It's Melina, isn't it?"

"Yes."

"She attacked. But before she reached me a tiger came out of nowhere. Not Canino. This one was larger than he is. The fight was over in seconds. There was nothing I could do. He stood over her, roaring, and then he left."

Rebekka pressed her face to his chest. Her body continued to shake as tears wet his skin. "I can't stay here. I have to go back to Oakland."

A wave of agony slammed into him with her words, drenching him in failure at the realization she no longer trusted him to keep her safe. He shook it off, or tried to, denying it would end this way.

"This won't happen again," he told her.

She tilted her head, revealing eyes wet with pain but shimmering with resolve and pleading. The sight of her face was like a slash through his chest, a ripping out of his heart even before she whispered, "Come with me. Please come back to Oakland with me."

The pain crashing through him increased as it occurred to him Melina's attack might only have cemented an earlier decision, might only be an excuse. That Rebekka had already chosen the outcast prostitutes over a future with him.

He wanted to latch onto the explanation, so it wouldn't be his own failure to keep her safe from attack that was responsible for her desire to return to the human world.

His throat clogged with emotion. She had to know he couldn't leave Were lands.

He was an enforcer. He was needed here, now more than ever if he wanted to keep his vision of a far-reaching alliance between Were groups alive.

Had she forgotten what Nahuatl said only a short time ago? As long as she remained on Were lands, becoming his mate was acceptable. To follow her to the human world and take her as a mate there would be a direct challenge to the ancestors' will.

Didn't she realize she was asking him to become outcast? He would be judged and punished.

Surely she had to know what the ultimate cost would be, the loss of his jaguar form when she was forced to heal him as she'd done Levi.

"I can't," he said, expecting the Jaguar to separate and add to his pain by raking savage claws through his chest and belly. But his two Earth-bound souls remained fully integrated, united against the idea of living among humans and outcasts. United in their suffering and braced to endure losing her now, especially if her choice to leave had nothing to do with Melina's attack.

Yet he couldn't let her go without one last attempt to make her stay. His mouth covered hers and, regardless of their audience, he poured all his emotion into the kiss.

It only made things worse.

She answered with like emotion.

Pain and desire.

Longing and hope and loss.

Love.

"Stay," he asked again, eyes burning as he suppressed his tears.

"Come with me." Her voice broke. "At least for a little while."

"I can't."

It would only prolong the suffering if he did.

Unlike him, she didn't try to stop her tears. They coursed down her cheeks. "I understand," she whispered.

He could see she did, that despite her request she'd known what his answer would be. Accepted it.

Pride made him release her and turn away.

This is her choice, he told himself, leaving her without a backward glance.

Thirty-one

REBEKKA hadn't thought she had any more tears to shed. But when she knelt next to Caius and solemnly took the amulet he'd found in the woods and kept safe for her, a new wave of pain washed through her and she felt the tightening of her throat.

His lips trembled and his chin jutted out. He already saw good-bye in her tearstained face and the shaking of her hands.

"I have to go back to Oakland," she said, her tears starting to flow again. "I'm needed there."

He swallowed, his small frame stiff as he tried to face yet another loss in his life. "Will you come back when you're done? And teach me to read like you promised?"

Rebekka wanted to say yes, even if it meant returning and finding Aryck mated to a Jaguar female. But she knew there was every chance she would be killed if Allende found out she was helping the prostitutes escape. And if she managed to avoid death, there would be other cities, other places.

She'd been created for a purpose and given a choice whether to embrace it or turn her back on it. She'd been forced to choose between the two things she had always wanted the most, and now she had to live with the choice, though it felt as though her heart was being ripped from her body.

Rebekka pulled Caius into a hug. "I can't promise anything except that I'll try to come back for a visit."

Caius gave a sob, his arms tightening around her and her shirt growing wet as he cried. Canino joined them, rubbing his side against them. Circling, purring in an offer of comfort and solidarity. Then finally butting his head against Caius's back and pressing his nose into the cub's armpit as if to say, "Enough is enough. You've got me."

Rebekka ended the hug. Words clogged in her throat. She couldn't bring herself to say good-bye. "You two should get back to Jaguar lands," she said, trying for a light tone and failing, though her effort was enough to help Caius stop crying.

He took a long shuddering breath and offered a tremulous smile. "I asked Phaedra if she thought I should take Canino to my house again. She said yes. She said it'd be a good thing to do every day if Canino is willing to let my mother chase him away."

"I'm glad," Rebekka said, managing a wobbly smile, though she felt frozen in this final moment of good-bye, the last of them before she and Levi began the trip to Oakland.

Caius didn't move away and neither did she. Canino came to the rescue again, pushing between them, grumbling deep in his chest and using his sheer size to reposition Caius so he faced Jaguar lands.

Rebekka swallowed hard and willed herself to turn toward where Levi waited and, beyond him, the Wolves who would ensure they made it to the border of Were lands safely. She forced herself to take one step, and then another, and another, to not turn around and look back one last time. She managed it until she heard the sound of running footsteps behind her.

She turned in time to have Caius barrel into her. He gave her a fierce hug. Then just as quickly released her and ran to Canino, climbing on the Tiger's back so Rebekka's last memory of him brought a smile instead of tears.

They traveled in silence. The Wolves almost never visible. Levi respecting her privacy, her need to deal with her heartbreak on her own, though she knew he wanted to ask what had happened to make her leave Aryck and the Were lands when she could have stayed.

Whether it was because of her father's gift, or her desire to escape thoughts of Aryck, Rebekka kept moving forward, her endurance matching the Weres'. Surprising them.

For a time loss drove her on relentlessly, barely allowing for eating or drinking. Denying the possibility of sleep and making her push the others to keep running through the night rather than stop.

And then it was anger keeping her going, that Aryck hadn't been willing to accompany her to Oakland, even for a little while. If he'd said yes, then he would *know* her reason for leaving and understand the choice she made.

Finally it was hope, excitement. Anticipation making it impossible to slow or stop until they reached the border of Were territory and the Barrens were visible in the distance, and, beyond them, Oakland.

She thought the Wolves accompanying them would leave without speaking. Other than appearing to mention the proximity of water or to call a halt long enough to cook and eat whatever game they'd killed, there'd been little sign of them.

Instead Jael emerged. He took her hands in his and met her gaze with piercing gold eyes, searched for something before giving a small shake of his head and saying, "I don't understand your choice but may the ancestors welcome you again to our lands, and if the Jaguars are so foolish not to make you one of them, then become Wolf."

He released her hands and turned, loping back into the forest. She and Levi traveled through the area where the ferals roamed and finally entered the blackened destruction of the Barrens. Levi broke his long silence then, asking, "Do you want to talk about it?"

She could hear compassion and caring in his voice, as well as anger and the desire to tear Aryck apart, with human fingers and knives if lion claws and teeth weren't available. She took Levi's hand, felt a lump rise in her throat at the prospect of returning to the place where it had begun, where she'd first seen the Jaguar barely clinging to life.

"Let's go to the shelter we spent the night in," she said, unsure of what would be involved in healing Levi and not wanting to do it out in the open.

He glanced upward and frowned. Opened his mouth, no doubt to say they could make it to the brothel if they pushed, but she stopped him by saying, "I want to try to heal you."

She couldn't tell him more, but he knew. It was there in his eyes, in his hoarse whisper. "The witches spoke the truth about your gift?"

"I won't know until I attempt it," Rebekka said, her palm growing damp against his. She didn't think her father had lied, either about the gift or not being demon, but she couldn't be sure.

Levi gave her hand a squeeze before releasing it. "It will only take a few minutes to get to the shelter. Should we walk?"

His nervous anticipation matched hers. She laughed, doubting she *could* walk now that she was so close to realizing a dream she'd had from the moment she'd stepped into a Were brothel and seen what life was like there for those trapped between forms.

"Race you," she said, feeling carefree, joyous in those moments it took to reach the structure of narrow passageways formed by twisting, rusted steel.

They climbed slowly, careful of the jagged edges. She avoided the tearing of flesh even as memories of Aryck sliced through her with each step.

He made his choice and I made mine, she told herself, but the anger she'd managed earlier was gone, leaving an aching, empty place behind.

Despite her attempts to suppress the pain, her eyes grew wet with tears as they entered the room where she'd healed Aryck. A sob escaped when Levi hugged her to him, his hand stroking her back, his cheek against her hair.

"This is why you left, isn't it? To heal the outcast." She felt him swallow. "To heal me."

"Yes."

"And Aryck feared the ancestors' wrath? He forbade you from doing it?"

"He doesn't know. I couldn't tell him unless he left Were lands."

"Then how—"

"I can't explain." She tightened her arms around him in a silent plea for him to accept without questioning further.

"Aryck is a fool for letting you go. And a coward for not being willing to see for himself what it means for outcasts to live among humans."

Part of her wanted to agree, to fill the empty, aching place with hate or anger, to use those emotions to eradicate the feelings of love and the pain of loss now accompanying it. Instead she found herself defending Aryck. "He's needed in Were lands. I think if the Weres are going to survive the war between supernaturals that Annalise Wainwright told me about, then they need to be united."

Somehow, speaking the words out loud erected a barrier, walling off everything except hope and anticipation. "Ready to try this?"

Levi gave her one final hug before dropping his arms and stepping back. "What do you want me to do?"

"Sitting would be best. Or lying down."

He stripped out of his clothing and put them on the floor, using them as a pad to sit on beneath the hole in the ceiling that allowed a beam of light to stream in.

Rebekka sat down cross-legged in front of him. Her hands lifted to the amulet, intending to take it off as she'd once had to in order to heal, but when her fingers touched the beads that were the same size and color as those braided into her father's hair, she hesitated.

The first time she'd healed after getting the amulet had been in this place, and her gift was changed. She'd suspected then that the amulet was tied to her father. Now she was sure of it.

Guided more by instinct than anything else, Rebekka left the amulet on. She gathered her will, imagined Levi as a Lion as she placed her hands on his shoulders and closed her eyes.

Nothing happened.

There was no tingling sensation followed by a gentle, unconscious blending of purpose and a desire to render aid as she'd once experienced. Nor was there the taking, as if she was nothing more than a tool, that she'd come to expect.

Rebekka exhaled on a sigh, thinking perhaps she'd been wrong about the amulet after all. Her hands slid from Levi's shoulders to his chest and her breath caught at hearing the faint beat of distant drums.

Her mouth went suddenly dry. Her own heart began thundering as various pieces of what had been an unsolvable puzzle fell into place.

The reason why she couldn't attempt this on Were lands.

The reason why outcasts who entered Were territory had to seek out the shaman.

The reason why she was accepted without undergoing the Rite of Trial but warned against the dangers of coming back to the human world and the risk of having her spirit corrupted.

And the reason why Levi had been warned against presenting himself for judgment in Lion territory. So he could face the ancestors now, her desire to heal him leading to this moment, this choice, because this was not to be a healing of the body, but a healing of the soul, and her gift had been changed to enable it

Her eyes opened and went to Levi's face. His features were taut, his jaw clenched and breathing carefully controlled. She licked dry lips, knew the answer by what she saw in his face but asked the question anyway. "You hear them?"

"Do it, Rebekka. I'm willing to be the first so you'll know what the cost is to yourself and to others."

Once again she closed her eyes, consciously allowing her right palm to slide lower. The beating grew louder, more insistent, and when her hand finally lay over Levi's heart, the surge of power came like a wind at her back, pushing her spirit from her body and against a gale force battering her as if trying to keep her from answering the call of the drums.

Gray nothingness swirled around her, and she knew, from her visit with Aisling the night before she and Levi entered the maze to free Cyrin and the others, that this was the ghostlands. Fear tried to turn her back, but she'd endured too much since the Wainwright witches set this in motion with their summons and the offer of the token, and she'd lost too much to turn away from the path now.

The drums called and she willed herself toward them, felt a spike of primal terror when out of nothingness an opening formed in front of her, a yawning chasm filled with howling, shrieking wind, a place symbolized in the physical world by a dark cave filled with sun-bleached bones.

She entered it and took form. Became transfixed in horror, unable to look away from the throbbing, pulsing heart she held in her hand. Levi's.

The sound of chanting joined that of the drums, broke her trance and pulled her deeper into the cave until she reached a fire, and around it men and women representing Weres of more species than she could count.

Some wore headdresses and capes, as Nahuatl did. Others were marked by facial brands, as the Lion shaman was. Still others wore beads of bone in their hair and bore scars across their chests as she'd seen on the Wolf shaman.

Rebekka became aware of her own nakedness then. She wore nothing except for the amulet resting against her illusionary flesh. And as the fire glinted off the ancestors' eyes, she knew instinctively that without her father's protection she could be harmed in this place.

The chanting stopped. The beat of the drums faded to the background as did all of those gathered except for a man draped in the pelt of a bear.

His face was hidden, though yellow eyes shone through the snarling headdress. His human arms disappeared into folds of fur so his hands and fingers become bear claws. "You ask us to render a judgment?"

His voice was a deep growl that seemed to be picked up by wind and carried throughout the cavern. *Yes* was on the tip of Rebekka's tongue, but unbidden she remembered the argument she'd had with Aryck, her claim that not all outcasts became so because of the ancestors, and her belief that Levi didn't deserve this fate, not when he could have chosen a lion's form as Cyrin had and been free to live among the Were.

Hoping in being bold she wasn't damning Levi further, Rebekka said, "I'm here to heal a soul."

Yellow eyes gleamed. "As long as your gift remains untainted by evil, you have that power."

A furred arm lifted and pointed to the opening behind her. "The part of the Lion's soul once living among us now roams the ghostlands.

If you choose healing over judgment, then you must be the one to suffer the pain that comes with bringing it back to our world."

The conversation with her father whispered through Rebekka's mind. The remembered shine of approval in his eyes when she'd asked, "And the cost to me of making a Were whole?"

No more than you can bear. Nothing the life you've led hasn't prepared you for.

Since accepting the amulet she'd endured pain, accepted it as the price to be paid for the use of her gift. "I choose healing over judgment."

The drums grew louder in response. Their beat was joined by human voices, rising and falling in a chanted song as the Bear ancestor stepped forward.

"Know this, then. Those you stand with draw our attention to them by accepting what you offer. You might come before us by your own choice to heal, but there are others who come at our bidding, and kill at our command. Pass this warning on to the ones who would benefit from your gift, so they can understand the risk accompanying their redemption."

He jabbed one end of the staff he carried into the fire then touched the other to Levi's heart. Flames engulfed it, a searing agony Rebekka felt not in her hand, but in her chest.

She fell to her knees, screaming as her heart burned. Her voice blended with the drum and song, becoming part of a spirit wind that poured from the darkness and plunged into the ghostlands in search of Levi.

She knew the moment he was found because with the pain came images from his life since being made outcast. Terrible scenes of being tortured and twisted into a monstrous shape.

With it came the horror of witnessing the same thing happening to Cyrin. The cruelty perpetrated on them both and that Levi had perpetrated in turn, when insanity and hate made him truly soulless as he hunted those who ran the maze.

Tears streamed from Rebekka's eyes. She fought the urge to curl into a ball, to hide from the dark evil that could find its way into even the best of hearts.

She was struggling to breathe when the pain stopped abruptly, the fire in her chest and hand suddenly doused. She felt wind on her face and saw through puffy, swollen eyes a figure coming toward her, man shifting to lion and back again in endless succession. Levi.

He reached her and took her hand. The drums ceased, as did the world around them.

Rebekka opened her eyes. A lion lay next to her, his breathing as fast as her own, his heart pounding against her palm.

"Levi," she whispered through parched lips, hardly daring to believe it had been real and they'd both survived the attention of the Were ancestors.

She rose to her feet when he did. Felt herself calming as he shook and stretched, padded around the room and pounced, barely missing a scurrying mouse. A smile formed, his happiness in wearing fur again after so long making the memory of the pain she'd endured fade along with the scenes she witnessed.

He returned to stand in front of her. *Changed.* The transition seemingly easy.

Joy lit his face and he hugged her to him. His tears wet her neck. "I can never repay you for this, but I'll spend a lifetime trying."

She hugged him back. "Not a lifetime. Help me in Oakland. Then go back to your pride."

There would be other places; she knew it with certainty. Her father hadn't created her to help those in Oakland, only to turn her back on Weres elsewhere by returning to Jaguar lands and becoming a mate and mother.

Sadness threatened to eclipse joy at the thought of Aryck. She suppressed it ruthlessly.

Even if she could go back in time, she'd make the same choices if they led to this moment. "If we hurry, we can get back to the brothel before dark."

"Not the brothel," Levi said, releasing her and getting dressed. "Araña's boat."

Rebekka frowned and followed him out of the room, once again moving slowly down the staircase and through the narrow, twisting passageways. "I could start with those who look human and have earned the right to work more flexible hours. They could slip away at dawn and not be missed for a while."

Levi shook his head. "It's too risky to go to the brothel and be trapped there by the night. I can't hide my scent. The longer I'm there, the quicker the change in it will be noticed. Those who know about the Rite of Trial will guess I've gone through it and wonder why I've come back. The reason will become obvious when the brothels start emptying.

"Keeping what you're now capable of a secret will be impossible. We can't know for sure who spies for Allende. We need to be in a safe place. The outer harbor is Rimmon's territory. He might not protect anyone on board the *Constellation* while she's docked but he won't allow other boats near her if she's out in the water."

Rebekka considered enlisting the aid of The Iberá, as well as the Wainwright witches, then dismissed the idea. Maybe later. The witches would take payment in favors owed, and beyond that, the outer harbor was closer to the brothels and didn't require Weres to pass through the wards into the area set aside for the gifted—and more important, trust witches or one of the Founding Families.

"You're right. We'll go to Araña's boat."

Rebekka thought of Feliss as she'd see her last, broken and bloody, doe eyes holding so much pain, and knew she couldn't bear the thought of her friend being locked in the brothel for another night when freedom was so close. "Will you bring Feliss to the boat tonight?"

Thankfully she wasn't one of those restricted from leaving or requiring permission and a guard. Given Levi's absence, and the rumor circulating about him wanting to buy out Feliss's contract, his taking her away wouldn't rouse any suspicions for a few days.

"Yes. Just her tonight. Tomorrow I'll go back for others."

Thirty-two

ARYCK prowled around his home. Melina's scent lingered there like a malicious spirit taunting him, reminding him of his furious rush to Lion lands when he'd learned Rebekka was there with Levi. Tormenting him with images of them together now because he'd lacked the courage to go with her, because his pride had prevented him from considering what he was asking her to give up to remain in Were lands.

She was a healer filled with compassion, with the need to help others regardless of species or circumstances. From the very first she'd railed against his attitude when it came to the outcasts.

He'd become more flexible in his thinking. Yet at his core he'd still believed their fate was their own. He'd considered it enough to offer them a chance to come into Were territory and face the ancestors.

But how many of them were as Rebekka claimed, caught between forms without knowledge of the Were culture or the existence of the ancestors? How many would trust those who'd always reviled and excluded them? How many would come on what could easily be a rumor?

There'd been no guarantees of safe escort. No offer of protection or help extended to those who might desire to flee the brothels of the human world.

Aryck rubbed his hand over his bare chest, massaging the ache radiating from his heart as he remembered the trek through the Barrens that would have ended in his death if Rebekka hadn't come to him. The image of her tear-streaked face was a fist to the gut.

Come with me. At least for a little while, she'd said on a broken voice, and he'd refused, hadn't even stopped to fully consider her request.

Despite his arguments to his father about the ancestors favoring his taking Rebekka as a mate, he'd turned his back and walked away from her, wrapping his pride around him like another skin.

The bitter taste of self-recrimination and remorse filled his mouth. Was she meant to be his mate only if she chose him over those who desperately needed her? Was she meant to be his lover and the mother of his children only if she turned her back on the outcasts who were her friends? Left her world for his?

Was all the sacrifice to be hers? All the risk?

He'd failed her again, proven himself unworthy not just in protecting her physically, but in the safekeeping of her heart.

Resolve forced all other emotions to recede. The Jaguar, crouched in shame and sorrow deep within Aryck's psyche, rose, adding its strength of purpose to the man's, both of them finally fully accepting the risk, the necessity of possible sacrifice that came with tying their life and fate to Rebekka's.

She was their mate and no other would do. They would challenge the ancestors themselves to have her. They would go to Oakland and beg for her forgiveness, then spend a lifetime proving they were worthy of her trust and love.

Aryck left the cabin, sending a quick mental probe and locating his father at Phaedra's house. He found Caius sitting on a log there, drawing in the smooth dirt while Phaedra cooked the meal and Koren spoke with Nahuatl a few steps away.

Caius looked up as Aryck approached. His lips trembled despite the straightening of his spine. "I'm going to visit her when I get old enough," he said. "She'll see I still know all my letters, and she'll teach me how to read like she said she would."

It wasn't the way Aryck had meant to tell his father. If he'd wanted to avoid doing it face-to-face, he could have done it mind-to-mind instead of coming here. But Caius hurt too, and so Aryck knelt in front of the cub, pausing for a moment to look at the alphabet spread out between them. "I'm leaving for Oakland now. I'll tell her you're practicing. It'll make her happy."

"Are you going to bring her back?" The cub's face and voice held a wealth of hope.

"Maybe not right away, but in the future," Aryck said, ruffling the boy's hair before standing and facing his father and Nahuatl.

As if his father had been expecting it all along, Koren said, "You've made your choice. Go."

Addai

THE *Were might yet live up to the expectations of his ancestors*, Addai thought. He hadn't been certain the enforcer would follow Rebekka.

Of course, now that the Jaguar had finally made his choice, time worked against him. It was entirely possible he would arrive in Oakland only to find Rebekka dead.

Into the silence following the enforcer's departure, the shaman spoke, delivering lines crafted for him but forbidden until this moment. "If Aryck returns with Rebekka, it is because he has been judged worthy to serve more than a single pack. He is meant for greater things. The ancestors speak of a war coming for rule of the Earth. If the Weres are to survive it, there must be those who will lead us in a new direction, away from the past and into a future where we are united. The alliance with our neighbors is just the beginning, as is change when it comes to dealing with the outcast."

Addai smiled, satisfaction filling him, though this had yet to finish playing out. With Caphriel gone, and the delivery of the ancestors' message witnessed, his business here was done.

His focus shifted to the city. But unlike the Were's journey there, for Addai, Oakland required only a thought coupled to his will.

He chose the brothel, curious as to whether Rebekka remained free, or if the last of her father's testing had finally claimed her life.

He chose to wear flesh because it amused him to wander unstopped and unmolested among the prostitutes and their clients. And because the hot energy of the Were reminded him of what it had been like to live among Sajia's people, Djinn who were *mārdazmā*, able to change shape but who had no noncorporeal form.

On a catwalk above the dungeons Addai stopped to watch a scene unfold. A Were female was led into one of the open playrooms on a leash.

She wore nothing but a collar and tight clamps attached to her nipples. Luxurious black hair shimmered in waves down her back, not stopping until it curled around her buttocks and brushed against her bare mound.

The man who'd paid to own her for the session was wealthy. The cut of his clothing and the rings on his fingers made it evident.

He ordered the female onto a piece of equipment allowing him to bind her spread-eagled so he could step between her open thighs and fuck either orifice, or position himself next to her head and command her to take him into her mouth.

The slap of his hand against her bare cunt sent a door crashing open in Addai's mind. Memories flooded in and he hardened in a heartbeat, his cock swelling along with his need for the woman who had once been his.

Thousands of years should have made it easy to keep her from his thoughts, but now that he was close to possessing her again, she was never far from them. A hot wash of anticipation slid through him at the prospect of meeting her for the first time, of their being strangers again. It built as he imagined seeing a hint of fear in her eyes, instinctual on her part at being given over to a being who was her natural enemy.

Those feelings would soon be turned into something erotic. She would grow wet and ready as she knelt at his feet, her hands clasped behind her back, long black hair caressing her dusky buttocks as she looked up at him, pleading silently for him to allow her to worship him with her mouth.

Fantasizing about her was a sweet torment he knew better than to indulge in, a distraction he didn't need as this thread woven to solidify alliance grew close to being judged a success or a failure. He ached for her, dreamed of her, but in the end, there was no hurrying her arrival in his life. It would come, soon, and he would never allow her into the presence of danger again.

With great effort Addai closed the door opened by the carnal scene taking place in the dungeon beneath him. He forced his thoughts away from Sajia even as his gaze lingered on the darkened, flushed skin of the prostitute's bare mound before moving up to the still-clamped nipples.

His will betrayed him with the memory of other nipples, gripped long ago by delicate clasps shyly left for him to find. His cock throbbed, begging for relief.

He turned away from the sight of the dark-haired Were and left the catwalk, knowing he would seek neither companion nor even a release granted by his own hand. Only Sajia would satisfy him.

In the corridor between brothels Addai gave up the illusion of flesh and the temptations that came with it. He used his will to move to the building Rebekka lived and did the majority of her work in.

He sensed the hushed excitement immediately and saw the Lion, Levi, soon after. His manner said Rebekka was well, and though Addai could not *see* the Were's soul as some of the Djinn were said to be able to do, he could feel its completeness, its binding to a place even the angels given charge over the spiritlands didn't enter.

She'd healed him, as she'd been created to do. *It won't be long now*, Addai thought, watching Levi move among the outcasts. A touch here, a nod there, the signs as subtle as the slow exodus of the chosen. By his reckoning, Levi and Rebekka had been back at least a day or two, and if they were smart, the first to be freed were those who'd earned time off and wouldn't be missed for a while.

He wasn't the only one to notice. Two others did as well. Addai watched as Dorrit, the madam, busied herself, turning her attention to other matters, ignoring those who were slipping away. Far more interesting was the Lioness, Kala, who found a reason to be near Levi as he made his rounds through the brothels before exiting himself.

Addai lingered outside, curious to see if Kala would emerge after Levi had disappeared from sight. When she did, a small smile formed on his lips at having guessed from the outset she would be the one. *Betrayer.*

No doubt she would scream in fury to know she served the very ancestors who'd seen the darkness in her heart and marked her as outcast. Or perhaps the Djinn had a hand in her making. Addai didn't discount the possibility.

He followed the Lioness as she tracked Levi by scent, and wasn't surprised to find the trail led to Araña's boat. Rebekka stood on its deck, greeting each of the outcasts by name as they climbed aboard. Her friend, Feliss, jumped easily to the dock, going to Levi and shyly taking his hand.

Nearby several of Rimmon's men watched without interfering. Another smile played over Addai's lips with thoughts of the vice lord.

Oh how the mighty had become *Fallen*, and for a far lesser sin than he himself had committed in loving a Djinn. It would be amusing to watch Rimmon fight the net so carefully crafted for him with the birth of his Finder daughter, Saril.

In the end, he would be named ally or enemy. Neutrality was no longer an option.

The last of the Weres boarded. Rebekka motioned toward the cabin, sending one of them inside before entering and closing the door behind her.

Addai expected Levi to remain on guard, or return to the brothel. Instead Lion and Deer walked away hand in hand, as if going off to lie together.

Addai fought against a sharp bark of laughter. He almost regretted Caphriel wasn't here to witness it and deliver a quote.

With a thought he moved near to where the Lioness hid. A choice now, for her. Ambition or jealousy.

Jealousy won, at least for the moment.

He followed Kala as once again she trailed Levi, this time to the forests behind the rubble remains of the maze. *Circles within circles*, Addai thought, having seen the cycle repeat for thousands of years. So often beginnings and endings passed through the same place, nearly indistinguishable from one another.

From her hiding place the Lioness watched as Feliss shed her clothing, revealing a completely human form. Kala sneered, already guessing the Deer intended to flee the brothel and thinking that, mixed form or human, Feliss had no chance of escaping Allende.

Her expression darkened as Feliss clung to Levi, whispered, "I'm scared."

"I know, but it's too dangerous for you to remain with Rebekka and me any longer. I'm surprised the alarm hasn't already been raised. This is your chance to escape Oakland and the vice lord's easy reach. You've got to take it."

Levi kissed her tenderly before extricating himself from her arms. He bent over and gathered her discarded clothing, touching the pocket and smiling. "Rebekka gave you money?"

"Yes."

"Then do it, Feliss."

Tears fell. "Go with me."

"You know I can't."

Feliss gave a low cry of pain and slowly began changing from woman to deer as Levi twisted her clothing, using strips of leather to turn the bundle into a collar. When she stood trembling next to him, wet like a newborn fawn from the effort to shift forms, he placed the clothing around her neck and said, "Leave now."

She took the first tentative steps forward, tail flicking. Then several more that were bolder. A look back at Levi, eyes pleading, but he shook his head and turned away, his emotions hidden from Addai in a way the Lioness's weren't.

Kala's expression of shock slid into one of ambition and cunning. When she remained in the woods instead of following Levi out of them, a whisper of compassion moved through Addai.

The remembered pain of losing Sajia made him hesitate. But in the end he decided against interfering. War was coming and sacrifices were inevitable.

Thirty-three

ARYCK found the sights before him unpalatable and nightmarish. A short time in the brothels owned by the vice lord Allende and he understood Rebekka's choice to return. How could she turn her back on those she cared about when this was their fate?

He'd killed outcasts in the challenge circle when guilt drove them to continue fighting after Nahuatl ordered a halt to call for a change of form. He'd hunted those sentenced to death, but he'd never had to follow one of them into the human world. He'd never seen this for himself.

She'd described what life was like for the outcasts who lived in brothels, told him of the brutality and degradation. But even as he listened, a part of him had remained sure they lived as they deserved to live. He was no longer willing to make such a sweeping generalization.

Aryck turned away from the glass allowing him to watch as humans were serviced by those trapped between forms. Rebekka's scent lingered in this brothel more than it did in the others, a sweet blend of woman and compassion surviving in the cesspit stench of unwashed bodies and stale sex.

His purity of form along with the payment of coin allowed him to move unhindered from building to building. It gave him free rein to watch, though nothing he saw gave him pleasure or made his cock stir with desire.

This was the fifth brothel. There'd been no sight of Rebekka, and he could find none of the prostitutes she'd mentioned by name. It made his fear for her deepen.

In growing desperation he sought out the bore-tusked madam, Dorrit. Asked if she knew Levi's whereabouts, thinking she'd lie if he asked about Rebekka.

Small pig-eyes took his measure. There was calculation in Dorrit's gaze. Suspicion. But in the end she said, "Check the bar."

Aryck moved through the parlor where males and females alike lined up, suffering the meaty pawing of a merchant as bodyguards looked on and a second man whined about the poor selection.

He followed the smell of beer and unwashed bodies to a dark room where a waitress knelt in front of a chair, working a man's shaft in and out her mouth as he sprawled in his chair, swilling his drink and bragging to his companions about staving off release to make her earn her money.

Levi stood with his back to the scene. His head bent in a whispered conversation with the bartender.

He stiffened, feeling Aryck's eyes on him or catching his scent. Turned as Aryck neared, an unwelcome expression on his face. "Go away and stay away. You've hurt her enough. She deserves better."

Anger flashed through Aryck, mixed with jealousy. Levi's charge was well deserved, but he couldn't stop himself from inhaling, half fearing and half expecting to discover Rebekka had turned to the outcast in her pain and let him comfort her with physical intimacy.

Relief came at finding no sign they were lovers. Shock followed at the difference in the outcast's smell.

Not human with only a hint of Lion as it had been before. Not lion with only a hint of human as Cyrin's was, but an unmistakable blend of the two, the scent of a pure Were.

Rebekka. Though Aryck couldn't explain it, every instinct told him she was somehow responsible.

"Take me to her," he said, willing to put aside his pride. "I've failed her repeatedly, but let her be the one to decide if she's willing to give me another chance to prove myself."

Levi's eyes burned with harsh judgment. *No* hung in the air between them, if not permanently, then at least until the Lion judged Aryck had suffered in equal measure to Rebekka.

Addai

ADDAI watched as yet another naked female rose from her hands and knees and left Allende. Shadowing the Were vice lord was very nearly a punishment, but after thousands of years of waiting, what were a few hours more, a day or week of added torment?

A servant appeared in the doorway as if on cue. "Two of the brothel prostitutes are at the gate, my lord. One of them has her hands bound behind her and is gagged. The other says she has important business with you."

"Interesting," Allende said, idly picking up a knife at the corner of his desk and touching the hilt to his lips, half closing his eyes as he inhaled the scent of woman. "Do you recognize either of them?"

"No, my lord."

Allende stood. "I'm in the mood for exercise, perhaps even a little sport. Have them brought to the courtyard."

The servant hurried off to do the vice lord's bidding. Unseen, Addai followed Allende.

Moments later, escorted by bodyguards, Kala and Feliss were positioned in front of the Were who owned their lives. Allende's eyebrows rose in silent query then abruptly lowered.

He tilted his head, studying Feliss intently as if comparing her to a mental picture. His eyes narrowed and his mouth firmed, the good humor that had brought him to the courtyard disappearing.

"Turn her around," he told Kala.

The Lioness obeyed, and though Feliss shook with terror, she didn't resist or try to pull away from Kala's grip.

Allende lashed out with the knife, a swift, sure strike slicing through the back of Feliss's dress and bisecting the smooth flow of human skin between delicate shoulder blades, scoring just deeply enough so blood slowly welled to fill the cut.

Allende said nothing. Only when the blood gathered and began to slide downward did he take his eyes off his handiwork and look at Kala.

"This is hardly a matter to warrant coming to my home and interrupting me, even if Rebekka unwisely helped a prostitute who intended to flee and cheat me out of what's due on a contract."

"Feliss is not the only one Rebekka has helped. There are probably dozens by now."

"And you've come to me hoping I'll decide Dorrit or one of the others needs to be replaced as madam?"

Kala had enough sense to be frightened by the silky threat in his voice. But whatever conflicting emotions she might have wrestled with after witnessing what Rebekka was capable of, what Rebekka's gift might mean for *her*, in the end ambition had dominated.

"The scent doesn't lie. Rebekka did more than make Feliss look human. She healed her completely. I saw Feliss shift form."

Something passed through Allende's eyes. Not disbelief. Not surprise. It made Addai wonder. Speculate. Increased his interest in proceedings with a foregone conclusion.

Allende reached out and cut away the gag, then the leather ties around Feliss's wrists, before ordering her to face him. "Does Kala speak the truth?"

Feliss didn't answer. For all her terror and hopelessness, she refused to betray Rebekka.

Allende stroked her cheek with the back of his hand. "It would be a shame to destroy something so beautiful when it's not necessary." To Kala he said, "Do you know where Rebekka is?"

"Yes. I can take you to her."

Feliss whimpered and looked up, eyes filling with tears. Allende's smile was very nearly gentle as he stroked her cheek again. "There, see what I mean? Violence can be avoided. Capturing Rebekka will be an easy thing. Do you know what they say about healers like Rebekka?"

He didn't wait for an answer. "To hurt another, even in self-defense, ruins their gift. It taints it so instead of diminishing pain, their touch increases it. Rather than strengthening and restoring a body they try to heal, they turn it against itself, weakening the immune system, allowing infection and disease to spread throughout it."

Allende cut the material of Feliss's dress. It fell away, leaving her naked.

He placed the blade tip on a breast, lightly circled the nipple. "How long do you think Rebekka will keep her secrets when faced with the damage a knife can do? Or with the prospect of being taken to one of the brothel dungeons and paying for her silence and her betrayal there?"

He cupped Feliss's chin and forced her to meet his eyes. "So beautiful. So naturally submissive. There's no reason for you to suffer. Nothing you can do will change her fate, only your own." His voice dropped to a whisper. "Show me your other form."

Crying, Feliss shifted. She stood, a trembling Doe not looking behind her to the open archway or trying to make an escape.

Allende turned toward Kala. "Perhaps you should be made a madam after all. Let's see what you make of the choice everyone in that position faces."

He opened his hand, and the knife lay across his palm. "What do you think should be done with this one? Make an example out of her with a punishment that allows her to keep working, paying off her debt? Or kill her, so others will know death is the only way they'll escape before their obligation is met?"

The choice was offered without inflection. Addai thought that had it been any other at Kala's mercy, she might have chosen differently. But where ambition dominated when it came to capturing and bringing Feliss to the vice lord, jealousy ruled now.

The Lioness snatched the knife. And for the first time since arriving, Feliss's fear did something more than hinder her.

She tried to bound away, but it was too late. Kala's arm was around her neck, long talons digging in, causing the Deer to struggle and rear, providing a perfect target.

With the expertise of an experienced hunter, Kala unerringly slid the blade between Feliss's ribs and into her heart.

"Not the choice I would have made," Allende said, as the carcass landed on tiles painted in shades of blue and gold. "But not a waste either."

He turned to the servant who hovered behind him. "Deliver the Deer to the cook employed by Dorrit. Tell him I want the head and the hide for the brothel wall. He can do whatever he wishes with the rest."

"Should he be told who—"

"Not until I've seen to Rebekka. Take a few men with you and make sure word reaches all the madams and bouncers. Clients may enter and leave but those whose contracts I own may not. I'll be along shortly and I'll expect a head count as well as the names of any who are missing."

The servant stepped forward, picking up and shouldering the carcass. Allende turned his attention to Kala, then to the two bodyguards standing on either side of her. "Take her. Contact me when you've collected Rebekka. I've got arrangements to make regarding the healer's fate."

Addai didn't bother remaining with them. He returned to the harbor and found Rebekka had maneuvered the *Constellation* out to a buoy as a safety precaution.

Addai felt the presence of a Djinn nearby. Rebekka's father no doubt.

It didn't take long for a heavily armored car to arrive. It glided to a smooth halt several hundred yards away, hidden from the docks by the jungle of wrecked cranes and cargo containers left from the days of The Last War.

Darkly tinted windows shielded its occupants from view. The back doors opened and Kala emerged, accompanied by two armed men.

They made their way toward the harbor, careful not to be seen. The two men halted behind the last piece of rusting metal while Kala alone stepped from behind it and crossed the open space to the water's edge.

Addai had to admire her show of courage and confidence. She barely looked at Rimmon's men nearby, one standing with an automatic weapon while the other did maintenance work on the engine of a speedboat.

Kala waved at Rebekka, yelled, "I saw Feliss in her fur when I was in the woods."

A laugh followed, amused, believable. "Good thing she changed before she ended up on the dinner table! Help me too, Rebekka. I want more than to spend my life as a whore to humans."

Addai could read the briefest hesitation in Rebekka before she started the boat's motor and carefully guided the *Constellation* to the dock.

Kala leapt on board, pausing only long enough to look into the cabin to be sure Rebekka was alone before pulling a knife and holding it to Rebekka's throat.

"Turn off the engine," she said, her attention on Rimmon's men, waiting to see what they would do.

Neither made a move toward the boat until Kala had forced Rebekka off it.

The Lioness backed away, using Rebekka as a shield. She didn't turn from the dock until it was no longer in view and by then it was obvious that beyond securing the boat, Rimmon's men didn't intend to get involved.

One of Allende's guards stepped forward, locking his fingers around Rebekka's upper arm. "We'll take her from here," he said to Kala. "You're to return to the brothel."

Kala's knife left Rebekka's throat.

Rebekka's eyes were wide with fear and the pain of betrayal. "Why?" she asked.

The Lioness gave no answer.

"Where's Feliss?"

Kala's smile held vicious satisfaction. "Dead."

The men led Rebekka away.

As soon as she was out of sight, the Djinn materialized behind Kala. The Lioness had only enough time to register the arm around her chest and a hand across her face before he broke her neck.

Addai manifested in human form, clothed in flesh and dark material, his thumbs tucked into the front pockets of his pants instead of pressed to the hilt of a sword. "You are quick to destroy your tools, my friend."

Torquel let the body fall to the ground. "This one has served its use. If my daughter survives, I'll not risk her life and all we've worked for by leaving this enemy in place."

"So I see. I will tell Tir to be ready to finish his part in this."

Thirty-four

THE arrival of the tusked madam cut Aryck's penance short. She stopped in front of him and spoke as if discussing business with a brothel visitor but her words were directed at Levi. "I smell Jaguar. He's the one?"

An upward flick of Levi's eyes answered her question. She said, "Allende knows. His men are here. As soon as one of them finds me, I'll be ordered to lock down the brothel."

A brief hesitation and she added, "They brought the body of a Doe with them. Feliss is dead."

"Come with us, Dorrit," Levi murmured, lips barely moving.

"It's too late. Do what you can for those of us trapped here but don't put Rebekka at risk."

She moved on, stopping to talk to others, customers and prostitutes alike, as if merely making her rounds.

Regret slammed into Aryck. Shame, for a lifetime of judging those he knew nothing about.

"Let's go," Levi said, escorting Aryck along public and hidden walkways until finally reaching an exit doorway guarded by hard-eyed Jackals who let them pass to freedom.

Away from the brothel the scent of grief and fear poured off Levi. Breaking into a run he said, "We may already be too late. The moment

Allende learned Rebekka can stand before the ancestors and return an outcast's eternal soul to the shadowlands, he would have sent his men to capture her."

Aryck stumbled. Shocked despite having guessed Rebekka was responsible for the change in Levi.

"This is why she left," he said, feeling the sting of failure as he remembered eyes wet with pain, silently pleading as she asked him to come back to Oakland with her.

"She couldn't tell you. She shouldn't have had to."

Hostility was back in Levi's voice.

"I won't fail her again," Aryck said. "I'll give up my life before I do."

The Lion didn't respond, only continued running. The salt-laden scent and the sound of water lapping against metal and wood and rocky shore intensified as they neared the bay. They entered the metal ruin of what had long ago been a port for container ships from around the world, and soon came upon a body.

Levi glanced down at it, his steps faltering, though he didn't stop. Aryck followed, dread arrowing straight through him at the sight of the outcast female Lion.

They cleared the last of the metal jungle. A boat bobbed gently where it was tied to the dock. The cabin door stood open. Even at a distance the only feeling emanating from the *Constellation* was one of emptiness.

Agony clawed up Aryck's throat, making it impossible to call Rebekka's name. He reached the boat and climbed aboard. The healer's journal lay on a seat, as if she'd been reading it but laid it aside before she was taken.

Seeing it abandoned nearly drove Aryck to his knees. Hopelessness and failure tried to crush him. He shook them off, refusing to acknowledge the possibility it was already too late.

He'd found her in the encampment and saved her before she could be raped. Against all odds they'd not only left it alive, but because of her, the threat posed to the Weres was over and the slaughter of innocent humans avoided.

This wasn't a world he could navigate. For a second time Aryck swallowed his pride where the Lion he'd once thought *less* was con-cerned. "She must have allies who can help us find her. Who do you suggest we approach?"

"There are only two choices. The Wainwright witches, who drew her into their games and dangled the lure of being able to heal the outcast in front of her. Or the Iberás, one of the Founding Families. They're rich and powerful, with allies in the Guard and no doubt spies in the red zone."

"The witches first," Aryck said, spitting the words.

"There'll be a price to pay," Levi warned. Adding a challenge. "Are you willing to pay it to get her back? I am."

Aryck's lips pulled back, baring his teeth. The Jaguar rose in his eyes, staring down the Lion. "She'll never belong to you. She's my mate."

"If she'll have you," Levi said, satisfaction in his voice at having baited Aryck.

Aryck reverently picked up the journal, the movement loosening Rebekka's scent and making him wish the warmth trapped in its cover came from her holding it and not from the sun.

REBEKKA sat between the two Weres who were Allende's personal guards. On either side of the car, there was nothing but the forest that began where the red zone ended to the north.

She thought they must be going to Allende's estate but it barely mattered to her. She felt overwhelmed with grief at Feliss's death, with the shock and hurt of Kala's betrayal, and the sense of failure at having so quickly been discovered and captured.

The events at the dock played over and over in her mind. Silently she berated herself for ignoring the tiny, hesitant internal voice urging her not to take the *Constellation* in until Levi returned.

The thought of Levi jarred Rebekka out of failure and pain-induced apathy, bringing with it fear, not just over her own fate, but his. Had Kala told Allende about his involvement? Was he already dead?

Sweat trickled down her back and sides at the prospect of being at Allende's mercy. He wasn't known for his compassion.

She took a deep breath, fisting her hands in her lap so tightly her short nails dug into her palms. The physical pain helped. It reminded her of all she'd endured.

Since Levi, she'd healed many, many others, not all of them brothel workers. Most were like Feliss, victims instead of victimizers. Those who'd been born with a part of their soul wandering in the ghostlands instead of cast there by the ancestors. But some had deserved their fates.

What she'd felt as she held their metaphysical hearts had been an agony more excruciating than what she'd endured on Levi's behalf. Though in the end, after she'd witnessed the events of their lives, she'd felt their redemption was equally deserved.

A shudder went through her. There was a difference between pain borne psychically and that endured physically. If Allende intended to kill her, she'd already be dead.

Death was too quick a punishment. And she was still a valuable tool even if she couldn't be trusted.

Bile rose in her throat as she imagined what he'd do in order to make an example of her. He had only to say the word and she'd become a prisoner in the brothel, forced into serving as healer as well as prostitute.

Rebekka looked out the window, wishing desperately her father would appear. Surely he hadn't abandoned her now even if she hadn't seen the cardinal since making her choice to return to Oakland.

If only she could summon him. He'd saved her twice already. He'd touched his mouth to hers and given a part of himself.

My spirit to yours. Surely that meant they were somehow linked.

Could she find him? Signal her need for him in a way similar to how she'd been led to the infected goats?

Rebekka gathered her will and closed her eyes. Focused on him only to have nothing happen.

There was no tingling, no surge of power, no icy emptiness in her chest. She realized then why he'd refused to give her his name when she'd asked for it, guessed that with it, she did have the power to call him to her.

Her mouth went dry as another possibility came to her. Each visit to the Were ancestors had started the same way, with the ritual question, "You ask us to render a judgment?"

What if she were to touch the guards and enter the shadowlands with their spirits? What if she were to stand before the ancestors and answer *yes* instead of saying she was there to heal?

Would it destroy her gift if the ancestors chose punishment? If, rather than healing, her touch led to the making of an outcast?

Rebekka trembled at the prospect of risking it. Healers who killed or willfully harmed another corrupted their gift. Everyone knew it.

She was as frightened of turning her gift into a thing that destroyed others as she was of whatever Allende had in store for her.

Rebekka wavered, hands clenching and unclenching in uncertainty. If she attempted it, she'd have to be quick and accurate. Even then there was no guarantee it would work without the touch of her palms to the bare skin over the guards' hearts.

Every choice seemed ultimately to lead to death—either spiritual or physical.

To taint her gift was to taint her soul. How could it be otherwise? Gift and spirit for a healer were the same.

To taint her soul was to never be able to stand before the Were ancestors, to never again be welcomed in Were lands. She'd been warned about both.

And yet to go meekly, in the hopes she could endure whatever punishment Allende intended to mete out . . .

The slowing of the car sent a raw panic through her. Visceral terror followed with the sight of a man standing by the side of the road, an apparition dressed in a black, hooded cloak and wearing a leather mask to conceal his face.

Too late she attempted to place her hands over the guards' hearts. They grabbed her wrists, keeping her palms from contacting their skin as if they'd guessed she might be capable of bringing them to the attention of the ancestors.

She struggled against being removed from the car. Struggled then to escape and flee into the woods, but she was no match for even a single Were, much less two of them.

Thick arms tightened around her chest with enough force to make breathing impossible. Immobilized her with the silent, ruthless promise that continued resistance would lead to broken ribs as she was taken to where the man waited.

"Good, she has some instinct for self-preservation," he said, his voice making Rebekka think of jagged, metal edges. "I was afraid she'd hardly be worth the money when your lord said she was a healer."

A gloved hand emerged from the cape, a velvet bag in its palm. With the flick of a wrist he tossed it to Allende's man.

The guard caught it, and Rebekka heard the unmistakable sound of coins. He pocketed it then accepted a length of rope.

"Bind her wrists in front of her and put her in the sidecar. There's a metal loop in the floor. Secure her to it."

Rebekka looked to the right and noticed the narrow path for the first time, and in the center of it, several yards away and hidden from the road, the motorcycle. She began struggling again, only to feel the sharp pain of ribs being compressed almost to the breaking point.

She stopped fighting, tears streaming down her face, breath whooshing in and out of her lungs as the grip around her chest loosened. Pride kept her from pleading, from begging as the guards carried out the masked man's instructions.

When she was bound in place, secured so she couldn't escape the sidecar, the man pulled a strip of cloth from his cloak. Rather than order the guard to do it, he wrapped it around her head, blindfolding her.

The bike shifted with his weight. The engine started and they began moving.

"WITCHES," Aryck spat again as pain engulfed him when he crossed the wards separating the red zone from the area Levi said was set aside for gifted humans.

The same curse sounded in his thoughts but remained unspoken a short time later when they found one of the Wainwrights in the doorway of a sigil-marked house, there to usher them inside with ominous words. "Levanna waits. She *saw* your coming and knows the reason you seek her out."

The matriarch sat in a darkened parlor. An ancient, sightless crone who made Aryck think of midnight horror stories told to shivering cubs around the fire pit.

"Time runs out for the healer," Levanna said. "It runs out in the brothel as well. After Allende metes out the punishment he wants witnessed to those he feels betrayed him, or intended to, he plans to sell their contracts to the *Pleasure Venture*. It arrives in port shortly."

"What do you want?" Aryck asked, unwilling to drag the bargaining process out and risk being too late to save Rebekka.

The matriarch turned white-moon eyes on him and the hairs rose at the back of his neck. "A favor owed. One from each of you."

"Accepted," Levi said, Lion stare offering the same challenge it had on the *Constellation*.

This time Aryck couldn't be goaded. He was the enforcer. Son of the alpha. His life, his eternal soul, he could forfeit. But even for Rebekka he wouldn't betray the Weres, or destroy the very thing her presence on their lands had brought about. "I won't become a tool to use against the pack or those it forms alliances with."

Laughter greeted his pronouncement, making his skin crawl as though he'd landed in a spider's nest. "Done," the witch said.

From the depths of her black garments she pulled a small willow cutting, the ends brought around and lashed together to form a circle reminding Aryck of Rebekka's amulet. A red cardinal feather hung in the center, attached to the frame by a beaded string.

Levanna cupped the charm, holding it against her lips and whispering a spell. When she was done she held it between her thumb and forefinger.

An unnatural wind stirred, moving through the willow circle and carrying the feather to the end of the string at the same height as the hand holding it. It continued to point in the same direction when she transferred it to Aryck.

"I *saw* only one man with Rebekka," Levanna said. "Perhaps you'll reach her in time. Perhaps not. Annalise will show you out."

As Aryck followed the witch with the skunk-striped hair to the front door, he said to Levi, "Do what you can to save the outcasts. Rebekka would want it. Seek help from the Iberás you spoke of earlier. I'll go to Rebekka."

Thirty-five

LIKE the day she'd been blindfolded by Annalise and taken to a client, Rebekka couldn't guess how far they traveled, or where they were when they stopped and the motorcycle engine was silenced.

She expected to be left blindfolded. Instead the man removed it, and she immediately knew why.

It took effort to keep from whimpering at the sight of the house. It sat in isolation, surrounded by a dense forest of pines. Every window was covered by bars, not to keep the predators out, but to keep the prey in.

Behind the mask, pleasure emanated from the man. "Should I tell you what's in store for you now, or would you prefer to take a tour of the house first?"

"Now," Rebekka said, somehow managing to force the word out.

He laughed, a sound resonating with such pure evil her skin chilled and broke out in gooseflesh.

"You're going to be quite a bit more fun for our potential initiate than I anticipated."

She couldn't stop herself from shivering, from desperately searching the woods for a flash of cardinal red. He saw both actions and laughed again.

"No one will come to rescue you. But it would hardly be sporting if you didn't have a chance to save yourself."

The man moved around the motorcycle, leaned down, and untied the rope from the metal loop welded into the floor of the sidecar. "I've changed my mind. I think you'll better appreciate your situation from inside the house."

He stepped away and jerked hard, using the rope binding her wrists like a leash. "Come along. Your company will arrive shortly and I'm sure you want to be ready for your guest."

Rebekka knew she should preserve her strength and energy, but she couldn't bring herself to go passively into the house. She fought like a fish at the end of a line.

It was a hopeless battle, leaving her shoulders aching and her wrists raw and bloody. It was a struggle that ended with the rope draped over a staircase banister and tied there, forcing her hands to remain raised above her head.

"This will do as a starting point," the man said, breathing heavily, not from physical exertion as a result of her fighting him, but from his excitement over it.

He dangled a key in front of her face. It was threaded onto a velvet ribbon.

"This opens the front door," he said, demonstrating the truth of it by walking over and inserting the key into the lock, twisting it so she heard a telltale click.

He unlocked the door and removed the key, separated the ribbon strands so he could wear it around his neck.

"Your visitor will let himself into the house. He will disrobe if he so chooses, though I've found few potential members choose to do so, not when they're so very aware of being captured on camera initially."

Rebekka's attention jerked to the ceiling. Cameras were mounted there, sickening her, reminding her of the maze and the gambling clubs that profited from those running in it.

Cold, evil laughter made her look at the masked figure once again. "Your face is so expressive. I can tell you're thinking about Anton's little venture. It might amuse you to know that for a while he served as the family priest for several of our members.

"In some ways this is similar to his sadly defunct operation. But in all the ways that count, it's different. Only those among the crème of Oakland society are invited to run in our houses and join the elite who make up our membership. To be accepted they must do one thing, prove they really do enjoy the combination of murder and sex."

He waved at the cameras. "If the prospect loses his nerve, this little film catching him in the act of rape buys his silence. It unfortunately doesn't buy your freedom, or save your life, unless you're able to capitalize on your visitor's weakness and get the key—which by club rule must be worn around a guest's neck—and leave the house. If you accomplish that, then you will be given money enough to start a new life elsewhere.

"You will be escorted to that new life by men in our employ. Any whisper of what took place here will end in a death meted out by a professional in such matters.

"If, despite the lack of nerve and initiative to end things with a kill, your guest manages to keep the key in his possession and prevent you from escaping, it merely buys you time to regain your strength so you'll provide at least somewhat of a challenge to your next visitor."

He touched the key. "Somehow I don't think you'll get a second run, not unless you're willing to sacrifice your gift for your life. I suspect that's why Allende offered you to me, because in some way, your talent for healing has become a problem to him. Would you care to satisfy my curiosity on the matter?"

When she didn't answer, he shrugged and returned to the staircase. He climbed the few steps necessary to untie the rope serving as a leash.

"We'll forgo a tour of the upstairs, I think. There are several rooms with beds and a few with assorted clutter to add excitement to the chase. There are even a couple of them with doors that close and lock from the inside, though you've got to reach them first."

He paused to study the staircase. Cold chills went through Rebekka when he said, "A lot of very satisfying, dramatic scenes have concluded with a desperate attempt to get to the second floor. But now it's time for a quick tour of the downstairs before getting you prepared for your visitor."

He led her through the house, jerking the leash if she didn't follow quickly enough to suit him. Living room, dining room, bathroom, except for the cameras, they appeared perfectly normal, like a house owned by a merchant, comfortable but not luxurious.

In the kitchen, skillets hung from the wall but the cabinets and pantries were bare. The drawers were empty, save for the long, sharp knife he extracted from one of them.

"In the usual situation you'd be allowed some time to prepare your defense. You'd simply be set free in the house and left with the knowledge that at some point there would be an 'intruder' if that was the particular fantasy being played out, or perhaps an angry husband returning home to deal with an unfaithful wife, or—"

With a laugh he interrupted himself. "My apologies for giving you needless things to consider. As the House Master and Director of Scenes for this particular dwelling, I tend toward enthusiasm when it comes to all the delightful possibilities. To be a bit more succinct, normally you'd be set free and left to your own devices. But since this is essentially an initiation into our club, we don't want to make things too challenging for our prospective member. And yet at the same time, our rules *do* require you have a chance to save yourself."

He flipped the knife into the air and caught it, repeating the action as he tugged her into the room at the end of the hallway. It was a bedroom.

Rebekka fought him again when he looped his end of the rope through a metal ring set into the wall next to the door. Her wrists began bleeding but she didn't stop until her arms were once again forced into position above her head and the rope secured to a second loop several feet below and to the right of the first.

The man shook his head and tsked. "A waste of effort on your part, though I suppose it doesn't really matter. As I said a moment ago, we *want* our candidate to succeed."

He moved closer and touched the knife to her throat, making small, imaginary cuts there before slowly unbuttoning her shirt with his free hand. Instinctively she tried to drive him away with her knee. He backhanded her hard enough her ears rang and for a moment she was dizzy.

"You're safe enough from me, unless you continue to be difficult," he said, leaning in so the leather of his mask touched her cheek. "But persist and I promise you I will have you before the prospect gets his chance to. It's not against our rules for the House Master to enjoy the fruits of his labor before a scene runs."

She shuddered. Forced herself to remain passive as he used the knife to strip away her clothing and leave them in useless pieces on the floor at her feet.

He touched the tip of the blade to the tattoo, traced the black circle and the red *P*. "This is unexpected." His voice was heavy with displeasure. "It makes me wonder if you're a discarded whore instead of a gifted healer as Allende claimed. Tell me, did he lie?"

Rebekka hesitated, trying to work out which answer might be more to her advantage. He backhanded her again, hard enough to split her lip.

"The truth," he said. "There's time enough for me to make a few discreet inquires, and time after I do it to teach you a lesson, even if it's a short-lived one."

"I'm one of the gifted."

"Good. See how easy that was?" He was breathing fast again, excited by hitting her while she was naked and defenseless.

She trembled, and his eyes seemed to glitter. The tip of the knife left the tattoo, snaking upward in a slow, sinuous journey that made her skin crawl.

It finally stopped at the leather cord attached to the amulet. "I'm tempted to leave this as decoration but I'm afraid it might be an unfair advantage since it's obviously witch-crafted."

He slid the knife underneath and cut, catching the amulet and tucking it into a pocket rather than letting it fall to the floor.

"Perhaps I'd better make sure I didn't miss anything," he said, crouching down and quickly going through her clothing, finding the Wainwright token. "Ah, good thing I checked."

He tossed the garments from the room then stood. "Now then, here's the scene I've arranged for you. In a moment I will escort you to the bed and retie you there, leaving enough slack in the rope to allow movement on your part. I will then place the knife at the end of the mattress.

"If you're careful, and even remotely coordinated, rather than kick it off the bed you should be able to use your feet and body to work it upward, toward your hands. How you approach cutting through the bindings at your wrists, I'll leave up to you.

"If you work quickly, you should be free before your visitor arrives. If not . . . well the failure is yours. Our rules were honored and you were given a chance to save yourself."

This time Rebekka didn't fight him. She went docilely, lying down as directed and trying to blank her mind to his presence, to the possibility he'd rape her before he left.

When he was finished arranging the scene to his liking, he caressed her cheek with the back of his gloved hand. "I'm looking forward to seeing just what your choice will be. Your gift. Or your life. Assuming of course, you free yourself first and manage to maneuver into a position where you can use the knife against your guest."

Icy numbness replaced a terror that couldn't be sustained any longer. But it didn't suppress Rebekka's will to live. Even as he left the room, his footsteps sounding in the hallway, she was working the knife upward, losing all track of time as she raced to free herself.

Slashes soon marked her forearms where she'd cut herself on the knife's blade. And by the time the bloodstained rope fell away from her wrists, her skin was slick with sweat.

Rebekka rushed from the room, anxious to get away from the bed, though she knew it didn't matter. A lifetime of witnessing how closely knit violence and sexual satisfaction were for some had demonstrated how unimportant comfort was when it came to sating those needs.

The shredded remains of her clothing no longer lay in the hall-way. Like cold, merciless eyes, she was aware of the cameras captur-ing her nakedness, her every movement, and what might be the last minutes and hours of her life—all for the twisted, sick entertainment of others.

She considered returning to the kitchen and taking a skillet but discarded the idea. Effectively wielding it in one hand and the knife in the other would be impossible.

Her throat closed on the icy horror of the choice confronting her. When it came to what it would cost her, there would be no difference between injuring the man coming here or killing him.

Tears formed, unwanted but unstoppable. They fell as she heard the Bear ancestor's voice in her mind, saying as long as her gift remained untainted, she had the power to fully restore Were souls.

Was it better to die than live without being able to use her gift? For so long, it was how she'd defined herself.

The final scene with Aryck played out in her mind, the choice she'd made then, sacrificing the role of mother and mate for that of healer.

I can have that kind of life with someone else, she told herself, though a part of her doubted she could ever trust another man enough to open her heart to him.

She brushed away the tears and steeled herself against shedding more of them. First she had to survive long enough to escape.

The door was locked, as she expected it to be. From there she moved into the living room to look out the window.

She tried to think as her attacker would. To consider what he would expect, how his own nervousness and excitement and fear might be used to her advantage.

Would he be told she was one of the gifted? Would he expect plead-ing and discount the potential for violence?

A hot wash of bile crawled up her throat as she imagined his thoughts, his feelings, his desire to rape a woman then kill her after-ward. Her heart felt as though it would leap out of her chest when she heard the sound of a motorcycle.

Through the window she saw it approach, the masked man driving while another, younger and barefaced, rode in the sidecar. They slowed to a stop, though the driver didn't turn off the engine or dismount.

The club prospect got out of the sidecar. He stood next to it, body vibrating with excitement as he listened to the other man give final instructions, or remind him of the rules.

Rebekka's mind raced, panic getting the better of her, freezing her at the window until she saw the driver lift his arms and remove the velvet ribbon with the key on it, passing it to the younger man.

She hurried to the stairs then, climbed just far enough to gain momentum, knowing she couldn't hesitate, couldn't falter. Surprise was her greatest weapon. Her only chance lay in a quick, unexpected strike, one deep enough to sever an artery.

Outside the sound of the motorcycle engine grew fainter as it drove away. Her would-be rapist and murderer entered the house cautiously, as she'd expected him to.

He reached the foot of the staircase, eyes going to the knife, her grip on it so tight her fingers paled against the dark hilt. There was no need to feign fear, to force it into her voice. "Please don't do this," she said, taking a step back as if she intended retreat. "I'm a healer."

A sneer formed when his gaze moved to the tattoo. His body telegraphed his intention to charge a heartbeat before he did it.

Rebekka leapt forward with only one thought, one emotion. To do whatever it took to survive.

They collided. The knife held low, already thrusting forward between his thighs, her knowledge of anatomy making her accurate.

His expression went from surprise to shock to terrified understanding in the instant before he grabbed her, pushing her away from him instead of to the ground beneath him. Blood already soaking his pants.

He tried desperately to staunch the flow. But it pulsed through his fingers with the pounding of his heart.

"Please, help me," he begged. "Please. My family has money. They can make you rich."

Rebekka stood motionless, watching in frozen, sickened horror as he bled out, his panic growing and his pleading little more than sobbing at the end.

Despite knowing there was no other choice, that he intended far worse for her, she threw up when he ceased breathing. Continued to retch until the instinct for survival kicked in, urging her to get out of the house, to get as far away from it as quickly as possible, before the man wearing the mask arrived.

She liberated the key. A shudder went through her at the thought of wearing the dead man's shirt, but without it she'd be naked.

It took effort to get it off him. She was panting, hearing the phantom approach of a motorcycle by the time she escaped the house and ran for the forest, seeking refuge in the thick press of trees so anyone who pursued her would have to be on foot.

Healer

UNSEEN, Tir watched as Levi approached the Iberá estate. Days ago thoughts of retribution would have dominated; now he found irony at events playing out here, between a family that had once paid coin to purchase him and prolong his enslavement, and a Were who'd left him free but shackled by chains in the woods.

Behind the high, gated walls of the compound, lions began roaring as if scenting a being who could take their form. On the walkway along the top, men stopped patrolling and pointed automatic weapons down at Levi as others emerged from the gatehouse with pistols drawn, witch-amulets glowing in the presence of a Were.

"What brings you here?" one of them asked, his eyes going to Levi then skittering away, searching the area behind him as if fearing a surprise attack.

"I'm here to speak to the Iberá patriarch."

"And you are?"

"My name won't mean anything to him. But the healer Rebekka's does. And maybe, if the guardsman Captain Orst mentioned it since returning from a salvage operation in Were lands, the patriarch might know the name Aryck."

The guard's expression remained suspicious despite obviously recognizing at least one of the names Levi used. He returned to the guard-house, not bothering to close the door as he placed a call and repeated what Levi had said.

A moment later a heavy door swung open, offering a glimpse of manicured lawns and a magnificent house. Levi was motioned through it and escorted to the front door by guards. The butler took over, inviting Levi in and leading him to the patriarch's study.

Tir followed, lips curved in dark amusement. So Addai spoke the truth even if he didn't elaborate on it. In the end, Caphriel's game had been turned to their advantage.

The patriarch sat behind his desk. At the corner of it, a militiaman wearing the stripes of one in command stood at ease, as if there to listen rather than guard.

"Why did you come to me?" The Iberá asked.

Levi's hands clenched into fists. "Rebekka forgave you for holding her here against her will because she believed you were sincere in your desire to see the guard cleaned up and the red zone made a thing of the past. I'm here on her behalf.

"Since she was sixteen, Rebekka has been a healer in the Were brothels. We were working to help those we could to escape life as a prostitute. The vice lord Allende learned of it. Now the buildings are locked down and he plans to make an example of anyone who intended to leave or turned a blind eye to what was going on. He'll sell their contracts to the *Pleasure Venture* when it arrives in port. Will you help the Weres Rebekka cares about? Or do you care *only* about the fate of humans in this city?"

In answer The Iberá picked up a slim phone. His hand trembled slightly, the effects of disease rather than emotion as he touched a button and spoke to someone on the other end. "Use what contacts you have to reach the vice lord Allende. He plans to sell some of the contracts he holds to the *Pleasure Venture* when it reaches port. Find out if he is willing to sell those same contracts to me. Let him know I intend to remove the shapeshifters from the area."

The patriarch set the phone down. To Levi he said, "Often victory is more easily achieved using money instead of soldiers. While we wait for Allende's answer you can accompany Colonel Peña to the planning room. If force becomes necessary—"

He stopped speaking as a dark-haired beauty appeared in the doorway. She frowned, either at having caught his mention of force or at finding he had a visitor. But when Levi turned, her eyes widened and her mouth formed a small *O* in seeming recognition.

There was a flash between them. Physical attraction and something else, an inevitability reminding Tir all too well of the first time he'd seen Araña.

"Isobel," the patriarch said, the sharp crack of his voice enough to divert her attention and raise a blush to her cheeks.

"I'm to tell you everyone is gathered for the birthday party."

"I will be there momentarily."

"I'll let them know," she said, careful not to look at Levi as she turned away and retreated down the hallway.

"As I was saying," The Iberá continued, "while we wait for Allende's answer, you can accompany Colonel Peña to the planning room and provide information about the layout of the brothels as well as security measures. If force becomes necessary to extract those who wish to escape, then you—and any other ally you can personally vouch for— will need to go with the colonel and his men. I won't risk having them killed by the very ones they're attempting to rescue."

"I understand."

The patriarch's hand settled on the controls operating the wheelchair. A motor hummed to life quietly in a signal of dismissal.

Colonel Peña moved to Levi's side, and the two left the room. Tir waited, allowing The Iberá to maneuver the chair out from behind the desk before materializing, blocking the old man's path in a display of angelic glory, of power and shimmering, unfolded wings.

If the patriarch guessed the being now standing before him was the very one his grandson had offered coin for, there was no sign of it in his face. He paled but didn't cower as his good hand grasped the crucifix worn beneath his tailored shirt.

Restoring the old man to good health would once have required Tir's blood. Now, free of the sigil-inscribed collar, it required only his will.

He felt Araña's presence in his mind a heartbeat before her voice whispered through it like a caress. *Addai says it's time to finish this and go to Rebekka.*

"Your fate is bound to the healer's," Tir told the patriarch, amused by the subtle, dual meaning contained in the words. "You have proven yourself worthy of being called an ally."

He bent forward and touched The Iberá's useless hand where it lay on the arm of the wheelchair.

"Be healed," he said, willing it so.

And so it became.

Thirty-six

ARYCK smelled death moments before he saw the house. The scent of it escaped through a barred window, blood and bowel and urine.

Flies were already gathering for the feast. Their buzz seemed loud in the sudden, oppressive quiet of the forest.

Instinct urged caution even as man and Jaguar raged, feared. Screamed silently at the prospect of finding Rebekka inside, always and forever gone from their lives.

The weight of it nearly crushed Aryck. The knowledge he'd failed her yet again felt like a mortal blow.

He tucked the witch's pathfinder into the clothing collar he'd fashioned upon entering the woods and left the cover provided by the trees. His ears told him there was no one alive in the house but he still approached it carefully. The isolated location, the barred windows, the cameras mounted near the roof, all made him think this could be a trap.

Rebekka's scent slammed into him like a fist to the gut when he neared the front door. It made her presence real, overrode the tiny, flickering hope the witch-produced tool was wrong, the hint of suspicion they had betrayed him—either of which would have been preferable to finding Rebekka inside.

Two men had been here before him. Aryck crouched, committing their scents to memory before picking up a handful of twigs and going to the door.

It was unlocked, adding to his sense this was somehow a trap. He stepped to the side and opened it, alert for any change in sound, for movement at the edge of the forest.

The smell of death intensified.

Aryck wedged the twigs under the door, holding it open as he cautiously entered the house. The Jaguar part of him raged, wanting a form that lent itself to ripping and slashing in a venting of fury.

Reason prevailed up until the moment Aryck saw the man's corpse. In a glance he read what had happened by the blood pools and spatters on the stairs and walls, knew Rebekka lived, and, regardless of the cameras perched in the corners, *changed*.

He left the house at a run, following her path around and into the woods. It became easier the farther he went. She was barefoot, her feet bleeding.

Pride filled his chest when she came to a stream and began traveling in it. Making it more difficult to be tracked by humans. Not for him.

The water was shallow and the bed rocky. But the breeze carried her scent and it grew stronger with each step he took. He loped, his heart pounding not from exertion but from anticipation, from the knowledge he was only moments away from her.

He would never let her ago again. Regardless of what had happened to her since being taken prisoner, he wouldn't leave her side or let her push him away.

She was his mate. He knew now the true depth of the word.

He rounded a curve and heard her running out of sight ahead of him. She was whimpering in pain, her breathing coming in fast pants.

A cry of denial screamed through him. Remorse followed when he realized the sound of his splashing pursuit had reached her, driving her forward in fear for her life.

He stopped. Shifted. Yelled, "Rebekka! Rebekka! Stop. It's me."

Rebekka stumbled and nearly went down to her knees at the sound of Aryck's voice. *It can't be*, she told herself, afraid she was hallucinating, then worse, that maybe with the taint to her gift came madness, insanity.

A chill swept through her. She kept going, only to falter when she heard him say, "Please stop, Rebekka! Let me catch up to you. I was with Levi earlier. I know you healed him. I know you can stand before the ancestors. The brothels are locked down, and Levi's gone to the Iberá estate to ask for help freeing the outcasts."

She did stop then, her grief over the loss of her gift making it impossible to go on. She stepped onto the bank and turned. Waited, almost expecting a phantom, a spirit apparition, not the flesh-and-blood man who appeared moments later, moving so stealthily she hadn't heard his approach.

"Aryck," she whispered, tears freed with the reality of his presence.

He closed the distance between them at a run. Discarding the clothing collar steps away from her before hugging her to him with a fierceness at odds to the trembling of his body.

She held him just as tightly. Didn't try to stop crying as she closed her eyes and pressed her face to the crook of his neck, breathed in the scent of him, allowing herself the illusion everything would be all right now.

"You came after me," she said, touching her mouth to the bite mark on his skin, remembering how he'd wanted her mark on him.

"Too late," he said, loathing in his voice. "I failed you again. First in letting you leave without me, then in not getting here in time to protect you."

Her throat went tight imagining what would have happened if he'd been on the *Constellation* with her when Kala arrived. He'd be dead. Led into an ambush because of the knife held to her throat, or killed by a bullet where he stood on the deck.

At least this way he lived. Even if she could no longer enter Were lands, or be his mate, or heal, at least he hadn't lost his life because of her.

"You came after me. I'll never forget it," she said, her heart breaking with the knowledge she was only going to lose him again.

She lifted her face, wanting one last kiss, needing to soak in a little more of his body heat to offset the chill at her core. Through the blur of tears she saw the starkness of emotions laid bare, love and desire, remorse and gratitude.

And then his mouth was on hers, his tongue thrusting, rubbing against hers, emotional hunger rousing a physical one in a burst of hot flame centered between her thighs.

Her hands roamed his back. His did the same to hers, their lips parting only long enough for him to rid her of the dead man's shirt so they were skin to skin.

He hardened against her belly and she desperately wanted to feel him inside her, his body joined to hers. But when he lifted her, as if to thrust into her where they stood, her thoughts flashed to the Were ancestors and reality drenched her like frigid water.

"No," she said, stiffening in his arms, hating the pain that returned to his eyes at her rejection.

"Give me a chance to prove myself to you," he pleaded, his voice gravelly with unshed tears.

"It's too late," she whispered, understanding Aryck's respect of the Were ancestors and his fear of being made outcast in a way she hadn't until she healed Levi.

She saw the shimmer of tears on his cheeks as he allowed her to see what the thought of losing her did to him. "It doesn't have to be too late. I'll stay with you. I'll work with you and Levi to help the brothel workers escape Allende."

"My gift is useless now. Tainted because I killed a man. I can't go before the ancestors again. I can't return to Were lands. I can't be your mate."

"You killed to save your life; how can it be wrong?" Aryck asked, challenging her in the same way she'd challenged him about the outcasts.

He pressed kiss after soft kiss to her cheeks, her lips, her ears, trying to convey the strength of his belief and his refusal to accept defeat when it came to her. "No Were, living or dead, would judge your soul tainted for defending yourself. If you doubt it, I'll bring a shaman to you. I'll go before the ancestors myself on your behalf and ask for a judgment."

Her arms tightened around his waist. "They can't help. I'm not Were."

Aryck touched his forehead to hers. "Then we'll go to the witches. Levi took me to the Wainwright house. We bargained with them to find out if you lived and where you were. I'll bargain with them again if it means we can be together." He thought he saw a flash of hope in her eyes, then wondered if he was mistaken when he felt the subtle bracing of her body.

"What if the cost of restoring my gift is that after Oakland I have to go to another city, and then another, and another? Twice I've met my father. He says he's not demon, but I have no proof he's telling the truth. He paid my mother to carry me to term and keep me safe while I was still a child. He created me for a purpose."

"Then I'll come with you and keep you safe. I'll help you with your work and at the same time continue lobbying for an alliance among all Were groups."

"And if the witches can't help me? If Nahuatl or another shaman says you'll be made outcast if you remain with me?"

"It doesn't matter. I've already given you my heart and my body, my Jaguar soul and my human one. You're my mate, Rebekka. Wherever you are, that's where I want to be, in life and in death."

Aryck took her lips in a kiss that conveyed the strength of his conviction even as he silently begged her to believe in him despite his failing her, to feel for him what he felt for her. He plundered her mouth with the thrust of his tongue against hers, boldly claimed her as belonging to him, and didn't stop until she was clinging to him, her body melded to his in a softening that shouted acceptance.

He didn't know how desperately he needed to hear the words until she whispered them. "I couldn't tell you why I had to leave Were lands, not if I wanted to be able to heal Levi and the others. I hated leaving you. I hated knowing my choice hurt you. I love you."

"Weres rarely speak of love," he said, tenderly brushing his lips against hers. "We say instead, everything I am and have belongs to you."

"It is so among the Djinn as well," a male voice said, and Aryck spun, putting himself between Rebekka and the sharp-featured man who'd managed to sneak up on them.

"My father," Rebekka murmured, touching Aryck's shoulder and stepping to the side.

The man registered as human on every one of Aryck's senses. But there was no doubting he was something else when in the blink of an eye he became a cardinal, and then the tiger whose scent was left behind with Melina's corpse, and then a man again, only closer, a step away, as if he'd moved when he had no form.

Aryck's fingers flexed in Jaguar reaction, but he neither attacked nor stepped backward as the stranger studied him with critical eyes, judged him, then ignored him completely in favor of directing all his attention to Rebekka.

"In every way you have made me proud, daughter. Our kind has always tested their children. Even those born in our prison kingdom set deep in the ghostlands must prove their worthiness. No one will ever question the rightness of entering your name in the Book of the Djinn."

He stepped closer, curled his fingers around Rebekka's upper arm, pulling her toward him. The Jaguar soul rose in challenge and growled in warning while the human one snarled and took possession of her other arm.

Rebekka's father ignored the display. "The enforcer spoke the truth. No Were, living or dead, would judge your soul tainted for defending yourself.

"So it is for the Djinn too. At the moment, your spirit is locked in a human shape, but you are not limited by the rules applied to the gifted. Because you're of my House, I can make you *mārdazmā*, Djinn, able to shift between living, sentient forms. You are only so limited because an ancient enemy's blood runs diluted in your mother's line, commingling with mine, though it's his blood that allows you to stand in the entranceway between ghostlands and shadowlands."

Rebekka glanced at Aryck, tugged on the arm in his grip until he loosened his hold on it enough so she could slide her hand into his before meeting her father's eyes again. She knew the face of one of his enemies and was sickened by the possibility of being related to an entity who could so casually use plague for nothing more than entertainment purposes, but she forced herself to ask, "The urchin with the rat on his shoulder. Who is he? What is he?"

There was a glorious flash of light as if in answer, and standing next to her father was Tir—not as he'd been before, but in his true form, an angel with black wings spread, the light shimmering off them in the same way as it had the feather on the amulet she'd worn.

"My brother," Tir said, and Rebekka knew his name, had noticed the likeness when he appeared at the Fellowship of the Sign and offered to cleanse her gift of any taint.

"Caphriel."

Tir inclined his head. "I was once like him. But now I join others of my kind in an alliance that will see the return of the Djinn and a change in who rules this world. Araña and I will come back to Oakland in the future. Aisling and Zurael remain there. Seek any of us out if you need us."

He disappeared in another flash, and her father leaned forward. "To those willing to make the greatest sacrifice should go the greatest rewards. My spirit to yours, daughter."

He touched his mouth to hers as he had in Lion territory. And it was like being on the receiving end of her own gift.

Power poured down her throat, raw and primordial. Like molten stone coming from the Earth itself. She healed as though she'd never been injured. The place where her skin was inked in a prostitute's tattoo burned as if it was on fire. And at the very last came knowledge of his name. *Torquel en Sahon.*

When he stepped away from her she looked down. Where the ugly black circle and red *P* had once been, there was now an image of a cardinal, its wings outstretched.

Her eyes lifted to her father's face. He said, "Among the Weres there is no true, unbreakable mate-bond until a child is conceived. Among our kind it takes only the sharing of breath, done with absolute conviction and intent.

"The Were ancestors have already chosen the Djinn as allies. We cement it with the uniting of our children. You are but one of them. The responsibility that comes with your gift does not preclude having children or spending time in Were lands."

He tilted his head in Aryck's direction. "Is he your choice then, Rebekka en Sahon, daughter of the House of the Cardinal?"

"Yes. He's my choice."

"So be it then. I will enter his name next to yours in the Book of the Djinn."

Her father disappeared as suddenly as he'd arrived.

Rebekka turned toward Aryck, going willingly into his arms. "It's not over," she said.

"No, it's just beginning. There are brothel workers to liberate and heal. There is justice to be served on the man who wasn't there when you killed his companion."

Rebekka started to tell him about the club, only to realize there would be time for it later. This moment belonged to them.

"My spirit to yours," she whispered, touching her lips to his, sharing breath.

She felt the bond slide into place and, when the kiss ended, saw evidence of it in a small cardinal on his skin, its wings outstretched above his heart. And in the look in his eyes as his voice sounded in her mind. *Become Jaguar. Mate with me. Love me.*

Yes, she said, changing as if she'd always had another form.